The Diary of a College Rebel

THE DIARY OF A COLLEGE REBEL

STUART "SANDY" CARSON AS TOLD BY RICHARD MASON

BWM Books Pty Ltd

For Millie

Contents

INTRODUCTION

"Yeah, I guess I should have written this book under a pen name, or maybe just have moved to Texas when it came out. My God, I can't believe some of the crap I pulled during those four short years. But, hey, nobody's perfect, and if all those goodie-two-shoes who will stick up their noses when they read this book, really told what they did in college, I'll bet it would open some eyes.

My guess is, that you'll read this book, and then start asking questions—just like my wife did. "Did you really do that?" Or "Who was Millie? Or "Did you really play poker all the way through college?" Or maybe you might wonder just where fiction ends and non-fiction begins? That's a hell of a question, because as I wrote this book, I wrote both. Yes, parts of this book are non-fiction, but as any publisher will tell you, if there's one sentence in the book that's fiction, then the whole work is fiction. So, I'll leave that one up to you. You decide if "Sandy" really was the rascal I made him out to be, or was "Sandy" a victim or maybe both. And when it comes to breaking and entering, or just ordinary cheating on a test, is there any difference in how you do it? Or, if a young man is desperate, is that an excuse for illegal behavior?

So, my recommendation is, for you the reader, to just sit back and not worry if this or that is fiction or non-fiction. Actually, it might be more fun to read, if you read this book as a non-fiction diary of a college rebel—which it could be—of course, one sentence of fiction, makes it a work of fiction."

ACKNOWLEDGEMENTS

My wonderful wife, Vertis, worked tirelessly with me to depict the realistic setting for this book, including how students dressed, acted, and reacted during the late 50s and early 60s. Her eye for the little details and her frank—sometimes blunt criticism—made the manuscript better in many ways.

1.

Regrets?

I guess it was my fault. Yeah, damn right it was, but who likes to admit they screwed up? It'd been a hell of a week for me. Oh, I don't mean stuff with my business or problems with my grown kids. It was a lot deeper than that. Over the years, I've gone through periods of depression, and that week I kept sinking lower and lower until, on Friday, I was barely able to function at work.

Of course, I really didn't even need to show up for my business to carry on. My staff could keep things running quite well without me, so I spent most of Friday brooding with my office door shut. When my door is shut, it's like a red flag that the boss is out of sorts. Yeah, I was going through one of those dark moods again. Hell, I walk around town like a self-made man, always in control, but that's just posturing. I've secretly been seeing a psychiatrist for over a year. It's taken her most of the year to dig through all the barriers I'd put up, but during our last visit she brought out some things that disturbed me. Hell, let me be honest: It was a lot more than just 'disturbing' to me, and, after that session, I was shaking with regret.

By about two that afternoon I couldn't stand it any longer, and I bolted out of the office, leaving my staff wondering what was going on. I knew exactly where to go. There's a place down on the Ouachita River called Pigeon Hill, where giant beech and pin oak trees are clustered around a steep bluff. When the first settlers arrived in south Arkansas, it was a roost for Passenger Pigeons. As a boy, I had hunted squirrels up and down the river, and that spot always had a calming, head-clearing effect on me.

In a few minutes I'd pulled off the pavement, and, after another fifteen, I arrived at a locked gate meant to keep trespassers off the property. I ignored the gate, walked around it, and was soon leaning back against one of the big beech trees, looking out over the river. For a while things were better. Maybe it was the peace and calm, which assured me that everything was going to be all right. There have been times when I've pulled away from my family and my work just to contemplate life. Am I going in the right direction? Should I do this or that? The questions over the years have changed, but they have always been there.

Questions—always questions, and sometimes I have reflected back and wondered if some of the choices I'd made in life were the right ones. But, you know, it's human nature to try and justify your choices. We all do it, and, after you've justified those choices long enough, you actually believe that you made the right ones, even if you didn't. Well, a good psychiatrist, will sooner or later make you face up to those decisions, especially the ones that have been really bothering you. And when that happens, it can be very therapeutic—or very troubling. Deep in my past was a choice that had tormented me for years.

It was almost dark when I walked back out of the woods. I wish I could say, as I have so many times, that I felt refreshed and sure of my direction in life. However, the depression was even worse, and I was mumbling some long-suppressed regrets. I felt as if I had no direction in my life.

My habits are so rutted that being two-hours late coming home from work, and missing from the office since two o'clock, had my wife fuming. With the irritable attitude I was bringing home, I knew we were in for a rocky night, but I never dreamed that it would turn out as badly as it did.

"Hey, I'm home," I yelled as I walked in from the garage. The back door banged behind me, shaking the pictures on the wall in the hallway. My wife wheeled around with her hands on her hips. Not a good sign, but she let the door-slamming slide.

Our conversation was civil for a few minutes. I thought maybe we could relax over a martini and manage to get though the evening, but, before I could mix the drinks, she said in a flat, mater-of-fact manner, "Not even going to have the courtesy to tell me where you've been?"

You know, when you've been married as long as we have, you're able to pick up little nuances. Sure enough it was there, that tight-lipped, cocked-head attitude. I could feel the prick of disgust, but I held my temper.

"Had to drive over to El Dorado to look at a geologic log—How about a martini?" Hell, I figured a little gin might salvage the evening.

My wife was shaking her head before the words were even out of my mouth, and it wasn't because she didn't want a martini. I pulled out the Plymouth gin and started to make our martinis.

"You're lying, Sandy. Your secretary said you've been in one of your rotten moods all day, and then you just walked out. Looking at a log in El Dorado? Now come on; were your iPhone and fax down?"

Hell, I knew better than to push the lie after that.

"Damn, can't I go to the pot without checking in?" I turned my back to her and went back to pouring the gin.

"What's wrong with you, Sandy?"

She had that look that has always been able to melt me. I swear, if she didn't have such a forgiving heart, we'd have been divorced years ago. Most of the time I'll soften up and put my bad mood aside, but for some reason I couldn't shake it.

"Nothing—still want that damn martini?"

The sharp comment made her shake her head and turn toward the living room. She muttered, "I guess," before walking away.

Over the years, my wife and I have developed a habit of having one martini before dinner, sitting back listening to jazz, and relaxing while we unwind. That night didn't look very promising, but, hell, I thought maybe a martini would give me some relief. We sat down, and things went smoothly for about half an hour, but trouble was brewing right under the surface, and we both knew it. Usually, we sip our drinks slowly while we talk, but I finished my drink quickly and cut off the conversation.

"Hey, let's have another martini. I really need it tonight." That wasn't a question; it was more of a demand, and I saw her take a deep breath before she answered.

"Sandy, we always stop at one. We'll feel terrible tomorrow if we drink another."

"I don't care about tomorrow. Do you want one or not?" I knew that was a snappy, rude response, but she took a deep breath and said, through tight lips, "Well, I guess if you're having one, fix me one, too."

I didn't answer her except for a shrug of my shoulders. Tension was rising, and we could both feel it.

Looking back on that evening, I've always been tempted to blame what happened on the second martini. But it wasn't the second or even the third martini that caused the problem. The problem was there, and even stone-cold sober, sooner or later it was bound to boil to the surface.

Normally we talk nonstop about our day, the latest town gossip, or where we're going on vacation. But we drank that second martini without saying a word. The room almost felt suffocating to me. And as my wife's lips got tighter and tighter, I knew it was only a matter of time until we went into one of our classic, screaming fights.

"Hey, I'm having another. How 'bout you?"

She looked at me, her head tilted slightly back, and her steely gaze told the whole story—wow, was she mad. I knew I'd crossed the line, and now the woman who loved me dearly had been pushed too far.

"Sure, why not?"

She spit out the words out like bullets.

That surprised me, because my wife is an exercise freak, and having something extra to drink is one thing she never does. Now more than a hint of disgust, barely hidden below the surface, came with that "Sure..."

She crossed her legs, leaned forward on her elbows, and waited for me to sit down. Hell, I knew what was coming. That was her attack posture. I straightened my back and waited for the blast. She grabbed the third martini out of my hand, spilled about a quarter of it, and started in on me.

"Sandy, I've just about had it with these moods!"

Damn, when she started out with that high-pitched near-scream, I knew she was about rip into me. Looking back on that night, I sure couldn't blame her.

"Sandy, you're not even good company drunk. What's wrong with you?"

Of course, she didn't wait for a reply. She kept digging, and in seconds she had ended up exactly where I didn't want her to go.

"Let's see, you're not drilling anything, so it can't be a dry hole. Hmmm..."

That woman had more insight than anyone I've ever seen, and, after a few minutes of probing, she managed to zero in on the problem. But she didn't understand, not one little bit. I guess I couldn't blame her. With a nod of her head, she said, in a near-whisper, "I'll bet I know."

I could feel the assault coming like a rushing wind as she raised her voice to a shout.

"Depressed about her again, aren't ya?" The words had a cutting, shrill edge and promised more of the same. Then she went through the irritating motion of raking her fingers through her hair. God, when I saw that, the warm-up for a real blast, I gritted my teeth and got ready. That was just her opening salvo, and, knowing my wife as I do, I knew she was going to have a lot more to say. Of course, I tried to cut it off, but she was wound up.

"Oh, please, surely you're not going to go through that again? Don't overreact!" I yelled. "I mean it! Don't overreact!" I've hit her with that line for years, and I knew just what the response would be. Yeah, I had just punched one of her hot buttons.

"Overreact? Why not? God, how can I not react to someone who's been hanging over this marriage for decades? Let's talk about her! Get her out on the table! I want you to talk about her until you're blue in the face! Come on, Sandy, get it out! Say you made the wrong choice!"

Maybe it was my imagination, but the word "choice" seemed to echo through the room.

She'd punched my hot button now, and I responded just as I had hundreds of times before. But tonight I was on another level of anger and depression, and—yes—I was drunk.

"Hey, don't you mention her again, you hear me, Mrs. Fat Ass!" Ha! I could see her seethe when "fat" hit her. That was another one of my favorite buttons of hers to push, and I smirked as I leaned back on the couch and took a sip of my martini. Take that! I thought.

She glared at me, spitting her words out through pursed lips.

"Bring her up again? Look, Sandy, you've brought her up for the last forty-five years! My God, last week when they put you under for that little colonoscopy you mumbled her name!" Then she leaned back, carefully enunciating her words. "Can't forget that last night in Fayetteville, can you?" Those words just slipped out of her mouth like slime.

"Fayetteville" was loud enough to break glass. Hell, over the years we've tried to forget that night, and we'd never really talked about it, but now, after forty-five years, she'd finally brought it up. It was as if a knife had been driven into my chest. I barely breathed for a few seconds as the words penetrated the depths of my soul.

I tried to recover, but my breath was coming in short jerks, and my face turned from a splotchy, drunken red to a pale, sallow white. My hands shook, but I managed to take another swallow of my martini while glaring at her. I couldn't believe how that woman could jerk me around. It was all I could do to just sit there.

"You're lying! Lying!" I slurred, beginning to lose control.

There it was—that look of disgust I'd seen so many times. Then she pointed her finger at me, twirling her head as if she were speaking to a lowlife dog, and threw another zinger.

"God, you're so sick and obsessed that nothing goes through that pea brain of yours! You strut around town like you're some big deal—God's gift to Magnolia! Don't you know people think you're just rich, trailer-park trash?"

I'm not kidding, that really ticked me off. Well, I guess I do have a thin skin when it comes to how people in Magnolia think of me. I've worked like a dog to pull myself up from the pits of poverty, and I've given that town more than you can imagine—a lot more than so-called "old" Magnolia. First, she brings up that last night in Fayetteville, and now she belittles everything I've done for the past thirty years. I was so mad and out of control that I could hardly speak.

"You worthless!—Worthless!"—I couldn't think of anything else to say for a few seconds. Then I added, "I ought to throw this martini in that double-chinned face of yours!" Boy, did that double-chin punch nail her. Hell, she had to put her martini down, she was so mad. Yeah, that's a good comeback, I thought as I leaned back on the couch and gave her a little smirk.

It took her a few seconds, but then she tossed off the double-chin remark like it didn't matter. She shook her head and laughed as she pointed to where my martini was sitting.

"Ha! You haven't got the guts to throw that martini! If you so much as touch me, you'll regret it for the rest of your sorry life! How would you like the divorce papers to read, 'spousal abuse?' Try to live that down, Mr. Magnolia! So get out of my sight!"

She took a big sip of her martini as she flipped her hair back, knowing that she had pretty much nullified everything I'd just said. God, I loved that woman, but she could absolutely drive me crazy. Of course, I was speechless. What do you say after someone has nailed you with the absolute facts, and you both know that they're true? I'll show her I thought. Then I reacted like some stupid drunk. I walked over to where she was sitting, and threw the last half of my martini in her face.

Of all the rash things I've done over the years, I've never regretted anything as much. I knew I'd crossed the line. She looked shocked for a second because in all of the arguments and fights we've had, I'd never touched her. She slowly wiped the gin from her face, and I immediately began to feel remorse about what I'd done. There was a fiery glare in her eyes, so intense that it made me step back. Then she leaned forward, made a sweep of her arm, and cleared the table of her martini glass, two candles, and a vase full of flowers.

"Wait! Stop! Are you crazy?" I began waving my hands, but she was so mad that I had to take another step back to get out of swinging range. I yanked out a handkerchief to wipe her face as I tried to mouth the words "I'm sorry," but it was way too late for that. She was out of control, looking for something, and then her eyes fixed on the glass-top coffee table in front of her.

"Hey! Stop! What in the hell are you doing?"

She'd picked up a big, trilobite fossil that I'd brought back from Morocco, and I thought for a moment that she was going to throw it at me. I backed off another couple of steps and raised my arms to catch it. I'd been deep in the Atlas Mountains, doing surface geology for Exxon, when a young boy came up to my car and held out the most perfect specimen of a large trilobite that I'd ever seen. It was about eight inches long and maybe four inches thick of solid rock. God, don't let her break that fossil, flashed through my mind.

"Don't throw that! It's a perfect trilobite, and I'll never find another one like it!" I jumped around in front of her and put up my hands to deflect or catch the heavy rock. But she stared at me, and, without saying a word, turned toward a tall glass case that contained my collection of Pre-Columbian figurines and pottery.

I'd spent twenty years buying them at Sotheby's, Santa Fe, and even in central Belize. I had collected four shelves of figurines and pots—mostly Mayan and Colima. Then, a few years ago, I had found an eight foot tall glass case in an antique store, and managed to get my entire collection in one display. The case had a solid front of curved glass, good lighting, and a motion-detector alarm.

"No! No!" It all happened so suddenly that just the thought of what she was about to do froze me in my tracks. I gasped and watched in horror. She drew back and threw, and I dived toward the case. I've played out the scene in my mind many times over the last several months, and that moment always seems to be in slow motion—the heavy fossil rock flying out of her hand and heading for the case. I could feel my body tense as I reached for the fossil, which cleared my outstretched hands by inches. I fell sprawled out on the floor in front of the case. I remember hearing one thundering crash followed by more and more crashes, and then glass and pieces of Mayan pots cascaded down on me. The fossil had hit the glass case above the top shelf, shattered the front of the case, and then collided with a priceless Mayan pot, smashing it to pieces.

But what happened next was unbelievable. The rock smashed against the next glass shelf, breaking it, and the contents of that shelf toppled down onto the next shelf, which also broke. Then everything from the top two shelves hit the third, and the whole mess collapsed in a pile of rubble. Pieces of Mayan figurines and broken pottery were scattered across the base of the case, and the living room floor, and the motion detector railed an alarm.

I staggered to my feet, brushing off glass and fragments of Pre-Columbian pottery. Then I stood there in a drunken shock as I looked at my priceless collection, destroyed in an instant. It took a few seconds for it to sink in: my wife had destroyed Pre-Columbian art worth about half a million dollars.

"Oh, my God, Sandy, I didn't mean to do it! Oh, God, no!"

She staggered back, sank down on the couch, and buried her head in her hands, sobbing.

When I looked at my pride and joy, destroyed in such an irrational act, I knew that I couldn't live with her for another minute. I walked out the front door and never looked back, and the next day I filed divorce papers.

Maybe, when she destroyed my Pre-Columbian pottery collection, it gave me the reason I needed to file the divorce I'd been wanting for years. She was right about one thing: That last night in Fayetteville was still as vivid in my mind as if it had happened a week ago.

2.

The Journal

T hat night I remember storming out the front door as my wife ran after me, crying, "Sandy, please don't leave! I'm sorry. Don't leave me, please!"

I wanted to turn around and go back in, but the martinis and the cussing fight we'd just gone through sent me up the tile walk toward my car, and then I felt a feeling of relief as the weight of that marriage lifted from my mind. Yes! Finally! Finally, I thought. I was shaking my fist in the air, and, just for a few minutes, I had an exhilarating surge of emotion, which gave me a fleeting feeling that I was on the verge of reversing the choice I'd made forty-five years ago. Then, as I backed out of the turnaround and drove up the driveway toward the street through a grove of oak trees, my hands began to shake. Should I stop and go back in the house? Am I making a mistake? That fight was my fault! She's such a wonderful woman!

Those thoughts flooded my mind, and, as I drove up the long driveway, a desolate hollowness seemed to fill my chest. My memories—kids—my wife. It was as if I'd closed a chapter of my life and instantly regretted it. I slowed the car down and paused at the end of the driveway, trying to sort out my emotions. Then, overriding the urge to return home, I recognized another feeling, one that my psychiatrist and my wife had laid bare. It came surging through the depths of my soul and drove me away into the night.

***

Several months passed since that night, and my emotions were on edge to the point that I could hardly function. Even going to work became difficult, and there wasn't a day that I didn't think about returning to my wife. However, separation has an effect on a person, and each day I grew a little stronger until, finally, I could face my friends again without an embarrassing silence.

I guess the hardest part was actually going through the motions of a divorce, which I would desperately want one day, but not the next. As I look back on those times, I realize that to actually go through with the divorce I needed to build up resentment. I tied to dream up my wife's every conceivable flaw, but finally my imagination turned me into such a short-tempered person no one wanted to be around me. God, I was awful.

***

The phone was ringing as I walked back into my apartment at The Pines.

"Yeah! Oh, hey, John—uh huh, no, and I don't care! She can have every bit of it!" It was John Dickerson, an old friend and attorney, who told me my wife was getting the house. I had one last morning to pick up any personal items. Hell, the way the divorce was moving, that might be it. Of course, in my frame of mind, I'd just yelled at my attorney to give it all to my wife. I guess that's why you need an attorney. For the next ten minutes, he calmed me down and convinced me I should at least go through my personal belongings.

"Hell, Sandy, you know damn well there are things in that house you're gonna want. Listen to me, boy, you may never set foot in that house again, so get your ass over there and at least look things over."

That was John: profane, kick-ass attorney and good friend. So the next morning I went through my desk in the main house, and that afternoon I was told that I had four hours to clean out personal items from our guest house, which also served as my home office. I couldn't believe it had come to this, and I was in a lousy mood as I walked down to the guesthouse, knowing this was probably the last time I'd walk through the door of a place I really held dear.

First, I went to my old desk in the front-room office. Aside from some oil and gas leases, nothing in the desk was worth taking. I was about to call it a day when I went into the main guest bedroom, where I'd built a row of storage closets. I started yanking open each closet door, letting them bang against each other as I thought about how mad that would make my wife. By the time I reached the last of the four, I was slamming and closing them while yelling, "Yeah! Nothing here!" I was going to be through in minutes, but, when I opened the last closet door, something caught my eye. I hesitated.

"My God, I can't believe I saved all of this stuff."

There they were; stacks and stacks of old college notebooks, annuals, and other keepsakes from my days at the University of Arkansas. Why in God's name I saved all that crap I'll never know, but there it was, three shelves full of assorted junk. Well, that's me, a junk dealer. Hell, I save everything. I'm a geologist and a pack-rat and, believe it or not, they go together. Instead of throwing anything away, geologists just add a file cabinet.

Curiosity got the best of me, and I reached in and began to rummage through the papers on top. There, beside the notebooks, was a letter from the now long-gone Humble Oil and Refining Company, offering me a job in south Texas, and right beside it a copy of the first royalty check I received after I quit Humble and started my own business.

Successful, too, I thought as I contemplated dividing a multi-million dollar estate with my wife. Of course, just that thought put me in an even worse mood. Over to the side of the first storage closet shelf I saw a nameplate with, "Sandy Carson, President," on it. One of my kids had given it to me for Christmas a few years ago, but I'd never put it out. Being president of Empire Resources, a family company, didn't seem to be that much of a deal.

Then I saw it: Shoved to the back of the bottom storage shelf against the cabinet wall was a thick, three-ring notebook. I recognized it immediately. It was The Journal.

"Oh, my God! Where did that come from?" I murmured aloud, pulling it out from under a pile of notebooks. "I thought I threw that away—guess I didn't." Hell, I was almost yelling as I stood there shaking my head.

For a few minutes, I stared at the dusty cover of the three-ring binder, and I felt my breath quicken. "Shit, what's wrong with me?" I muttered. Yeah, more of those choices came drifting back, and, as I looked at The Journal, I couldn't resist sitting down and thumbing through it. I wiped off the dust, opened it, and frowned as I looked at a notation in the last part of the notebook.

"Shit!" It was an especially sordid memory—one of the really bad ones I'd been trying to forget for forty-five years had just hit me in the face, and I shivered involuntarily. I started to put the notebook back in the storage closet, but something about it made me hesitate. It was as if The Journal was an addictive drug that I couldn't resist, and now I eagerly flipped through it, glancing at the entries.

"Oh, my God!" I shook my head in disgust, and then flipped a few pages over to a different entry. Looking at it, I laughed for the first time in several months, and it startled me so much that I looked around, embarrassed at myself.

Well, one thing I knew for sure: I wasn't about to leave The Journal there for my wife to read. She'd probably use some of that stuff to nail me at the final divorce proceedings. But what am I going to do with it? And then I glanced over at the trashcan and nodded my head as I tossed it in. My aim was excellent, and the notebook hit the top rim, bounced up and plunked down. However, as it cascaded into the can, something popped out and landed on the floor. As picky as I am about a messy house, I compulsively walked over to tidy up. I recognized it immediately: It was an envelope with a key in it, the key to the side door of the Delta Chi sorority house.

"God Almighty, I can't believe I still have that key," I muttered.

I guess that was enough to suck me in again, and I put the Delta Chi key and envelope back in The Journal and started to read from page one.

Three hours later, I was still turning pages. I laughed, swore, and—yeah, I cried as I relived the years I had spent at the University of Arkansas. Everything written in The Journal had always been a well-kept secret. I'd never told anyone what I did during those four years, and, when I graduated and got married, the last thing on earth I wanted was for all that stuff to be made public. I don't know, maybe it was the bitter life that had suddenly come upon me since I walked out that night. Or maybe it was the divorce, which I was beginning to dread.

As I sat there reminiscing and wallowing in my misery, a compelling urge to tell this story swept over me. My mind raced. But what would my kids think? What if my wife and I reconciled? What would my church think, and my friends and business acquaintances? It took another hour to sort through all those questions, but even while I was going through that process, I knew that the outcome was settled. What did I have to lose? I was in a failing marriage. I was rich and self-employed. But overriding everything was a strange impulse to tell the world my story, and even though I had changed from my college days, there were things in The Journal that would be embarrassing to everyone concerned. Could I take the comments? After all, I had become a pillar of the community and some of the things that happened during my college life weren't exactly what someone of my status would be proud of. But there's something, and I guess it's the desire to confess, which spurred me on. From that moment, I started preparing to write this book. I tucked The Journal under my arm and left the guesthouse.

Before leaving, I took a long look back at my house. I saw my wife standing in the doorway, watching me drive away. I thought she held up her hand, and I felt a wave of remorse, which I quickly pushed out of my mind. I had a project, and, for the first time in years, I was excited.

3.

Lawyer John

Well, after I'd thought about it for a few days, some of the excitement about writing my book was replaced by the cold realization that it was really going to tick off some people in a big way. I guess there are plenty of times in a person's life when just the idea that you would upset a lot of people by revealing personal information would be enough to call a halt to a project. This wasn't one of those times. Hell, I'd pulled away from all of my friends, my wife was about to nail me for millions of dollars in a divorce settlement, and I had nothing but time on my hands.

Late one afternoon I had a martini and made my decision: Yes, I was going to write the book. But, after I decided that, the question came up about using actual names. Well, I'll admit it: I backed down a bit and decided I wasn't going to use real names, or real sororities or fraternities, but I was going to set this story at the school where it happened. And, most importantly, I sure wasn't going to use my own name.

It all boils down to this: Because of the sensitive nature of what I have revealed in my book, names have been changed to protect the innocent, and, yes, the guilty, and to dissuade any lawsuits, which might be filed.

It's been almost fifty years since those events occurred, and, although The Journal records a detailed account of various conversations, actions, and incidents that occurred during this time period, I know the sequence of events and the conversations I had will be difficult to record exactly as they happened. However, I did write in the notebook almost every day during my four years at the university, and the tone and nature of those hectic days is clearly expressed in this writing.

I've been in business long enough to know I needed to run a crazy project like this by a lawyer. My soon-to-be ex-wife was going to get a lot of my money, so I sure didn't want some jerk suing me for what I had left. On Monday morning, I gave John Dickerson The Journal, told him to read it, and then set up an appointment. John is a confirmed bachelor who's overweight, sloppy, and chews an unlit cigar most of the time. Going into his office is like wading through a minefield of paper. I got a lot more advice than I wanted. John began yelling at me when I walked through the door.

"Sandy, what in the hell is this? You can't be serious! I spent most of the night readin' through that journal of yours. Let me get this straight: You've either got the best imagination in the world, or your college life at the University of Arkansas was off the damn wall." He tossed the The Journal back to me, and I laid it on a chair.

"Which is it?"

"John, I was eighteen to twenty-two years old, and impression-able as hell. I probably exaggerated some stuff, but, overall, that's about like it happened."

"Really? Well, I'll be damned. Now, are you serious about putting all of this out for public consumption?—You know, every-body's gonna read it, especially anybody that ever attended the university. Ready for your preacher to read all that stuff about women and stolen test papers?"

"I don't care who reads it, John. I've thought that through. What I don't want is to have to cough up more dough if I'm sued. That's your job, old buddy. To help Sandy keep what little money is left after the divorce."

Lawyers don't like to be told that you only hired them to save your ass, and John winced as if I'd just stuck him with a pin.

"Bull, Sandy. Don't give me that crap! Sit down and let's talk about this." John plopped back in his chair and shoved some papers aside. In a few seconds, he'd uncovered his notes. He was still shaking his head when he started in on me.

"Okay, then, let's get right to the point. You'd be all right tellin' 'bout most of the crap that's in there, but I'd like to find out if some of the principal characters you paint as real losers are still alive. Keep this in mind, Sandy: You can't libel the dead, and you can't be sued for telling the truth, if you can prove that it's the truth, but you sure can have your ass cleaned out if one of those guys you talk about is still living. And if you can't convince a jury you're tellin' the truth, they'll hang you out to dry."

"Damn, John, I'm not about to use their real names."

"Sandy, if you describe someone to the point where a person can recognize 'em, then that's as good as usin' their name."

"Okay, I got it. Make a list of people you want me to leave out if they're not dead, and I'll check 'em out."

"You think that's it? For God's sake, Sandy, you're overlooking the real problem here."

"What?"

"Sandy, there's stuff in that journal that'll have some people in this state ready to shoot you. Hell, some of the things you did in college, even if the statute of limitations has run out, will make you look like crap. Can you handle that?"

"I think so. Hell, I'm not about to write it under my own name, and, after my divorce goes through, I'll probably never see Arkansas again. Let me tell you something, John. I'm at the point in my life where nothing really matters anymore."

"Oh, come on, Sandy, you're not being realistic. Number one, I don't care how careful you are, sooner or later you'll be exposed as the author. And, hell, when that happens, you'd better have a tough hide. You might say you don't care if you tick off the whole state, but, when the hate mail and snide comments start peppering your ass, it'll be different. And some redneck really might shoot you."

"Well, John, if it gets too tough, I'll just say I was a ghost writer for someone else, or that this is really a novel. Made it all up, just fiction."

"Bull, Sandy, it won't be difficult to figure out most of the characters in your book, no matter what names you use. And Lacy and Vi? Sandy, if you make all this crap public those two women will kill you."

"Fiction, John. Remember, it's just fiction."

"You're dreaming, Sandy. Some of the Deltas will remember this, and when you put that stuff about the Texas game in there, you're going to hear screaming all over the state. Fiction, hell! You can tell 'em it's fiction till you're blue in the face, but you're not gonna convince some people. My advice to you, as your attorney and friend, is to forget that journal, or put it away, and let one of your kids let it out after you, Lacy, and Vi are dead. Sandy, right now, you're really not yourself. You're depressed about your divorce. Give this thing some time, and you'll see what I mean. Please don't write this until you've cooled off."

John and I sat there looking at each other for a few minutes, and then I said, "Give me your list of people I need to check out. I am going to write the book."

John shook his head and reached for a file. "Sandy, I've known you long enough to know you were gonna write the damn thing no matter what I said. Here, I've already made out the list. Check these people out, and don't include 'em if they're not dead."

I took the list, put it in my suit pocket, and smiled.

"Thanks, John. I'll let you read a first draft before I send it off to a publisher." I tucked The Journal under my arm and stood up to leave.

"I hope the hell you do. Maybe you'll have cooled off by then, and, when I spot some problems, we can cut 'em out of the book before the lid blows off this pile of crap." John got up from his desk, walked around to where I was standing, and put his arm around my shoulder.

"Sandy, we've been friends for over thirty years, and I can see how much this divorce has hurt you. I've handled more divorces than I can remember, and I've never seen anyone take it so hard."

John paused and shook his head. "I don't know. Maybe it's because you've been married to one of the most gorgeous women in the state, and your marriage looked perfect to everybody who knew you."

John looked at me and then at The Journal, which I had tucked under my arm.

"You didn't let some of that stuff that happened to you in college get to you, did you?"

"No, John," I lied. "Little things, then her lawyers got involved, and before I knew it I'd had become bitter and cynical and wanted out. Hell, I know I'm not myself, and I'm probably writing this book just to get some things off my chest, but can't help myself."

I wasn't about to tell John the real reason we were splitting up. John smiled and shook his head, and I turned to leave.

"Keep me posted, Sandy. And, hey, don't give up on your marriage yet. You never know, y'all still might still make it."

I shook my head and shut the door behind me.

That afternoon I opened The Journal and started typing. This is the story as I remember it.

4.

Uncle Hosie

Well, I found out real quick that it was a lot easier to posture about writing a book based on The Journal than to actually put the damn thing on paper. I had a bad case of writer's block when I sat down, because if I started with my first day in college it was going to be hard for a reader to figure out some of the things I did. So, after thinking things through, I decided to include some of the stuff that happened when I was a senior in high school—things that sure influenced my college life.

When I started my senior year in high school I had dark, blond hair, which bleached out that summer from working in the sun. Thanks to my hair, I had long since been tagged with the nickname "Sandy." Of course, my mother had tried to stop that nickname from sticking by insisting that everyone call me Stuart, my given name. But, after a few years, she was the only person I knew who still used it. When I was in my teens, Stuart Carson sounded like some stuck-up guy from the East Coast. I liked being called Sandy. It had the right sound. I was almost as tall as I am now, six-foot-two, but instead of weighing 175 pounds, I weighed less than 140; I was skinny as a rail and ornery as hell.

I probably should have regrets about the stuff I pulled in high school, but I don't. "Just coming of age" is the best excuse I can come up with. That year I lived with my mother in a pitiful, unpainted little farm house a mile outside of the small, south Arkansas village of Pine Valley, a little hick town of about 1200. When I was fifteen, my father was killed in a car wreck on the Magnolia Highway. Since it was on a Friday night, naturally he was drunk. All Mother received from his estate was $2000 from an insurance policy, which didn't go very far, since my alcoholic father's estate was sued for $5000. It took almost a year to clean up everything from my dad's death. The lawyers took everything, and we had to declare bankruptcy.

To get by, we moved to a little farm about a mile out of town, which was owned by a family friend. He didn't charge us rent, and Mother took a job in Magnolia, working at a dry cleaner's, which allowed us to get by. Money was pretty scarce, but I worked part time during the school year, and every summer I worked in the woods or baled hay for our neighbor, Mr. Purvis. Baling hay and stacking hay on a wagon is one tough job. Well, we managed to get by, but it wasn't easy.

Pine Valley had been a much bigger town during the south Arkansas oil boom of the 1920s, but by the time I graduated from the little consolidated high school of Mount Union, the town had dwindled down to a single row of dilapidated businesses, most of which seemed to be propped up by a row of tobacco-chewing old-timers. Pine Valley is only eight miles from Magnolia, a much bigger town.

In the summer before my senior year, I worked on a hay-baling crew. I don't remember much about stacking that hay on the back of a big flatbed trailer except that it was hard as hell, but I do remember the noon lunch hours, when the crew sat around under a tree and played poker. I started the summer really getting cleaned out, and it was beginning to look like I was going to work all summer for nothing. But by mid-July I could hold my own, and when Labor Day rolled around I was winning almost every day, which, considering the crew of rednecks I was working with, wasn't much of a deal. Hell, most of those guys had to use their toes to count to 20.

The hay-baling job finished up right after Labor Day, and I was glad to have a few days off before school started to rest up from some of the hardest work I'd ever done.

It was one of those early September days, a week before my senior year began, when we had a visit from a relative of ours, an uncle I'd never heard of. I was sitting on the front porch when I saw this skinny, bent-over man walking up the road toward our house, dragging an old, beat-up cardboard suitcase. My God, he looked like death warmed over. The temperature was at least 95 degrees, and I could tell he was really struggling. He'd stop every thirty yards or so to puff on a cigarette and wipe the sweat off his brow. He was wearing a gray, felt hat, an old, blue sports coat, and some khaki slacks that looked four sizes too big. We lived a mile from Pine Valley, and it was unusual for someone to be walking along the road by our house. I really took notice when he looked at the number on our rural mailbox, turned up the driveway, and walked up to the porch where I was sitting. I was shaking my head as he tried to catch his breath.

"Son, is this here the Carson home?" he wheezed, sucking on his cigarette as he gasped for air.

"Yes, sir, it is. What can I do for you?"

The man smiled, wiped the sweat off his brow, and cocked his head, as he looked me over.

"Yep, I'd have guessed it, a-lookin' at you. You is shore a Carson if I ever seed one."

"Huh?"

"You don't know me, do you, boy?"

"No, sir, I don't."

"Son, I'm yore Uncle Hosie."

What is he talking about, I thought.

"Stuart, who is it?" Mother yelled from the kitchen.

"Mother, you need to come here," I yelled back. "There's a man out here who says he's my uncle." Well, let me be honest: If that shriveled-up old geezer was my uncle, then our family was sure a rung further down on the ladder from where I thought we were. Mother was through the door in seconds. She took one look and said, "Hosie, what are you doing here?"

"Now, Sister, don't get all riled up, 'cause I ain't escaped or nothin'. They let me out on parole."

Mother was wringing her hands and had started to tap her foot, a habit she had when she was upset. She walked to the edge of the porch and leaned over, right in Uncle Hosie's face.

"Hosie, are you telling me the truth?"

Uncle Hosie spit some tobacco juice on the front step and said, "Sister, I swear to God, I is. Got out of Tucker this mornin', rode the bus to Magnolia, and hitched me a ride to Pine Valley. I been walkin' to yer place ever since I got to town, and my ass is plum worn out."

There was something about old Uncle Hosie that I liked. He seemed, on the one hand, like a rundown, old man, but he had a way of talking and a glint in his eyes that said otherwise. Of course, I couldn't believe the conversation I was hearing. This sweaty, crusty old coot was calling my mother, "Sister," and she was acting as if she knew him. What in the world is going on? Is he really my uncle?

I gave Mother a puzzled look, and she took a deep breath and said, "Stuart, this is Hosie Lee Davis, your uncle."

"What?" It was hard to hold back a smile, because Mother had had to make herself say those words. She just shook her head and didn't answer my question.

Uncle Hosie smiled, spit some more tobacco juice, and said, "Sister, let me tell Stuart."

"Uh, call me Sandy."

Mother frowned, but Uncle Hosie grinned a tobacco-stained, toothy grin and nodded.

"You bet, Sandy. Shoot, that name suits you a whole lot better than that phony soundin' 'Stuart.'"

Mother looked a little uncomfortable, but she was calming down as Uncle Hosie started in on a tale about some really "damned bad luck," as he called it, which ended up with him in Tucker Penitentiary, serving ten to twenty years. He'd been paroled and was released that very morning. I couldn't figure out the bad luck part of the story, unless it was bad luck that he'd been caught.

He finished up with, "Guess, yer momma didn't want to admit to no black sheep in the family." Uncle Hosie lit another Camel, leaned back against the porch, and wiped his brow with a dirty handkerchief.

"Oh, Hosie, I just thought Stuart didn't need to know about having an uncle in the penitentiary. Well, I'm glad you're out, and thanks for stopping by to see us. What are you going to do now?"

Momma had a worried look because she knew the answer to that question.

"Oh, I don't know, Sister. Maybe get a job in the oil fields or cuttin' timber, but, uh...uh...I need a place to stay. Course, just till I find a job."

Mother gave him a cold stare, and her foot began to tap again as she considered the prospect of a pardoned criminal staying with us while he looked for a job.

"No, Hosie, it wouldn't look right to have a convicted felon living here with us. What would people say?"

"Oh, Sister, it'll be just a few days. I promise. Shoot, I'll be gone by the weekend. If I don't stay with y'all, I'll have to sleep out in the woods. Would you make yore brother sleep out there with all them mosquitoes?"

Mother wanted to say no, but she had a heart of gold, and turning away her brother, even if he was a convicted criminal, was more than she could do. Finally, he nodded her head, and Uncle Hosie followed her into the house, dragging his suitcase.

Uncle Hosie's weekend stay lasted much longer than a couple of days. Actually, I liked having a man around the house to talk with, and we became good friends. After he'd been with us for a week, he settled into a routine. He slept late every morning, and I never saw him until late afternoon. Usually sometime after three o'clock, he'd sit out on the front porch, smoke, and whittle, while

I sat on the steps, and we talked. Almost every night after supper he'd walk the mile into Pine Valley and be gone until well after midnight.

One Saturday afternoon was especially interesting to me. When I came home from a trip to Magnolia, he was sitting on the porch swing filing a long, thin, round piece of metal. It had a handle like a knife, and it had been filed down until it looked like a long, thin toothpick with a little hook on the end. I walked up and asked him what he was making.

"Well, Sandy, this here's a lock pick. Never know when you'll find a locked door that needs to be opened." He flipped the lock pick around for me to see.

"A lock pick?"

"Yep, I broke off my good one the other night in an old rusty lock. In a few minutes, I'll have this 'un ready. Ain't no lock 'round that'll stand up to this little baby."

Thoughts swirled through my head as I watched Uncle Hosie file the long piece of metal, and, finally, I had to ask the question that I'd avoided. "Uh, Uncle Hosie, why were you sent to the penitentiary?"

Uncle Hosie never said a word. He just smiled, puffed on his Camel, and twirled the lock pick around. I got the message. The old man was a lock-picking crook—and my uncle.

For some reason the idea of picking a lock fascinated me, and, after a little pleading, Uncle Hosie took me out to the barn, where we had several locked doors, and showed me how to work the pick.

The next afternoon I had the file and another long strip of metal, and was filing away under the supervision of Uncle Hosie. Soon I had a well-honed lock pick and lock jammer. After several tries, I managed to open the locks on our barn doors, our house, and even a padlock on an old trunk.

Late one afternoon, a few days later, Uncle Hosie and I were sitting on the front porch. He was talking to me about some of the finer points of lock picking when the Columbia County Sheriff pulled up in front of our house. Uncle Hosie looked a little concerned as the Sheriff approached our porch. Everybody in the county knew Sheriff Benjamin "Bud" Taunton. When he walked up to the front porch, he called me by name and nodded to Uncle Hosie, who was fidgeting in his rocking chair.

"Hosie, where were you last night?"

Uncle Hosie nervously lit another Camel, leaned back in the rocking chair, and pretended he was relaxing and just visiting with the Sheriff.

"I went into town, had a beer at Pop's Place, and came right back here. I was in bed by ten o'clock."

Well, I knew the having a beer part was probably true, but I didn't go to sleep until after eleven, and Uncle Hosie had come in long after that.

"Hmmm, didn't go to Magnolia last night?" asked Sheriff Taunton. He took off his hat, wiped the sweat from his forehead, and stepped up closer to the porch.

"Nope, I stayed right in Pine Valley. Never left the city limits."

"I guess the skinny old man someone saw runnin' down the alley after the jewelry store alarm went off wasn't you, huh?" Sheriff Taunton leaned over against the porch, almost touching Uncle Hosie, and I noticed Uncle Hosie take a deep breath before he answered.

"Naw, Bud, couldn't have been me, 'cause I's right here when that robbery happened, and that's the God's truth. Ain't that right, Sandy?"

I must have looked like a startled rabbit, and I mumbled something like, "Uh, well, uh, huh," but the Sheriff just ignored me. He was honing in on Uncle Hosie.

Sheriff Taunton frowned and stared straight into Uncle Hosie's eyes.

"You sure?"

"Yes, sir, I'm positive, and I'll swear on a stack of Bibles! Ask Sandy!" Uncle Hosie was beginning to get rattled.

My God, stop trying to bring me in for an alibi, I thought.

Sheriff Taunton ignored me again and got right up in Uncle Hosie's face.

"Well, Hosie, someone picked the lock on the back door of Murphy's Jewelry store, ran in, grabbed up a gold watch and some other little stuff, and took off down the alley with the alarm ringin'. That pickin' job looked an awful lot like something you'd do."

"Bud, that man might have looked like me, and might have been able to pick a lock like me, but I'll swear on my sainted mother's name, it weren't me. I's right here, ask Sandy."

My gosh, every time Uncle Hosie mentioned my name I nearly fell off the porch. He was lying through his teeth, and, of course, the Sheriff knew it.

"Hosie, empty your pockets."

Uncle Hosie almost swallowed that Camel.—He slowly started pulling things out of his pockets and putting them down on the porch. When he finished he smiled at the Sheriff.

"See, Bud, done told you: I didn't have nothin' to do with that job," he boasted as the Sheriff looked through the contents of Uncle Hosie's pockets.

Just when I thought the Sheriff was about to walk away, he reached over and patted the right front pocket of Uncle Hosie's overalls.

"Hosie, what's the lump in that pocket?"

"Aw, it's just chewing tobacco, Bud."

"Let's take a look."

I saw a slight shake of the head, and Uncle Hosie's shoulders slumped as he reached in his pocket and pulled out a gold watch and chain.

"Well, Hosie, just can't stop, can ya?" And the Sheriff motioned for Uncle Hosie to come with him.

Uncle Hosie stood up, leaned over the porch rail, and shook his head.

"I don't know what it is. Something deep inside of me just

makes me go after 'em locks. I've sworn off so many times I've lost count. I just can't help it."

I stood there and thought about what Uncle Hosie had said: "Just can't help it."

Maybe he can't, I thought.

Uncle Hosie walked down the porch steps and then turned to look at me.

"Sandy, tell yer momma I've had a little run-in with the law, and I won't make supper." He followed the Sheriff to his car, opened the door, and slid in the back seat.

The Sheriff smiled and nodded to me as he walked around to the front of the car. "Hosie won't make supper for another ten years."

5.

High School

Mother seemed relieved after Uncle Hosie was taken back to prison. I think she was beginning to think he'd be with us permanently. A few days after Uncle Hosie left us, I started my senior year in high school. On the first day of classes, I walked into Biology class, planning to sit as far back and away from Coach Simmons, our worthless teacher, as I could. I tried to slip by, but he motioned for me to come over to his desk before taking my seat. As I stood there in front of the class, he started to go on about the football team, as usual.

"Uh, Sandy, I noticed y'all didn't dress out last week for football practice." Coach Simmons always used the plural "y'all" when he talked to folks. It didn't matter if it was one person or a hundred.

"No, sir, Mr. Simmons, I didn't."

Well, it hacked off Coach Simmons when I didn't call him "Coach," which, of course, I did deliberately, but he regained his composure and smiled.

"Sandy, we could really use y'all. We don't have many boys to pick from in this little school, and if somebody gets bunged up, y'all could see lots of playin' time."

"No, thanks, Mr. Simmons. I tried football last year, and it's just not my sport." A 137 pounds hanging on a six-foot-two frame is not your ideal size for playing football.

"Now, Sandy, you owe it to Mount Union. This school's been good to y'all."

Owe it to Mount Union? Well, I knew one thing for sure: I didn't owe Mount Union anything.

"Mr. Simmons, I think football is just about the dumbest sport I can think of, and I wouldn't go out this year if Marilyn Monroe were the coach." My smart mouth got me detention for the rest of the week, but, hey, that was par for the course. I was the world-class troublemaker of Mount Union High School.

Coach Simmons made his little note about detention, turned away from me, and reached down to pick up the Biology textbook as I went to the back of the room, catching some glares from the football players and a few giggles from the girls.

Well, I breezed through my classes that year, never carrying a book home, and only studied during study hall right before a test. The only time I spent on what might be called studying were the hours I spent in the school library. I absolutely love history, and I read every book that had anything to do with history. But that was it; nothing else even got a glance.

As the year passed, my tendency to shirk homework and only study enough to get a C almost caught up with me. During the spring semester, I studied Biology in the study hall right before a big mid-term test, and I figured I had an easy C. However, there were six A's, all from football players, which set the curve so high that I made a D. Something was sure fishy. A week later, I walked into the classroom as Coach Simmons and the same football players were standing around his desk. He quickly shoved a paper in his top desk drawer and motioned for everybody to sit down.

My God, I thought, he's showing them the test questions. Sure enough, he was, and when a pop quiz was given later that period the damn football players whizzed right through it. I made an F.

Something had to be done. I was so mad I was steaming. That sorry coach was letting his players cheat. The rest of the day, I schemed, trying to come up with a way to get even. If I told the principal, he'd brush it off since it came from me, Mr. Trouble-maker. If he did take it seriously and talked with Coach Simmons, it would be even worse. My name would surely come out, and, boy, I could just see the rest of the year with a bunch of ticked-off football players and their coach on my butt.

It finally came down to getting even, which meant acing the test. However, I decided that, even if I studied non-stop, I couldn't possibly out-score guys who had seen the actual test. All after-noon I wondered what to do, and then, late in the afternoon, when I was daydreaming in class as I usually did, I thought of Uncle Hosie. Then it hit me: Yeah, I could ace that test—if I really wanted to.

For the rest of the day I considered whether or not I should break into the school the night before the next big test and copy the questions. I felt uneasy and guilty as I sat there and schemed, but along with that uneasiness was a sense of excitement. It was a funny feeling, unlike anything I'd ever had. Something was pulling me to break into the school, if only to see if I could. Look-ing back on that time in my life I can remember thinking, Maybe Uncle Hosie can't help it—and maybe I can't either. I guess those Uncle Hosie genes had something to do with me wanting to pick the school lock and break in. Well, whether it was Uncle Hosie's blood or just Sandy the troublemaker I don't know, but I couldn't resist.

That afternoon all I could think about was breaking into the high school. The very thought of it had me excited, and at nine-thirty that night I was standing outside the building with the two lock-picking tools that Uncle Hosie had helped me make. My hands were sweating and shaking so badly I could hardly get the pick into the lock. Finally, I did, and, with one quick rake, pins rat-tled, the lock jammer turned, and the door opened. A few seconds later, I was in the building. As I walked down the dark hallway, the strangest sensation came over me. It was something like being on an exciting ride at a carnival, but different. I felt powerful, smart, on top of the world, in charge—almost giddy from the experience. Halfway down the hall I turned into Coach Simmons's office and started going through his desk. The test was right on top of some papers in the front desk drawer, probably where he had put it after showing it to those football players. I pulled out a little flashlight and, in a few minutes, I'd copied it.

As soon as the school door clicked behind me and I headed back home, I began to feel terrible about breaking in and stealing the test. I'd never stolen anything in my life. I had a restless night, but the next day I whizzed through the test and made a perfect score. Coach Simmons was puzzled, but he wasn't smart enough to think I'd stolen the test. After I got my test back and had a chance to flaunt it to the football players, I began to feel really guilty. Never, never, will I do something like this again, I told myself as I tried to justify the theft by thinking about how Coach Simmons was letting the football players see the test. Thinking about Uncle Hosie, who was a convicted felon, put me on a terrible guilt trip, and for several weeks, I worried that one day I'd end up just like him.

As my senior year slowly drifted into history, I started thinking about what I'd do after graduation. However, I didn't really have a choice in that matter. My mother was adamant.

"Stuart, you're going to college, so you might as well pick one. If you want to stay close to home, Southern State College, in Magnolia, is close by.

Yeah, I thought, and it's less than ten miles from Pine Valley. I didn't have a plan about what to do after high school graduation, but what few I had were far, far away from Pine Valley and that sorry Mount Union High School.

"Well, Mother, I was thinking about the University of Arkansas."

"Stuart, that's all the way up in Fayetteville. Are you sure you want to be that far away from home?"

"Yes, ma'am, and I think it's a better school."

"Well, it's up to you, but I can't afford to pay all the college costs. You know how tight money is around here."

I sure did. Mother worked as a presser at a Magnolia dry cleaner's to make ends meet. And working in that hot shop, pressing shirts all day, had caused her to drop fifteen pounds off an already thin body. Smoking further deteriorated her health, and I dreaded seeing her go to work, where she sweated all day in that dry cleaner's, and then came home in the afternoon exhausted, smoking one cigarette after another. I developed a strong dislike for cigarettes as I watched them sap my mother's strength. I knew if I went to college, I'd have to earn at least half of the $1200 a year it would take.

That summer, after I graduated from high school, I worked for Mr. Purvis's hay-baling crew again. After a summer's worth of work and day after day of noon hour poker playing, I had $350 in the bank, an expanded vocabulary of cuss words, and a good tan. When I put my poker winnings in with my hay-baling wages, and Mother gave me enough for a semester's room and board, I still didn't have enough money for a whole year of college, but at least I could get started. I'd have to find a part-time job after I registered for classes.

6.

Fayetteville and The University...and Doris

Of course, being accepted into the University of Arkansas wasn't a big deal, because they had to accept all Arkansas high school graduates with a 2.0 GPA. As the registration date for classes approached, I started checking around southern Arkansas, looking for another student who'd be attending. I was trying to find someone with a car in order to get my stuff to school.

After being turned down by a couple of boys from Magnolia, who didn't have room in their car, I gave up and went to the Greyhound Bus Station in Magnolia and bought a ticket to Fayetteville. I'd never been to the campus; in fact, I'd never been north of Little Rock. I was a little apprehensive, but just the idea of leaving Pine Valley and starting a new life had me anxious to go. Well, riding an old, smelly bus nearly ten hours to Fayetteville wasn't my favorite way to get to college, but the idea of actually having a car was so remote that it was laughable.

A week later I boarded the bus, dragging an old, beat-up, cloth suitcase and some extra clothes rolled up and tied in a piece of canvas. After a hellacious bus ride in a dirty, bus reeking of diesel fumes, packed with some really low-rent people—topped off with a two-hour layover in Little Rock—I stepped off the bus in downtown Fayetteville, hoping the university would be close to the bus station. But it wasn't. There was a café inside the station, and I went in to ask a lady at the cash register how to get to campus. She looked at me, sweat-soaked, bedraggled, and barely coherent, with my hair matted down, dragging my old cloth suitcase and a rolled-up canvas pouch, and I'm sure she was wondering how such a country bumpkin had made it to the University of Arkansas. She pointed north.

"Boy, you-ah, looks a-like you could use a drank."

Well, I looked a little puzzled and she said, "You know, a drank uv water."

"Yes, ma'am, that'd be fine." I sat at the counter, sipped a cold glass of ice water, and she continued to talk. Hell, I needed a translator. I thought south Arkansas was pretty far back in the sticks, but my first taste of northwest Arkansas had me thinking I'd arrived in another country—Dogpatch.

"I thank them a-Hogs is a-gonna win a bunch of ballgames this year. Don't you?"

Well, I picked up "Hogs" and "ballgames" so I gulped my water down and said, "Yes, ma'am, I sure 'nough do."

"Shor better win six, or that danged new coach is a gonner."

"Yes, ma'am. Well, I'd better head on over to the school. Can you give me some directions?"

"Just walk right down College Avenue—that there street yonder—two blocks to Dixon Street and turn left, keep a-walkin' through Schuler Town—which ain't no town a-tall—and you'll walk right up to that there school. It's 'bout a mile. Sure you don't wanta take no taxi?"

"No, ma'am, I don't have much in my bags. I can make it."

My suitcase and canvas bag were heavy, but, since I'd never taken a taxi before, I sure didn't feel confident enough to start. And, of course, I didn't have a clue how much a taxi would cost.

As I walked along College Avenue, I began to get depressed. I was sharing the sidewalk with young, barefoot girls, who looked about twelve, with babies on their hips, lanky hillbillies wearing overalls and beat-up straw hats, and farm couples in town to shop, which brought to mind the old joke: "If they get a divorce, are they still brother and sister?" Well, that was Fayetteville in 1957, before an infusion of money and fresh genes improved the economy and the I.Q. of the population.

I walked down Dixon Street into Shuler Town, which was just a railroad crossing, some burger joints, low-rent motels, and used car lots—not the best gateway to the state's premier university. As I trudged on down Dixon Street and started up a long hill, I could see a cluster of buildings, which, I found out later, were the original campus buildings. They formed a semicircle around the main administration building, known as Old Main.

When I finally arrived on campus, I started to feel better about being there. After asking a couple of students, I found Razorback Hall, my dorm. I checked in at a desk on the first floor and walked up the stairs to room 201. My roommate, Benny Blevins, from Mountain View, Arkansas, was sitting on one of the beds when I walked in. Benny had black hair, cut in a tight burr. He was wearing a dirty, white t-shirt, blue jeans, and a pair of beat-up, tennis shoes. Benny was the exact opposite from me in size. He looked to be about five-feet-seven-inches tall, and he weighed a good 190-pounds, some of which was sagging around his middle. He had a fair case of adolescent pimples, and he could have used braces.

"Hi, I'm Sandy Carson, from Pine Valley—down in south Arkansas."

"Come on in and throw your stuff on that bed against the wall. I'm Benny Blevins from Mountain View. You just got here?"

"Yeah, it was a ten-hour bus ride."

"Hey, I'll bet you're hungry. Let's get something to eat. Wanta go out or eat here?"

"Uh, whatta you mean, 'eat here'?"

"Oh, we can call Jug Wheelers. They'll deliver anywhere in town, and it can be as little as a Coke."

"Are you kidding?"

"Naw. My brother's a junior, and I've been to visit him a bunch of times. They're always calling Jug's to deliver somethin'."

I sat down on the bed, savoring my first taste of freedom. My gosh, order something to be delivered, or go out and eat anywhere we wanted? It took a minute for it to sink in.

"Well, are you hungry or not?"

"Yeah, I'm hungry. Let's call that Jug Wheeler person and get some hamburgers."

"Ha, it ain't a person; Jugs is a drive-in burger joint that delivers."

"Okay, whatever. You call, and order me a hamburger, onion rings, and a Coke."

"You got it."

In less than fifteen minutes, the delivery boy was hollering in the hall, "Jugs! Jugs!"

Benny opened the door and motioned him down as the rest of the guys on our floor looked curiously at what was going on. Jugs' delivery boy was soon on his way to another dorm, and about half the boys on our floor had come down the hall to our room to see what the delivery was all about. We were sitting on our beds, chowing down on our hamburgers, as the crowd of boys looked in on us.

"I'm Sandy, and this is Benny," I said, looking up from my burger. "That was Jug Wheeler's delivery boy. Want something? Just phone 'em and they'll have it here in fifteen minutes. Don't matter how little the order." We sat there, waving every now and then as boys introduced themselves. This tiny bit of knowledge made us self-assured, since we seemed to know a little more than most of the freshmen who were curiously peeking into our room. Twenty minutes later, the delivery boy was back with a huge sack of burgers and fries.

Well, that was my first taste of college, and there was something about being with a bunch of guys who were away from home for the first time and excited about their newfound freedom, which was very satisfying to me. I could tell from that first weekend I was going to enjoy college. After goofing off all week-end with my newfound friends, however, I had to face the reality that college was about more than partying.

I had a hellacious Monday and Tuesday as I took entrance tests, and if there had been any academic standards at all, it would've been my last two days at the university. But I was saved from being tossed out because there were so many of us in the same sorry shape. This was Arkansas in the late 1950s, and country boys from small towns were barely literate, especially when it came to math, chemistry, and foreign languages. To keep from sending about 50% of their prospective students back home, the university administrators had developed a system for students who couldn't pass the entrance tests. They'd come up with a whole raft of courses called X courses. Of course, my entrance scores were horrible, which meant I had to take the X-numbered courses, which didn't count as graduation hours. Oh well, hon-estly, I really didn't care that much about coursework, and the thought that I wasn't gaining graduation hours was pushed aside by the satisfaction that I was actually enrolled and away from south Arkansas.

On Wednesday, Benny and I walked down to the field house to register. For some dumb reason, which for the life of me I can't remember, I'd decided to major in Electrical Engineering, even though I was terrible in math and hadn't taken any classes in high school that would prepare me for engineering courses. I spent all day registering, and on Thursday I went to an Electrical Engineer-ing orientation lecture. Boy, was that an eye-opener. The next day I headed back down to the field house to change majors. Benny had told me the night before I didn't have to major in anything as a freshman. I could take general courses, which would apply to any degree, and wait until I was a sophomore to major.

I was re-registering in the College of Arts and Sciences, and, since I was changing majors, and almost everybody had already registered, most of the classes were full. My advisor, who was a graduate student and only three-years older than me, finally gave up trying to register me in X courses. He was desperate just to find courses that weren't full.

Soon I had dropped all the Engineering courses and had picked up Chemistry, German, and Advanced College Algebra. My advisor poured over the catalogue, trying to find another three-hour class.

"Hey, here's one, Creative Writing 106. Miss Doris Colton is teaching it."

"What's Creative Writing?"

"Oh, it's a snap course where you write a bunch of crap and get an A or B. You'll enjoy Doris Colton. She's a good-looking woman, for someone in her thirties. Heck, with Chemistry, German, and Advanced College Algebra, you're gonna need a snap course. Listen, Sandy, we show her class as full, so you'll have to take this card over to the Journalism Department and get her to initial it."

"Uh, what?"

"She has to okay any additions to a full class. Just go over to that sign that says 'English Department'—on the far table against the wall, and sitting under that sign you'll see a good-looking blonde. That's Doris Colton. Tell her you love creative writing, and you've been sick so you're registering late. Then ask her to let you in her class. Got it? Hey—just a minute, Sandy. Listen, wave your hands around like you're really excited about creative writing. Being excited about a course usually gets you in."

I made my way over to the Journalism table, and, sure enough, there was an older blonde woman leaning back in her chair and smoking a cigarette. She smiled as I walked up.

"Uh, Miss Colton?"

"Yes."

"I'm Sandy Carson, from Pine Valley down in south Arkansas, and I just love creative writing." Then I remembered what my advisor had told me, and I started waving my hands around like a

Baptist preacher. "I've been sick for a few days, and I'm registering late. Please let me in your class?"

As I started my stupid spiel she began to smile, and, after I started waving my hands, she laughed out loud.

"Uh, what is it?" I asked. My palms were sweating, and I know my face had to have been beet red. Thank God, she finally stopped laughing. She took a drag on her cigarette, smiled at me, and said, "What's your name?"

"Sandy Carson."

"Okay, Sandy, tell me the truth. Why do you want in my class?"

I'd had it. I was so beat down and tired from trying to re-register that I'd given up hope. Miss Colton had seen right through me, and I was ready to throw in the towel. Finally, I confessed, "My advisor and I were desperate. Your course is about my last hope of getting registered."

Miss Colton smiled as she looked at me, a desperate, bewildered freshman, and I guess she took pity on me.

"Sandy, my class is full, but I'm going to let you in. There's something about you that I like."

"Oh, Miss Colton, thank you, thank you," I gushed as she initialed my registration card. So I was re-registered, but why I picked those other courses, German, Chemistry, and Advanced College Algebra, which were almost my undoing, I'll never know. I was no more prepared to take them than I was to fly.

As I walked back to the dorm after buying books and paying my fees, I remembered what Mother had told me about having to get a part-time job to help pay for college. Books and tuition had already cut into the $350 I'd saved from that summer's hay-baling job and my poker winnings, and I was already dreading running out of money before the semester was over. I had to find a part-time job, or I'd be leaving college at the end of the fall semester.

That night when I finished eating supper at the dining hall, which was right across the street from Razorback Hall, I walked back behind the food service area to talk with the manager about a job. The manager, Jim Norton, was a tall, lanky man of about fifty-five, wearing a long, white smock tucked into a pair of khakis that were belted up so high the belt was right under his armpits. His nickname, "Beak," which, of course, no one would call him to his face, was perfect. Wow, what a nose! Mr. Norton had a huge Roman nose, which seemed to take up most of his narrow face. To make matters worse, he had broken it years ago, and when it healed there was a pronounced bump right in the middle. It was hard to stand there and talk to him without staring at it.

Beak sized me up and started talking out of one side of his mouth while he puffed away on a cigarette, which was hanging out the other side.

"Well, son, there ain't but one job available, a tray grabber—May be more job than you want."

Well, I couldn't imagine a job that was inside being worse than that hay-baling job I had during the summer.

"Uh, what's a tray grabber?"

"Come over here and see."

We walked over to the side of the kitchen, where a guy was standing behind an open window. In a few seconds, several guys walked up and shoved their trays, with dirty plates and half-full glasses of tea, across a stainless steel counter to him. About every other one would put a little too much shove on the tray, and it would bang into the end of the counter, sending food, tea, and sometimes silverware flying toward the guy standing there. I could hear him yelling when we walked up.

"Hey, I saw that!" he yelled at a guy after a particularly bad shove. "Man, I'll be so glad to get outta this food shootin' gallery!" he said as he turned to Beak.

The guy was covered with splattered food, wet from the tea that had spilled, stacking dishes and trays in the dishwasher, and I started to reconsider. It was the worst job I could imagine.

"Billy Joe's quittin'. This is his last day. You still want a job?"

I hesitated a minute. I needed a job, but having to put up with the stuff that came at you about every five seconds was more than I'd bargained for.

"'Fraid of a little hard work? Don't wanta get your hands dirty? You're just like most of these kids who want a job, don't wanta work. Hell, I worked tray grabbin' for a whole year when I started workin' here."

"I don't believe that! Nobody could work here a year!" said Billy Joe. He grabbed a glass of tea that had bounced off the end of the counter and screamed, "You are so worthless!"

Beak shook his finger at Billy Joe and said, "Now, Billy Joe, you know we don't allow that kinda talk 'round here to our customers."

"Well, what're you going to do? Fire me?" he said, slamming an empty tray against the dishwasher.

Beak looked over at me, and I made my decision—I had to have a job. I nodded and said, "I'll take it."

"Hey, you got a new man? Then he's got the job, right now." Billy Joe said, walking away, as the trays piled up.

"Wait a minute. You can't quit right in the middle of a shift."

"The hell I can't. Put your new dummy here. I'm gone." And with that Billy Joe left.

"Uh...you...what's your name?"

"Sandy."

"Well, get to work. You're behind already, and don't put the silverware in with the dishes. It goes in this rack."

I was slamming and throwing silverware in the little basket when a big, burly guy stepped up to the window.

"Hey, new meat!" he hollered as he sent the tray, food plate, and silverware spinning across the stainless steel counter straight at me.

I managed to catch the tea glass when it hit the back rail, but the plate hit and dumped a half portion of turkey dressing right on the front of my jeans.

"Ahaa, look at my jeans!"

"Still want the job?" said Beak.

"Yeah, I gotta have it," I mumbled back.

"Okay, come by the office, fill out some forms, and pick up your time card after the serving line closes. The job pays eighty-five cents an hour, but your meals are free."

Well, the free meals proved to be a good bonus, and partly made up for such a crappy job. After a few weeks of loading up on the unlimited food at the dining hall and adding a pint of whipping cream to every meal, I was soon up to 160 pounds and gaining weight every day.

Working as a tray grabber was lousy, but other things were going pretty good. I'd made a lot of new friends in the dorm, and most of them were like me, small town boys free to do anything they wanted for the first time in their lives. No curfew, no one to tell you to study or do anything. It was a magical time. It was only the first week of school, but I was having the time of my life.

7.

Doris, Lacy...and Millie

My roommate's older brother, Bob, a big, square-faced guy with thick, hairy eyebrows, had turned twenty-one during the summer. The first Friday night after I arrived at the university, Benny invited me to join him and his brother for a beer at George's Majestic Lounge, and see if we could meet some girls. Actually, we'd talked of meeting some hot babes and taking them up to Mount Sequoia to park, but those were just guy thoughts, and we knew we'd probably just sit in a booth and talk for a couple of hours before heading back to our dorms.

George's was, and still is, a fixture on the west end of Dixon Street, just a few hundred-yards from the edge of campus. If George's ever closed, it'd put half the school into a deep depression. According to Bob, a man named George Pappas opened the place back in 1927 and ran it until he sold it to Mary and Joe Hinton in 1947. Mary and Joe ran the place back in the 1950s, and a lot of the guys called it Mary's. But, since Mary and Joe didn't change the name, it was George's to most of the students. Mary managed to keep her waitress staff stocked with attractive, older girls from Fayetteville, rather than from the university.

"Most college girls are just here for one thing, to get married, and I need dependable help. Shoot, I've seen 'um quit after one hot date," Mary told us one night.

Most of her girls were seasoned waitresses and had seen students come and go for several years. They tended to be a little on the saucy side, which sure added to the attraction of the place. Mary always sat behind the cash register on a little stool, and rarely came out from behind the counter unless there was the possibility of a fight. If you got in a fight at George's, she barred you from ever coming back in the place. Being barred from George's would be a terrible fate for a lot of guys.

Bob, Benny's older brother, looked a lot like an oversized Benny, except for his heavy, thick eyebrows, which were so shaggy that they gave his whole face a very mature look. Since he looked at least forty, he was never asked for an I.D.

We sat down in one of George's red booths, leaned forward with our elbows on the Formica tabletop, and were just talking away when Bob pointed out a waitress standing at the next booth.

"Hey, check out the little brunette right behind you," he whispered to Benny and me.

I glanced over my shoulder and spotted her nametag, which said, "Millie." According to Bob, Millie Mason was the hottest of George's hot waitresses. Well, she sure looked the part. I didn't know it then, but Millie would become a very special girl in my life.

"Listen, guys, last year she went home with a different guy almost every night," Bob whispered across the table.

Millie glanced over at our table, saw us staring at her, and gave me a big wink. I could feel my face starting to flush.

She was barely five-feet-tall, and had short, black hair, deep blue eyes, and a great figure. I watched her as she walked over to take an order from a booth full of guys, and, as she approached them, she gave them a big smile, winked, kidded around, and put her hand on the shoulder of the guy nearest to her. When full-figured Millie, wearing a low-cut blouse, put the menus on the table, she bent over and took her time. Then she straightened up, threw her shoulders back, and winked.

When Millie cleared a table, I could tell it was all she could do to carry a tray full of empty plates and beer mugs. I asked Bob why Millie didn't quit George's. It was a lot of hard work and a low-paying job.

"Ah, Sandy, Millie's from south of Elkins—back in the hills, and she ain't been in shoes but a few years. The gal can't do nothin' else. But let me tell you something else about her: There's more to Millie than just being a waitress. She works like a dog, but it's not 'cause she wants extra tips. She's helping to take care of her mother back home."

Well, I felt sorry for Millie, but, since I had a sorry job as a tray grabber, I understood how she felt.

I was starting to squirm because I was wondering how an eighteen-year-old with a baby face was going to buy a beer.

"What can I get ya?" Millie murmured, smiling, as she leaned against the table with her hand on Bob's shoulder.

"What's on tap, sugar?" said Bob.

"Schlitz, Bob. You know that's always what's on tap," said Millie as she winked at me.

"Yeah, I forgot. Okay, bring me a pitcher, and oh, this is Sandy, and you know my brother, Benny."

Yeah, hi, Benny. Good to see you again. Sandy, I can tell right now, you're gonna be one of my special customers." She moved over to my side of the table and placed her hand against the back of my neck. Wow, I can still remember the tingle that went right down my back. Well, Millie believed in touching. As we watched her work our table and then, later, the rest of the room, we saw her causally touching the guy sitting on the outside of the booth. I can tell you from first-hand experience a touch from Millie made your night.

"Uh, well, sure," I mumbled as I began to blush.

"Whatta y'all want?" She looked at Benny and then smiled at me. I didn't know whether to order a beer or not. I sure didn't want another Coke. I wanted a beer, but it'd be the end of the evening for me if I showed her my I.D.

"Uh, well..." I started to mumble, turning redder by the second.

Before I could answer, Benny kicked me under the table and said, "Just water for both of us."

"Gotcha," Millie said, giving me another wink as she walked off. Wow, the way she walked and wiggled had every guy in the place gawking. College was getting better by the minute.

"Hey, what'd I tell ya," said Bob. Bob acted as if he were an old pro in sizing up women as he nodded his head in satisfaction.

"Bob, have you been out with Millie?" I asked.

"Maybe."

"Maybe? What does that mean?"

"Well, Sandy, some girls that you take out you ain't gonna hang out for your momma to see. Millie is one of 'em. Let's just say I've gotten to know Millie pretty good the last two years."

Benny and I smiled as Millie walked back over to our booth with a pitcher of beer, a glass for Bob, and glasses of water for Benny and me. I looked at my glass of water and frowned. Sitting there, drinking water while Bob sipped beer wasn't exactly what I had in mind.

"Here's one pitcher of beer and two glasses of water. Anything else?"

"Naw, Millie, but don't go too far. I'm thirsty tonight," said Bob.

Millie smiled and nodded. Bob poured himself a glass of beer and looked over at me.

"Drink your water, Sandy, and I'll give you a refill."

Well, that surprised me, and I said, "We're not twenty-one, Bob. Won't Mary get on us if we start drinking beer?"

"Nahaaa, if there's someone at the table that's twenty-one, she don't care. Anyway, Mary didn't sell you beer. She sold it to me, and if I want to give some of my beer away, it ain't against the law."

Well, I'm not sure Bob was right about giving beer to minors, but Benny and I gulped down our water, and Bob filled our glasses with beer.

"Had much beer, Sandy?" he said.

"Uh, well, not a lot," I mumbled. Actually, as I raised my glass, I was about to take my first sip of beer. I sure didn't want them to think it was my first time, so I took a big gulp, about half of the glass, and leaned back against the booth. My eyes watered slightly, and I choked on the last swallow, but I managed to get it down and conceal my choking from Benny and Bob.

"Hey, Sandy, don't chug-a-lug it," said Benny.

I smiled, unable to speak for a few seconds. In a few minutes, a warm feeling eased over me, and, as we finished the pitcher of beer, I was happier than I had been any time in my life. College was more fun than I'd ever imagined.

"Hey, look who's comin' in the door," said Bob. He was so excited that we all turned around to look.

I guess some things will always stay in my memory, and the sight of that gorgeous girl with shoulder-length blonde hair, accompanied by two guys, walking over to the booth across from us is a scene that is vividly etched in my mind. I'll never forget it. I was stunned.

"My gosh, who's that?" I managed to say.

"That's Lacy Darnell, a hot new freshman. They say she's a nympho."

"Huh? What's a nympho?" Benny and I both asked.

"Y'all don't know what a nympho is?" laughed Bob.

We shook our heads.

"I was talking to some guy she fooled around with during Rush Week, and he said someone from Tulsa, where Lacy graduated from high school, told him she was a nymphomaniac. That's a woman who can't say no to sex."

"Huh?" I said. "What's her name again?" A drop-dead, gorgeous woman who couldn't say no to sex sure had my interest, but it more than good looks and sex made me notice her. I couldn't put my finger on it, but she was different. The university was full of pretty girls, and I'd met and seen dozens the first week I was there, but none of them had the effect that Lacy had on me.

Lacy Darnell, Lacy Darnell, Lacy Darnell, I thought over and over again. I was determined to meet Lacy, and not only because she was beautiful. As she glanced over to where I was seated, only a booth away, our eyes locked for just a moment, and she pressed her wonderful lips together and smiled at me. I was mesmerized by those pale blue, washed-out eyes, which seemed to light up her face. We sat facing each other for another hour, and time after time I'd catch her eyes, or she'd catch mine. Over the years, I've thought about seeing Lacy that first time, and I honestly don't know if it was love or lust at first sight. All I can tell you is that we both felt an attraction, and neither one of us ever forgot the first time we saw each other.

When we left George's, all I could think about was Lacy. Why is she so intoxicating to me? Why can't I get her out of my mind? Is it her eyes, lips, or her wonderful figure? No, it was more than that—a lot more.

When I got back to the dorm, I walked down the hall to Skeeter Anderson's room, where a wild poker game was under way. Well, maybe "wild" isn't the word for it, but there was a lot of yelling and throwing of cards, even though the maximum bet was a nickel. Skeeter had pulled his bed out away from the wall, and six guys were gathered around it.

"Sandy, we need one more player, sit your ass down and get out some of that south Arkansas money," yelled Skeeter. Skeeter was a thin, wiry guy with long arms and funny-looking hair. He'd tried to have his hair cut in a flattop, but his thin hair wasn't suited for it, so about half stuck up and half didn't. When he talked, he waved his hands around, reminding you of a mosquito's wings. He smoked like a fiend and was nervous as a cat. The nickname, Skeeter, fit him perfectly.

"Aw, I'm no good at poker," I lied. Actually, since I'd played poker several hundred times the last two summers with the hay-baling crew I worked with, I knew every possible poker variation.

I pulled out a couple of dollars, smiled, and sat down to play with those green freshmen. I could almost feel my billfold fattening up.

"Does three of a kind beat two pair?" said a little freshman, who didn't look twelve.

"Does a cat have an ass? Hell yes, stupid!" said Skeeter as he blew smoke across the table.

"Okay, fresh meat!" yelled Skeeter. "Here, country boy, let's see if you can deal."

Skeeter shoved the cards over to me. I smiled and said, "Seven card stud, high-low splits the pot, black queens are wild."

"Huh, what kind of south Arkansas poker is that!" Skeeter hollered. He sat there, looking puzzled and sucking on his cigarette. Of course, most of the guys were playing poker for their first time, and a crazy game like that really threw them.

"It's dealer's choice, isn't it?" I said.

"Yeah, but—"

I could hardly hold back a big grin. When you're playing with beginners, the more complicated the game, the easier it is to take their money.

"Okay, here's how you play. The high-low part: After the last bet, you have to declare which you're going for, the high hand or the low hand. Aces can be used as either high or low, but not both. The wild, black queens can be anything you call 'em. Got it?"

No, I can tell you, they didn't get it, but they were too intimidated to say so. There was a mumbling of unsure yeses. I smiled and started dealing. After some stumbling around with various combinations of cards, they started to catch on, and it became the game of choice for the rest of the evening. Well, maybe 'catching on' is stretching the point, but they did at least figure out how to play. However, the real danger in learning how to play high-low poker with wild cards in the deck is failing to understand the odds and staying in pot after pot, hoping to luck out. I stayed in about one out of four pots, and by the time we'd finished I was up $8.75. I know that doesn't sound like much, but when the highest bet is a nickel, it meant I cleaned up. The nightly poker games at the dorm would keep me in spending money, especially if the same group of green freshmen kept playing. Things had begun to look up.

The following Monday classes started, and I spent a long, long morning sitting in Chemistry, German, and Algebra classes, listening to boring professors drone on and on about subjects I knew or cared very little about. College was beginning to stink, but late in the day things picked up. My last class of the day was an English class, Creative Writing, which began at four o'clock in Old Main, the oldest building on campus. Old Main was the first building constructed when the university was founded back in 1871. There were five floors, if you counted the basement, which was about half underground. The first floor had the registrar's office and all student records. The top floor was the University Museum, and the middle floors were classrooms. The construction was red brick with white trim, and the lower rear steps, which went to the first floor of the building, were sheathed with Ozark flagstone, a stark contrast with the red brick. Actually, the flagstone looks like a bad afterthought. "Oh, why don't we put some flagstone on the building to reflect our Ozark heritage?" And they did, and it looks like crap.

I'd met my Creative Writing instructor, Doris Colton, when I registered, but evidently my memory must have slipped. I was sitting toward the back of the class when she walked in, looking very different than she had down at the field house. God, I must have been really tired.

This blonde, sexy woman can't be our teacher, I thought. She was tall and willowy, with tight-cut, short blonde hair, wonderful long legs, and a figure that sure caught your eye. None of which I'd noticed when I first met her. I know I must have been sitting there with my mouth open as she started to talk.

"Good afternoon, class, I'm Doris Colton, and this is Creative Writing 106. I want our class to be as informal as possible, so please address me as Doris. As I get to know you, I'll call you by your first name. My goal as an instructor is to help you express yourself through writing, and to impart the basics of creative expression."

This unconventional teacher, who was now sitting on the front of her desk with her legs crossed and had just lit a cigarette, mesmerized me. She raked her hand through her short blonde hair, walked around to the blackboard, and began to write down a list of required reading. Doris was in her thirties, but my gosh! With the tight sweater and skirt she was wearing stretched over her excellent figure, she could have passed for a student.

She walked around the front of the room, waving her cigarette around like a baton, and my eyes followed her every move. Except for Lacy Darnell, the girl from George's, she was the sexiest woman I'd ever seen. After watching my mother smoke herself into poor health, I couldn't stand cigarettes, but somehow, the way Doris smoked added to her sexiness.

She finished writing the required reading list on the blackboard and walked around to the front of her desk again. As she smiled and looked at the class she said, "Today, I want you to get a taste of creative writing. Take out your notebook and start writing about your senior year in high school. I want you to write nonstop for the next forty-five minutes, and then, as your homework assignment, you are to reread, correct your composition, and place it in a three-ring notebook. Your writing is a personal expression, and I won't ask you to share it with the class or me. During the semester, I want you to keep adding to your notebook, which will serve as a place where you can review your first writings and compare them with your later ones. I hope that you'll see some improvement. Class, you may begin to write."

I opened my notebook, thought about that first day of my senior year at Mount Union High School, and started to write. Well, since I wasn't going to have to turn in the writing, I covered everything I did that year, including the break-in to steal the Biology test. If that paper had fallen into the wrong hands, I'd have been in deep trouble. At the end of class, I stayed a few minutes after the bell rang to finish a paragraph, and, when I closed my notebook to leave, Doris was standing by the door. I smiled a sickly smile, still a little embarrassed about the ass I had made of myself when I was registering. She gave me a big smile and said, "Your name is?"

"Stuart Carson, but everybody calls me Sandy. I'm from Pine Valley, down in south Arkansas."

"Oh, yes, and you love creative writing and you've been sick," she said as she grinned and waved her hands. "It's nice to see you again, Sandy. Do you really like to write?"

Damn, I almost swallowed the gum I'd been chewing and turned Razorback red. I stumbled through an answer, trying to regain my composure. "Uh, well, honestly, I've never written much more than an English theme, but I enjoyed writing today."

"Good. If you enjoy writing, you might become a good writer. Sometimes it works that way."

"Really?" I finally got my breath and started to relax.

"Yes, not but not every time," she said, focusing her deep blue eyes intently on me. "Well, Sandy, maybe I can help you develop as a writer this semester, but I need to go right now. If you have any questions about writing, I can stay after class. This is my last period of the day."

"Thanks, Miss Colton."

"Doris, Sandy."

"Uh, Doris."

Doris smiled and nodded as she lit another cigarette and left the room.

Later, when I was back in my room, I read the eight pages of composition for the first time, marking the errors, changing up a few things, and adding details. Yeah, and I did write an extra page about sexy Doris Colton. Of course, some of it was pure teenage hormones surging through me. It sounded so corny when I reread it while writing this book that I almost threw up. The next day I stopped by the university bookstore, bought a three-ring note-book, and put the writing about my high school senior year inside. On the front I printed, in heavy black letters, The Journal. Well,

I'd intended to keep The Journal exactly as Doris had suggested and make it a record of my writings in her class. But after putting in the first entry, I remembered Millie and seeing Lacy, and I added almost a page telling about these two women I saw at George's. Then I thought some more about sexy Doris Colton, and I added another page telling about seeing her at registration. After only a few days at school, I found myself pulling The Journal out of my desk to write about things that had happened to me that day. It became a detailed record of my life in college, my personal diary, something that only my attorney and I have ever read—thank God.

The next day Benny and I were walking across campus, heading for the University Bookstore to buy some school supplies, when he grabbed my elbow.

"Hey, Sandy, look who's coming—it's Lacy Darnell," he whispered.

Lacy had just left the library and was walking toward Old Main, coming right toward us.

As she approached, she recognized me, hesitated for a moment, flipped her long blonde hair back over her shoulder, and gave me a big smile.

"Hi."

"Uh, uh, hi," I managed to mumble. I know I should have stopped and introduced myself to her, but I missed my chance as Lacy smiled again and then walked on.

"You know Lacy?" Benny said in amazement.

"Yeah, but not very well," I lied. "But, my Lord, did you see those lips? I'd sure like to go out with her."

"Ha, yeah, you and every other guy on campus. Bob said she's hanging around with a whole raft of guys. Probably makin' out with most of 'em."

"You're kidding?"

"Naw, according to one of the guys Bob talked with, she got laid the first weekend she arrived at school."

"Wow, she must be something else."

Lacy continued across the street and then started up the stairs into Old Main. My God, even after nearly fifty years I can still see her sauntering up those stairs.

I ran into Lacy several more times during the next two-weeks, and she always gave me a big smile and usually said, 'Hi.' I thought about how to introduce myself to her, but I was intimidated by her. She was overpowering.

8.

R. Richard Barnett
IV..."Dickie"

Friday morning I was sitting in German class talking with a new friend, Jeff Hunsinger, a sophomore from Eudora, who belonged to the Sigma Delta fraternity, or the "Deltas," as they were called around campus. Jeff was just a little shorter than me, but a little more filled out, and a rather nice-looking guy. He had the perfect college look: button-down collar, khaki slacks, and a white shirt. We'd hit it off almost from the day we met, and, as we talked, it turned out we were a lot alike and from very similar backgrounds. Although his folks really couldn't afford for him to be in a fraternity, he had an uncle who was a Delta legacy, and the uncle had anted up the extra dough.

The Deltas had a big house, right across the street from the west corner of the campus. Even though I'd been on campus for only a short time, I knew about their reputation. They were an off-the-wall bunch of guys who were already on probation because of their wild parties and test swapping. Of course, other fraternities and independents had parties, swapped tests, and did crazy stuff, but the Deltas were in a class by themselves. Those guys had an attitude problem, and, if you were looking for somebody to dislike, they'd easily fit the bill.

"Whatta ya gonna do this weekend, Sandy?"

"Not much, probably go down to George's and drink a little beer with my roommate and then come back and play poker."

"You play a lot of poker?"

"Well, yeah, but only with the guys at the dorm. It's not much of a game, nickel-and-dime stuff."

"Say, why don't you come by the Delta house at eight o'clock Saturday night. We lost a regular player this week. I'll save you a seat, and I'll guarantee you one thing: It'll be more of a game than a bunch of independents can get up."

"What's your limit?"

"Twenty-five-cents, with three-raises, and some of those pots have nearly five bucks in 'em."

"Really?"

"Yeah, is it too rich for you?"

"Naw, I can handle it. What kind of a game is it?"

"Dealer's choice, and you won't believe some of the crap those guys come up with."

I couldn't believe my ears, dealer's choice for a five dollar pot. With my playing experience; it was my poker dream coming true.

I tried not to act too anxious.

"Uh, well, if it's all right with the rest of the guys, save me a seat."

"You got it, but remember, eight o'clock, and we start right on time. When you walk in the house, just say, 'Where's the game?'"

I was holding back a smile when Dr. Hans Hoffer, our German professor, walked in. My other teachers would saunter into the room, put their papers on the desk, and nod at the class. Not "Herr Hoffer," as he liked to be called. His entrance was always dramatic. The classroom door always seemed to fly open, and Herr Hoffer marched in. Yeah, that's the only word for it. He marched into class and almost clicked his heels as he made a right-face, turning like clockwork to face the class.

"Guten morgan!"

Well, at first we were mesmerized by his demeanor, but, after a while, it was all we could do not to laugh when he wheeled in and started the class. He was a tall man with sharp features—black hair and a ramrod straight posture—a former German Panzer officer, who had commanded the German 10th Panzer Division during the Second World War. He was now teaching at the university on an exchange program. His jet-black hair was always cut short, and his demeanor became even more imposing when he stuck out his chin, raising it slightly as he spoke. He'd learned his English in an American POW camp in east Arkansas, and he liked the townspeople and guards so much that, after the war was over, he applied to teach in Fayetteville.

Well, Herr Hoffer made German the most interesting of all my classes. Of course, I hated trying to learn German as a language, but, as our class found out very quickly, a question about the War would send Herr Hoffer strutting around in front of the class, launching into a detailed discussion about how his Panzer Division had rolled across France, scattering those Frenchies in their wake. I wasn't learning much German, but I was sure getting the German perspective on the war.

I settled back in my seat and began to daydream about Lacy. Then I'd think about Millie, down at George's, and wonder if she'd date someone as young as me. Before the class was over, my daydream fantasies had included Doris Colton, my Creative Writing professor. No, I didn't take notes or even listen to Herr Hoffer. Nothing could be more boring than trying to learn German.

I could hardly wait to sit down at that poker table. The next Saturday night, Benny, Bob, and I went down to George's, and, after an hour or so of drinking beer, flirting with Millie, and talking about school, I walked up the street to the Delta house. A pledge was waxing the banister and he looked up as I walked in.

"Are you looking for somebody?

"Naw, just the game," I said.

He looked up and nodded toward the stairs to the basement.

"Go down to the basement and turn left, they're in the reading room."

"Thanks,"

When I reached the bottom of the stairs, I saw an open door. Looking in, I could see guys gathered around a big, round table. There was a lot of smoke, and you could hear the bunch mouthing off from out in the hall. I stood in the doorway until Jeff saw me and motioned for me to come in. I looked the table over as I walked in, sizing up the group. Fat guy—won't be much of a player—that quiet one might be—wow, what a big mouth, I thought as I looked across the table at a particularly loud and obnoxious guy.

"Hey, Sandy, come over here; I saved you a seat. Guys, this is Sandy, fresh meat. He's an Independent."

A few nods and a mumble of names came from around the table, and then the loud-mouthed guy sitting across the table started talking to Jeff as if I didn't exist.

"For God's sake, Jeff, you'll drag up anybody. The poor joker probably doesn't have two bucks to his name. He'll be out of here in thirty minutes. I thought this was a frat-only game."

Well, I was ready to go when I heard that. I wanted to play, but I wasn't about to put up with a pile of crap like that from anybody.

That anybody was Dickie. Actually, as I found out later, his name was R. Richard Barnett IV, and he was what Jeff called a Trust Baby. Of course, I didn't have a clue what he meant by that until Jeff told me that Dickie's father was a rich oil man from Dallas, and he'd created a trust fund for Dickie. Dickie was always bragging to everybody in the fraternity that he could buy the place, and he probably could. He was a freshman with a large, almost oversized head, a permanent cigarette hanging out of his mouth, and a flattop trimmed to perfection. It didn't take long to find out that Dickie was one of those guys who was always trying to prove himself. He was stocky and well-built, and had played a little high school football back in Dallas, but he wasn't big enough or good enough to play college ball. His "I'm better than you" air permeated everything he did. He was one of those guys who could talk to someone standing right beside you and treat you as if you were a piece of wood. I couldn't stand the blowhard.

"Since when? Billy Bob Evans played last week, and he sure ain't a fraternity man," said Jeff.

"Yeah, but he's a big deal football player. Whatta you say, guys? Shall we tell this skinny independent to crawl back up the hill to his dorm?"

God, I was so mad that I could hardly keep from walking around the table and hitting that big mouth. I'm out of here, I thought.

I stood up, as ticked off as I've ever been, red in the face and ready to leave.

"Aw, come on Dickie. He's Jeff's friend, and I say we start playing and quit this mouthing. Hell, we need another player," said Peter Fuller, an upperclassman and a friend of Jeff's. "Sit down Sandy. You're welcome to join the game."

I calmed down a little bit and waited to see if the group was going to let me in the game.

That loudmouth, Dickie, leaned back, sucked on his cigarette, and said, as he blew a smoke ring, "If you want him to play, Peter, it's all right with me. I was just trying to keep a little class in the house."

You sorry, worthless...One day I'm going to knock that cigarette down your throat, I thought.

"Sit down, Sandy, and ignore Dickie. He's all mouth," said Jeff.

Well, that little zinger stung Mr. Big Mouth, and I felt a little better.

"All mouth? You want some of this?" he shouted at Jeff, pumping his fist.

"For God's sake, shut up, you two, and let's get started," said Peter. "It's eight o'clock. Time to start playing."

Peter pulled out a deck of cards and proceeded to shuffle.

"It's dealer's choice, cut for the deal," he said, putting the cards out in the middle of the table. Peter was a junior and president of the fraternity. He looked more mature than the rest of the group, which consisted of eighteen and nineteen-year-old freshmen and sophomores. Peter controlled the game and made the call if a hand was contested, and, since we played with several extra wild cards, there was sure to be controversy. Jeff turned over a king of spades and won the right to deal first.

I took a deep breath and started to relax as the game progressed. After an hour, I was comfortably involved in the game—moving steadily into the winner's circle. As I got to know the players, I realized they were really a nice bunch of guys—except for that asshole Dickie.

It wasn't long until, during a conversation about what everybody did last summer, I mentioned I lived on a farm and had worked on a hay-baling crew all summer. Well, that brought a laugh from big-mouth Dickie.

"A farm boy? Well, listen to me, Mr. Farm Boy, I'm gonna clean your plow tonight and get a little of that hard-earned money."

I smiled, looking across the table at Dickie, who had already proven that he was a lousy poker player. I couldn't stand the conceited so-in-so, and I said, "Oh, I don't think so. It takes more than a big mouth to win a pot."

That got a laugh from the rest of the table.

"We'll see, Mr. Farm Boy," he muttered.

After another hour of playing, I began to relax and analyze the players. Dickie was by far the most flamboyant, but he was a terrible poker player, hated to get out of a pot, and consistently bluffed, which almost guaranteed he'd come out a loser sooner or later. The fat freshman sitting beside me was just as I had pegged him, a true novice who'd misjudge a bad hand, and then, later, bet over the top when he got anything decent. He was a sure loser, and since he was a pledge, he was only in the game to contribute cash.

The rest of the table included steady Peter, the upperclassman, who wasn't going to set the world on fire with his playing, but who also wasn't going to be in the losing column at the end of the night. There were two sophomores sitting by Dickie who had played a fair amount of poker, but one of them had a giveaway twitch when he had a decent hand, and the other had a tendency to bluff too much. They'd be somewhere in the middle of the pack when the night was over. I was confident I had a lot more experience playing the wild dealer's choice games, and, unless I hit an unlucky streak, I'd win some dough from this bunch.

It was around two o'clock and everybody was about ready to quit, when I got the makings of a great hand. After the fourth card, I had a pair of kings in the hole and a pair of sixes up. Dickie had a pair of queens up and started betting like crazy.

Three queens or two pair—probably just two pair, the way he's betting—maybe just a pair of queens—trying to buy the pot, I thought. The fifth card came up. Dickie got a seven, and I got another king. I had my full house, which was a sure thing to win the pot.

Okay, Big Mouth, let's see how much I can squeeze out of your sorry ass, I thought. Hell, the odds that I'd win the pot were out of sight, and all I could think about was how much I could get out of that sorry guy.

The sixth card was dealt. Dickie got a five, and Jeff, who was still in, got a queen.

Hot dog! The last queen is gone, flashed through my mind. Dickie can't have four queens!

Now, the best hand Dickie could possibly have would have been a full house of queens and something else. Dickie's next bet ran Jeff out, and I raised him. He hesitated but called, and the seventh card, a down card, was dealt. Dickie's hand twitched as he peeked at the card. He started biting his cigarette and picked up his chips to bet even before it was his turn. My God, talk about giving away a hand.

Well, he's made his full house, and he thinks he's got this pot. He's gonna die when I turn over these two kings in the hole.

"I bet a quarter," I said, knowing that Dickie was certainly going to call and would probably raise me back.

Keep raising me, you moron. Every nickel you put in that pot is gonna go in my pocket, I thought.

Dickie called and raised; I called and raised; Dickie called and raised. Our rules allowed for only three raises.

I called his third raise and Dickie flipped his cards over.

"Full house, Farm Boy, queens and sevens," he said, triumphantly raising his hands over his head as he took a bow. "That's plow cleaning," he hooted.

After the embarrassing start, I'd been waiting all night to get even with that guy. All eyes were on me as I slowly turned over my cards.

"Here are a couple of sixes, and let's see, yeah, here are a couple of kings." I hesitated and Dickie reached for the pot, hollering and laughing.

"Wait a minute," I said, "look, here's another king. Full house kings and sixes."

A roar went up from the other players as Dickie pulled his hands back and bit down on his cigarette so hard that the end dropped off on the table. His mouth dropped open. He let out a string of cuss words and slapped the cards, scattering them all over the floor.

"By God, you hick, wait till next week! I'm gonna clean your plow if it's the last thing I do!" he screamed as I started raking in the pot.

I gave Dickie a big, open-mouthed grin, rolling my head and stacking the chips as I pulled in the big pot. Dickie and I were instantly bitter enemies after that poker game, and, over the four-years I spent at the university, it would only get worse.

9.

Vi!

The next Friday night Benny, Bob, and I were down at George's having a beer before they drove down to Greenland, a little town on the outskirts of Fayetteville, to pick up a couple of high school girls they'd met the week before. Of course, Benny had been bragging all week that they were going to pick up some hot high school girls, but nobody in their right minds would believe that a dud like Benny was about to even find a pick-up date. Yes, I wanted to go, but as Bob said, "Sandy, we'd love to take you, but they ain't enough room in my old Ford if we get to foolin' 'round, and anyway, we don't know but two girls."

A few minutes later they gulped down a beer, hopped up, and headed out, leaving me a couple of bucks to pay for the beer. I was by myself on a Friday night without a thing to do. I was sitting there, feeling sorry for myself as I lingered over my beer, watching girls come and go with guys, wishing I had a car so I could go out on a real date. I finally got bored and waved at Millie to come over and give me the check. She'd been busy all night and, after dropping off the pitcher of beer and two glasses of water when we arrived, she hadn't said a word to me, which sure didn't help my attitude. Millie headed my way, swaying her hips and giving me a sexy smile, and my down-in-the-mouth attitude started to improve.

"Sandy, sorry I've ignored you, but they've been running my ass off tonight. Are you by yourself?"

"Yeah, Benny and Bob found a couple of hot high school girls down at Greenland, and they're off to see 'em."

Millie moved over close to me, touching my shoulder with her hip as she rubbed her left hand around the side of my neck. Damn, that woman really knew how to turn a man on.

"Well, those little high school tarts aren't getting the best of the bunch," she said and winked at me. Millie picked up the empty beer pitcher and headed back to the bar. I thought she'd be right back with my check, but she reached across the bar, added another glass of beer to the pitcher, and put it back on my table.

"Compliments of Millie," she said, grinning as she bent over the table, exposing some well-developed cleavage.

For the rest of the evening Millie flirted back and forth with me. When I finally left, she put her arm around my waist as I walked to the door and, before I walked out, reached up and kissed me on the cheek. My sour mood had changed with all the touching and flirting. That girl really knew how to turn a man on, and I went to sleep that Friday night fantasizing about a date with her.

She was still on my mind when I went to German class that next Monday, and I paid very little attention as Herr Hoffer went on and on about German verbs. I was sitting there considering whether a thirty-year-old waitress would go out with an eighteen-year-old freshman. A date with Millie moved up to a strong maybe before class ended.

On Mondays, I had an empty period between my German and Algebra classes, and, since both of those classes were in Old Main, and the Student Union was right next door, I usually spent the hour between classes in the Student Union Grill with friends.

That Monday morning I left my German class still fantasizing about sexy Millie. I was walking down the steps into the basement of the Student Union, which housed the University Bookstore and the café, when several girls came up the steps carrying books they'd just bought. I stood back and held the door open. They smiled, and I started to go in. Then, about six feet behind them, a very tall, attractive brunette approached the door. I know my mouth must have dropped open when I looked at her. She was breathtaking. That's a moment in my life I'll never forget.

Evidently, she'd purchased books for an entire semester. From the looks of the stack, she had enough for a couple of years. They were a load, and she was having trouble. I backed up, opened the door, and she looked at me and smiled a thank you. There was a moment when our eyes met, she smiled again, and then she held that look for just a second too long. She stumbled on the threshold and books went everywhere. I caught her arm and steadied her, and she looked down at the books and papers strewn all over the floor.

"Oh, my God, I'll never make it back to my room with all these books!"

"Here, let me help you." I was on my knees in seconds, scooping up books and papers while students almost ran over me in the narrow hallway.

"I don't have a class till eleven. Let me help carry these books for you."

"No, thanks, I can manage. Here, let me have them." She held out her arms for me to stack the books on, and our eyes met again. Her face was flushed. She had a slight smile on her lips, and I could tell that she was still a little chagrined from her last look at me, which had caused her to drop all her books.

"Are you sure?" I asked.

"Yeah, that Western Civ book just slid off the top. I can handle them."

I shook my head as I looked at the thick stack of textbooks. That Western Civ book was three-inches-thick, and it was stacked right on top of several other monsters, which would weigh anybody down. She got her balance and started out the door, weaving a bit as she approached the steps leading out of the basement.

I waited, thinking, she'll never make it up those fifteen steps.

Sure enough, about halfway up, she began to wobble and lean against the rail. It was just what I'd been waiting for. I ran up the steps in time to stop another avalanche of books.

"Hey, give me some of those." I took three big, thick ones off the top and held my hand on the others in the stack until she got her balance.

She steadied herself and smiled. "Okay, you're right, I need some help."

"Where are you going?"

"To the Delta Chi House. It's not far, just across and up the street, but these books weigh a ton."

I took another couple of books, and we started walking toward the crosswalk. We walked in silence for a few seconds, and then I said, "Uh, my name is Stuart Carson, but everybody calls me Sandy."

"I'm Virginia Botner, and I'm a Delta Chi from Monticello. My friends call me Vi."

I didn't know it then, but during those last few minutes, I'd been with a woman who would never leave my mind. She was tall, almost as tall as me, and her eyes, my God, they were a vivid, violet blue, and framed by the longest eyelashes I've ever seen. When she smiled, it took my breath away. Of all the girls I'd met at the university, none of them had a more captivating smile. Her coal-black hair curled tightly around her ears and short bangs came down midway on her forehead. And boy, did she have a figure. She was wearing a light pink sweater that set off her pale, ivory complexion. I wished we were walking across campus instead of right across the street.

We were less than hundred yards from the Student Union when we came to a crosswalk. As we were standing there, talking about how much traffic was whizzing by, a stray dog tried to cross the street. Vi screamed as the dog tried to dodge one car only to dart into the path of another.

"No! Oh, my God!" she screamed.

The car knocked the dog halfway across the street. Cars stopped and Vi dashed out in the street heading for the dog, who looked as if it would never move again.

"Sandy, help me move this dog out of the street," yelled Vi, who was kneeling over the dog rubbing its head.

Initially, I was stunned that Vi had run out into traffic to help a stray dog, and now I didn't know what to do after she yelled at me. It didn't take me but a few seconds to respond. Refuse to assist a beautiful girl help a dog, that had been hit by a car? Of course, I couldn't refuse, and I headed for Vi. By the time I got to her and to what I thought was a dead dog, she had pulled off her blue blazer and was trying to ease the dog onto it.

"Vi, stop; you're going to ruin your jacket. Just let me pull the dog off the street. I think it's dead."

"No, Sandy, it's not dead, it's still breathing, and if you just pull it off the street you might injure it more. Here, help me slip my jacket under it."

We finally got Vi's jacket under the dog and by holding the four corners we started to carry it toward the sidewalk. Traffic on that side of the street had been stalled for at least ten minutes, while we were trying to get the dog off the street. Just as we started for the sidewalk, some jerk honked his horn.

Vi looked at me and said, "Put the dog down, Sandy."

"What? In the middle of the street?"

"Yes!"

Wow, that yes was so firm I almost dropped the dog. We eased the dog down, and Vi started for the car that honked.

Oh, my God, what is she going to do? Crossed my mind.

Vi walked up to the driver's side of the car and yelled, "Are you the person who honked at us while we were trying to care for an injured animal?"

I could see the smartass guy who honked face turn red as Vi eyed him. He managed to mumble something, before Vi gave him a two-minute lecture about carrying for animals. Then she turned and walked back to where I was standing over that damned, dead dog.

"Come on, Sandy, let's get this poor animal to the sidewalk."

We picked up the corners of Vi's jacket and managed to carry it to the sidewalk. I was wondering, What now? When a miracle happened. The dog opened its eyes and raised its head.

"Look, Sandy! The dog's alive!"

Well, I'll admit it, I was shocked, but even more so when the dog stood up and started to move.

"Sandy, it still might need to be taken to the vet to see if it has internal injuries. I'll go borrow one of my sorority sister's cars."

However, before Vi could cross the street the dog hopped off, limping a little, but considering it had been knocked halfway across the street, it was in pretty good shape.

"Vi, it's okay," I yelled before she could cross the street. In a few seconds, the dog disappeared into some bushes by the library.

"Well, it's gone. Let's pick up your books and head for your sorority house."

Vi nodded, and we gathered the books and her jacket and started to walk.

"Sandy, I'm sorry I caused you so much trouble, but I can't stand to see animals suffer. There's just something about me that has to help an animal that is injured."

I nodded. In less than ten minutes my opinion of someone, who I had looked at as only a beautiful girl, had changed drastically. We walked along in silence until we reached Vi's sorority house.

"Sandy, thanks for helping me out. I can manage from here." She picked up the books I was carrying and started into the sorority house.

"Uh, wait a minute, Vi. If you don't have a class, let's go back to the Union and have a Coke."

Vi stood there a minute while I held my breath. Finally, nodding and smiling, she said, "Okay, let me put these books in my room. I'll be right back down—maybe we can check on the dog on the way to the Union."

I can still remember the tingle that went up my spine when she said, "Okay." I couldn't have been more excited if it had been a date with Marilyn Monroe. And yeah, I was hoping the damn dog was long gone.

We walked back across the street, and in a few minutes, we were in a booth, drinking our Cokes. Vi sat across from me, and, after her deep blue eyes had mesmerized me for a few seconds, I finally started talking.

"Are you a freshman?"

"Yes, what about you?"

"Uh huh, me too."

We sat and talked for the rest of the hour. I listened as Vi talked about going to a finishing school in Paris the previous summer, and then about all the fun she had during rush week. She went over all of her awards and wins in various beauty contests. After a few minutes, I figured out that I was having a Coke date with Miss Everything. I couldn't believe all the stuff she'd done.

Vi was from Monticello, a small, southeast Arkansas town of about 5500. She was an only child, and I could tell from the way she talked about her father that he pretty much ran her life. I really didn't know how much he controlled her and how domineering he was until a few years later. However, I remember her voice had an unusual edge to it when she referred to him.

She'd accomplished so much during her high school years that I was embarrassed to tell her how little I'd done. My high school annual picture had less than ten words beside my picture. From what Vi told me, I bet her write-up took most of a page. Every time she talked about something she'd done, it was punctuated by, "Daddy was so proud of me!" Of course, that started to sound a little weird after about ten times, but I didn't care how much of a daddy's girl she was. As I sat there in the booth, I knew one thing for sure: I'd never met a girl who affected me the way she did.

Her father owned the largest bank in town, and her mother

had been a Delta Chi when she attended school there. Vi was a Delta Chi legacy.

"Actually, Sandy, I could be here on a twirling scholarship, but Daddy didn't want me to spend all my time practicing. I was head majorette for our high school band, and I won the state twirling title my senior year."

"Uh, well, I guess you're a pretty good twirler." Then, hoping to change the subject, and since she was so tall, I said, "Did you play basketball?"

"Didn't you see my picture in the Gazette?"

"No, why was it in the Gazette?"

"I was All-State, silly."

"Oh, well, I don't pay much attention to sports, and we don't take the Gazette where I live, down in Pine Valley."

"You don't pay any attention to sports? That's hard to believe. I thought everybody in the state was a Razorback fan."

"Oh, the Hogs are okay, but they're no big deal to me. Have you been to any of their games?" I was getting a little tired of hearing about Super Vi, but she kept talking and talking.

"Have I been to any of their games? Are you kidding? Of course I have. Daddy has season tickets, and we haven't missed a Little Rock game in years."

"Uh, well, sounds like you and your father are big fans. Did you go through rush last week?"

"Yes, Sandy, you wouldn't believe all the parties and all the fun I had. I got a bid from every sorority I visited, but, since I'm a Delta Chi legacy, my mother would have just died if I hadn't pledged Delta Chi. Daddy said to humor her. Mother has lost something the last few years, and she stays home most of the time. And guess what? You never know who you'll meet at a rush party. I met Bill Tucker. Can you believe that? And guess what? He asked me out the first night, and now I'm dating Bill Tucker. You know, he's a starter on the football team, and he told me the other night Coach is expecting him to be an All-American. Can you believe that, me dating Bill Tucker?"

"Uh, well, is he a nice guy?" Well, that Coke date was sinking to a new low, and I was beginning to regret being there.

"Well—oh, never mind, but I still think he's great. All the girls at the house are so jealous, and my daddy was just beside himself when I told him. Daddy calls me after every date, and I tell him everything we talked about."

Tell your daddy everything about a date?—I'd never do that, I thought.

I knew Bill Tucker from my work in the dining hall. He'd shove his tray into the area where I was standing with a "Here you go, sport," bouncing the tray filled with silverware, a glass of tea, and food off the end of the stainless steel counter, splattering the stuff all over me. He rated a big zero as far as I was concerned.

But even I knew who big-shot Bill Tucker was long before I went to work at the dining hall. Super Bill, as he was called by the papers, was a graduate of Little Rock Central High School, and had been one of the most widely recruited athletes in Arkansas history. When he decided to attend the University of Arkansas, it was headlined in our two state newspapers. The Second Coming won't get bigger headlines. He was a short, cocky, one-hundred-eighty-five pound quarterback with great moves, and had set a state record for points scored his senior year in high school. Arkansas moved him from quarterback to running back his freshman year, and he was set to become a starter this year. However, Bill wasn't the best of students, and it took a full-time tutor to keep him eligible.

Well, the Coke date was going downhill fast. First it seemed I'd picked Miss Everything, who had the most distorted set of values I'd ever known, and not only that, but she was dominated by some live-his-daughter's-life father. My God, I thought when I got up from that booth, I'd forget about that girl. But...as we sat there, she smiled and kidded with me, and talked about how we had worked together to save a poor dog, and I forgot all about not seeing her again. When we started to leave, she reached over, squeezed my hand, and said, "Sandy, thanks again for carrying my books, and I'll always remember you helping me save that poor dog's life. Maybe we'll see each other again."

She'd set the hook, and all she had to do was reel me in, but I tried to act nonchalant.

"Sure, it was nothing. Say, where's your next class?"

"Old Main, third floor."

"So is mine, I'll walk with you." That was a bald-faced lie, of course, but it would only take a few minutes to walk her to class and then run over to the Business Administration Building to my Algebra class.

As we walked to our classes, I managed to find out her entire schedule. "Maybe we'll see each other again" was going to become a certainty.

That night, as I made my notes in The Journal, I only had Vi on my mind, and I filled three-pages with comments about her. Yeah, and as much as I hate to admit it, saving that damned dog connected us and helped me understand Vi was a lot more than just a good-looking woman.

I've thought back to our first meeting hundreds of times, and maybe it wasn't love at first sight, but it was damn close to it. I believe there's a deep, inner attraction between some men and women, and, when we met that day, it was like electricity was in the air, and I think Vi felt it. I couldn't wait until I "accidentally" ran into her again. It would always be right as she finished her Western Civ class, when she'd have an empty period. At least we could have Coke dates, and, since I didn't have a car, that was going to be it for a while.

It didn't take long for me to come up with a sure-fire way to convince Vi to meet me in the Union. Girls like to give advice, and, when I walked up to her as she left class, I always started a line of bullshit by saying, "Vi, I need your advice, do you have a few minutes?" She could never resist. I never really had anything to ask her advice about, but I'd come up with something, such as my imaginary girlfriend. I figured if I could be with her for three-hours a week, surely I could make some headway toward a real date.

The only other girl on campus I was paying any attention to was Lacy. Well, there wasn't a guy on campus who didn't notice her. It seemed I bumped into her almost everywhere I went. Lacy, who was outgoing and friendly to everyone, always gave me a big smile, and we started saying "Hi, good morning," as we passed. I wanted to introduce myself to her, but I never felt it was the right time. Actually, I was pretty pathetic.

I kept hearing about her from other guys on campus. She was getting quite a reputation—all bad, or all good. It depends on what you're looking for in a girl.

10.

Bill Tucker...'Mr. Football'

Those first few weeks of college were some of the most enjoyable of my life. I was having a ball going by George's on Friday nights, playing poker every Saturday night, and flirting with Vi over Coke dates during the week. There was just one problem: I treated my classes the same way I did in high school, never studying or taking notes, day-dreaming through lecture after lecture, and expecting to make a C. Back then, most classes had three major tests: Four Weeks, Ten Weeks, and the Final. They each made up one-third of your grade. After Four Weeks Tests were over, I was shocked: all F's except for Creative Writing. I was stunned. After getting the last of my Four Weeks grades, I sat down with Benny, my roommate.

"Look at these grades, Benny! I can't believe it! I've never made F's before."

"Hell, Sandy, what did you expect? You never study."

"Uh, well, yeah, but I didn't study in high school either, and I never made F's."

"Well, let me tell you something. This ain't high school, Buster, and if you don't pull those grades up to a two point by the end of the semester, they're gonna flunk your ass right out of school."

"What?"

"Yeah, you'll be on probation, and the way you're going now you won't be back next year."

Flunking out of college, me, flunking out? I couldn't believe it, but I knew Benny was right. I'd tried to ignore that possibility, but Four Weeks Tests pulled me up short. I remember seeing my grade for Chemistry posted on the bulletin board outside of the classroom: Stuart Carson—42—F. The embarrassment, as I stood there with everybody carping about their grades when I had the lowest grade posted, was humiliating.

The Creative Writing class was my only bright spot. Doris was a great teacher and certainly a radical departure from my high school English teacher. The second week of class, after we turned in our compositions, entitled "Living in the Ghetto," she pranced back and forth in front of the class, waving her cigarette, swinging those sexy hips, and scolding us.

"Class, do you know the name of this course? Sandy?" she said, pointing at me.

"Creative Writing, 106."

"Did you say creative?—Creative?"

"Yes, ma'am."

"Oh, hell, Sandy, don't ma'am me. Doris is my name," she said as her eyes flashed.

"Yes, Doris," I said as she smiled.

"I'm going to read from one of your papers, and you tell me what's not creative and what is. Do you understand?"

A nod of heads, and Doris started reading.

"Page two, Leroy approached two of his friends standing on the corner and waved, 'Hi, guys, what are you doing?' A member of a rival gang was across the street, and they yelled at him, 'Hey, you better get out of our territory!'"

A couple of girls tried to add some adjectives, but Doris shook her head.

"Okay, I don't know if you're hesitant, or if you don't get it. This is how I want you to write dialogue.

"Yo, what's up?"

"'Hey, Bo, better get your ass outta here, or we gonna cut you up!'"

There was a twitter of giggles from the boys, and most of the girls just gasped. My God, I just sat there with my mouth open. Yeah, it did sound like trash talk from the ghetto, but who in the world would have expected that to come from a college professor?

Doris sat on the corner of her desk, crossing and uncrossing her legs and waving her cigarette, as she did most days.

"Be creative. If someone is a worthless so-in-so, call him one. If you need to say a profane word in a conversation, don't hesitate. Got it?"

I was sitting beside this little Pentecostal freshman girl (you know, no lipstick, long dress, etc), and, as Doris reeled off some of the 'bad words,' the little freshman nearly slipped under her chair. Well, most of the guys were a little red-faced, but we were eating it up, looking around the room and grinning like we'd never heard some of those words before. Well, we hadn't—not in class and not from a teacher. I was really thinking I might enjoy Creative Writing. Doris continued to talk and walk in front of the class, pointing her cigarette at individual class members to drive home her point.

"Okay? Do you understand? Now I'm going to hand these papers back, and on Wednesday bring them back corrected, using colorful, descriptive dialogue."

Wow, my mind just flooded with words I'd heard working with the hay-baling crew. Of course, living in south Arkansas, I had a number of black friends who spouted some very colorful language. I couldn't wait to add those words to my composition.

That night I went overboard correcting my composition, using some of the most off-color language you can imagine. In fact, I was hesitant to turn in my corrected paper, but since I was pretty off-the-wall anyway, I thought I might as well shock her. After all, she'd opened the door for nearly anything, language wise. The next Friday Doris told me to come by her desk after class.

Shit, I was nervous. I figured I'd gone too far, and she was going to give me a lecture about using too much profanity. When she handed me my paper she nodded and smiled. I quickly opened it. I couldn't believe the grade. It was an A with two underlines. When class was over, I hung back until everyone had left and then stopped by her desk on my way out.

"Sandy, your composition was outstanding," she said, lighting a cigarette.

"Where on earth did you come up with all those colorful phrases and words?"

"Uh, well, ma'am...uh, I mean, Doris, I worked on a hay-baling crew all summer, and those guys can cuss and swear like you wouldn't believe. Of course, just being around some of my colored friends helped me pick up some of their words."

"Humm, I guess that's it. I've never heard some of those words before."

Doris took a long drag from her cigarette, as she smiled and looked me in the eye. I could feel the blood rushing to my face.

She smiled as she saw my red face.

"Sandy, those words are just words. Get used to using them. Words are words, there are no bad words or good words: There are just words. Get comfortable with being creative."

"Uh, well, yeah, I'll remember that."

"Good, Sandy, now remember this lesson in being creative. Express yourself. And, by the way, your composition was excellent. You need to work on your spelling and grammar a bit, but other than that, it was outstanding. I love having students with talent in my class. Maybe before the semester is over we can get together after class and talk about creative writing."

She squeezed my arm and smiled as she walked behind her desk to pick up the rest of her papers.

"Thanks, Doris, I'd love to talk with you about creative writing. Just let me know when it would be convenient."

"I will, Sandy."

Wow, I thought as I left the room, a teacher who encourages her students to say words that would have gotten my mouth washed out with soap back home. When you're eighteen, a conversation like that will stick with you for a while. My daydreams took on a decidedly different slant, with sexy Doris front and center.

***

After the shock of the F's on Four Weeks Tests, I started working desperately to improve my grades. I could just imagine flunking out of school and having to go back to Pine Valley to a dead-end life—working in the woods or oil fields. The next day, after my talk with Benny, I borrowed notes to catch up and actually started studying at the library almost every weeknight. My God, walking in that library for the first time was about the last thing on earth I could have imagined doing before those F's hit me in the face.

Studying in the library allowed me to concentrate without being interrupted by my roommate or someone from down the hall who was just goofing off. However, library studying didn't always allow me to concentrate. It was a Monday night, and I made myself go to the library at seven o'clock. I stumbled in, grumbling to myself about having to sit for three hours as I studied the most boring subject imaginable, Chemistry. I didn't pay any attention to anything but finding an empty seat, away from the group of freshman fraternity and sorority pledges who had been forced to come.

Dummies, I thought, and then it occurred to me that if someone had made me study four-weeks ago I wouldn't be in the mess I was in. Maybe they're not so dumb.

After I settled in and stared at my Chemistry notes for thirty minutes or so, I raised my eyes and looked across two tables, right into Lacy's eyes. I was so surprised that I know my mouth dropped open. She winked, puckered those wonderful lips, and smiled. Well, we eye-flirted for most of the study time, and I got very little studying done. It was getting late, and I decided that, when the librarian flashed the lights, which meant the library was closing in ten minutes, I'd walk over and introduce myself. The lights flashed. I got my courage up and headed for Lacy. In my mind I had rehearsed exactly what I was going to say. As I walked past the first table between us a guy stood up, and I stopped to let him pass by. He walked straight over to Lacy and began to whisper something to her.

Ahaa, damn it. Get the hell out of here. But he stayed and stayed, whispered and giggled, and, after a couple of awkward minutes, I left the library. Of course, I was back every night for several days, but Lacy didn't show up. My gosh, just seeing Lacy put her in my mind for days. I couldn't quit thinking about her, and in my daydreams she quickly replaced Doris.

Well, even with all the studying I was doing, I wasn't about to quit playing poker. I still played on Saturday nights, and I continued to see Vi several times a week at the Union between classes, but other than that I studied during every available moment.

It was shortly after the shock of all those F's at Four Weeks that I started having dreams—or, hell, nightmares. I'd wake up in the middle of the night in a cold sweat from a dream about working on a hay-baling crew from daylight to dark, and then going home to a little shack out in the country. Those dreams were miserable, but they sure gave me an incentive to study.

Chemistry was by far my hardest course and German was a close second. I spent night after night at the library studying those courses, and, as Ten Weeks Tests approached, I began to understand them a little better, but only a little better. Chemistry was about to do me in. It was still two weeks until exams, and I had decided to study that Saturday morning. That was until I got a call from Vi.

"Sandy, I hate to ask you, but will you do me a big favor?"

Well, or course, I said yes. But when I heard about the favor I had agreed to, I instantly regretted it.

I'm signed up to work at the Humane Society this Saturday morning, and I need some help."

"Help? Doing what?"

"I'll be cleaning out the kennels, and I need someone to help with the hose. You know, to wash out the stuff. I can't stand to see animals suffer, and for those poor dogs to live in a dirty pen when I could clean it out is just more than I can stand."

God, what a sorry way to spend Saturday morning. The damn dogs snarled at me, and I came away from about three hours of washing out dog pens with a bad attitude and smelly tennis shoes. But I'll say one thing about Vi: I've never seen anyone who cared more about those dogs, and they were some of the worst looking, filthy mutts that you've ever seen. Hell, I was so busy I barely got to talk to her. Not the best Saturday I've ever had.

***

The Saturday night poker games at the Delta house were about my only source of entertainment and, as the weeks passed, my spending money. That worthless Dickie was bound and determined to, as he had said, "clean my plow," and the weekly poker games became a time when he obsessed about doing just that. I realized that, over the weeks that I'd played poker at the Delta house, the bitterness between Dickie and myself was festering until Dickie was almost fanatical about it, and I wasn't far behind. I've never had many enemies, but I couldn't stand that sorry guy. Hell, I had to hold myself back and not let anger fowl up my poker playing.

I knew I should have gone to the library to study the last Saturday night before Ten Weeks Exams started on Monday, but the urge to play poker and win some of Dickie's money overcame the need to study, and at eight o'clock I was in my seat, counting my chips and giving Dickie a "Go to hell" look.

"Gonna get your sorry hick ass tonight," muttered Dickie as we sat down to play.

"Shove it!"

"Don't you tell me to shove it, you hayseed!" shouted Dickie.

"For God's sake, if you two don't stop mouthing off, I'm gonna kick your asses out of the game!" said Peter.

We settled down until Dickie lit a cigarette and blew smoke across the table at me. He knew I couldn't stand cigarettes.

"Blow that smoke somewhere else, you worthless scumbag!"

"Make me, hillbilly!"

"That's two. You guys have one more to go. Three strikes and you're out of the game, understand?" Peter yelled at us.

A couple of "yeahs," and we proceeded to play.

The first hand began a run of the crappiest poker I've ever been a part of. I've had runs of bad luck before, but that night beat all I've ever seen. I was losing steadily, and even though I got more and more conservative in my playing, I could tell that that sorry ass Dickie and the rest of the guys at the table were going to walk away with some of my money. Then it happened, the making of a great hand, two aces down and two sevens up with only four cards dealt.

I took a deep breath and started figuring how I could build a big pot and get some of my money back. When the seventh card, a down card, was dealt, I peeked and held my breath; an ace. Aha, full house! That should do it! I raised the limit, thinking my raises would be enough to drive out most of the players. They did, and it was down to Dickie. I couldn't wait to turn over the three aces in the hole and win the biggest pot of the night when Dickie stopped before his last raise.

"Hey, farm boy, since it's just me and you, how 'bout we make a side bet on this hand?"

I could hardly hold myself. The best I could tell was that Dickie had maybe a full house, probably kings and something. Three aces in the hole would send Dickie into shock. Hell, he would have to have four kings to win the pot, and the odds against that were out of sight.

"Uh, maybe. What do you have in mind?"

"This ten dollar bill," he said, throwing the ten into the pot.

"Sandy, you don't have to call that bet," said Peter. "You can just call a twenty-five cent raise if you want to."

I was in shock for a couple of moments. My God, ten dollars was a lot of money. I couldn't imagine betting that much on one hand of poker, but I thought, Why not? I've got this hand won. I reached in my pocket and dug through some bills until I found enough to make ten dollars, and I tossed them in the pot.

"Call," I said.

Dickie turned over a king to make a full house of kings and jacks. I breathed a sigh of relief and was about to turn over my aces when Dickie flipped over his last hole card. It was another king. He had four kings.

"Ohooooo! Ho! Ho! Yeah! Finally got you, cleaned your plow, Farm Boy!" hooted Dickie as I pushed my cards out to the center of the table.

"Good hand, you lucky moron. That about cleans me out. I'll see you guys next Saturday."

Dickie was still yelling and carrying on about that last hand as I walked up the stairs. That bad night had cost me nearly thirty dollars, but, looking back on eight weeks of winning, I knew I was still ahead by a bunch. That last hand would lead that worthless Dickie into some deep poker water, and next time he ventured in, I'd be ready for him.

***

Monday I was standing at the foot of the stairs in Old Main when Vi left her Western Civ class. I was planning another 'accidental' meeting with her.

"Vi, how 'bout a Coke? I need to ask your advice about something," I lied as she paused at the foot of the stairs.

Vi was still dating Mr. Football, Bill Tucker, and had told me the last time we were together she was a little nervous that he'd find out she was seeing me, even though it was only for a Coke between classes. But she justified the Coke dates by assuring me that we were friends and only friends. Ha, I sure didn't believe that, and I don't think she did either.

"Oh, Sandy, I can't today. Can't it wait?"

"It won't take ten minutes, Vi, come on."

"Well, it better be important."

We walked out the side door of Old Main and headed for the Union, with Vi striding out in front and elbowing her way through the throng of students. I smiled as I watched her. She was always competing, even if it was just to get to the door of the Union. There was something about that edge she had that fascinated me. She was a tall girl, but she never dropped her shoulders, and her demeanor just oozed with confidence. I had fallen in love with Vi over the past few weeks, and I absolutely adored everything she did.

Of course, I didn't need any advice; I just wanted to be with her. We sat down and she said, "Oh, Sandy, before we get started, I want to thank you again for helping me clean the dog pens last Saturday. Didn't it make you feel good?"

"Uh, yeah." I lied.

"Well, what do want to ask me about?"

"Uh, what?"

"What do you need advice on, Sandy? You said you needed advice about something."

"Yeah, oh, I remember now. I'm considering majoring in geology. You know, studying rocks and stuff like that. They say there's a bunch of geology jobs right now."

"Geology? You're kidding. That's the dumbest major I've ever heard of. You should major in business or finance. Only real dorks major in geology."

"I don't like business stuff; it's the most boring thing I can think of."

"Well, you probably aren't the type to major in business. I can't see you in a suit. Maybe you should major in engineering."

"No, I started out in engineering. After hearing from the head of the department on the first day of class, I knew that wasn't for me."

"Well, if you were a good athlete like Bill, you could major in P.E."

"Ha, and be a small town coach some day? No thanks."

"Bill won't be a coach. He'll probably play pro ball, retire at thirty-five, and travel around the country."

"Oh, come on Vi, you know he's not going to be an All-American. The girl that marries Bill Tucker is gonna be a coach's wife in some hick southern town."

"Sandy, I can't believe you. Bill's a very good athlete, and my daddy says I should do everything I can to keep going out with him."

"Well Vi, you should tell your daddy to start dating Mr. Football. He treats you terrible. You said so yourself."

"Oh, Sandy, I was exaggerating. He's just forceful sometimes, and occasionally he forgets when we have a date. And did you know, he's an assistant scoutmaster? He works with a Boy Scout Troup every Saturday. That's why he couldn't help me clean out the dog pens."

I tried to dismiss the Boy Scout comment with a comment about the louse standing Vi up on a date.

"If I had a date with you, I wouldn't forget."

Vi looked at me, slowly shaking her head, and said, "No, Sandy, I don't think you would. But we're just friends. And anyway, Daddy has told me more than one time to date only fraternity guys. He said they're from better families."

"Better families?" Is she kidding?

The blood was rising in my face as Vi continued to extol what her daddy said about the virtues of fraternities and sororities. She glanced at my red face and knew I was upset.

"Sandy, I didn't mean you. You're different. If your family had money, you could have pledged, and I think you might have gotten a bid."

"Might have?" Boy, was I getting ticked. I gritted my teeth and said, "I wouldn't have taken it."

"What? Why?"

"Oh, I don't know, maybe I like being independent."

"Well, it doesn't make any difference, does it? You're not ever going to be in a fraternity, and one day you'll probably regret it."

"Listen to me, Vi!" I almost shouted. "There are some great guys in fraternities and some wonderful girls in sororities. But surely to God you don't think all independents are second-class students? Is that what I am?"

"Oh, Sandy, don't be silly, and don't get so worked up. There are some neat independents. You sure are. That was just my daddy talking. You know he's a little strange the way he thinks."

Well, I melted when Vi said that because she gave me that wonderful smile and squeezed my hand.

"Shoot, let's change the subject. Are you and Mr. Football serious?"

"Don't call Bill 'Mr. Football,' and, yes."

"Yes?"

"Very serious. And if you promise not to tell a soul, I'll let you in on a little secret."

"Yeah, okay."

"We're going steady."

"You're kidding."

"No, he asked me a week ago. I'm so excited, I can hardly believe it."

"Why is it a secret?"

"Well, he said Coach didn't want any starters to get involved with girls. It might affect their game."

"Oh, Vi, that's baloney. Mr. Football was down at George's a couple of nights ago with Lacy Darnell." I knew Vi had heard about Lacy. Hell, almost everybody on campus had. Actually, I was lying about Mr. Football and Lacy, but, since Lacy dated so many guys, I knew it would hit a nerve with Vi.

"Sandy, that's not true! You're just making that up!"

"No, I'm not, I swear to God! And Vi, you know why he cooked up this going steady bit."

I slammed my hand down on the table as I made my point. My God, I thought, the oldest make-out trick known to man. Surely, Vi's not that dumb.

Vi stammered and blushed. I knew I'd hit the nail on the head, and I was disgusted with her.

"Hey, I've gotta head to class," I said, jumping up, "see you later."

Vi sat there for a minute, and as I turned and looked back at her from the door, she wiped her eyes and picked up her books.

I was so mad I could hardly sit still in class. My mind was on nothing else. That damn jock promising to go steady and God knows what else, and for what? Damn! Damn! Yeah, I was jealous.

I was so disgusted with Vi for believing Mr. Football's line that I didn't see her for the next week. Ten Weeks Tests were barreling down on us, and I was using every possible minute to study. The week before Ten Weeks Tests I decided that I'd ignored Vi for as long as I could stand it, and I was waiting for her when she finished Western Civ that Monday morning.

"Vi, hey, let's go have a Coke. I haven't seen you in a while."

She had her head down and was turning toward the door when she heard me call out to her. Usually when we met, she'd flash that wonderful smile and yell something back to me, and we'd gab for a few minutes before going to the Union. That day she didn't say a word. When she saw me she smiled a small smile and nodded her head as she walked toward the Union. I followed and soon was beside her. Something was bothering her.

"Hey, you look down in the dumps, what's wrong?"

"Oh, I don't know, I guess I'm thinking about next week's tests and some other stuff."

For God's sake, I knew Vi well enough to know that school

was the last thing she'd ever worry about. She had a memory like a steel trap, and her grades were outstanding. We sat down and talked about a few things, sipped our Cokes, and then the conversation just seemed to die. She was quiet for a couple of minutes, her eyes half closed, staring at her Coke, when I noticed something. There was something dark under her makeup, a round, dark spot above her temple. I looked closely. She noticed and put her hand up to cover it. A bruise, she has a bruise and she's tried to cover it with makeup, I thought.

"Vi, you've got a bruise above your right eye."

"No, no, I haven't, it's the light in here. It's a shadow—a shadow."

"No, it's not."

"Oh, Sandy, it's nothing, nothing."

"How did it happen?"

"Uh, well, I bumped my head...on the closet door."

"No, you didn't."

"What?"

"I know you, Vi, and you're not telling me the truth. You didn't get that bruise from bumping your head on the closet door."

"Oh, Sandy, I..."

Tears filled her eyes, and she pulled out a tissue.

"Vi, you can tell me. What happened?"

She shook her head and softly said, "Sandy, I can't tell you. I just can't."

Every possible scenario raced through my mind as I looked at Vi, a dark bruise on her forehead and tears streaming down her face.

I thought of it in a flash.

"He did it, didn't he? Didn't he?"

There was no answer from Vi, who sat across the table with tight lips, unable to speak. She finally dropped her head, and I heard a soft, "Yes."

"That sorry, big-shot football player hitting a woman! You should have had him arrested!"

Vi shook her head. "Sandy, he didn't mean to. It was, well, he'd been drinking, and we stopped down at the stadium parking lot before he took me back to the house, and, well, uh, he got mad, and oh, Sandy, I can't talk about it anymore. Daddy said to just forget it. Anyway, it's behind us now, and he sent me roses the next day with the sweetest card."

"What? Roses? And now everything's hunky-dory again? You're kidding! Vi, surely you're not going out with him again?"

"Sandy, he didn't mean to hit me, it was the beer. Daddy said to not even think about breaking up with Bill—But I have some wonderful news. Bill has nominated me for Homecoming Queen, and, since he made the nomination, I'm sure to win. Can you believe that? Virginia Botner, Homecoming Queen."

Vi's eyes lit up, and she smiled for the first time.

I was stunned. The worthless guy hits her and bruises her, but instead of having him arrested, or at the very least dropping him, she's still going to date him. Mr. Football, roses, and a Homecoming Queen nomination. I can't win.

For the rest of our Coke date, Vi told me how many yards Bill gained last Saturday, and how, when he stopped by the sorority house on his way to a Boy Scout meeting, all the girls ran out and clapped when he came in the door. I wanted to throw up.

"Un huh, and that's the same guy who took you out and beat you up. Is that right?"

Vi just tightened her lips and looked at the table.

"But Daddy..."

"Vi, any man who'd hit a woman is worthless! He should be in jail! Forget your damned daddy!"

"Sandy, I believe you're the only person in this whole state who doesn't think Bill Tucker is wonderful."

"Wonderful? Huh, maybe, if they knew the woman-beater Bill Tucker I know, they'd feel a lot different."

"Oh, Sandy, nobody's perfect. Bill is really a good person. Did you know he's a blood donor when it's not football season? Anyway, you and I are good friends, so you should be glad I'll be Homecoming Queen. Daddy was so excited he could hardly talk when I told him. He thinks it's great for me to date Bill."

"What's your daddy got to do with your life, Vi? Surely you can make some decisions without him directing them."

Vi frowned when I mentioned her daddy and tried to shake the comment off, but I could tell that the words had hit home. My God, he must have an unbelievable grip on her. How can he possible control her that much?

"Well, even if you don't think it's a big deal, everybody else thinks it is."

"Humm. So you may be Homecoming Queen, and your daddy just loves Mr. Football. Do you like him?"

"Well, yes, I do. Of course, there are some things I don't particularly like about him, but yes, I like Bill."

The date had gone from bad to worse. I couldn't wait to head to my German class. Anything would beat sitting there listening to Vi extol some jock who had beat her up. I was in a bad mood when I walked into German class that day. However, after Herr Hoffer got off the subject and started talking about how he and his troops lived it up in Paris with girls from the Follies, everybody laughed, and I put Vi and Mr. Football out of my mind for a while.

11.

Tests and Poker

Thank God German was going a little better, and, after I started meeting after class with Herr Hoffer, my weekly test scores began to improve. I hated that class, but at least I could memorize the German vocabulary assignments, so I thought I might have a chance for a good C on Ten Weeks Tests. Of course, I didn't have a clue about sentence structure.

However, Chemistry was another story. I'd memorized all my notes, but the equations and molecular structure problems still had me stumped. I never seemed to catch up with the class. As soon as I began to understand one part of the course, our professor would move on to something entirely different, and I'd be lost again. I've never worked so hard on anything.

Ten Weeks Tests arrived, and I was living on NoDoz tablets, desperately trying to bring all the F's up, at least to C's. My God, I was waking up in the middle of the night in a cold sweat, dreaming about flunking out and having to go back to Pine Valley. I was miserable.

The Creative Writing test, which was a writing assignment, was on Monday, and I breezed through it, confident that I'd made at least a high B, or, the way Doris was encouraging me, maybe even an A. As I turned in my composition, I took a good look at Doris in her light yellow sweater. I was trying to visualize her without the sweater when she gestured for me to stop by her desk. She said softly, "If you don't have a five o'clock class, hang around, and we can talk about your writing."

I sat back down, and in a few minutes the classroom was empty. Doris got up, sat on the end of her desk, and crossed her legs. She lit a cigarette and smiled at me. What a sexy woman. God, when you're eighteen, every thought in the world goes through your mind, and most of them have to do with sex. I tried to act relaxed, but my body wasn't cooperating.

"Sandy, I always look forward to reading your compositions. You have a way with words that a lot of my senior students don't have. Of course, your subject matter always seems to revolve around sex, so it sure keeps my interest." She crossed and uncrossed her legs, grinning at me. Of course my mind was every-where except on creative writing, but I faked a casual conversa-tion.

"Well, ever since we had that talk about being creative and about how words are just words, I've tried to write that way."

"Oh, you mean the colorful word talk?"

Of course, just Doris saying "colorful word" had an immediate effect on me, but I took a deep breath and tried to carry on a nor-mal conversation.

"Yes, I won't forget that little talk for a while."

"Good, I'm glad you're letting yourself go. I can't wait to read your composition."

Our talk continued for another thirty minutes, bantering about words, creative writing, and life on campus, until I got up the nerve to say, "Doris, let's walk over to the Union and continue this conversation over a Coke." My God, I almost choked—asking a thirty-six year old teacher to have a Coke? I couldn't believe I'd said that. Doris gave me a big smile, but she was shaking her head.

"I'd love to, Sandy, but the administration frowns on students and faculty going out together. Of course, I disagree, but if we see each other after class it'll have to be in private."

"Oh, I didn't know that."

"Yeah, some of the students will do almost anything for a grade. The administration is just trying to make it less obvious. Maybe some night we can meet at my apartment, have a beer, and talk about creative writing."

"That sounds great, Doris. I'll look forward to it."

"It can't be this week. I'm covered up with test papers to grade, but I'll let you know when I get caught up. Well, I need to go. See you Wednesday."

I walked back to the dorm. I was anticipating something from Doris, but I didn't understand what. Maybe it would just be to talk about creative writing. She sure loved creative writing, and I was her best student, but there was something else. When we talked in private, her language and body movements were suggestive, but I sure didn't think a thirty-six year old teacher would be flirting with an eighteen year old freshman.

College Algebra came next, and the studying paid off. At least a C, I thought as I finished up early and handed in my paper. However, the big two were looming ahead, German on Thursday and Chemistry test on Friday.

The night before the German test I stayed up most of the night, memorizing every vocabulary word we'd been given. I knew sentence structure would be a problem, but if I got the words right maybe I could get at least a C. The test went about like I expected, and, even though my sentence structure was atrocious, I left the class hoping to pass.

Chemistry was another story. I still didn't have a complete understanding of problem-solving, and, even though I had memorized everything in my notes, I was in serious trouble. Finally, after hours of studying, I walked into class, sat down, and opened the Chemistry Ten Weeks Test. My heart sank. The test was full of problem solving, my weakest area. If I made a D, I'd be lucky.

Boy, was I relieved those tests were finished. The Chemistry test grades were posted on Friday, and, sure enough, I had a D, a middle D. Six more points and I would have had a C. The final would be the deciding factor.

I got up Saturday morning in a good mood. Tests were over, and, even though I'd continued to play poker every Saturday night right through Ten Weeks Tests, tonight I was anxious to play. Nothing but poker was on my mind, and even that scum Dickie Barnett wasn't going to keep me from having a good time.

The game started at eight o'clock as usual, and there was Dickie, sitting across from me, dragging on a cigarette, blowing rings, and mouthing off about everything. God, what a detestable person. Only Mr. Football fell lower on my list.

"Hey, Farm Boy, hope you brought an extra ten bucks tonight. I feel like I'm gonna clean your plow again. Ha, ha, ha," mouthed Dickie.

"It's right here, you blowhard," I said, patting my pocket, "but I don't think it's going anywhere."

Dickie reached over, took the deck of cards, flipped through them until he found all four kings, and then demonstrated how he'd won the big pot.

"Now you see three kings, and, just as old Farm Boy reaches for the pot, I flip over this fourth king! Whooooo! Whoooo! Hoo! Boys, that's how you clean a farm boy's plow," he yelled, waving a ten dollar bill.

Everybody had a good laugh at my expense, but I smiled and looked back at Dickie.

"That was just a little of your money coming back home, loser. I've still got a billfold full from all those other Saturday nights you lost your dumb ass."

Another big laugh, but this time at Dickie, who was red-faced, knowing that I was right on target.

"You smart-mouth hick, I oughta stick these cards down your throat!"

"Come try it! You're all mouth!"

"Damn it, you two can't just sit down and play poker, can you?" said Peter. "Come on Dickie, give me the cards. It's eight o'clock and time for this game to get under way." We played most of the night without an incident, and I was comfortably ahead when an interesting hand came up. Dickie began to twitch and bet, giving away what looked like a winning hand. I'd called him just to see if I could help a pair of deuces, and, much to my surprise, the next card dealt was another deuce. Now I had three deuces, two of them face down. Dickie's hand looked as if he might have two pair.

The bets skyrocketed after the sixth card, and everybody dropped out but Dickie and me. I looked at Dickie. He was the worst I've ever seen at concealing his hand. He was twitching, reaching for chips to bet, and sucking on his cigarette. Confidence oozed from every pore. Without a doubt, he'd made his full house. I had three deuces, and, even if I filled my full house, his would beat it. I should have folded my hand. The odds of me getting another duce were out of sight.

"Hey, Farm Boy, too rich for ya?" cackled Dickie.

I ignored his mouthing and continued to look around the table. All the cards that had been dealt to the other players were showing, and the fourth deuce wasn't there. Should I call his last bet and probably waste fifty cents? The odds weren't in my favor, and normally I'd have folded. However, sometimes in poker you play hunches. That's what I did as I threw fifty cents in the pot. If I didn't get that fourth deuce, I'd fold when Dickie bet. The cards were dealt, and I peeked at mine. I'll be. It was the fourth deuce.

Now the betting and raising flourished as Dickie and I raised each other until, at Dickie's last raise, he stopped and pulled out the ten dollar bill.

"Okay, Farm Boy, here's your ten bucks. Want a chance to win it back?"

"It's up to you, you creep."

"Okay, ten bucks, my last bet. Got the guts to call?" Dickie made a big show of throwing in the ten dollar bill in the pot and then leaned back in his chair, blowing smoke rings. He'd looked at my up cards long enough to be convinced there wasn't any way I could have a winning hand. The three deuces in the hole were going to shock the hell out of him.

"You're damn right I do!" I still had one raise left, and I pulled out two tens and threw them in the pot. "Call and raise you ten, you worthless moron!"

"Well, looks like Farm Boy has a decent hand, but not as good as mine. Call your bluff!" he said, tossing another ten in the pot.

Dickie had called, and I was supposed to show my hand first, but he was so anxious and sure that he had a winning hand that he flipped his cards over and yelled, "Okay, Farm Boy, read 'em and weep. Full house, kings and eights!"

I savored the moment for a few seconds, and then I took the one deuce from my up-cards and slowly started pulling the deuces out, placing them carefully beside the other deuce.

"Hey, dumb-ass, can you count?" I taunted. Dickie suddenly paled as he saw the third deuce flip up. "One, two, three..." I hesitated and then said, "four!"

Dickie sat there with his mouth open, and the rest of the players yelled and laughed.

"I can't believe you're that lucky!"

"Yeah, I feel it. I'm lucky, lucky tonight. Wanta cut for another ten? Or maybe there's a little chicken clucking across the table!" I taunted.

Dickie squirmed as I pulled the cards over, and, as I stacked them up to cut, I used a trick one of the guys on the hay-baling crew had taught me; I palmed an ace.

"Come on, put up or shut up."

"Okay, here's my ten," Dickie said, pulling out another ten and putting it in the pot.

"Go ahead, big shot, I'll let you cut first."

Dickie reached over, picked up the cards, shuffled them, and cut.

"Hey, a queen, all right!"

I reached over and took the deck of cards, slapping my hand with the concealed ace on top of the deck, and cut the deck, stacking the equal piles up beside each other. Then I turned the ace over.

"Well, I told you I felt lucky—an ace. Thanks for another ten dollar donation, loser."

"You lucky hick! I can't believe it!"

The game wound down in another forty-five minutes, and I left with a record take courtesy of Dickie. I thought about cheating Dickie as I walked back to the dorm, but I considered that cheating him was justice done. He deserved it.

12.

The Chemistry Test

Monday night I was having a beer in George's with Benny and Bob, and I told them about clipping Dickie for thirty bucks on one hand. We were still laughing about the sneaky cutting of the cards when Millie walked up. I was sitting on the outside edge of the booth, and Millie stood with her hip touching my shoulder. Her hand was rubbing the back of my neck. My gosh, Millie could turn a guy on in an instant.

"Hi, guys. The usual?" she said, smiling as she gave me a big wink.

"Yeah, Millie, but don't give these guys another big glass of water. Heck, they spend half the night running back and forth to the head. Just bring 'em an empty glass," said Bob.

"Sure, Bob. These guys are big boys, especially this tall drink of water," Millie said, giving me a little back rub as she joked with Bob. Well, I was enjoying the attention, and Benny and Bob were grinning like a couple of possums. As soon as Millie left the booth, Benny and Bob both began kidding me about her.

"You're Millie's next date, Sandy," hooted Bob.

I blushed and tried to deny it, but I knew Millie had started giving me a lot more attention than any of the other guys.

"Oh, hell, guys. Millie flirts with everybody. Helps her tips."

"Yeah, but there's flirting and then there's flirting. When Millie starts touching and rubbing, it's beyond flirting," said Bob.

"Damn, Sandy, why don't you try to take her out?" said Benny.

"Come on, guys, Millie is just being Millie. And anyway, with no car and very little money, I'm not going to be doing any dating for a while."

Well, they both laughed and nodded at that remark, and we settled down to shoot the breeze and drink beer. At about ten o'clock, Benny and Bob left, and I sat there a few minutes, finishing the last half glass of beer from the pitcher. Millie came over, and, instead of flirting, she sat down across from me, shaking her head.

"Sandy, I'm so tired I can hardly put one foot in front of the other. One of the girls didn't make it in tonight, and I've been handling eight tables."

Millie did look beat, but as I looked across the table at her, sitting there and resting her feet, I thought she was one of the cutest girls I'd ever seen, tired or not. She might have been a country girl from the hills south of Elkins, but she wasn't dumb. For the next fifteen minutes we quipped back and forth about everything from the football team to Fidel Castro. We were still sitting there kidding around when the short order cook yelled at her, "Millie! Order up!"

"Gotta go, Sandy. Enjoyed talkin' to ya. See ya around."

She slipped out of the booth and cleaned off a table before she picked up her order. Millie was so cute that I was still watching as she picked up a full tray of plates and bottles. She didn't weigh a hundred pounds, and she was dead tired. She wobbled slightly as she lifted the heavy tray over her head, but she steadied herself like a good waitress and headed for the kitchen. I was about to finish my beer and leave when Millie walked by a table where several jocks were sitting. One of the guys reached over and patted her on the butt as she passed. Millie jerked slightly, and she'd have made it if it hadn't been for some spilt beer on the tile floor. She stepped sideways, her foot came down on the wet tile, and Millie fell. The tray full of plates and bottles shattered on the floor, and she sprawled out against the edge of the bar. I was on my feet in an instant and ran over to help. She bit her lip as I picked her up, but she couldn't hold the tears back.

"Millie, it's okay. It's okay." I pulled her up and put my arm around her shoulder. Millie turned and sobbed on my shoulder, and Mary, the owner, came storming around the counter.

"Damn it, Millie! I've told you not to carry so much! Those plates are coming out of your salary!"

Millie was still crying, unable to answer, and the guy who had patted her on the butt had turned around in his chair, trying not to look at her or the mess on the floor.

I was getting madder by the second.

"Wait a minute!" I yelled at Mary. "That wasn't Millie's fault! That big goon patted her on the butt and caused the whole thing!"

I shoved the big jock on the shoulder, and he turned around, trying to deny that he had had anything to do with Millie falling.

"I didn't touch the girl, Mary. I swear."

"You liar! You sorry, lyin' numb-brained jock!" I screamed right in his face. Those words had no more than gotten out of my mouth before I regretted them. The rest of the guys looked surprised, even shocked, that I had called one of the biggest men on the Arkansas football team a liar. There was a shaking of heads as though they were thinking, Oh, my God, is he ever going to get his ass kicked.

"You called me a liar and a what?" he roared as he stood up.

"A numb-brained jock; are you deaf!" Then I realized my big mouth was about to get me killed, but for some reason my brain just kicked out of reality, and I stepped right up in his face and yelled, "You stupid, worthless prick, you made Millie fall!" I had my finger right in his face, pointing it at him as if I was going to poke him in the eye. "Now get your sorry ass down on the floor and clean up this mess! And when you get through, apologize to Millie!"

Well, I guess if you're as big as that guy, there are very few living people who have ever said anything like that to you. I could see one ticked-off jock getting ready to knock me across the room as his shoulders lifted and he took a deep breath.

Oh God!

Mary was getting anxious as the big jock doubled up his fist, but, just when I knew he was going to knock my head off, Millie pushed me back and stepped over in front of him. She had quit crying now, and her eyes were flashing. Wow, I could hear her teeth grinding.

"Don't you ever touch me again, you worthless piece of trash!" she screamed. And then, to the shock of everyone, especially the big jock, she drew back and slapped him in the mouth with the back of her hand. Wow, you could hear that slap all the way across the room. Well, if I'd slugged him, I'd be dead right now, but he was stunned when a small woman really whacked him, and he began to back away. Millie turned around to Mary, who had her hands up like a referee at a football game, and got right up in her face. Boy, I've seen some mad women in my life, but I don't think I've ever seen anyone who was as furious as Millie.

"Listen to me, Mary!" Millie yelled right in her face. "He patted me on my butt and made me slip on that wet tile!" she screamed loud enough for everyone in the place to hear and pointed at him. The guy was really embarrassed, and he was backing away. I think he thought Millie was going to hit him again, and he knew he couldn't do a thing about it.

Mary nodded and walked around Millie to face the big jock.

"You're out of here!" Mary yelled as she pointed toward the door. The guy was trying to leave, and his friends were already slipping out the door when Mary grabbed him by the arm.

"Wait a minute, Mister. You're paying for those plates. Let's see—two dollars, plus three—the glasses—plates. Okay, twelve-fifty will do it," said Mary as she held out her hand.

A big, tough guy had been humiliated and embarrassed by two little women not half his size. I snickered and quickly covered my mouth. Too late: He saw me and shook his fist at me.

"Your ass is mud!" he yelled at me.

"Get out of this restaurant, or I'm calling the police!" screamed Mary.

He gave me one more "Gonna get your ass" look, and I gave him the finger. Mary still had her hand out, and finally he opened his billfold and handed Mary the money. I gave him a little snort of a laugh, and Mary shook her head at me, knowing I was pushing a little too far. When sanity returned I leaned back in the booth, realizing I'd better avoid him for the rest of the semester, or he'd break my face.

"Millie, go get the broom, and Sandy, that's enough out of you."

Millie walked back to get the broom, and Mary yelled at the jock one last time, "Listen, fellow, don't come back in this place!"

Millie spent a few minutes cleaning up the mess and then walked over to my booth. I wasn't about to follow that bunch out the door and get my ass kicked.

"Sandy, you were wonderful! I won't ever forget tonight."

Of course, I knew Millie was the real lifesaver. If she hadn't stepped in front of him, he'd have knocked me across the room in about two seconds.

Millie and I talked for a few more minutes, and then I left. That night we had bonded, and our relationship was never the same. We'd shared a moment where we both intervened on each other's behalf when it really mattered. I never did tell Millie how thankful I was when she stepped in front of that big guy and saved me from a sure beating, but to this day I'll always remember a woman with more courage than any ten men I've ever known. Millie was some woman.

I didn't see her again for a couple of weeks, but when I did she treated me like a king, hugging me when I walked in the door and hanging all over me after we sat down. Benny and Bob were with me, and, of course, Millie bragged on me and told them how I had stood up to Robert Ray Schmidt, the big 270 pound defensive tackle.

"You called Robert Ray a what?" said Bob.

"A numb-headed jock."

"God, Sandy, I don't even want to be standing close to you when Robert Ray gets a-holt of you."

Well, I sat there trying to act as if I could care less about what Robert Ray was going to do to me, but I knew that he'd have to be a fast runner to catch me. I wasn't going to get near the big jerk for the rest of the semester. Of course, I didn't tell Benny and Bob that I was scared to death, or that Millie had saved my ass.

***

Outside of the Friday nights at George's and the Saturday poker games at the Delta House, I was still spending almost every night at the library studying, trying desperately to pull up my grades.

The next few weeks seemed to fly by, and before I knew it the Christmas holidays arrived. After I spent two weeks back in Pine Valley, bored out of my mind, I was glad to return to the university. Finals would start in two weeks, and my grade point was shaky, but not hopeless. It finally boiled down to the Chemistry test.

I probably had a D in German because I was spending so much time studying Chemistry. I was okay in English, Algebra, and Creative Writing, but if I didn't make a C in Chemistry, with a D in German, I'd be below a two point and be on academic probation. My God, every time I thought about flunking out of school I got nauseated.

Two days before the Chemistry final, I finished studying at midnight. The NoDoz tablets had my eyes wired open, and, after a few minutes of trying to sleep, I got up, walked out of the dorm, and started strolling across the campus, just killing time. As I passed the Chemistry building, I shook my head, dreading the almost certain outcome of the final. I just couldn't get all the background I needed in one semester, and, no matter how hard I studied, I could see a D looming.

The big, gray limestone building cast an eerie shadow in the flickering street light. Then, for some reason, I thought the Chemistry building looked like the high school building at Mount Union High School. And then it hit me like a brick. I knew how I could pass Chemistry with a C—get the test and make a high B. Oh, my God!

I was so stunned that I'd even thought of stealing the test that I just stood there. There was a bench in front of the building, and I slumped down and thought about the possibilities. What if I get caught and expelled from school? Do I want a C bad enough to break into a university building, into a professor's desk, and steal the test? I had the deepest feeling of anxiety, and I stood up and walked over to the side entrance of the building. As soon as I touched the door, handle a feeling of exhilaration swept over me, just like when I broke into the Mount Union High School building. It was the most addictive feeling I've ever had. It's criminal. It defeats the purpose of college. I'll never be able to live with myself if I do this, I thought. Then I started thinking about all the cheating I'd observed in some of my other classes. Some of my classmates in Algebra had cards with the math formulas on them, and about a third of my German class was regularly using cheat cards to remember vocabulary. I'll admit it; I was trying to come up with anything I could to justify my desire to steal the Chemistry test. Maybe stealing the test is just another form of cheating, I thought. I knew better than that, but a person's mind sometimes justifies the person's actions in spite of the facts. Maybe I had some of Uncle Hosie in me, and I couldn't help it. I don't know, and I guess I never will. All I can say is that the urge was overpowering, and, when combined with the thought of actually flunking out of school and having to go back to Pine Valley to some menial job, I couldn't resist.

After I'd made up my mind, I thought about the lock jammer and the lock pick that I'd tossed in my bag when I'd packed for college, as well as the clothing and the time I would need to complete the break-in. I spent another hour walking around the building, peering in windows, trying to determine if there was an alarm system and if there was a night watchman on duty. After an hour, I saw someone walking toward the building, shining a flashlight into the windows and bushes. He walked up to the front door, shook it, and then walked around to the side door and tried it, too. I was standing in the bushes behind a tree, and, as he walked off, I checked my watch; two o'clock exactly. It was a campus cop making his rounds. I'd gotten there a little after one o'clock, so I figured he must not come by more frequently than every hour. I'd need to go into the building shortly after one o'clock, be sure that the door was locked behind me, get the test, and leave before two o'clock.

Well, I couldn't believe I was actually plotting a break-in of a university building. Every few minutes I'd change my mind and worry about something, usually getting caught and expelled from school. But, after calming down, I'd continue on. When I left the Chemistry building that night, I knew that, twenty-four hours later, I'd be crouched by the side door, trying to pick the lock.

The next morning at about ten o'clock, I left the dorm and headed downtown to the Salvation Army Thrift Shop. An hour later I came away with a black shirt, pants, and even a black beret. I spent the rest of the afternoon reviewing and planning the mission.

Benny had a test the next morning, and he was studying when I came in from working at the dining hall that afternoon.

"Dang, Sandy, you better get to studying Chemistry. You know if you don't make a decent grade on the final, you're gonna be on probation."

"Yeah, I've been working on it, and later tonight I'm going over to Brian Littleton's apartment to study with him."

Benny nodded, and I proceeded to pack my tools and clothes for the break-in. I sat at my desk studying until almost nine o'clock. Then I picked up my stuff and left the dorm.

However, instead of going to study, I walked to the Greek Theatre, which is right down the hill from the Chemistry building, and stashed my break-in clothes and tools under the back steps that led off the stage. Then I walked down Dixon Street to the UARK Theater and took in a late movie. When the movie was over, I walked across the street to the bowling alley, had a hamburger, and then strolled back onto campus. It was almost midnight when I slipped behind the back wall of the Greek Theatre to change clothes and pick up the tools I'd left there. I could never tell you how nervous I was. My knees were shaking so badly I could hardly walk, and my breath was coming in short, shallow spurts.

I checked my watch: 12:45. Fifteen minutes later, I'd changed clothes and slipped through the bushes at the back of the Greek Theatre, climbed the hill by the Chemistry building, and was standing in the bushes directly behind the building. I crouched there, dressed in black, a rubber hammer tucked in my belt, holding my lock jammer and lock pick, and waited until I saw the flashlight of the campus cop heading down the sidewalk toward the Chemistry building. A rattling of the door, a sweep of the light along the side of the building, and he was gone. I stood at the corner of the building for a few minutes to be sure no one was coming, and then I walked hurriedly up to the side door and inserted the lock jammer far enough into the keyhole to turn the lock. I turned it a quarter of a turn in the direction you would turn a key, and then I slipped the lock pick into the keyhole and started racking it as I kept pressure on the lock jammer. Finally, after some deep breathing, my hands steadied, and I began to hear the individual pins click into place one at a time. Then, with a hard turn, the lock jammer turned the lock, and the door was unlocked. I pulled the door open and stepped inside.

The break-in at Mount Union High School had been exciting, but nothing like this. Never had I felt more excitement, fear, and apprehension than I felt standing in that dark hallway. In a few seconds, I was standing in front of my professor's office. Pulling out a small flashlight, I looked at the lock. It was a simple snap lock, which I opened with my screwdriver blade. Professor Arnold's desk was against the far wall, and it was unlocked. I looked in the front and side drawers, and there, in the right side drawer, was a big stack of mimeographed tests.

"That's it," I gasped as I tried to catch my breath. I pulled one of the papers out and scanned it quickly. Yes, it was the Chemistry final, and it was in my hands. Suddenly, a flashlight beam swept across the room, and I dropped to the floor.

Damn, I thought, I've taken too long and the campus cop is back. Did he see me? Did I relock the door? Will he be coming down the hall in a few minutes? When he sees the door open, will he walk right into this office and arrest me? My college life might be ending in the next five minutes. The side door rattled. Oh, my God, I hope I locked it back. I held my breath for what seemed like an eternity, and then I crept up to the window and looked out. The flashlight of the campus cop was bobbing along as he headed away from the Chemistry building.

"Oh, my God," I gasped, "if I get out of here, I'll never do anything like this again! Never!"

Then I got lucky; I happened to glance in the wastebasket beside the desk, and there, partially wadded up, was one of the tests. The mimeograph machine had smeared one of the copies, and, even though you could easily read it, Professor Arnold had culled it and tossed it in the wastebasket. I picked it up, stuffed it in my pocket, and carefully closed his desk. In less than a minute, I was out of the building and heading for the Greek Theatre to change clothes.

Afterwards I sat down on one of the back steps that led up to the stage, and, as I sat there and thought about what I'd just done, I began to feel so depressed that I couldn't hold my head up. I was no better than Uncle Hosie, who was sitting in Tucker Penitentiary for picking locks. A wave of regret and depression swept over me, and I slumped down on the steps and held my head in my hands.

Finally, I stuck the test in my shirt and headed for the dorm. When I got to my room, I pulled out my Chemistry book and started working on the test. There were no surprises, but, as I looked at the twenty problems, I knew that the best I could possibly have hoped for, if I hadn't stolen the test, was a low C. I picked out three of the hardest problems and decided I'd deliberately miss them. If I got the other seventeen correct, that would give me an eighty-five. In an hour, I'd figured out the answers to the other seventeen, and I began to memorize them. By test time, ten o'clock, I had them down pat and breezed through the test, finishing before anyone else in the class.

I picked up my test, checked to be sure my name was on the top of the page, and walked up to my professor's desk to hand it in.

"Hi, Sandy. How do you think you did?" questioned Professor Arnold, who had begun to appreciate my hard work during the last half of the semester.

"Well, pretty good, I think. Maybe all the hard work will pay off." I had a little queasy feeling when I lied to Professor Arnold, and I wanted to get out of his sight as soon as I could.

Professor Arnold nodded and opened my exam paper.

"Just a minute, Sandy, and I'll grade your test," he said as he moved his finger down the page.

"Hummm, no—no—no."

I held my breath. He'd already marked wrong the three problems that I'd deliberately missed. Had I missed anything else? If I had, I was headed for probation.

"Well, I'm pleasantly surprised, an 85," he said, nodding in satisfaction.

"Yes!" The guilt of what I'd done momentarily left me, and all I could think about was not being on probation.

The C in Chemistry took a big load off my mind, but the guilt I felt after stealing the test kept sweeping over me in the days ahead. No matter how I tried to justify it, I knew I was a thief and a petty crook. I could've gone to jail, just like Uncle Hosie, if I'd been caught. It could've ruined my life. What would Vi have thought if she'd found out? Hell, she would never have spoken to me again.

Of course, to make myself feel a little better, I kept telling myself that it was only a one-time thing and that lots of students were cheating.—but I was lying to myself again.

13.

An Old Main Meeting

SPRING SEMESTER, FRESHMAN YEAR, 1958

I was dead-dog tired after Finals ended, so I spent the semester break in Fayetteville, resting up from all-night studying while I tried erase the guilt of stealing the Chemistry test from my mind. Every time I passed the Chemistry building, I had a sinking feeling of remorse, quickly followed by a surge of adrenalin as I thought about walking down that dark hallway after picking the lock. Of course, I tried to justify my thievery by thinking of how many other students were actively cheating, and I kept thinking that I really did know a C's worth of Chemistry. I deserved a C, I told myself, but I knew that I'd committed a serious crime to get it. I couldn't shake it. It bothered me constantly.

However, after a few days, I managed to at least push that theft back into the recesses of my mind. Other things were keeping me busy. With classes starting back in less than a week I was determined to find better work than the sorry tray-grabbing job I had had at the dining hall. Then I got a lucky break. Two days before classes started, I was in the University Bookstore and overheard the manager tell one of the student clerks they needed a couple of extra workers. I dashed back to the dorm, cleaned up, put on my best pants and shirt, and hurried back to the bookstore. I asked to see Mr. Conroe, the manager, and thirty minutes later, I was hired.

Vi came in the day registration started. I took her registration card and managed to move her in front of a long line of students by lying and saying that she'd been in line all morning, and had forgotten to bring her schedule.

"Hey, Vi," I whispered, "I'll be finished for the day in fifteen minutes. How about catching up at the Union?" I handed her a stack of books, and she started shaking her head.

"Sandy, you know Bill and I are going steady, and he found out I've been meeting you in the Union. Of course, I told him we were just friends, but he still doesn't want us to meet, even if it's just in the Union. I'd better not."

Damn muscle-headed jock, flashed through my mind. Vi started to turn away, but I caught her sleeve and whispered, "That's okay. Let's meet tonight in front of Old Main. We can sit on the steps and talk. I've got something really interesting to tell you." Of course, the something interesting was a lie, but Vi looked interested.

"Sandy, Bill would have a fit if he knew that I met you at night."

"Well, sure he would, but he'd never know. Anyway, he shouldn't stop you from meeting and talking with friends. Come on, Vi, we need to catch up on a bunch of stuff."

"I don't know, Sandy."

"Listen, Vi, we'll just talk, and it's just up the street from your sorority house. I've really got something interesting to tell you.—Oh, by the way, I'll help you at the Humane Society Saturday." Vi's eyes lit up, and I thought, Damn, I'm offering to clean up dog crap to be with her. I'll be there at seven o'clock. Hey, I've got to wait on that guy over there. See you tonight."

Vi stood there a minute, waved goodbye, and smiled. My chances looked good. I'd have to invent something interesting to tell her. I thought about it for the rest of the day, trying to come up with something good.

That night, at ten minutes till seven, I was sitting on the top step at the front entrance to Old Main, looking out on the big lawn area. I didn't just pull that meeting place out of thin air. I'd picked it because it was completely private. From the steps of the building to the street were at least three-hundred yards of open lawn flanked by trees. It was, and still is, one of the most secluded places on campus.

I sat on the top step, wearing a light jacket, shivering from the early January cold, still thinking about what I could tell Vi that was really interesting. I couldn't think of a thing. Maybe we'd just talk about stuff, and it wouldn't come up.

The minutes passed, and I was grumbling under my breath about her not coming. It was ten minutes after seven, and I'd about given up when I saw a shadow moving out of the dim light behind Old Main.

"Sandy?"

"Vi?"

She walked over, all bundled up, and we sat down on the top step and began to talk about our new classes. A few minutes later, she brought up the reason we were there, the very interesting bit of news I had to tell her.

"Vi." I moved close to her. She looked at me, and then I leaned forward and kissed her. We kissed for a few seconds before she pulled away.

"Sandy!"

"Oh, Vi, I couldn't help it. You looked so gorgeous, sitting there in the moonlight."

"Sandy, I'm going steady. You know that."

"Yeah, you're right, but don't be upset, Vi. I just couldn't resist."

"Okay, but don't you breathe a word of us meeting here. Bill would drop me in a minute if he found out, and you can't imagine how upset Daddy would be."

We talked for another twenty minutes before Vi had to go, but, as she said goodbye, we kissed again, this time a little longer and more passionately. She walked away, leaving me sitting on the steps, utterly frustrated. On the plus side, we'd kissed twice, and she'd kissed back, but on the other hand, she was more concerned about Mr. Football finding out than she was about our relationship. Damn, what's it going to take to get her to ditch that worthless creep? That was all I had on my mind as I walked back to the dorm.

14.

Doris!

The day before second semester classes started, I saw Doris, my Creative Writing teacher, crossing the street in front of the library. I'll tell you one thing, with those long legs and that sexy walk you couldn't miss her—if you were a guy. I'd made my first college A in her class, and during the last part of the semester Doris and I had become good friends as we talked after class. During the course of our conversations, I found out that she'd decided never to marry, but that was really hard for me to believe. She was flirtatious and one of the sexiest women I'd ever met. I couldn't imagine her not wanting to be around a man. However, one afternoon she told me about a relationship that had occurred a couple of years ago. My God, when she finished telling me about this guy, I know my mouth must have been hanging open. It was Jim Jenkins, one of the football coaches, a big, square-shoulders guy, somewhat overweight, with thick, black, dyed hair, and rather attractive in a rough sort of way. The players had nicknamed him "Bull" because of his short temper, which would frequently send him into a wild, bull-like rampage. Hell, I didn't care much about football, but I knew Bull's reputation.

According to Doris, they had had a relationship that was hot and heavy for most of a school year, but it was beginning to go sour as Bull became more and more irrational and possessive.

From the way Doris talked about it, I think she'd become afraid of him. Then a scandal of epic proportions hit the campus, and I'm not kidding. Wow, when she told me about what happened, I was shocked speechless. A campus police officer was patrolling the area behind the Fine Arts Center and heard some noises in the bushes near the building. He shined his flashlight to see what was going on, and there was Bull, fooling around with a guy. Well, he hauled them in and filled out an indecent exposure charge. Of course, this charge was squelched the next day, but not before a part-time student cop leaked it out. It was all over campus by the end of the day. Bull managed to pull some strings and wasn't charged, but it was obvious to everyone on campus, especially Doris, that he was bisexual. She was humiliated and broke off the relationship.

Bull was in his fifties, fat and out of shape, and, according to Doris, not only did he have a thing for young boys, but, as she found out later, he was constantly trying to pick up girls on campus. I'd seen Bull cruising around campus from time to time, slowing down every time he passed a decent-looking girl. He was easy to spot, since he drove a new custom- painted, metallic blue, '57 Chevy. Every Sunday afternoon he was out behind Carson Terrace, the apartment complex, waxing and polishing his car. God, he was obsessed with that car. According to Doris, if one of the girls accepted a ride from Bull, she would invariably end up on some secluded back road, where he'd demand sex in return for a ride back to campus. On a weekend when he didn't pick anyone up, he'd end up down at the bowling alley, playing the pinball machines. Benny and I had seen him there several times, and, just from watching him manhandle one of the machines, we could tell that he had a terrible temper.

It had been a few days since I'd seen Doris, and, when I saw her walking toward me, I stopped and waited for her to approach. She was wearing a charcoal-colored trench coat, which was unbuttoned, revealing a light pink sweater and skirt. Doris's outstanding figure looked great in that tight pink sweater.

"How's my favorite student today?" She reached out, took both of my hands and gave me a big smile.

"Just great, Doris, and thanks for the A. It's my first."

"Don't thank me, Sandy, you deserved it."

We stood and talked for at least fifteen minutes, and, when I was about to leave, Doris stepped closer to me and put her hand on my arm.

"Say, Sandy, I'm caught up, why don't you stop by my apartment tonight? We can have a glass of wine together and talk about creative writing."

Doris gave my arm a little squeeze. I took a deep breath and managed to act as if being asked to visit a sexy woman in her apartment didn't excite me.

"Sure, I don't have a thing going on either. Where do you live? And what time?" I managed to say, holding my breath.

"The address is 323 East Maple Street, apartment four. The complex is called The Maples. Come by around seven."

"Okay, I'll see you tonight."

Doris gave my arm another squeeze, smiled, and walked away.

I stood there for a minute, stunned that she had actually asked me to come to her apartment. On my way back to the dorm I thought about meeting Doris in her apartment, and my mind filled with possibilities. Did she really want to talk about creative writing? That could be it. Teaching the subject was her whole life. Or did she enjoy being with me and wanted some company during this dead time between semesters? Of course, as a young man of nineteen, the idea of meeting an attractive woman in her apartment had me thinking other thoughts. I wondered, after all the kidding and flirting with me, if she had other things in mind. My God, we might kiss, or who knows what might happen? Well, to be honest, I thought that was a long shot, but she was such a good-looking woman I couldn't help fantasizing about her.

That night I left the campus and walked east up Maple Street until I spotted the Maples apartments. The Maples was one of several large apartment complexes that ringed the university, and apartment four was in the back of a twelve unit building. It was a ground floor apartment with parking next to the front door. I rang the doorbell and heard Doris walking to the door.

"Sandy, come in and have a seat—sit over there on the couch—can I get you a beer or a glass of wine?"

"Sure, a beer will be fine." A beer? What? She knows I'm only nineteen. A teacher serving beer to a minor? Well, that only excited me more as I sat there, waiting for Doris to get me my beer.

She walked back to the refrigerator for the beer, and I sat on the couch, breathing a little heavily, not knowing what to expect. When she opened the door, I'd been surprised by what she was wearing. In class she always wore a sweater and a matching tight skirt, but tonight she looked so different, wearing a pink jumpsuit with a zippered collar that was opened down the front. She was showing cleavage! My thoughts were interrupted as Doris returned from the kitchen with a beer.

Doris sat down beside me, smiled, and started talking about writing. "Sandy, I've been meaning to have you over all semester. I think you have a lot of potential as a writer. Have you ever written anything before?"

"Well, just a few things in high school. Your class is the first one I've taken with any writing assignments." Of course, my mind wasn't on writing, but I covered my nervousness by telling her how much I enjoyed her class. Actually, it was my favorite class, but when compared with German, Algebra, and Chemistry class, Creative Writing didn't have to come up very high.

I finally relaxed, and, after a couple of hours and several beers, we were laughing and kidding around about some of the more off-the-wall writing assignments that had been turned in that semester. We sat and talked for several hours, and, as the evening progressed, Doris pulled out some essays that were examples of good writing and scooted over closer to me. We read them together as she pointed out good examples of dialogue and descriptive terms that the various writers had used. Several of the papers had descriptions of sexual activities, and Doris made a point of stopping to outline how the author used key words to highlight each paragraph and to give the reader a clear picture of what was happening. By the time the evening was over, she was sitting very close to me, with one arm draped across my lap as we turned the pages and read the essays together.

Well, after Doris snuggled up beside me and started reading, I began to feel my breath quicken. Damn, I hope I don't have to stand up any time soon, crossed my mind. However, when the next essay, which was about eighteenth century England, came up, I calmed down and relaxed again.

It was late in the evening, after Doris had finished her third glass of wine, when she leaned back on the couch, looked up at the ceiling, and said, "Sandy, you know I like teaching Creative Writing, but guess what I'd really like to do?"

Of course, I didn't have a clue. Doris said, still looking at the ceiling, "I'd like to walk out of this stuffy school and go to southern California and write. Maybe I'd write those cheap romance novels."

"Really? You could write something a lot classier than that."

"Oh, Sandy, I think it would be fun just to sit at the typewriter and hammer out one sex and violence novel after another."

"You should do it, Doris. Hey, you only get one chance in this life to do what you want."

When I said that, Doris looked over at me and, for a few seconds, gave me the faintest smile, as if she were drinking in the possibility.

"You're right, Sandy," she said, slowly nodding her head, "but you know very few people do what they want they really want to do."

Doris got up, walked over to a cabinet, pulled out a second batch of essays, and scooted up close to me so that we could read them together.

"Well, since I'm not going to run off to southern California, we might as well review some more good writing," she said as she began to go over the various papers.

After the second batch of essays, I glanced at my watch.

"Gosh, Doris, it's after eleven. I didn't realize it was so late. I'd better get going."

Doris started to get up, and, as she did, she slipped and her hand pressed down on my thigh to catch herself. Of course, that might have been an accident, but, at age nineteen, every touch from an attractive woman, especially anywhere near the thighs, is enough to turn on most guys. I can still remember that touch—yeah, it did turn me on.

"Sandy, it's been fun. Next time I'll make you a new drink, called a Margarita. My Margaritas are the best. Ever had one?"

"Uh, no, I don't think so." Of course, Margaritas were the last thing on my mind right then, but I just smiled and nodded my head.

"There're mostly tequila and lime juice. I'll fix you one next time."

"Sure, sounds good."

However, my thoughts weren't on Margaritas, or the touch on my thigh. I was trying to figure out how to say goodnight. God, what am I going to do now? This wasn't a date, and she was my thirty-six year-old teacher, but shaking hands didn't seem right, since we'd been so close while sitting on the couch. But I was afraid to kiss her like I would a regular date. What if I made her mad?—maybe a little hug. I could feel little beads of sweat popping out on my forehead, and I had almost stopped breathing.

Doris walked to the door with me and put her arm around my waist as I hesitated.

"Uh, Doris, I had a great time. I didn't realize there were so many ways to write," I mumbled, trying to retain my composure.

"Oh, we've just scratched the surface, Sandy. There's so much more."

This was the awkward moment I'd been dreading. I turned around and faced her, thinking I'd give her a little hug around the shoulders unless she stuck out her hand to shake hands. Then, as I reached out to do my little hug, Doris moved closer, turned her face up to mine, and kissed me on the lips. It wasn't the most passionate kiss I've ever had, but it was certainly the most surprising: a soft, subtle kiss as she pressed against me.

"Goodnight, Sandy. We'll do it again sometime, maybe next Friday," she said as she stepped back, leaving me stunned. I finally managed to acknowledge her as I backed out the door.

"Sure, Doris, sounds great."

After a few more mumbled thank you's, I walked back down Maple Street to campus, thinking about the evening. For God's sake, I'd never been in a situation even remotely similar to that, and my thoughts swirled as everything you could imagine passed through my mind. I'd been with a very attractive but older woman—hell, she was almost old enough to be my mother—for several hours, reading suggestive essays, and then, when I left, we'd kissed. What? What? Well, what a nineteen-year-old freshman thinks about every fifteen seconds filled my mind. I was confused, but I was excited just thinking about my next visit.

15.

Three Queens

By Monday, the bitter cold of a north Arkansas winter had settled across the area, and the howling, north wind penetrated every fiber in me as I walked across campus between classes. I met Vi when she finished her civics class, and we sat in the Union, drinking hot chocolate and trying to stay warm. I tried to steer the conversation around to us, but Mr. Football had come to visit her at home after Christmas, and Vi's dad had squired him out to the country club. Her dad was so pleased. That was all I could get her to talk about: "Pleasing Daddy, pleasing Daddy." I thought I'd throw up if she said that one more time.

I guess Vi's giving in to her dominating father, was about all that kept her from being perfect—at least as far as I was concerned. She was warm and friendly and was one of the best people I've ever known, except for that one flaw. She wanted to please her father so badly that it was screwing up her life. It made absolutely no sense.

"Sandy, did you know Bill was voted All Southwest Conference?"

Well, I could care less, but I mumbled, "Nope, I don't pay any attention to the sports page."

"Well, you should. Everybody in this state is a Razorbacks fan but you."

"Vi, there's a lot more to school and life than football. Football's okay, but if I had a choice to float the Buffalo River or see a football game, I'd float the Buffalo."

"Well, if you did, you'd be by yourself."

We sparred back and forth about Mr. Football, football in general, and life without football until it was time for class. Vi went out the main door of the Union, and I headed for the side door, still thinking about Vi and Mr. Football. My God, can't she see what a dead-end marriage she'd have if she married that dumb football player?

As I was leaving the Union, I saw Lacy coming in the door. I took a deep breath. This was a perfect time to introduce myself, and I was thinking like crazy about what to say. I held the door open for her and blurted out, "Hi, uh, uh, whooo, I'm freezing. Cold enough for ya?" Damn, how stupid can a person sound, I thought.

She grinned, puckered those wonderful lips, and said with a wink, "I'll bet I could warm you up."

Maybe we could have carried on a conversation and I could have introduced myself, but as I usually am when I'm shocked—and I was sure shocked at that comeback—I turned into a mute.

"Uh, uh, yeah," I managed to mumble as Lacy walked into the Union.

I walked back to my dorm thinking about ways to meet Lacy, but nothing seemed to be right. She was so intimidating and gorgeous that I couldn't get up the courage to just stop her and introduce myself. Of course, I felt a little uneasy about pursuing Vi when I couldn't get Lacy off my mind, but it seemed I was attracted to Vi in a different way than I was attracted to Lacy.

While Vi, a former beauty queen, was a real beauty, she couldn't hold a candle to Lacy when it came to sex appeal. But there was something else that I thought was appealing about Lacy. She seemed like me in so many ways as she ignored how a freshman sorority girl was supposed to act and look on campus. I think she was the only girl on campus who refused to wear loafers and white socks, and, in a school where almost every girl's hair was bobbed and short, her long, golden blonde hair really stood out. She didn't conform, and I liked that.

***

My Creative Writing class was the last class of the day that next Monday, and as I walked into Old Main, I was anxious to see Doris. How is she going to react? Will she invite me over again? Those thoughts and many more flashed through my mind as I walked down the hall to her class. Of course, I thought she'd make a fuss over me all through class since we'd become so close, and I was sure expecting her to ask me to stay after class and talk.

However, Doris didn't even look up when I entered the room, and she didn't call on me or make eye contact during the class. When the class was over, she left with the rest of the class, leaving me standing there, feeling like an idiot. Oh, my gosh, she's mad because we kissed. Damn, she'll probably nail me on the next writing assignment. I was confused, and, to be honest, really let down.

Wednesday's Creative Writing class was almost identical, and now I was certain that I'd crossed the line when we kissed. The friendship we'd developed was gone. I was depressed. Nineteen-year-old guys can whip up an infatuation with an older woman in an instant, and I'd daydreamed about Doris since our 'date' at her apartment. It seemed it was over as quickly as it had started.

On Friday, I considered cutting class and going squirrel hunting with Benny, but at the last minute, I changed my mind and slipped into class about five minutes late. Doris didn't pay any attention to me when I walked in, and I slouched into a chair toward the back of the room. When the bell rang, I took an extra minute to make myself a couple of notes before I left, and then started for the door, only glancing over at Doris. Then, much to my surprise, she said softly, "Sandy."

She nodded for me to wait. The room emptied in a couple of minutes, and I walked over to her desk.

Doris had a big smile on her face and said, "Sandy, come over tonight, and I'll make you one of my margaritas."

"Huh?"

I know I must have looked shocked because she said, "Sandy, when we're in class together I'm not going to give you any attention. You know what I said about the administration frowning on students and faculty seeing each other socially. Well, I'm up for tenure, but don't think that I'm ignoring you because I don't like you."

Those words lifted a load off my shoulders, and my spirits soared.

"Well, Doris, I'm really glad you said that, because I've been worried all week that I'd offended you somehow."

"No, of course not. You didn't do one thing that offended me, but remember what I just said: If we see each other after class it must be private and confidential. Don't tell your roommate, or anybody else, that you've been coming over to my apartment. Now, Sandy, that's very important. I hope you understand why."

"Yes, I do, Doris. I understand, and I promise I won't tell a soul."

"Good. Well, how about a margarita tonight?"

"Sure, what time?"

"Seven o'clock."

Doris leaned back in her chair, lit a cigarette, and smiled at me as I thought about how sexy she looked as she crossed her legs and waved her cigarette around. Gosh, I was smiling and grinning, kidding around as if Doris wasn't my teacher, just an attractive woman. It had been such a relief when she told me that she wasn't mad at me, and, looking back at that time, I can see that my infatuation with this sexy woman was getting serious.

We made small talk for a few minutes, and then I walked back toward the dorm. I was relieved after Doris explained to me about keeping our meetings private, but why private? I couldn't figure it out. It seemed to me that we had talked almost non-stop about creative writing, and, outside of that little kiss when I left, we hadn't done anything out of the ordinary. But, since she was so firm about keeping our meetings a secret, I wasn't going to tell anyone. However, I was so excited about seeing her on Friday night that I wrote a couple of extra pages in The Journal.

I sat around for a couple of hours, propped up on my bed, thinking about having margaritas with Doris, and yes, every conceivable thing that could happen crossed my mind. Later that afternoon I ran into both Vi and Lacy and barely spoke to them. Only Doris was on my mind, and I couldn't wait to be with her that night.

A little before seven, I walked across campus, bending my head into a bitter, north wind as I trudged up Maple Street to the Maples Apartments. I hurried up the steps, knocked on the door, and glanced through the window beside the door. In a few seconds, Doris walked into the front room, and, as she walked toward the door, I saw her zip down the front of her jumpsuit so that I could make out the rounded tops of her breasts. She'd shown cleavage before, but not like that.

"Sandy! Come in before you freeze to death."

Doris welcomed me with open arms, and, after a welcome hug and a kiss on the cheek, she led me over to the couch.

"Sandy, just lean back and relax while I mix up the margaritas. I won't be but a minute."

I can still remember the thoughts I had as I leaned back on the couch. I'm nineteen, and Doris is thirty-six and my teacher. Then I thought about my high school sexual fantasies with Miss Harris, my English teacher, and, for gosh sakes, that was sure just my imagination. Yeah, Doris just wants to talk about creative writing, and I'm just making something out of nothing.

"I'm almost finished, Sandy."

In a couple of minutes, she walked back into the living room, carrying two margaritas and a blanket tucked under her arm.

"Sandy, you look like an icicle. Here, take these margaritas while I spread out this blanket."

I guess there've been times in my life when I was more nervous, but I sure can't think of any. Doris was acting like anything but my teacher.

I took the margaritas with shaky hands, and Doris spread out the blanket, sitting down close by me, and pulled it up around us.

"There, is that better?" she said.

"Gosh yes, I thought I was going to freeze to death walking over here."

"Well, these margaritas will warm you up, even if they are cold."

"They sure are small."

Doris smiled and said, "You'll find out they're big enough. Cheers!"

We clicked our glasses and I took a big sip. The almost pure tequila with a dash of limejuice took me off guard, and I must have looked startled as it hit bottom.

"Wow, these are powerful," I said, taking another sip. Thank goodness for the tequila, because as the alcohol passed into my bloodstream I could finally start breathing normally again, and my hands quit shaking.

We sat under the blanket, cuddling together to keep warm as we drank the margaritas. Our talk drifted from creative writing to campus gossip about various professors and their sexual preferences. Doris ticked off the gay and lesbian professors as we talked. Some of them were obvious, but several others surprised me. Then she talked about Bull Jenkins. Doris had mentioned him before, but hadn't filled in the details.

"That sorry guy almost soured me on men, and some of the old gossips around campus have whispered that I'm a lesbian, since I'm thirty-six and not married. But let me assure you, I'm not a lesbian. After taking some time to get over Bull Jenkins, I've decided that I'm not ready to give up on all men. I just need to be a little more selective."

"Doris, if you're a lesbian, you're sure concealing it well."

She laughed and took my margarita glass into the kitchen for a refill. In a few minutes, we were back under the blanket, sipping our second drinks, laughing and touching.

That second margarita warmed us up—hell, more than that. Two margaritas had me loosened up and about half-drunk. We pulled the blanket back as Doris went over to her stereo and put on a record. There'd be no essay reading that night.

"Come on, Sandy, let's dance."

"Oh, Doris, I'm left-handed, and I guess left-footed; I'm a terrible dancer."

"Come on, Sandy, we'll slow dance. It's easy, I'll show you how."

I reluctantly got up and steadied myself, as the room seemed to be swaying. That second margarita had taken its toll, and I'd gone from nervous to almost silly as I kidded around with Doris. I don't know, maybe it was the margaritas, but it seemed I was just with an attractive, sexy woman, not my thirty-six-year-old Creative Writing teacher. Well, I couldn't dance, but I could care less. Doris took me in her arms, and in a few minutes, she was almost holding me up as we moved around the room, slow dancing and rubbing against each other. It only took a few seconds of slow dancing for me, even in my condition, to realize that Doris wasn't wearing anything under that black jumpsuit and that the full figure the guys in class admired was all real. I could feel Doris's soft breasts pressed against my chest, and I started to become aroused. Oh, my gosh, I thought, but that idea quickly left my mind.

The song ended with us in a tight embrace; she raised her head and kissed me, first softly, and then, as we kissed again, there was an intensity that I had never experienced before. My God, kissing a little junior in high school was about my only kissing experience, and Doris was on another level. After a few minutes of passionately kissing and rubbing, while we stood there in the middle of the room, we moved over to the couch, where we French-kissed for several minutes, as my hand slipped down inside her jumpsuit and the touching and feeling moved to a new level. There was nothing that she or I didn't rub or touch as we sat there. As I pulled away from an unusually passionate embrace, with her hand on my groin, she whispered in my ear, "Let's go to the bedroom. I don't think we'll be comfortable on this little couch."

I guess you could say I was in shock because things had gone so fast, and the margaritas had me dazed. She led me by the hand into her bedroom, where, in the dim light, I could see that her bed was already turned down and classical music was softly playing on the radio. It didn't occur to me then, but, looking back on it, there was no doubt that Doris had had the evening planned.

She quickly slipped off her warm-up and slid under the sheets.

"Come on, Sandy, get in bed and I'll keep you warm."

As I quickly undressed, thoughts about having sex with Doris swept over me, and it was almost enough to sober me up. This would be my first time, and it wasn't going to be with some young girl who was as inexperienced as I was. It would be with a mature, sexy woman who was very experienced. Naturally, I was concerned about my ability, but not concerned enough to hesitate for very long. I wasn't sure what to expect as I slid between the sheets and felt her move over to face me. Soon Doris was rubbing and cuddling me under the bedcovers, embracing, and becoming more intimate by the second. Hell, my thoughts of seducing Doris were just a fantasy, because I wasn't doing any of the seducing. She was in total control. She pulled me on top of her, and soon we were in the throes of lovemaking. Thank goodness the margaritas had me almost drunk, or I'd have finished in seconds. The first time it was passionate and quick, very quick, but the second and third times lasted longer.

I left Doris's apartment that night in a complete daze, thinking about the most wonderful woman I'd ever known. I'd just made love three times to a passionate, uninhibited woman who had literally taken my breath away. It took me hours to fall asleep that night as I relived each second with her, and the next morning I wrote in The Journal for over an hour, listing everything I could think of that made Doris so special.

Well, my interest in both Vi and Lacy almost disappeared, and all I could think about was the affair I was having with Doris. I couldn't get her off my mind. She was the most fascinating and desirable woman I'd ever known. At least, that's what I thought during that semester. My Coke dates with Vi were almost void of affection, and meeting Lacy on campus didn't consist of much more than a nod.

As the semester passed, the Friday night visits to Doris's apartment became the highlight of my week. I guess it was infatuation with such a sexy woman and the pleasure I had having sex with her that caused me to fall head-over-heels in love. When we were having sex, and then afterwards, I started whispering to her about my love, telling her that I wanted to be with her for the rest of my life. Maybe it wasn't love, but it sure was desire. I'd come back to my dorm, prop up on a pillow, and think about our relationship. Of course, I always dismissed our age difference, telling myself that it didn't make any difference if we loved each other, and I'd fantasize about how we could get married and maybe move to another town, where people didn't know us. However, there was one slight problem with our relationship. As much as Doris seemed to enjoy our affair, she had never said more than "Oh, you're so sweet, Sandy" when I professed my love. Naturally, I thought she felt just as I did, but I was wrong. Doris set me straight one Friday night when I was about to leave.

"Sandy, before you go, I want to talk to you about something."

"Sure, Doris, go ahead."

"Sandy, you're getting too emotionally involved in our relationship."

"What?"

"That's right. If we can't keep our sexual activities strictly casual, then I'm afraid I'll have to end it."

"Doris, I—" It was a blow I hadn't foreseen, and it almost devastated me.

"Sandy, don't apologize. The feelings you have for your sex partner are perfectly natural, but I'm your professor, thirty-six years old, and scheduled for tenure next year. If our relationship goes any further than it is right now, it would be a disaster for both of us. Do you understand?"

I nodded and left her house depressed—hell, I was more than depressed; I was broken-hearted.

It took a few days to understand that she was right, but it was the hardest thing I ever did to fall out of love with her. Of course, I took the second part of Doris's Creative Writing class the second semester just to be around her, but toward the end of that semester, my visits to her apartment grew shorter and shorter. She would be waiting for me, and, after a brief conversation, we'd head for the bedroom. I guess that, after a while, discussing creative writing with a nineteen-year-old could get pretty boring. We continued our relationship for the rest of the school year, always on Friday nights.

16.

Mr. Botner

I couldn't believe how quickly the time passed that second semester. It seemed we'd just finished a horrible winter when another beautiful Arkansas spring arrived, and Final Tests were upon us. That semester wasn't a panic situation like the first semester, and, as finals approached, I was almost certain that I had an easy two point five, or, maybe, if everything fell into place, a three point.

However, every time I walked by the Chemistry building, I felt my breath quicken and my hands get clammy, but I managed to resist another break-in. Of course, the stealing of the Chemistry final was something I wanted to put behind me, but it was hard to do. There was still the thrill and adrenalin rush that hit me as I walked down that hallway months later. I kept telling myself that I was a good person, and I had never stolen anything before. It wasn't going to happen again. But even though I kept telling myself that, the urge to experience the thrill of breaking in wouldn't leave me.

Well, that was my first year at the university, and, as I reflected back on it during the summer, I considered it a success. At least I was a survivor, and that was an accomplishment, considering that, out of 125 guys in the dorm, a third had flunked out. In the 1950s, small Arkansas high schools were more interested in their football teams than they were in getting students ready for college.

I spent the summer working for Mr. Pervis again, baling hay, and, by the time August ended, I was more than ready to go back to school. Throwing bales of hay on the flatbed trailer had beefed up my shoulders and added ten pounds of muscle to my thin frame. The only highlight of my summer was a Saturday trip over to Monticello to see Vi. I borrowed Mr. Purvis's truck and called her the day before, making up some excuse about how I'd be coming through town on my way to Pine Bluff to pick up something for Mr. Pervis, but of course that was an out and out lie. Actually, my trip was to see Vi and no one else. Vi met me downtown, and we went into a little café to have a Coke. She introduced me to a couple of her friends, who were sitting at various tables, and right before we left her dad walked in to get a cup of coffee.

Vi waved at him, and he walked over.

"Daddy, I want you to meet Sandy Carson. He's one of my best friends at the university."

"Hi, SANDY, nice to meet you. Fraternity man?"

"Uh, no, sir, I'm an independent."

"Humm. Where did you go to high school?"

"Mount Union High School, sir. It's over in Pine Valley, near Magnolia."

"Uh, huh, I know the town. Is your father in the oil business?"

"No, sir, my father was killed in a car wreck when I was fifteen. I live on a little farm with my mother, who works for a dry cleaner in Magnolia."

Damn. Question after question, grilling me like some criminal.

Vi was looking a little uncomfortable, and I was beginning to get nervous, since I knew that every answer I'd given him had deepened his frown. Not good enough for Vi, huh? Yeah, you're making that very clear! crossed my mind.

There wasn't a doubt in my mind that Mr. Botner didn't approve of my visit to see Vi. It was obvious that I didn't measure up, and neither did my family. He was frowning, but suddenly he smiled and made small talk about the Razorbacks.

"Think Bill Tucker will make All-American, Sandy?"

"I don't have a clue, sir. I don't pay much attention to football." Well, that stupid comment was no more than out of my mouth before I regretted it. Wow, he looked as if I'd slapped him across the face. God, the way he reacted was bizarre.

"You don't support the Razorbacks?"

Mr. Botner was ticked off, and Vi was shaking her head and making a cutting motion across her throat. I started backpedaling, trying to think of some way out of the hole I'd dug for myself—and I did. I smiled, and my ornery self began to emerge.

"Well, sure I support 'em. I'm just a bigger basketball fan—never miss a game. I was All-State back in high school."

Vi's eyes widened, and she covered her mouth with her hand to keep from laughing.

I was just getting started.

"Huh? All-State? Is that right? Why didn't you play college ball?"

I didn't anticipate that question, but I was into the joke, and I thought, What would keep a six-foot-two-inch All-State basketball player from playing college ball? Then it hit me. Yeah, I got it. I started rubbing my knee and made a little frown, as if I was hurting.

"See this knee, Mr. Botner?" He nodded. I moved my leg from under the table and pulled up my pants. My knee had a scar across one side, which I pointed to.

"Tore it up playing in the All-Star game; it'll never be the same. Three operations and I still can't put any weight on it." The scar was from a bicycle wreck back in the tenth grade, but Mr. Botner nodded seriously. It had been just a cut, and, of course, I hadn't had three knee operations—not even one. Heck, I was beginning to enjoy this little joke. You know, when I got the idea I was pulling a crazy guy's leg, I started getting carried away. I liked jerking that off-the-wall football fan around.

Vi looked at me and shook her head as if I'd just told her dad that I was from Mars.

"Well, that's too bad, Sandy. With your height, you might have been a good player."

"Yes, sir, in the All-Star game I'd already made forty-four points when I hurt my knee. Heck, I'd have hit fifty if that kid from Pea Ridge hadn't tripped me. That's when I got hurt."

I looked across the table at Vi, who I swear wasn't breathing, and tilted my head, rubbing my knee as I tried to keep a straight face.

"You don't say. Damn, that's really bad luck."

Mr. Botner was back in a fair mood now, and he nodded, smiled, and walked over to pick up his coffee.

"Sandy," Vi whispered. "Daddy's the head of the local Razorback club. I thought he was going to have a heart attack when you said that you didn't care about football. Thank goodness you covered yourself with that lie about basketball but you almost carried it too far with that wild story about the All-Star game and tearing up your knee. I thought I was going to either faint or burst out laughing, listening to you go on."

I laughed and squeezed her hand.

Mr. Botner walked back up and I smiled. Shoot, I was just getting started.

"Mr. Botner, what just tears me up is missing out on playing for the Razorbacks. Coach Rose had already offered me a scholarship, and I could have really helped the team. He'd already told me I'd start my freshman year."

Vi made a little gasp and kicked me under the table. She could tell I was getting carried away pulling crazy Mr. Botner's leg, and, sure enough, I'd almost stretched my lie a little too far.

"Sandy, I'm on the scholarship committee, and I don't remember seeing your name."

Whoa, I didn't expect that, but I just took a deep breath and kept lying, "No sir, as soon as I hurt my knee, I asked Coach to pull my name and give my scholarship to someone else." Well, that was a little lame, and I was beginning to panic because Mr. Botner was starting to shake his head as if he didn't believe me. It was time to leave Monticello.

"I've got to head on over to Pine Bluff, Vi. I'd better get going."

I said goodbye to a puzzled Mr. Botner, who was muttering to himself, and Vi and I walked out and down the street to Mr. Purvis's truck. Before I turned to open the door I leaned back toward Vi, and I'm sure she thought I was going to give her a peck on the cheek, but instead I put my hand behind her head, turned her to me, and kissed her right on the lips. She hesitated for a few seconds before pulling back.

"Sandy!"

"I couldn't resist, again."

Vi smiled and shook her head.

"Sandy, you're going to get us both in trouble one day."

"I hope so—see you in Fayetteville in a few weeks." I got in the truck, looked out the window, and there was Mr. Botner, standing in the doorway of the café and holding his cup of coffee, his mouth wide open. I gave him a big wave, put the truck in low, and spun out as Vi walked back toward her father. Oh, look out, Vi. You're going to have a tough time explaining to your father that we're just friends. I drove back to Pine Valley thinking about the startled look on Vi's face when I kissed her, but, more importantly, about how she had kissed back for a few seconds and pressed against me. Maybe there's hope. I was glad her phony, big shot daddy saw us.

17.

Guys and Dolls

For the rest of the summer our hay-baling crew worked all across south Arkansas, and I picked up more poker-playing tips when we played during our lunch hour. Except for that brief visit to see Vi, my mind was on Doris and the torrid affair we'd had last year. After the little talk about tenure and keeping our emotions under control, my love for Doris had cooled off somewhat, but I still fantasized about her all summer. When I finally got ready to return to Fayetteville, I was anxious to see her.

I called the University Bookstore and Mr. Conroe, the manager, offered to let me work before classes started, stocking the new textbooks for the fall semester. Thank God. I'd have done anything to get off that hay-baling crew. I rode back to school with Bobby Thompson, a friend from Magnolia. Bobby sat beside me in Chemistry, and he'd let me copy his notes, which probably saved my ass by letting me catch up. As he drove along on those Arkansas back roads through the Ouachita Mountains, I thought about school. The one thought that kept worrying me was breaking into the Chemistry building and stealing the final. Hell, to be honest, I wasn't as worried about actually stealing the test as I was about feeling the adrenalin rush as I broke into the building.

Some of Uncle Hosie's genes were certainly at work in me, and he was in Tucker Prison because he couldn't control his desire to break in. Was that going to happen to me? I kept telling myself that I was a good person, and I would never do that again, but I wasn't convinced.

When I arrived back on campus it was Rush Week, and all the Greeks were already back in town to help with Rush. I'd checked into Williams House, an upper-class-man's dorm, and I was crossing the campus on the first day after I had gotten back, heading for the bookstore, when I saw Vi ahead of me.

"Vi, wait up," I called out.

Vi stopped and turned around.

"Hi, Sandy. Why are you back on campus early? Are you going through Rush?"

"No, just working at the bookstore, stocking books for this semester. How was the rest of your summer?"

"It was absolutely wonderful. Bill came to visit me a few times, and Daddy took him downtown and went in every store on Main Street to introduce him. He was so proud. Daddy has been going on and on about Bill ever since. And guess what?"

"Uh, I don't know."

"Bill's been hinting about giving me a ring."

"Really?"

"Yes, and I think Daddy would absolutely faint if he did."

My God, her crazy daddy again. "Vi, your damn daddy wouldn't be the one to marry Mr. Football. Are you sure you want to marry that guy?"

Vi frowned when I called Bill "Mr. Football."

There was a moment of hesitation, and that moment told me more than anything she was willing to say. She really didn't like him.

"Uh, well, yes, I think Bill is a...well...uh...a neat guy, and he sure is a great football player."

I nodded, frowning slightly. "You don't seem all that sure about him."

"Well, I am, and every girl in the house would jump at the chance to date Bill Tucker. Say, I've got to go, Sandy. I'll stop by the bookstore later, and we can catch up on what you did this summer."

"Okay, see you."

"Oh, Sandy, just a minute. Could you possible help me clean the dog pens this Saturday?'

Hell, cleaning out dog pens was about the last thing on earth I wanted to do on Saturday, but since Vi asked, I nodded, "Sure, Vi. What time?"

"I'll be there at seven, but you don't have to come that early."

Damn, seven—on a Saturday morning! "Oh, that's not too early; see you there."

"Sandy, I know caring for those poor dogs isn't something you really like to do, but thanks for helping me."

Well, when Vi said that and looked at me, I would have cleaned dog pens for a week. That woman has a heart of gold. Vi walked on toward Old Main and I headed for the bookstore, still thinking about Mr. Football.

Ahaaa, that sorry worthless jock, was all I could think about as I walked on to the bookstore. My desire for Vi looked like a hopeless cause. Maybe I should have started dating one of the girls I met while working at the bookstore. Several had made a point to come in almost daily to flirt with me, but every time I decided to ask one of those girls out, Vi would happen to come by and lean over the counter, kidding and flirting with me. When she left, I'd forget all about anyone but Vi.

***

The first poker game of the fall semester kicked off the next Saturday night, and almost the same bunch of players showed up. Dickie bragged all night about spending the summer in Europe, making out with Italian girls. I had thought he was obnoxious the year before, but that first night, he reached a new high. The game turned out about like all our other games, and I walked away with $18.00 in quarters. The poker-playing season was off to a good start.

I'd been back on campus for only a few days when Lacy walked into the bookstore. My God, she looked gorgeous. Of course, I made a beeline to wait on her, figuring I'd have a chance to introduce myself, but Bob, the assistant manager, grabbed my arm.

"Uh, Sandy, take those used books back to the stocking area. I'll wait on this customer." Bob pointed to a two foot stack of used books on the counter.

I could have choked Bob, but he was the boss, so I grabbed all the books and sprinted for the back. It didn't take long for me to toss the used books back on the table and rush to the front of the store. Lacy had the textbook she had come in for and was paying at the cash register when I walked back in.

I walked over, smiling, and asked if she needed anything else.

"Oh, no, I don't believe I do, but you're so nice to offer."

Then those lips puckered, and she tossed her blonde hair back over her shoulder and gave me the most wonderful smile.

"Bye," she whispered as I stood there, gawking.

"Uh, oh, yeah, bye," I managed to mumble. Why I didn't introduce myself I'll never know, but all I did was act like a mute again. I'd spent an entire year trying to get up the courage to meet Lacy, but every time I had the opportunity, I choked.

I did have one other girl, or I might say woman, on my mind: Doris. After a summer without sex, I couldn't wait for us to get together again. However, my phone calls to her were a puzzle. At first, she seemed glad that I had called, but when I suggested that we get together, she put me off. After a couple more calls the following week, I realized that our affair was over. I didn't understand it then, and even after I stopped her on campus one day to talk, I still didn't have a clue.

Twenty years later, I finally found out why Doris dropped me. It was some time during the spring of 1979. I'd been in Houston all day, presenting an oil prospect to various companies, and late that afternoon I met a business acquaintance for a drink in the Houston Petroleum Club. He had a friend with him and, after introductions; we discovered we were both graduates of the university. I'd graduated a couple of years ahead of him, but we overlapped and knew several of the same teachers and students. Our conversation flowed back and forth as we reminisced about various things, and then, for some reason, I asked, "Did you ever have a class under Doris Colton, the Creative Writing instructor?"

"No, but I wish I had. My roommate in Razorback Hall was her special student his freshman year."

"What?"

"You know, she'd pick out a freshman from one of her classes each year and have sex with him, then drop him and take another one the next year."

I sat there stunned, as I thought back on my time with Doris. I had just been another freshman she used for her sexual gratification. She picked a new partner each year so that she could stay emotionally unattached.

"Well, I'll be damned," I muttered.

"What?"

"Oh, nothing, I was just thinking back."

18.

Lacy!

That fall semester I took an American History course as an elective and enjoyed it so much that I considered changing my major. However, it wasn't only my love for American History that made that class exciting. It was the girl sitting right beside me: Lacy Darnell.

I'd been trying to meet Lacy for a year, and when she walked into class that first day I almost dropped dead. To say she was well known on campus, especially among the guys, was a gross understatement: Man, what a reputation! Lacy was just plain sexy, and she knew it. Her clothes always seemed a size small and cut deep in the front, and her light-blue eyes glistened when she talked, perfectly matching her soft peaches and cream complexion and long, blonde hair. But the real attraction, as far as I was concerned, were her fabulous lips. Lacy had big, full lips, and a habit of puckering, almost pouting as she talked. When I saw Lacy, I couldn't keep from staring at those wonderful lips.

Lacy and Vi were both pretty girls, but Vi was pretty in a different way. Vi always dressed exactly as the average girl on campus, looking as if she had been stamped out of a cookie cutter, but Lacy didn't conform. She was just a sophomore, but she had already been a maid on the homecoming court and a yearbook beauty. Of course, I always felt a little guilty pursuing Vi one minute and then lusting after Lacy the next. My desire for those two girls was completely different. From the first moment I'd met Vi, I was sure that she was the woman I was supposed to be with for the rest of my life. Lacy? Well, I guess it was her sexual magnetism that drew me to her. But it was more than that. I couldn't put my finger on it, but my desire to be with her was overwhelming. When she walked into American History class that day, I couldn't take my eyes off her.

I said a little prayer, hoping that she'd take the empty seat beside me. She stood in the doorway a moment, checked out the room, and then walked across the front of the class with every guy's eyes following her every move. She walked right by me, and I smiled at her as she passed. Oh well, another prayer that's not going to be answered. Then she stopped, turned around, walked back, and sat in the empty seat beside me. Wow, I know my mouth was still open when she slowly turned her head, looked at me, puckered her lips, and smiled a melting smile.

"Hi, I'm Lacy," she purred. "I guess we're finally going to meet."

There was a coy turn of her head, and she looked deep into my eyes. Of course, I tried to act as if it was just anyone who had sat down, but for a few seconds it was hard to say anything.

"Uh," I finally stammered, unable to keep my eyes off her lips and bosom. "I'm Sandy." Gosh, her face lit up as if I'd said I was Prince Charles, and then she gushed, "Oh, what an absolutely beautiful name. And you look like a Sandy!"

"Well, actually my name is Stuart, but I've been called Sandy ever since grade school." I was beginning to breathe again, and I tried to relax and carry on a decent conversation.

"It's absolutely a perfect name for you, Sandy. Sandy, Sandy. I just love the way it rolls off my tongue."

"Uh, well, uh, thanks, Lacy."

"Sandy, are you any good at American History?"

"Well, I think so. The textbook is pretty interesting. I read it this past weekend."

"You've already read the entire textbook?"

"Yeah, I didn't have anything else to do."

"Well, I'm sure glad I'm sitting by you, 'cause I just can't abide history. Who wants to know 'bout those old dead people anyway? Would you help me get through this class?"

"Sure, Lacy, but I don't think this is a tough course."

"Oh, it will be for me."

She was sure right about that.

I got to know Lacy a lot better over the next few weeks, and, even though I still considered her the sexiest woman alive, I found out that there was more to her than just being sexy. She had an ornery streak, much like I did, and liked to kid around and play jokes. Talking with her was so much fun that we started to arrive in class early just to spend time together. She hated history, but she wasn't dumb. It was just a subject she cared nothing about. Every day before class, we talked non-stop about everything from campus gossip to our hometowns and our folks.

Lacy and I had a lot in common in our backgrounds. She was from Tulsa, a much larger town than Pine Valley, and she'd grown up helping her single mother by working during the summers to help her make ends meet. Her mother had divorced her father when she was ten and then remarried. Her stepfather had lived with them until she was in high school. She only mentioned her stepfather once, and, from her expression, I could tell that she detested him. Evidently, he'd walked out on her and her mother when Lacy was still in high school. She was still close to her natural father, and he was paying for college.

Lacy was right about one thing: she sure hated history. Her test scores on the pop quizzes were the pits. I tried to help her, but the little things I recommended—like actually reading the coursework—were ignored. When Four Weeks Tests approached, I gave her a list of things that I knew would be on the test. I handed her the list the Friday before the test.

"Lacy, just memorize these dates, names, and places. You're going to get nailed on Four Weeks Tests if you don't."

"Sandy, I'm so busy this weekend, I don't think I'll have time to study."

"Huh? Doing what?" I said.

Lacy gave me that little turn of the head smile and lowered her voice. "Dating. I'm busy every night, if you know what I mean."

Yeah, I knew exactly what she meant.

"For God's sake, Lacy, if you'll just spend an hour memorizing this list you might not flunk the test. You don't need an F on your transcript."

"You're right. I'll do it."

Well, she did work in an hour or so of studying between hot dates and surprised herself with a C.

***

That was a good semester for me. I only had one Saturday class, which let out at nine-thirty, and, since I loved being in the woods, especially during the fall, I joined a club called the Ozark Hikers; a group of students who went out exploring the Ozarks every Saturday. We didn't do a lot of hiking; it was mostly going into the many caves that dotted the limestone hills around Fayetteville. You wouldn't believe some of the holes we crawled into.

It was the second Saturday in October, and the Ozark Hikers went to explore a big cave a few miles from the Buffalo River, near the small town of Boxley. It was a great outing, and we walked for miles deep inside a huge cave, where an underground river had created waterfalls and massive stalagmites. I got back to my dorm at about six o'clock and headed to George's for a beer. When I got there it was packed, and people had spilled out into the street. I saw my freshman roommate, Benny, standing with some guys near the door. Benny saw me and yelled, "Hey, Sandy, how 'bout them Hogs? We kicked some horns' ass today, didn't we? Yeah! Go Hogs!"

Then it hit me. The big game of the year, the Texas game, was over, and Arkansas had won. Well, I hung around and helped celebrate the big Arkansas victory. The celebration continued until the wee hours of the night, and I never did get a beer. Finally, I gave up and went back to my room.

The next Monday I was leaning over the counter at the bookstore when Vi walked up. I could tell she was excited before she even got to the counter.

"Sandy, wasn't that the most exciting game you've ever heard? Can you believe it? We beat Texas! That's two years in a row!"

Vi was almost shouting, she was so worked up. I smiled and tried to act interested. Hell, I knew Mr. Football was about to come on the scene, and I was right.

"Could you believe Bill caught that pass and scored when we were tied, and with only a minute to go? Oh, I almost had a heart attack."

"Well, I was busy, and I didn't listen to the game."

"What? What on God's earth was more important than listening to the Texas-Arkansas game?"

Vi acted as if I'd slapped her in the face.

"Vi, about fifteen of us...you know, the Ozark Hikers I told you about? Well, we spent the day in one of the biggest caves in the Ozarks. You wouldn't believe some of the things we saw." I was trying to tell her about how big the cave was and how hard it was to get down the fifty foot drop to the river, but Vi broke in: "Oh, my God, Sandy, surely you're kidding. You spent the day in a cave when the Razorbacks were playing?"

Well, three or four customers looked around to see who was yelling, and I whispered, "There's more to life than football, Vi."

"Oh, I'll never understand you, Sandy! The big game of the year—and we won!—and you're acting like it's nothing!"

"For gosh sakes, Vi, it was just a football game!" I was getting a little loud and upset, and when I said that she shook her head and almost screamed, "But it was the Texas game!"

Well, I knew that conversation wasn't going anywhere, so I finally changed the subject. We talked for another few minutes about our classes, and Vi finally cooled down before she had to leave. Actually, I'd been a Razorback fan since I was old enough to listen to them on the radio, and I did feel a little funny with everybody so worked up about beating Texas, but I guess that sorry Mr. Football had soured Arkansas football for me. It's funny how love and jealousy can overcome almost every other desire.

As I stood there fuming about Mr. Football, I tried to come up with anything I could do to win Vi away from that louse, but I'll admit that it looked like a hopeless cause. However, over the years it seems that I've tackled a lot of hopeless causes, and, as I look back over my career, I can truthfully say one of my strongest qualities is hanging in there and never giving up. When I was a starving, independent geologist, I put up $5000 to buy some oil and gas leases that almost everyone else had given up on. Dry holes were everywhere, but I felt that oil was there, and I persisted and bought the leases with nearly the last dollars I had in the bank. They turned out to be extremely valuable and gave my career a substantial boost. I guess that, at age nineteen, I was pursuing Vi like I did those oil and gas leases. I wasn't going to quit. One day, Vi and I would be together. I wasn't going to give up.

19.

A Date

As soon as Vi left the bookstore, I clocked out early and headed for American History class, where I could have a few extra minutes to talk with Lacy. We'd been coming to class early for the past couple of weeks, and I'd been trying to get up enough nerve to ask her out. We laughed and talked for about fifteen minutes before class, and after class ended that Monday, I motioned to her.

"Lacy, sit back down, I need to ask you something."

"Sure, Sandy. What?"

"How about taking in a movie with me tomorrow night?"

"Oh, Sandy, you're such a good friend, and it's so sweet of you to ask me out, but I'm busy." She reached and squeezed my hand, while with the other hand she rubbed my arm.

I tried not to look too disappointed as I said, "Okay, maybe some other time."

"I don't know, Sandy. I'm really busy. Listen, can you keep a secret?"

"Well, sure. What?"

"I'm going steady—with two guys."

"Two guys?" Oh, for God's sake!

"Yes, you know, they're both so sweet, I just couldn't say no, and two guys are all I can handle right now, if you know what I mean—you know, I'm just so busy." Lacy winked, and I blushed.

My God, just thinking about Lacy going steady with two guys, who probably didn't really care if she was dating around, had my head spinning. Yeah, I was disappointed because I thought she'd surely go out with me. I didn't know what to say, but I acted as if I didn't care that much. It was hard to sit there with a straight face. I finally mumbled, "Uh, okay, but I've sure enjoyed sitting and talking with you for the last few weeks."

"I have too, Sandy. Let's stay friends, okay, and I still want us to have our little talks before class. You're really my best friend."

Best friend! Well, being Lacy's best friend wasn't exactly what I had in mind. "Yeah, we'll just be friends," I said half-heartedly. It had taken me a year to meet Lacy, and now, after all the waiting, I was regulated to being just a friend. Boy, was I disappointed.

"See you Wednesday," she said. Lacy walked out of the class with me sitting there, watching her hips sway. I finally got up and headed down to the bookstore, in a crump over being turned down by Lacy.

Vi came by the bookstore later in the day to buy some supplies, and we talked for almost half an hour. She kidded and flirted with me, and, when she left, I felt guilty about asking Lacy out. Of course, it was hard to justify pursuing Lacy when I was in love with Vi, but, as hard as I might try, I couldn't resist Lacy. Her sexual magnetism was intoxicating to me. I've never been around any woman who could stir me up like Lacy Darnell.

***

The semester flew by, and Ten Weeks Tests were there before I knew it. Lacy and I had developed a close friendship, and, although she eventually told me that she'd like to go out with me sometime, I knew I was way down on her list of possible dates. Actually, I'd almost given up the idea of dating Lacy and had started to just enjoy our talks and friendship.

It was the week before Ten Weeks Tests, and I was breezing through American History. It looked as if I'd have an easy A if I didn't blow a big test. Lacy, on the other hand, was faced with a D, or maybe even an F, if she didn't pull up her grade. Lacy was a smart girl, but she absolutely detested History.

The Friday before the Ten Weeks Tests on Monday, Lacy and I got to class a few minutes early, as usual, and we talked about Monday's test. I can still remember that pink sweater she was wearing. Wow, did she fill it out! We had started going on about the upcoming Ten Weeks Tests when Lacy blurted out, "Sandy, I'd give anything to get that test. I need a B in the worst way."

Well, I was just kidding when I winked and said, "Anything?" And then I mouthed off, "Shoot, I could get that test if I really wanted it."

I saw Lacy's eyes light up, and she moved a little closer to me. I felt her hand squeeze my leg as she emphatically said, "Anything, Sandy, anything."

For God's sake! I'd just been kidding about being able to get that test. Her response caught me off-guard, and I was so flustered and surprised that I could barely mumble, but I did manage to say, "Uh, well, yeah, we'll see. Let me think about that."

Dr. Pearson walked in and Lacy moved her hand, winked at me, and leaned back in her chair.

The class got under way, and, boy, talk about having your mind on something else. Occasionally, she'd pucker those sensual lips and look at me. I sat there, wondering if she really thought I could get her the American History test. Maybe I'd bragged that if I really wanted a test I could get it, but heck, I was just kidding. Was she kidding about doing anything for the test, or did she really mean anything? I'll tell you one thing: She sure didn't seem to be kidding. When class finally ended, I motioned for Lacy to stay seated.

It had taken me almost a year to put the break-in of the Chemistry building and stealing the Chemistry test behind me, and it hadn't been easy. Now, as I sat there and thought about breaking into another building and stealing a test, my feelings surged first one way and then the other. Finally, as the period ended and I looked over at Lacy, I knew I wouldn't be able to resist. Lacy's sex appeal and Uncle Hosie's genes were about to do me in.

"Lacy, I might be able to get the Ten Weeks Test."

She reached over, put her hand on my arm, and softly murmured, "Oh, Sandy, I'd be so, so grateful."

Damn, I didn't know what to say then. Grateful was one thing, but not what I was thinking of, and maybe she really did mean that she would just appreciate having the test. I think I was looking for a way out when I said, "Uh, well, I don't know for sure if I can get it." There was a moment of silence as Lacy slowly raised her head and smiled.

"Sandy," she giggled, "are you wondering how grateful I'll be?"

I could feel the blood rushing to my face. She had me hooked now, and all she had to do was reel me in. Hell, there have been few times in my life when I have felt more helpless.

"Uh, uh," was all I could say until Lacy squeezed my arm again and said, "Didn't I say, 'Anything?'"

"Uh, well, yeah, but..." My mind was flashing through all of the possibilities as Lacy zeroed in on me. At first, I tried to back away from getting the test, but then I thought of a hot date with her, and she puckered those lips, and I melted. She had me, and she knew it.

"I meant anything." She was as serious as a person could be, and we both knew what "anything" meant.

I sat straight up as Lacy released my arm; she smiled and whispered as she said, "Am I going to have the Ten Weeks American History Test tomorrow?"

Well, hell, I'd have said yes to anything Lacy had asked me right then. I took a deep breath, regained my composure somewhat, and said, "Yes, you are," and after a pause, "and do we have a date tomorrow night?"

"We sure do, Sandy," she purred.

I left the classroom, breathing heavily as Lacy waved and walked away. Her hips swayed as she walked down the sidewalk, heading for Old Main, and I stood there and watched until she was out of sight. All the guilt that had built up as a result of stealing the Chemistry test and all the promises I had made that I would never steal another test disappeared in an instant. They were replaced by the strongest of human emotions; sexual desire. However, I had a nagging feeling that I was betraying Vi. What if she found out that I had a date with Lacy? She sure knew Lacy's reputation, and, even though Vi might be fooling around with Mr. Football, Lacy, the college tramp, was different. She was not only dating the two guys she was supposed to be going steady with, but several others.

Even thought Vi claimed we were just friends I knew it was more than that. Was I willing to give up ever having Vi? She would never speak to me again if she found out. But, by the end of the day, all I could think about was the date with Lacy, and any feelings of guilt were pushed to the back recesses of my mind.

I could hardly wait, and, that night at one o'clock, I changed clothes behind the Greek Theatre and headed for Dr. Pearson's office. There was something about changing into those black clothes that gave me a tinge of guilt, but I was committed. The overwhelming desire to have the date with Lacy overshadowed everything. I was risking being caught, expelled from school, and losing the woman I dearly loved just to be with Lacy. It was irrational, and I knew it, but I couldn't stop myself.

The walk from the Greek Theatre took only a few minutes, and soon I was sitting on a concrete bench across from the Business Administration Building's front door, checking to make sure that no one was around. After a few minutes of watching, I eased to my feet and started walking toward the building as if I were going to go right by it on my way back to one of the dorms. Then, as I got to the steps leading up to the entrance, I turned off and briskly walked up to the locked door. My lock jammer was already out as I approached the door, and I slipped it into the keyhole and gave it a quarter turn, holding the pressure on it as I started flipping the pins with my lock pick. It opened easily, and I jumped inside, closing the door behind me. I stood there motionless for a couple of minutes, holding my breath. No alarm. I eased down the hall as my adrenalin soared and my palms sweated. My breathing was coming in little short breaths, and I could feel my knees trembling. Oh my God, it was that old Uncle Hosie feeling, just like I'd felt when I had broken into my first building back at Mount Union High School.

Suddenly a beam of light flashed down the hall, and I dropped to the floor, lying face down while the campus cop shined his flashlight around the side of the building. I heard a rattle as he shook the door, and then a beam of light moved down the hall, heading straight for me as I hugged the wall. Damn, he's going to see me. Just before the light hit me I rolled across the hall to the other wall, and the beam of light missed me by less than a foot. I scampered down the hall and around the corner before he got to the side door, and stood there shaking as I watched the light shine down the hall that I had just vacated.

It seemed like hours before he left the area, but it was only a few minutes. I took a minute to regain my composure, and then I crawled down the hall to Dr. Pearson's office and pulled out my lock jammer and lock pick. After a couple of rakes, the pins rattled and the office door opened.

I slumped down in Dr. Pearson's desk chair, breathing as if I had just run a marathon as my heart raced. Is Lacy worth it? Well, the fear of being caught and kicked out of school was quickly replaced with desire, and I thought, Yeah, she sure is. I looked the desk over and started checking the drawers. There was nothing in the center drawer, but when I opened the right-hand drawer, I found what I was looking for. There were the 25 tests neatly stacked, ready to be handed out next Monday. After spending fifteen minutes on the floor, copying the test by the light of a small flashlight, I closed the drawer, slipped out of the building, and headed back to the Greek Theatre to change clothes. Then when I got back to my dorm room, I typed the test that I'd copied and managed to sleep a couple of hours before my Saturday morning Mineralogy class. When I got out of class, I called Lacy and told her that the date was on and that I had what she wanted. She laughed and said, "Good, I've got what you want." For the rest of the day I could only think of Lacy and our date, but I still had one more hurdle to jump before we could go out—I had to borrow or rent a car.

Earlier that semester one of the guys living in Williams House, Billy Roy Sorenson, had passed the word around that, for ten dollars, he'd let any of us use his old 1950 Ford. I was standing in front of his door on Saturday morning when he got back from class.

"Billy Roy, I need to rent your car in the worst way. Is it available tonight?"

"Naw, I'm thinking about going to the drive-in."

"Damn. Say, do you think you'd change your mind for fifteen?"

"Humm, I might for a twenty."

"Oh for crying out loud, that'll break me."

"Well, you don't have to rent the car, you know."

"Okay," I said, pulling out my billfold. "Here's twenty bucks. Let me have the keys."

"Hey, I haven't been charging enough," he laughed as he dug the keys out. Hell, he was right. I'd have given him every nickel I had to get that car.

"Remember, any damage, you pay, and you'd better not park it in a no-parking zone when you return it."

"Yeah, I know. Don't worry, I'm not going far."

"Must be a hot date for tight-ass Sandy Carson to cough up twenty bucks."

"Lacy Darnell." Hey, why not brag a little? A date with Lacy was worth a lot of bragging rights.

"Are you kidding?"

"That's right."

"You lucky son-of-a-gun."

I pocketed the keys and walked into my room to get ready. Questions were already swirling around in my head. Would we really make out? Well, I didn't have much doubt about that. And the biggest question of all: would I be any good? Would she laugh? Finally, I got my confidence up by thinking about my experience with Doris. After Doris and I had had sex a couple of times, I'd found an article in Playboy magazine about how to please a woman. I put the highlights on a five-by-seven note card and memorized them, and, as the semester passed, my lovemaking with Doris got a whole lot better. Tonight, I decided, I'd use the same methods on Lacy.

At seven o'clock exactly, I walked into Lacy's sorority house and asked the housemother to tell Lacy that I was downstairs. At 7:15 Lacy came down the stairwell. It had been unseasonably cool all week, and Lacy was wearing a tight-fitting red sweater and a full skirt. Her blonde hair was combed out over her shoulders, and her wonderful lips were a bright red. She looked breathtaking.

"Hi, Sandy, sorry to keep you waiting," she said, smiling as she started for the door.

We pulled away from the sorority house and started talking about where to go. I had only one place in mind, the drive-in theater, but I didn't want to sound anxious. Finally, I said, rather offhandedly, "We could go to the drive-in. There's a William Holden movie playing. I hear it's great."

"Oh, Sandy, that sounds super, and we can discuss the History test during the previews."

Ha, discuss the History test! After chasing Lacy for over a year, I only had one thing on my mind, and it wasn't a History test.

I took a deep breath and smiled.

"Okay, let's go." I pulled out on Highway 71 and drove north of town to the drive-in theater.

I pulled into a parking place toward the back of the lot, reached in the back seat were I'd laid the History test, and handed it to her.

"Here you go, Dr. Pearson's Ten Weeks History Test."

"Oh, Sandy, I can't believe it. You actually got the test!" squealed Lacy.

"Yep, I'll guarantee it."

Lacy thumbed through the test and then laid it on the floor-board.

"I guess I owe you a little something," she grinned, sliding over next to me.

She turned toward me, and I kissed her softly, and then again and again as I rubbed her breasts and legs. She leaned back in the seat, and soon we were prone in the seat of the car. I touched her thighs, and then, as I moved up her leg, I looked at her in surprise. She laughed, "No panties, they just get in the way." I rubbed and touched until we were both steaming with desire.

Then Lacy pulled her legs up, put one on the dashboard and the other on top of the seat. I was fumbling, trying to unbutton my pants and pull them down at the same time, when Lacy reached up and pulled me to her. With more than a little help from her, we began to make love. So much for the Playboy method.

"Don't worry about getting me pregnant. I've taken care of that," she whispered in my ear.

We'd barely gotten started when I finished.

I sat up in the seat, a little chagrined, and Lacy whispered in my ear, "Don't worry, you were just excited. You'll do better next time." Then she turned and French-kissed me. "Anyway, it was probably my fault. I hope I was good," she said after the kiss.

"Oh, Lacy, you were wonderful. It wasn't you, it was me."

"Are you sure? You really thought I was good?"

"Yes, Lacy, of course I did." Well, Lacy kept on asking me if she was any good, and if I'd enjoyed it, and on and on. I was a little puzzled by her attitude.

We started watching the movie, but after a few minutes, we were courting again. I started using techniques from Playboy on Lacy, and we slipped down in the seat again. This time things went a whole lot better. We finished, and Lacy sat up in the seat with a big smile on her face.

"Sandy, that was absolutely out of this world. You were really good!"

"Lacy, I couldn't believe how you made love."

"Oh, Sandy, do you really think I was any good? Are you sure? I hope you enjoyed it."

"Lacy, I couldn't have enjoyed it more. You're a great lover."

"Well, I guess practice makes perfect," she giggled.

After I dropped Lacy off, I thought about making love to her. It had been everything I'd ever imagined and more. Lacy was totally uninhibited, and she made love in a physical way that was so spontaneous, I could hardly hold on. However, there was one puzzle to Lacy's lovemaking. After we finished she seemed worried, and asked over and over if she had pleased me. It was totally out of character for Lacy. I couldn't figure out that part.

I was on cloud nine when I got back to the dorm. Of course, I envisioned a torrid continuing relationship with the girl whom most guys considered the sexiest woman on campus. As far as I was concerned, she definitely was.

The following Wednesday, after the Ten Weeks Tests on Monday, Lacy walked into class, gave me a big smile as usual, and sat down. I couldn't wait to talk with her after Saturday night.

"Hi, Lacy. You look stunning this morning."

"Oh, thanks, Sandy, and thanks again for the help."

"It was my pleasure," I said and winked. "Can we get together sometime this week?"

Lacy puckered her gorgeous lips and gave me a smile, but her head was shaking no.

"Sandy, I'm so busy, and you know I'm already going steady with two guys. I just can't work you in. I'd like to, but...oh, well, let's just stay friends."

I was stunned. Saturday night had meant nothing. I was speechless.

Lacy saw that I was in shock and squeezed my arm as she whispered in my ear, "I don't mean forever. Maybe we'll get together again."

So Saturday night was nothing more than returning a favor. It was such a letdown. I nodded my understanding, and Lacy whispered again.

"Sandy, you were wonderful, especially that second time, but we're just friends, good friends. Can we still be friends, even if I don't go out with you for a while?"

"Uh, well, sure, it's just that...uh."

"I know," she whispered again, "I've felt that way when it was so good. You'll get over it. Oh, by the way, a couple of my sorority sisters were really envious when they found out that I got the Ten Weeks History Test early. They may give you a call when finals roll around."

"What? Call me for what?"

"A test, stupid," she whispered.

"Uh, you don't care?"

"No. Why should I?"

Well, of course, I couldn't answer that question, but I was saved an embarrassing stutter when Dr. Pearson walked into the class carrying the Ten Weeks Tests. He walked around, passing out the graded papers, and, when he came to me, he said, "Sandy, stop by my desk after class."

"Oh, my God!" I whispered to Lacy.

20.

Vi and Lacy

Oh, my God, he knows, flashed through my mind. Is that crazy desire to have sex with Lacy going to get me an F in history?

Lacy gave me a worried look, and I felt my palms begin to sweat. The next forty-five minutes were the longest of my life. Damn, I thought, I was an idiot to steal that test for Lacy. Dr. Pearson knows she couldn't possibly have made a B without me helping her. Finally the bell rang, and everybody, including Lacy—who was the first out the door—rushed out, leaving me still seated and wondering if I should go up to the desk.

"Sandy, come here. I want to talk to you about your test."

Well, here it comes.

I'd made a flat A, but I hadn't even glanced at the test I got for Lacy. History was easy for me, and I knew the questions backwards and forward. The walk from my desk to the front of the room was a painful experience, and I'd decided to take an F for helping Lacy, but I sure wasn't going to admit that I'd stolen the test. I'd just slipped her some answers, was what I would tell Dr. Pearson. I was certain that he was suspicious about Lacy scoring so high, and that he was going to give me a verbal thrashing about helping her cheat, but I was wrong.

"Sandy, it's been several years since I've had a student give such insightful answers to the essay questions. Most of the class gave rote, by-the-book answers, but you injected an insight into the real, underlying situations. Good work. Have you considered majoring in History?"

I started breathing again. Dr. Pearson didn't have a clue that I'd snitched the test and helped Lacy. My God, what a relief! Hell, I'll never put myself in a position like this again.

I let out a deep breath and said, "Yes, sir, I have. History is interesting, and I read the whole textbook before class started. I'd rather read history books than novels."

"Well, I can tell that you've got an excellent background in history. Where did you go to high school?"

"Mount Union High School down in south Arkansas; it's a small school, about 225 students."

"You got your history background at Mount Union High School?"

"Well, in a way. I only took Arkansas and American History, but I did read all the history books in our library."

"If you enjoy history that much, you should major in it."

"I've really considered it, Dr. Pearson."

"Good. You'd better get to class. Keep up the good work."

"Thanks, Dr. Pearson."

Well, I was breathing normally again as I left the classroom, but I had that nagging feeling of guilt about the whole, sordid mess. My God, what a lowlife—stealing a test to have sex with the college tramp! I'm lucky to still be in school.

I walked out, shaking my head, and headed for the bookstore to clock in. Standing outside was Lacy. She nodded and I stopped.

"What did he want?" Lacy looked like a frightened rabbit, wringing her hands and breathing as if she'd run up a flight of stairs.

I quickly shoved the guilty feeling into the back of my mind and smiled. "He wants me to major in history."

"That's it?"

"Yeah."

"I've been standing here sweating blood while you two talked about majoring in history. Thank God he didn't suspect anything."

"Oh, he didn't, not a thing."

"Great! See you on Friday, Sandy."

"Bye."

I walked back to the bookstore, still thinking about stealing the test, having sex with Lacy, and how upset I was when I thought that Dr. Pearson had caught us. By the time I got to the bookstore, I'd decided that Lacy was worth it all.

I'd just clocked in at the bookstore and was leaning back against a rack of books when Vi came in. She looked right at me, and I knew she was coming in for another long visit between periods when she didn't have a class. As she came toward me, that captivating smile made me melt. I had an uneasy feeling that I'd betrayed Vi by going out with Lacy, and my face probably showed it. Just trying to look Vi in the eye was painful.

"Sandy, you look like you've lost your best friend." She stopped, put her hands on her hips, and waited for my reply as she observed my dour expression.

"Oh, no, Vi, it's nothing. I was just thinking about the Ten Weeks Mineralogy Test."

"Huh? I don't believe you, Sandy. All that geology stuff is easy for you. What's really bothering you?"

My God, how can she see right through me like that?

Vi stood there, waiting for me to confess, but there was no way on earth that I was going to admit what I had on my mind. Finally, I started mumbling something about not ever having a date, and Vi started going on the defense because she knew I wanted to date her.

"Oh, Sandy, lots of girls would love to go out with you."

"Yeah, maybe, but I think you know why I'm not dating." Vi's smile left her face as the words sank in.

"Sandy, come help me unpack these books."

It was Bob, the assistant manager, who pulled me away from an embarrassing situation.

I walked over to the boxes to help Bob and thought, Sandy, that was a lowlife thing to do. Making Vi feel bad when you're the louse who had sex with Lacy.

***

Over the next several weeks, as a beautiful Arkansas fall settled in, Vi and I spent more and more time together. I could count on a Coke date every Tuesday and Thursday between her third and fourth periods, and every other Saturday I would go with her to the pound to clean dog pens. We were getting along great, but I wasn't making any progress in booting out Mr. Football. However, I'd walk away from those Coke dates convinced that sooner or later she'd drop that bum, and then we could start going out.

Lacy and I continued coming to class early so that we could talk, and, as the weeks passed, we became close friends, but there was something a little unusual about the way she treated me. She was always glad to see me, and we had the best time just talking. However, when we talked, her manner was different. I couldn't put my finger on it, but, well, she didn't seem as sexy. She shied away from any mention of dating, and I resigned myself to the fact that we'd just be friends. I couldn't figure out the dating part, since she dated constantly, and her reputation was about as wild as it could get.

I'd usually run into Lacy as she came out of the Chemistry building after Biology Lab, around four o'clock, on Mondays and Fridays. We'd stand there and talk, and later we started taking long walks around campus, going on and on about almost everything that crossed our minds. My God, it was some crap that I wouldn't have told anybody. However, when the conversation worked itself around to Lacy's high school years in Tulsa, I could tell that something in her background was troubling her, and every time she started talking about her teen years she'd almost cry and change the subject. I couldn't figure out what was bothering her, and she refused to tell me. However, one afternoon during the second week in November, on one of our long walks, I got the shock of my life.

It was late one cool, clear afternoon, and we'd walked south across campus past the Delta House until we came to the old Fayetteville cemetery. Years ago, someone had built a three foot tall rock wall around it and planted hundreds of red maple trees. That afternoon the fall foliage was at its peak.

We walked into the cemetery through the iron gate on the north side and started strolling down a narrow walk. We'd walked about a 100 yards from the entrance when I looked over to my right and spotted a marble bench about 30 yards off the road.

"Lacy, there's a bench over there under those trees. Let's go sit down."

"Sure, Sandy—gosh, have you ever seen anything as beautiful as these trees?"

"No, they're absolutely at their peak."

We walked over and sat down on the marble bench, which was right beside one of three maple trees grouped around a large, impressive tombstone with the word JIANT carved on it. It wasn't but a few minutes until we were into one of our long conversations, talking about everything you can imagine. But then we started comparing our high school experiences, and Lacy suddenly became very quiet and got up, shaking her head as she walked around the largest of the three maple trees.

Then she looked over at me and said, "Sandy, I've never told anybody what I'm about to tell you, but it's so painful that I can't hold it inside me any longer. I don't know, maybe I'll feel better if I can get this off my mind."

Of course, as close as Lacy and I had become, I knew that whatever she was about to tell me was going to be significant. It sure wasn't some girl stuff, or even about one of her dates. I looked at her and noticed that, before she even started talking, her lips were trembling.

"Lacy, we're friends, and you can tell me anything. I'd never even think of telling a soul."

"Okay, Sandy, but I'm not sure I can get through all of it, and if I can't, you'll just have to understand."

Lacy composed herself, and, after a couple of tries, she started telling me what was so painful.

"Sandy, it started when I was about eleven years old. I went through puberty early, and I was already developing at that age. The man my mother was married to at the time started giving me a lot of attention. At first, I was delighted for him to hug and touch me, but then, as I got a few years older, I realized that he was being overly familiar. Finally, after he touched me in a very intimate place, I told my mother. She confronted him, they had a big fight, and he accused me of lying and threatened to leave us. It was horrible, and I worried about it for days. As the weeks passed he seemed to have forgotten about the incident, and soon he was rubbing and touching me again. He got bolder and bolder because I was afraid to tell Mother. My mother was a frail person, and I worried about telling her. If I caused him to leave us, Mother would never forgive me.

I did the best I could to avoid being alone with him, but, living in a small apartment with three people, it was bound to happen sooner or later, no matter how careful I was. It happened one afternoon when I came home from school. I was 15, a sophomore in high school. Mother was supposed to be home, but she'd taken a bus downtown to shop. He was sitting in the living room drinking a beer when I walked in. As soon as I walked into the apartment and saw that Mother wasn't there I started for the door, but he jumped up and stopped me before I could leave. He told me point blank that he wanted to have sex with me. Then he threatened me, and said that if I didn't, he was going to leave my mother. I felt trapped, Sandy." Lacy dropped her head and mumbled through tears, "I can't go on, it hurts too much."

My God, I know my mouth must have been hanging open as Lacy told me that.

She began to cry, and it took her a few minutes to regain her composure.

"Lacy, it's all right." I stood up and put my arm around her, and she buried her head on my shoulder, sobbing. She cried for a few more minutes and then continued.

"It was horrible, just horrible, Sandy, but I thought maybe it would be just that one time, and he wouldn't bother me again, but it wasn't. He would find ways to catch me alone, threaten me, and then force me to have sex with him. Finally, I couldn't stand it any longer, and one night at the dinner table I stood up and blurted out the whole thing. There was a huge scene, and he called me the most horrible names and accused me of instigating it. Then he lifted up the end of the dinner table, dumped all the plates and food out on the floor, and walked out. We never saw him again—Mother went into a deep depression—blamed me for everything. She was suicidal."

Lacy was about to break up and could hardly get the words out of her mouth, but then she caught her breath and screamed, "The last two years I spent in that house were the most miserable of my life!"

Lacy stopped, turned away from me, and then began to shake. Soon she was sobbing uncontrollably.

"Lacy! Lacy! It's all right! Don't even think about it anymore. That's all behind you now." I'd never felt more sympathy for anyone in my life. Lacy was so distraught that she couldn't even form words. There was nothing to do but put my arms around her and hold her until she regained her composure. From that moment, my thoughts about Lacy were changed. My God, I felt like a low-life heel for getting the test to have sex with her. Finally, she stopped crying, wiped her eyes, and started to talk again.

"Sandy, I don't know why, but that terrible experience changed me. I've got something wrong with me now, and no matter how hard I try there's an overwhelming urge to do things that I really don't want to do. I can't explain it, and I've never told anybody else about it. Maybe the way I am around guys here at school has something to do with what happened to me when I was 15."

When Lacy said that, she dropped her head and cried again,

partly from being so upset as she remembered that horrible situation, and partly from being embarrassed for telling me all of the intimate details.

"Sandy, I need help! I'm not sure I have the strength to go on! You'll never guess how hard it is to pretend and pretend—then play as if you're somebody else—always trying to please—but always feeling guilty. I don't know if I can keep on. Sometimes I think about suicide."

"Lacy, don't say things like that. You can stop. Just turn down those guys. You don't have to do any of that stuff."

"Sandy, you don't understand. It's not that I want to go out and do what I do; it's just that I can't keep myself from doing it. I can't say no. I come back from a date feeling so dirty, and I swear that I won't go out again, but then when one of the guys calls and begs me for a date, I go out telling myself that we won't have sex, but then I can't stop myself. Oh, God! Will I get through this, or will I end up as a hooker somewhere?"

"Lacy! Don't say that!"

"Well, Sandy, if I don't change, that's where I'll end up." Lacy stood there a minute, collected her thoughts, and slowly said, "Because of how I've acted, I can't have a normal date. All the guys on campus look at me one way—and you know what they're thinking."

There was a long pause in the conversation, and, for the life of me, I couldn't think of anything to say because I was as guilty as the rest of her dates. Then I walked over to the big tombstone with JIANT on it and stood there for a minute. About that time a gust of wind caused the leaves at my feet to swirl around, and I looked down. Then I looked at the tombstone.

"Lacy, come here! Read this!" I pointed to the inscription on the tombstone.

"Read an inscription on a tombstone?"

"Yeah, and Lacy, you're going to make it—one way or another."

Lacy walked over, bent down, and read, "The Lord will give strength to his people."

"Sandy! Oh, my gosh!"

Maybe it was a coincidence, but it was just the right word when Lacy really needed it. In a few minutes, Lacy was back to her old self, and she smiled at me.

"Sandy, I apologize for what I put you through, but I feel as if a weight has been lifted off my shoulders. Maybe I've got a future, and one day I'll straighten out my life."

"I know you will, Lacy, and thanks for telling me. You're a special girl, and I'll never forget this afternoon." Lacy smiled, and I hugged her as we sat there in the soft light of a late fall afternoon.

From that moment on, I thought I understood almost everything about Lacy.

***

The rest of the semester passed quickly, and, about a week before the History final, Lacy and I arrived in class ten minutes early and were carrying on a lively conversation when the subject of the final came up.

"Are you ready for the final, Lacy?"

"Of course not, you know how I can't stand this stupid class."

"Well, you better start studying. He's going to cover the entire book."

"It's hopeless, Sandy. Even if I studied non-stop, I couldn't cover everything."

Before I thought, I said, "Yeah, you're right. Want me to help you out?" Damn—I felt uneasy when I said that, and I wished I could have taken those words back. As close as Lacy and I were, she knew exactly what "help you out," meant. She gave me a look as if I had said something that had hurt her feelings. Then she dropped her head and softly said, "Sandy, we're friends, and I don't want you to do that again."

I was puzzled by how Lacy was acting, but, before we could

continue our conversation, Dr. Pearson walked in, and the class started.

The next Friday was the last regular class period before finals, and Lacy was absent. I talked with one of Lacy's sorority sisters as I walked out of class, and she told me that Lacy had a virus.

That night I was sitting around the dorm, still mulling over the "I don't want you to do that" comment from Lacy. It didn't make sense. She was sure to get an F on the final. What was the difference from Ten Weeks Tests to the Final? At first I couldn't answer those questions, but, after trying to fall asleep for a couple of hours, I got up, thought about the talk at the cemetery, and finally I understood why she didn't want me to get her the History final.

Hell, I don't know why I did it, but I walked down to the Greek Theatre, changed into my black clothes, and in less than an hour I had the History semester test in hand. For some reason I didn't feel guilty. It seemed that, this time, breaking into a university building and stealing a test was justified. Don't ask me how I came up with that—I've never figured it out. It was just the way it was.

Early Saturday morning I walked over to Lacy's sorority house and asked the housemother to tell Lacy that someone wanted to see her. In a few minutes, a sleepy Lacy stumbled down the stairs. She had pulled on a man's white shirt and blue jeans, and she had wrapped a scarf around her head. My God, she was still gorgeous, even dressed like that.

"Sandy, what are you doing here?"

"Oh, I just stopped by to give you something."

Lacy looked puzzled, and I handed her the test.

"Here's something that will help you in studying for your History final," I whispered.

She opened the folded paper and made a little gasp as she recognized it.

"Oh, Sandy..."

"Hey, I've got to go, see you Monday."

I was walking away, leaving Lacy standing there, holding the test, when she called me back.

"Sandy, wait, I need to tell you something," she said, running to catch me before I got out the door.

"What about-—you know—a date?"

I've never seen anything bother Lacy before, but, as I looked at her flushed face, I knew that for some reason she was embarrassed.

I moved close to Lacy and whispered to her, "Lacy, we're friends. I got you the test because we're friends. That's it: Friends don't expect something from friends."

I've never seen Lacy look prettier than she looked as she stood there smiling at me. She didn't say anything for a minute, and then, without a word, she gave me a big hug. I headed back to my dorm.

After stealing the test for Lacy and feeling the adrenalin surge as I slipped down that dark hall, I began to have the urge to do it again. However, I didn't have any courses that were giving me any trouble. In fact, after that hellacious freshman year, that semester was easy.

21.

A Monticello Cop

Finals passed quickly, and I decided to go home to Pine Valley between semesters. Hanging around the campus with everyone gone was the most boring thing imaginable. However, after being home, sitting out on the farm with absolutely nothing to do, I began to search for anything to break the boredom.

Then it hit me; go see Vi. Mother had a 1951 Ford, which she drove into Magnolia every day. If I took her to work and picked her up, I could have the car for the rest of the day. That night I called Vi, and, after a little small talk, told her that I'd like to stop by Monticello and see her on my way to Pine Bluff. Well, the Pine Bluff story was an out-and-out lie, but I knew Vi wouldn't accept that I was coming to Monticello just to see her.

"Sandy, Daddy would be upset if he sees me talking with you, and our downtown is so small that he'd know about it in a minute. You know how he is about Bill, and even though we're just friends, he doesn't want me to even talk to anyone but Bill."

"Yeah, I got the hint when I stopped by last summer."

"Sandy, Daddy saw you kiss me, and after you left he told me under no circumstances to ever see you again. He knows you were lying about the All-State basketball stuff. After you left, he was so angry I was frightened."

"But Vi, you're 20 years old. Surely you can talk to your friends without having to ask permission?"

"Oh, Sandy, I'd like to sit around and talk with you like we do at the Union, but we can't do it in downtown Monticello. It would be terrible for both of us."

"What?"

"Sandy, Daddy has become very different over the past few years, and he reacts to things very strongly."

"Hey, I've got an idea. Why don't I just drive through and pick you up, and we can drive out of town. Your daddy won't see us then."

"I don't know, Sandy."

"Oh, come on, Vi. I'm so bored I can't see straight. I need to talk to someone."

There was a long pause on the phone, and then Vi said, "Okay, we can go somewhere and talk, but it can't be long, an hour at the most."

I agreed, figuring that if we were somewhere talking and having a good time, Vi wouldn't be watching the clock.

The next day I dropped Mother off at the dry cleaners and headed for Monticello. Vi had told me that she'd be in the City Café at ten o'clock, and I should just pull up and stay in the car. She'd run out, jump in, and we would drive out of town and have our little talk.

Monticello is an hour and a half drive from Magnolia, and I gave myself plenty of time to make my ten o'clock date. I drove downtown and, at exactly ten o'clock, I pulled up in front of the City Café. Vi walked out and hopped into the car, and I pulled away. But as I did, I glanced back and saw Vi's father walking down the sidewalk. I spoke to Vi so she wouldn't turn her head and see him, but he sure saw her. He was standing there with his hands on his hips when we drove off. My God, I could see him fuming from half a block away.

"Sandy, I can't believe I'm sneaking off like this. You'd think we were going somewhere to make out."

"Maybe we are," I reached over and poked her in the ribs, and she laughed.

"Oh, Sandy, cut it out."

"Say, Vi, we just can't drive around for an hour and burn up gasoline. Where's a good place to park?"

"Sandy!"

"Oh, Vi, really. My mother will shoot me if I bring this car back empty."

Vi hesitated for a minute, and then nodded her head and said, "Okay, keep going on out of town until you cross the railroad tracks, then take a right and immediately take another right down a little logging road."

I nodded and smiled.

"Sandy, I know what you're thinking."

"Heck, Vi, what's wrong with knowing about a good parking place?"

"Nothing, but you weren't thinking about the parking place," Vi said as she laughed.

Well, for whatever reason, Vi knew a little logging road that led to a big pine tree where you could pull over and park. She looked a little embarrassed at being able to drive straight to an obvious parking place. I nodded my head and smiled as I pulled up and turned the motor off.

"Let's get out and walk around, Sandy. It's a nice day, and last week's bad weather kept me cooped up in the house."

We got out and walked over to the big pine tree, where we started to talk about school. On my way over to see Vi I'd thought about what to talk about, knowing that Mr. Football would be mentioned time after time. I'd planned out our conversation, and Mr. Football was the centerpiece of that plan.

"Well, did you make another four point?" I said, starting the conversation.

"No, I didn't. That old biddy Mrs. Love, my Western Civ teacher, gave me a B+ as a final grade. Nobody gives a B+. She's just horrible, and on top of that, if you're attractive and popular, she resents it. That B+ was just a slap in the face."

"Yeah, I've heard some stuff about her. I think you're right. All A's in everything else?"

"Yes, how did you do?"

"Well, a whole lot better than I did last year. If I get an A in Mineralogy, I'll have a three point."

"Sandy, that's wonderful. I was so worried about you last year. I thought you were going to be on probation for sure. It was a miracle you pulled an 85 on that Chemistry final."

I smiled as I thought about the Chemistry final and said, "More than a miracle, Vi. By the way, how did Mr. Football do?" Vi looked a little uncomfortable and hesitated as if there was something she didn't want to tell me.

"Uh, well, I think Bill is going to be all right. Coach Jenkins is talking to his Literature professor about letting Bill do some make-up work so he can raise his grade up to a C."

"Make-up work? Hell, Vi, there's no such thing as make-up work. Bull Jenkins is just strong-arming that poor professor. I can't believe Mr. Football can't make his grades. He's got this little nerd that the athletic department pays to walk around with him, take notes, and be sure he attends class. Mr. Football even makes him carry his books."

"Sandy, Bill has got a lot on his mind. So much depends on him that it's hard for him to concentrate on his studies."

"Bull, Vi. You know Mr. Football is as dumb as a fence post, and if he couldn't play football, he'd be pumping gas somewhere."

"Oh, Sandy, Bill may not be the best student, but he's smart in other ways."

"Really? Like what other ways? What do you talk about when you go out on a date with him?"

"Oh, I don't know, Sandy. Sometimes the weather, and Bill will tell me how practice went. And if there was a game on Saturday, he'll go over the plays with me."

"Huh, so you talk about the weather and football?"

"And other stuff."

"Vi, you're so smart. One of the reasons I like being around you is because we can have a deep conversation about all kind of things. I think about our talks for days afterwards."

"So do I, Sandy."

I smiled. It was time to move in for the kill.

"Vi, don't you see, Mr. Football is just a football machine with almost no other interests, and your life with him would be horrible. You can't have a meaningful relationship with someone who you have nothing in common with." Vi had a troubled look on her face, and I knew that she believed at least part of what I was telling her.

"Sandy, you're too hard on Bill. He's really a nice person when you get to know him, and the Boy Scouts he works with think he's great."

"Sure, Vi, I don't doubt it a bit, but if he wasn't a big-shot football player that your dad was pushing you to date, you wouldn't give him the time of day."

"Yes, I would, Sandy."

"No, you wouldn't, Vi, and you know it." I hesitated and then I said, "It's your father, isn't it?" Vi's eyes told it all, but she wouldn't let herself admit it. Her face paled with I mentioned her father.

"Oh, Sandy, let's quit talking about Bill. I can't understand why you don't like him."

"Well, Vi, even if he wasn't dating you, I wouldn't like him. He swaggers around campus like he's God's gift to Arkansas. Of course, that's part of the short man's complex he's trying to overcome."

"What?"

"Yeah, he's like a little Napoleon. He's a short guy trying to compensate. You know, Napoleon was just a little over four feet tall, and he finally made himself Emperor to make people look up to him."

"Napoleon was four feet tall?"

"Well, a little over four feet," I lied. Napoleon was actually at least a foot taller than four feet, but I wanted to make a point.

"How tall is Mr. Football?"

"He's five six."

"No, he's not. Heck, even with those lifts he wears, he's not five six."

"Lifts?"

"Yeah, those loafers he wears have built-up heels to give him a little more height." I didn't have a clue about the built-up heels, but Mr. Football was definitely short, and I wanted Vi to remember that every time she was around him. "How tall are you, Vi?" Vi could see where I was going with this conversation, and she hesitated, but finally answered.

"Five eleven."

"Haven't been able to wear high heels since you've been dating Mr. Football, have you?"

"No, Sandy, I haven't, but being tall is not that big of a deal."

"Well, Vi, you're right, it's not a big deal. But let's just say that Mr. Football took those lifts out of his shoes, and you wore high heels. Can you imagine how y'all would look walking into the spring dance?" I could see Vi visualizing herself towering over Mr. Football, and she frowned.

"Vi, just like people fit intellectually, they fit size-wise. Come over here and stand by me." I'm six feet two in my stocking feet, and that morning I'd deliberately worn cowboy boots with two inch heels. Vi was wearing flat brown loafers with white socks.

Vi looked a little unsure, but she walked over and stood facing me.

"Now, look at us, Vi. Doesn't this seem right? You're looking up at me instead of down at the top of someone's head. It just feels right."

Vi's head made a very slight nod as she looked up at me.

I'd planned the conversation right down to the last statement, and now it was time for more than words. Before Vi could say anything else, I reached over, put my hands on her shoulders, and pulled her forward as I reached down to kiss her. My hands moved down softly, caressing her back as she responded, pressing against me. She closed her eyes and we kissed again and again. She pulled back after a long and passionate kiss.

"Sandy, I should have known. You're just like all men, after one thing."

"No, Vi, I'm not."

"What?"

"Vi, if you think I like being around you because I want to make out with you, you've missed the whole point of our friendship." Vi was clearly on the defensive now. The friendship remark cut to the core.

"Heck, Vi, you're just so attractive that I couldn't hold back. But surely you realize that our friendship is a lot deeper than an occasional kiss." Vi smiled, and I knew big points had been made as she nodded her head. I took her in my arms again, and we kissed until both of us were gasping from all the kissing, touching, and rubbing.

Vi pulled away, smiling as she said, "We're going to be a lot more than friends if we keep this up."

I started to reach out to her again, but Vi glanced down at her watch.

"Oh, shit, Sandy, it's almost noon, and I'm supposed to meet Daddy at the café for lunch. Get in the car. We've got to get back to town."

Vi was clearly worried, and as I drove back to town our conversation was very brief. We pulled up in front of the City Café, and there stood her father. He was planted there just like when we left, scowling, with his arms crossed. Vi hopped out, said goodbye, and headed for the café.

"Vi, go get us a table. I'll be there in a minute," said Mr. Botner.

Oh, hell, I thought. He was coming over to my car.

"Hello, Sandy, how are you today?"

"Just fine, sir."

"Sandy, I want to tell you something, and I don't want to beat around the bush. I'm a plain-spoken man."

"Yes, sir."

"Do you know Vi is practically engaged to Bill Tucker?"

"Well, I know they're dating."

"Sandy, let me get right to the point. Stop pursuing Vi. I don't want you to ever talk with her again. Do you understand?"

"Mr. Botner, Vi's almost 21. Don't you think that's her decision?"

"What?"

"Yes, sir. Who Vi sees is up to her, not you."

I could see Mr. Botner's fists clench as his face turned red.

Well, I thought so much of that little comeback that I made a little smirk. I shouldn't have. Mr. Botner's hand was on my outside rearview mirror, and when I smarted off to him he gripped that mirror and his eyelids narrowed. Look out, here it comes.

"Listen, you little hayseed, if you think I'm going to sit back and let some low-rent piece of white trash break up Vi and Bill, you have another think coming! Now, get your ass out of my town! I don't want to ever see you in Monticello again! By God, you'll regret the hell out of it if you ever set foot in this town again!"

Well, I was shocked for a second, but soon I was fuming. He'd called me a hayseed and a low-rent piece of white trash, and I was burned up now. Mr. Big Shot Banker was threatening me like he owned the town.

"Mr. Botner, you may think you own this little town, but you don't, and I'll come to Monticello any time I want!"

Mr. Botner just stared at me for a few seconds, gritted his teeth, leaned forward, and gave me a go-to-hell look that was so weird it startled me. Then he turned around to go into the café, but, before he went in the door, he looked back over his shoulder and said, "We'll see."

I was so rattled by everything that had happened that I felt as if I were in a daze and couldn't enjoy thinking about the time

with Vi because of the encounter with Mr. Botner. Vi was probably getting the same chewing out I'd just received. As I left town I
was creeping along, going less than 25 miles-per-hour as I relived
my morning. Then, suddenly, a siren and a flashing red light shattered my thoughts. I glanced back, and there was a police car
right on my bumper. I pulled over and wondered why I was being
stopped. Was my license plate up to date? Maybe I was going too
slowly in a 45 mile-per-hour zone.

"Step out of the car, son." It was a Monticello police officer,
and, even though I was a mile out of the city limits, he'd pulled me
over.

"Sir, I wasn't speeding. Why did you stop me?"

"Boy, don't you get smart with me. I didn't pull you over for
nothin'."

"But I wasn't doing anything wrong, Officer. I'll bet I wasn't
going 20 miles-per-hour."

"Son, you can get yourself in a whole lotta trouble callin' a law
enforcement officer a liar!"

He'd raised his voice, which puzzled me.

"But why am I being stopped?"

"Boy, if you yell at me one more time, I'm gonna hafta subdue
you!" He was even louder and began to finger his nightstick. I
started to get concerned.

Yell, at him? I haven't yelled. Then it hit me. This was that out
of control Mr. Botner's way of showing me that he did own Monticello, and I was an instant away from being beaten senseless by
this crooked police officer. My God, I knew that I had to do something. My mind raced as I stood there, looking at a burly, police
officer with his hand on his nightstick. I dropped any pride about
being innocent and started trying to keep from being clubbed
with that nightstick.

"Sir, I want to apologize for questioning you. Maybe I wasn't
concentrating on my driving. You were exactly right to stop me,
and, if you think I deserve a ticket, then I'll be happy to pay it."

I held my breath. The officer grimaced and continued to finger his nightstick as he stared at me. Now it was obvious that he had intended to use it on me, but, after that exchange, he paused. Then, just when I thought he had changed his mind, he started to raise it.

"Sir, please! Please don't hit me! I have asthma, and if I'm injured, I won't be able to breathe!"

It's just a blur about what happened next. I couldn't even get my hand out to block his nightstick, as he whipped it out of his holster and with one continuous motion hit me right above my left ear.

"You faking little punk! I'm going to teach you a lesson you won't forget!"

The lick on the side of my head stunned me, but I still had enough sense to fall face down with my arms and hands covering my head. I don't know how many times he hit my arms and back, but I do remember when he stopped and turned me over with his boot.

"Listen to me, boy! That's just a taste of what you're going to get if I ever see you back in this town again! You understand?"

"Yes, sir! Yes, sir! I promise I won't ever set foot in Monticello again!" I screamed. God I would have promised to leave Arkansas if it would have kept from being beaten again.

"Okay, but just know you're getting off light this time. The Man said to beat the hell out of you, but I let you off light. Get up, boy. You just better watch it, or I'll pull this stick out again. Now, let's see," he said as he pulled out his ticket book. "60 in a 25 mile-per-hour zone, running two stops signs, cursin' a police officer, and resistin' arrest. I guess that about sums it up."

He spent a couple of minutes writing up the ticket, and then he handed it to me.

"Boy, you can call Judge Carelock's office. The number is right at the top of this ticket. Or you can come on back over to Monticello on the 25th and contest this ticket in court. It's up to you." He motioned for me to sign the ticket, which I did, and, as he started to walk away, he looked back over his shoulder and said,

"Boy, just a little advice. If I was you, I don't think I'd ever come back to Monticello...If you do, you might not leave. Do you understand me, boy?"

I sure did understand him, and I couldn't wait to drive out of Monticello. My hands were still shaking and my head and back were throbbing as I got in the car and headed back to Pine Valley. Mr. Botner was right: he did own that little town, and if I showed up again it would be a lot worse than the beating I'd just received. Right before I went back to school I called Judge Carelock and was informed that the fine was $150. That really made a dent in my small savings account. All because of an off-the-wall nut of a father.

A few days later, while riding back to school with a friend from Magnolia, I thought about the semester break. Was it worth it? A $150 fine and a beating from a crooked cop in exchange for a couple of kisses from Vi—yeah, it was worth it. She'll probably drop Mr. Football as soon as she gets back to school.

22.

Temptation

I was in a good mood when I got back to Fayetteville, certain that Vi and I were going to be together. After I'd settled in at my dorm, I went back to work in the bookstore, stocking books for the coming semester. The next week, after classes started, Vi stopped by the bookstore. I told her about the conversation I'd had with her father and about being stopped and beaten up by the crooked Monticello cop. She couldn't believe it until I showed her the bruises on the back of my arms.

"Sandy, surely you don't think Daddy had that policeman arrest you and then beat you up?"

"Vi, what do you think? I wasn't doing anything. I hadn't broken any law. That sorry cop said he had been told by the 'Man' to beat me half to death with his nightstick. He did and I got a $150 ticket on top of that."

It took a minute for that to sink in, and she frowned and said, "Maybe you're right, Sandy. Daddy was livid. I've never seen him so mad. He did make a phone call before he came to the table. Sandy, I'm so sorry. Daddy has some real mental problems, and sometimes he does some irrational things."

"Damn, Vi, your father's crazy and you know it!"

Vi's face paled and the look in her eyes confirmed exactly what I had just said. It was time to change the subject.

"Ah, let's forget about your father. How about meeting me tonight on the front steps of Old Main?" I thought Vi would smile and nod, but she was shaking her head no before I finished speaking.

"Sandy, I can't. You wouldn't believe how Daddy raved on and on after you drove off. I was in tears, and I promised him I wouldn't ever see you again. I'm disobeying Daddy right now by even talking to you."

I couldn't believe it. Vi was actually shaking as she stood there, going on about how her sorry daddy had made her promise she'd never see me again.

My God, trying to fight Mr. Football for Vi's time was hard enough, but I never thought prying her away from her crazy, domineering father could be so tough. Vi had a frightened look in her eyes as she told me about her father and the berating he'd given her after they went back into the café. Hell, I had never known anyone that was so verbally beat up. I was depressed.

"Surely, we can still be friends." Damn, I was almost begging.

"Well, we can, but we've got to cool it for right now. Daddy will calm down, and this will blow over in a few weeks, but right now I can't take a chance by meeting you. What if he found out?"

I nodded as if I understood, but I really didn't. Why can't Vi just do what she wants to? My God, her father must have an unbelievable grip on her. That was all I could think about as we talked.

For the next few weeks, I saw Vi only briefly. Sometimes she'd stop by the bookstore, or I'd run into her in the hall. We were still friends, but the fear of crossing her father was keeping us from any night meetings in front of Old Main, and, even when we just talked in the bookstore, she was nervous. I'd have to be patient.

***

It was an uneventful semester for the next several weeks, but that was about to change. Things started happening at the poker game the week before Ten Weeks Tests began. That Saturday night I showed up for the poker game, smiling and speaking to all the guys who were already sitting around the table, except Dickie. I'd made some good friends in the fraternity, but Dickie wasn't included in the bunch. There was an unspoken truce now between that worthless Dickie and me. Peter had made it clear that, if there were any more fights or cussing, we'd be kicked out of the game. The game was uneventful, and, at about 12:30, interest waned.

"Hey, let's get a beer and take a break," Dickie mumbled from across the table.

"Good idea. Holler at one of the pledges to bring us a six pack," said Peter.

We kicked back in our chairs and relaxed, talking about girls, school, and basketball. Then Bob Robert Persack, who was sitting next to me, started whining about Ten Weeks Tests, which were coming up the next week.

"By God, I'd give 50 bucks for a copy of my Western Civ test."

"Really?" I said. I suddenly felt the old Uncle Hosie urge hit me. Pay for a test? Would he really pay 50 bucks for a test?

"You're damn right I would. I need to nail at least a B on the Ten Weeks Test. The old coot gave me a flat F on Four Weeks."

"Okay, Dickie, break's over, your deal," said Peter.

The game started up before I could answer Bob Robert, but I sat there thinking about what he had said. My God, $50.00 was a lot of money, and I was struggling just to survive on my tiny bookstore salary and the weekly poker game winnings. It had never occurred to me that someone would pay for a test, and I couldn't get it out of my mind. Getting a test for Lacy was one thing, and I'd justified it by being overwhelmed by Lacy's sex appeal and charm, but I'd thought that stealing tests was behind me and that I'd never do it again. But when Bob Robert said he'd pay $50.00 for a test, a tingle went up my back, and the urge returned. Maybe the couple of beers I'd drunk had weakened my resolve. I don't know, but when the game was over I pulled Bob Robert aside.

"Were you serious about paying $50.00 for a copy of your Western Civ test?"

"Hell, yes. I'm sweating blood over that mother. Why are you asking?"

"Oh, I have a friend with some connections. He might be able to come up with the exam."

"Huh? Really? Come up with the test?"

"Yeah, he knows some people, and he just might be able to get it, but he'd sure want at least $50.00."

"Damn, I'd give him the 50, but it's gotta be the actual test, not one of last year's. Hell, we've got all of 'em from the past ten year's right here in the house."

"It would be the actual test."

"Well, tell your friend that I'm on."

"Okay, when's your exam, and who's your professor?"

"The test is next Thursday, and Dr. Scoggins is the teacher. He has an office in Old Main, 309, I think."

I made some notes on the back of a card and stuck it in my back pocket.

"I'll see what I can do, but if I come up with it, I'll only have it the day before the test."

"That's okay."

I left the Delta house, and, as I walked back to my dorm, I only had one thing on my mind. I couldn't think of anything but stealing that exam. It was an obsession, and just thinking about it made my heart race. I guess the money was the added incentive I couldn't resist. It was about to push me over the top.

Fits of guilt plagued me, but by the next day I'd forced them into the back recesses of my mind. I wanted the $50.00, but even more than that, I wanted to feel the thrill of doing the job.

The next day, after German class, I walked up to the third floor of Old Main, and, sure enough, there in the middle of a series of petitioned walls was #309, and, on the door, Dr. Ralph Scoggins.

The hall door to the offices was old, with a snap-button lock system that could be opened in less than ten seconds with a hooked clothes hanger. Old Main had 14 foot ceilings, and the petitioned walls inside the hall were only eight feet tall. It would be easy to step onto a chair and climb over one. When I left the building, I shook the side entrance door, examining the door facing and the lock. It all looked too easy.

For the next few days, I made a half-hearted effort to convince myself not to do the break-in, but it was no use. Tuesday night came, and I was behind the Greek Theatre again, changing clothes. I couldn't believe how easy it was to enter Old Main. The door was hinged so loosely and the lock was so old that, when I inserted the lock jammer into the lock, the door just opened. When I stepped into the dark hallway on the first floor the same feeling as before came over me. My palms were sweating, and the surge of adrenalin had me flying up the stairs to the third floor. My clothes-hanger hook clicked the button lock on the hall door on the first try, and, in less than a minute, I'd climbed over the petitioned wall and dropped down into Professor Scoggins's office. The test was in his right-hand desk drawer, and, after looking around, I found a discarded copy in his wastebasket. I was in and out of the building in less than fifteen minutes.

As I walked back to the Greek Theatre to change clothes, I thought about how easy it had been to make $50.00. 50 bucks for 15 minutes of work; not bad, crossed my mind. I was changing clothes in the bushes behind the theatre when I started to feel sick, and, by the time I got completely dressed, a cold sweat had broken out on my forehead. In a few minutes I was sitting on the back steps of the theatre, gagging. At first, I thought I was coming down with a virus, but then I realized that the revulsion of what I'd done was overcoming me. I dropped my head down on my knees in shame. Stealing a test for money, kept flooding through my mind. God, I'm a lowlife piece of trash! I sat there for at least an hour while I replayed the events of the night over and over in my head. Finally, resigned and feeling almost like a victim of Uncle

Hosie's curse, I walked back to the dorm and tried to get a little sleep. I got very little.

I called Bob Robert the next morning, and he met me across the street from the Delta house.

"Here's the test," I said, pulling it out of my folder.

"Are you sure? Is it this semester's Ten Week's Test? The one I'm taking Thursday?"

"It sure is, and I guarantee it. If it's not the test, I'll give you your money back."

"Huh, well, okay." He pulled out his billfold and handed me two twenties and a ten.

I felt as if I were holding dirty money, and I said, "Listen, Bob Robert, this is just between us. My friend would get upset if the word got around, and he said to tell you that this would be the only test he'd provide." I wanted to cut off any possibility that I would provide another test, and, at that moment, I was determined to put that sordid episode behind me.

"Yeah, I won't breathe it, see you Saturday night." He walked back across the street, and I stood there for a few minutes, holding the $50.00. I shook my head and stuffed it in my pocket. God, why did I do that?

Next Saturday night, after the poker game broke up, two of the players called me aside.

"Sandy, uh, well, we hear that you might be able to come up with a Ten Weeks Test for us?"

"Who told you that?"

"Hell, Sandy, Bob Robert was on cloud nine after he aced that Western Civ test. He blabbed it all over the house."

"Damn it, the guy that got the test is going to be all ticked off."

"Well, it's not our fault, we didn't do nothing but listen to Bob Robert."

"Yeah, I know, okay. But he told me that he wasn't interested in providing any more tests. He said it was too risky."

"Aw, come on, Sandy. Hell, 100 bucks is a lot of money. Are you sure he wouldn't do just one more job?"

As we talked, I felt my forehead pop out in sweat, and my hands began to shake.

"Uh, I don't know, maybe. Naw, he's said no, and I think he means it."

"Come on, Sandy, we'll throw in another 50."

I couldn't stand it any longer. I took a deep breath and said, "Give me the info, and I'll see what I can do."

One of the guys handed me a note card. It said, Civics 103, Mrs. Helen Sullivan, Room 223, Business Administration Building.

I was initially stunned when they asked me for the Civics test, and something inside of me screamed at me to walk away. But, as I listened to them, and as they started raising the price, I knew that I was hooked. Looking back on that time, I can truthfully say that I was as hooked as any heroin addict.

At one o'clock that night, I was behind the Greek Theatre, changing clothes. After watching in the bushes for the night watchman to pass, I crouched against the side door of the building, shoving my lock jammer into the lock and racking and flipping pins until the door opened. Of course, the guilt bothered me, but not as badly as it had the time before.

When I met the Deltas at nine the next morning out in front of Old Main, they gave me their $150.00, and I handed them the test.

That night I pulled out The Journal and printed: Boyd Taylor, Jimmy Faulkner—Sigma Delta Fraternity—$150.00 (Civics test) Pd.

After a sleepless night punctuated by nightmares, I swore that I would never steal another test. My God, you'll never know how depressed I felt just thinking about what I'd done. The guilt seemed to flow over me, and I would shake as I thought about what my addiction.

Ten Weeks Tests finished later that week, and, before the week was over, I'd turned down several Deltas who offered me as much as $200.00. But the word was out, and even Dickie was dropping hints that he might really need a test when finals came up. However, after turning down those offers, I began to feel as if I'd broken the habit and that it was all behind me. My depression lifted, and I could finally sleep at night.

The poker games had settled down to a routine in which I'd win fairly heavily for a couple of weeks, and then I'd deliberately lose and wail about how much I had lost.

About the only thing I enjoyed that semester were the long walks around campus with Lacy. As the weather warmed up, and as the redbud and dogwood trees bloomed, Lacy and I spent several hours a week just strolling around campus, talking, and enjoying each other's company. Ever since the cemetery talk, I felt a kinship with Lacy, because I also had an addiction—breaking and entering. We were different, but so much alike.

Finals were approaching, and, although the thought of stealing and selling a test occasionally crossed my mind, I wasn't greatly tempted. I really believed that I'd broken my addiction.

23.

Hooked Again

Vi frequently came by the bookstore to visit with me, and occasionally we'd talk about something other than sorry Bill Tucker, but not often. Mr. Football said he'd nominated her for Homecoming Queen again last fall, and she was almost elected. It was a damn lie, of course, but he had Vi fooled. My attempts to make out with Vi didn't seem to be getting anywhere either. After the kisses behind Old Main and the passionate Monticello parking, she wouldn't meet me after dark anymore. Her father sure had a hold on her, and nothing I could say would make her cross him. Hell, she acted as if talking with me in the bookstore was a big deal.

Mr. Football looked to be a sure bet to make All Southwest Conference next year, and, after the Gazette printed a full page spread on him, that was all Vi wanted to talk about—or "How proud Daddy was." God, it was sickening, and for the life of me, I can't believe I put up with all that crap. I guess I was convinced that Vi really did care for me, and sooner or later, she'd come around. I continued to press her to tell me if she really loved him, but her evasive answer always involved Homecoming Queen, her crazy daddy, or the possibility of Mr. Football being an All American—ha, fat chance of that happening. I had plenty of chances to date other girls, but I just wouldn't ask them out. It seemed like every time I'd decide to, Vi would come in and flirt and kid with me. When she left, the thought of going out with someone else always faded.

Finals were looming, and I began to be asked to provide tests, but I was adamant: There would be no more test stealing. That sordid bit of university life was behind me, and I wasn't about to start again.

That calmed everything down until Nikkei Dawson, a senior and good friend, who needed to make a B on the final in Organic Chemistry to graduate, cornered me after one of the Saturday night poker games.

"Sandy, I need to talk, come back to my room."

I followed Nikkei to his room, and he handed me a beer. Hell, I knew damn well why he'd called me in, and I was shaking my head before he even finished talking.

"Sandy, I know you managed to get several exams last Ten Weeks, and I need you to get the Organic Chemistry Test for me." Then Nikkei hesitated, shook his head, and said, "God, Sandy, I've gotta have it!"

"I can't help you, Nikkei. The guy I know who gets them won't do it anymore. Said it's too dangerous. You know, campus cops watching the building and stuff like that. Sorry."

"Come on, Sandy, I know you don't have a partner. You're the one getting those tests."

I was shaking my head no, but Nikkei continued.

"I'll make it worth your while, $200 bucks. Whatta ya say?"

"No, I won't...uh, he won't do it." I'd convinced myself that stealing and selling tests would end up horribly for me. I'd resisted up until now, and I was about to leave the room when Nikkei grabbed my arm and pulled me back.

"Sandy, please! For God's sake, I've got a job lined up as soon as I graduate, and if I don't make a B on the final my grade point will drop below a two point, and I'll have to come back next semester to bring it up. Hell, you're my only hope. I'll give you $500.00 to get that test. Please, Sandy."

"$500.00, are you kidding?" I was stunned. I'd never had that much money at one time in my whole life, but I could have it if I produced the Organic Chemistry final. Hell, it would almost pay for a semester of school.

"No I'm not: 500 in cash."

"Uh, well," I hesitated, but it wasn't just the thought of that much money that was sucking me in; it was also the desire to experience the thrill of doing another job. I succumbed. The damned Uncle Hosie curse had me in its grip again.

"Okay, give me the class details and the professor's office address."

Nikkei wrote it down; I stuffed the note in my pocket and started back across campus. Hell, just the thought of doing the job had me excited, and I was already breathing heavily, just thinking about what I was going to do. It was three days before the test, and I had plenty of time to case the Chemistry building and locate his professor's office.

Two nights before the test, I was behind the Greek Theatre, changing into my black clothes. Soon I was crouched over excitedly, picking the lock on the Organic Chemistry professor's desk.

When Nikkei counted out the money, I knew that I was completely hooked again. The guilt that I had felt when I stole the tests earlier in the year was pushed back into the recesses of my mind. Of course, Nikkei let the word out, and the calls and visits started. I was hooked and couldn't stop. I even deceived myself into believing I was operating a business by telling my customers I was running a test procurement service. I was busy almost every night, and, before finals finished, I'd sold three more tests. I didn't get $500.00 for any of those tests, but I did get $250.00 from an especially desperate Delta, who was on the verge of flunking out.

The finals were finally over. Nikkei made a B on his Organic Chemistry Exam, graduated, and my reputation soared. When I left the campus that semester it was a relief to be away from the horrible mess that I'd gotten myself into. There were times when I felt revulsion and depression when I thought about what I'd done.

Getting away from the university for the summer gave me hope that, next fall, I could put the test stealing behind me.

24.

Millie!

I spent the summer working as a roustabout on an offshore drilling rig, hanging over the side of the rig, chipping paint, hauling pipe, and slashing and pulling 100 pound cement sacks across a cutter. As I watched the geologists and engineers sit around fishing and goofing off, while the roughnecks and roustabouts were working themselves to death, it sure gave me an incentive to finish college. Hell, I thought, working on a hay-baling crew was hard, but that was a piece of cake compared to what I was doing as a roustabout. But it wasn't all work on the rig. During my off-hours, I played poker in a game that never stopped. Only the players changed, as the twelve hour shifts rotated men off the drilling rig floor and into the poker game.During that summer, I was exposed to some stellar south Louisiana poker players, and I walked away from many games a loser. However, as the summer progressed, I moved up in experience, and, by the time summer ended, I was playing with the best of them. I was licking my chops, thinking of the guys I'd be playing with when I got back to school.

I returned to the university early to work in the bookstore, and I moved back into Williams House, an upperclassmen's dorm.

During the summer, I'd tried to shake the desire to steal tests. That feeling of guilt came over me every time I thought about what I'd done. However, at times, a strange urge would sweep over me, and I'd forget about the depression and guilt as I thought about how exciting picking those locks had been. The Uncle Hosie curse had a grip on me, and I was going to have a damn tough time breaking it. I would tell myself over and over, You're a good person—you are not a thief!

I'd arrived on campus early, and almost no one I knew would be there for another week. There was no Saturday night poker game due to the lack of players. That Saturday night I stopped by George's, wondering if Millie would serve me a beer, if Bob wasn't with me. The place was almost empty. When I walked in the door, Millie spotted me before I even got to a booth, and she was over to take my order in an instant.

"The usual, Sandy?"

"Uh, well, yeah, sure." I wondered if she was going to bring me a glass of water or a beer, since she knew damn well I wasn't 21.

Millie drew a pitcher of beer, and soon she was back at my booth, making small talk. "Don't worry about the ABC" (the Arkansas Beverage Commission). She slid the pitcher over and moved closer to me. "Those guys won't start showing up and checking I.D.s until after classes start."

Millie spent the next 20 minutes standing beside me, her hip touching my shoulder while she caressed the back of my neck. Since the place was almost empty, she finally scooted into the booth beside me, and we talked for at least an hour. I was about to leave when Millie leaned over and whispered to me, "Sandy, if you're not busy later, stop by about midnight, walk me back to my apartment, and we'll have a nightcap." Millie winked at me when she stood up, and my eyes lit up. Oh, my gosh! Millie asking me to walk her home and have a beer? I couldn't wait, and at midnight I was standing beside the side door of George's as Millie slipped outside and grabbed my hand. Yeah, the thought that I was two-timing Vi did cross my mind, but hell, there were stronger urges in my body, which overcame the thought of an almost non-existent girlfriend.

"Come on, Sandy. I just live a couple of blocks south of here."

We hurried along until we reached a small garage apartment. Millie led me up the stairs, and, while I took our light jackets and put them on the kitchen table, she opened the refrigerator and pulled out two beers.

"Here, Sandy, have a beer. Gosh, I need something after this dull night. Mary didn't take in 50 bucks tonight, and she was mad as hell, yelling and hollering at everybody. I couldn't wait to get out of there."

Millie and I sat on her small couch and talked, sipping our beers. After a few minutes, she eased over closer, and we started to kiss, rub, touch, and wow; when I couldn't stand it any longer, Millie looked over at her bed and said, "Sandy, do you want to make love to me?"

"Yes, Millie, yes," I mumbled.

Millie pulled away, stood up, and said, "Well, Sandy, I noticed you the first night you came into George's, and I've always thought you were so cute, but Millie stopped for a minute, took my hand, and then said, "Sandy, I hope this won't bother you, but I've got to pay the rent, and God only knows what else. If we have sex, then I'll expect you to help me out."

"Help you out?"

"Oh, Sandy, do I have to spell it out for you?"

It was beginning to dawn on me as Millie spelled it out. "Sandy, you're cute, and I want to make love to you, but it'll cost you $10.00."

I looked stunned, and Millie pulled me close to her. "Oh, Sandy, don't make me feel so cheap. Mary only pays 75 cents an hour, and college boy's tips are almost nothing. I have to do this to get by. I'm sorry."

Well, Millie could have asked me to give her my whole billfold, as excited as I was about having sex with her. Before either of us could say another word, I'd pulled out my billfold and put a ten dollar bill on the table. Millie took me by the hand, and, in less than a minute, we were both nude under the sheets.

"Sandy, since this is your first time with me, you can spend the night here. We'll have a ball."

With that comment Millie pulled me over on top of her. I wish I could say that we had sex for 30 minutes, or even 10 minutes, but it was all over in less than a minute.

Millie grinned, "First time in a long time, Sandy?" I knew it would be stupid to deny the obvious. I nodded. "Well, you'll do better the next time, and the next time," she said. Millie rubbed her hand down my stomach and kissed me. Millie was right, and, before the night was over, I was able to last more than 10 minutes.

After spending the night with Millie, I found out that she had a completely different attitude about sex than Doris or Lacy, the only other women I'd been with. Sex was a game with Millie, a game to be enjoyed in the wildest way possible. Millie did everything but swing from a light fixture, and, as we had sex, she yelled, giggled, and generally seemed to be having the greatest time of her life. Damn, I thought after one wild episode, if she's enjoying it so much, why am I paying for it? However, I knew that, even though Millie and I were friends and she enjoyed sex as much as I did, she desperately needed the money. She was having a tough time, working for tips, keeping an apartment by herself, and having to take care of her invalid mother back in Elkins. I know selling sex technically made her a prostitute, but for some reason I never thought of Millie as one.

***

Classes finally started, and the bookstore was busy as students lined up down the hall to buy a semester's worth of books, or to sell back their old books at a greatly discounted price.

Finally, on a quiet day, I walked into the bookstore, clocked in, and was standing behind the counter when Vi came in. She picked up a notebook and walked over to where I was standing.

"Hi, Sandy, you look troubled. Anything wrong?"

"No, no, not a thing. I was just thinking about something."

"What?"

"Uh, well, uh," I mumbled. I didn't know what to say, because I was thinking about Millie.

"Come on, tell me."

"You."

"You were standing there, troubled, thinking about me?"

"Yeah."

"Well, why on earth?"

"Vi, I'm talking as a friend, but I was thinking that you should break up with Bill Tucker. He's not right for you. Remember the talk we had down in Monticello?"

"Yes, I remember the talk, but I still can't believe that you want me to break up with Bill. You've never liked him. I think you're jealous because he's such a good athlete."

"No, I'm not Vi. I think you're a neat girl who deserves someone better than a short, dumb jock."

There was a long moment of silence as she looked at me. I knew the short, dumb jock bit rang a bell.

"Uh, well, thanks for thinking I'm a neat girl, Sandy, but you're the only one who thinks I shouldn't date Bill. My father would have a heart attack if we broke up."

"My God, Vi, it's not your goofy daddy who's dating Mr. Football, it's you. Don't let someone else influence your personal life."

"Sandy, you know I don't like you calling Bill 'Mr. Football.' It's so demeaning, it's like that's all he is, a football player."

"Oh, what else is he?"

"Well, he's an assistant Scoutmaster, and just last week he gave blood. Bill is not just a football player."

I didn't expect Vi to hit me with the scoutmaster or blood donor bit, so I changed the subject.

"Ahh, let's quit talking about him. Say, I love that red sweater you have on." Vi laughed as I inadvertently stared at her bosom. Her figure was more pronounced since she was so tall, and that red sweater hugged every curve.

"You guys are all alike. I know why you like this sweater. Oh, by the way, can I count on you to help me with the kennels, Saturday?"

God, I hated that job with a passion, but I nodded "yes."

We kidded around for a few more minutes. Then another customer came in, and Vi left.

***

Millie was all over me the next several weeks when I was at George's. For a few weeks, I resisted, but late one Saturday night my resistance, which I'm sure was lowered by a pitcher of beer, broke down, and at 12 o'clock I was standing at the side door, waiting for her to get off. Millie was a little more business-like this time, and when we finished, she shooed me out the door, saying that she was worn out and needed her sleep. After finding out that Millie was selling what I'd at first thought was going to be free because she liked me or Bob or whoever, I realized that she had a rather extensive list of customers. I was one of many. As the semester passed, I found out that resisting Millie usually lasted about three weeks, and then I'd pull her over and whisper in her ear that I'd be waiting on her when she got off. Sometimes she'd shake her head and say, "Not tonight." I never knew for sure if it was her time of the month, or if she had another date.

25.

Lacy, Vi...and Bull

Classes had been going on for several weeks, and I was walking out of the bookstore to take a break when Lacy walked into the Union.

"Hey, Lacy! Come join me!" I yelled.

"Sandy! Gosh, it's good to see you. It's been weeks." Lacy smiled and gave me a big hug.

We took a seat. I picked up a couple of Cokes, and we started talking non-stop. I was about ready to leave when I saw Vi walk into the Union. She glanced my way, saw us, and stopped in the middle of the room with her hands on her hips, glaring at me. I acted as if I hadn't seen her, and soon she stalked off. It was definitely trouble.

About 30 minutes later, I was working in the bookstore when Vi walked in. She was tight-lipped and obviously mad. I tried to act nonchalant and waved to her as she walked over to me. God, get ready; here it comes. She didn't even acknowledge my wave, and in seconds those long legs had covered the ten yards from the bookstore door to where I was standing. No "hi" or anything. Her first words, through some of the tightest lips I've ever seen, were, "Sandy, I can't believe you're dating Lacy Darnell!"

"Dating Lacy? Are you crazy? We were just having a Coke and talking."

"Ha, you two love birds looked like you couldn't wait to get by yourselves—in the dark!"

"Vi, Lacy sat beside me in American History, and we got to know each other. We're friends. That's it."

"Friends? Sure, just like half the guys in your dorm!"

"Come on, Vi. Lacy and I just like to sit around and talk. What's wrong with that?"

"Nothing, if you want everybody to associate you with the biggest slut on campus!" she said, raising her voice.

"Bull! What about Mr. Football?"

"Bill?"

"Yeah, I told you I saw him with Lacy last year."

"You liar! You're always trying to trash Bill!" This time Vi almost shouted.

"The hell I am! I swear to God, he was in George's with Lacy!" Actually, that was a lie, but I couldn't resist saying it.

"Sandy, you're so jealous, I don't believe a word you're saying!" she yelled.

Vi's voice had picked up, and people in the store were turning around to see who was shouting. I saw Bob, the Assistant Manager, walking our way.

"Shusss, Vi, hold it down. People can hear you all over the store."

Vi just stood there fuming as Bob walked up.

"Sandy, don't you need to pack up some books in the storeroom?" he said as he tapped me on the shoulder.

"Yeah, Bob, I'll get right on it."

Vi stalked away, still mad as hell.

"Thanks, Bob, she was getting a little out of control." Vi left the bookstore in a huff as Bob and I watched her slam the door.

"Wasn't that Vi Botner, Bill Tucker's girlfriend?"

"Yeah."

"Well, what on earth were you two yelling at each other about?"

"Oh, I don't know. We've never dated, we're just friends, but she saw me having a Coke with Lacy Darnell and gave me hell about it."

"For God's sake Sandy, don't you know that if you're going out with Lacy you need to be a little more discreet? Lacy's a drive-in-movie girl."

"Bob, I'm not dating Lacy; we were just talking. What's wrong with that?"

"Nothing, Sandy, if you don't mind what people think about Lacy rubbing off on you."

I tried to ignore Bob's advice about Lacy, but he was right. Lacy had an almost unbelievable reputation. If you were seen with her, part of Lacy rubbed off on you. It irritated me that I couldn't sit around and talk to her. Our conversations were so lively that I thought about them for days afterward. The next week I was crossing from the Chemistry building to the library when I saw her coming my way.

"Hey, how's it going?"

"Oh, okay, I guess."

There was a troubled tone in Lacy's voice, and she wasn't her usual, outgoing self. I thought about the cemetery talk and nodded in understanding. As we talked, I noticed a concrete bench behind some bushes, next to the south side of the library.

"Lacy, if you've got a few minutes, let's sit on that bench and talk," I said, pointing to the bench.

"Sure, Sandy, I just finished classes for the morning."

We walked over and sat down. After a few minutes, Lacy relaxed, and we had a great conversation. For at least an hour, we talked almost nonstop, and I felt a little guilty about not asking Lacy to have a Coke in the Union. But maybe meeting on that bench, behind some bushes and away from nosy people, was best. Over the next few weeks, Lacy and I made a habit of meeting at the bench to talk. Soon we were just saying, "Let's go to the bench," or, "Meet me at the bench."

Vi was a little cool to me for a week or so after she saw me with

Lacy, but finally, when she hadn't seen us together for a while, she calmed down.

***

Four Weeks Tests would be starting in a few days, and I was determined not to get involved in stealing tests for the Deltas. Several guys approached me when I stopped by the Delta House to play poker, but I turned them down. I was going to put that sordid episode behind me, and anyway, not many guys wanted to pay for Four Weeks Tests, since they weren't under any pressure to pass. I felt a lot better about myself the week after Test Week, since I hadn't furnished the Deltas a single test. I really thought I had broken the Uncle Hosie curse.

***

It was a routine semester until I received a late-night call.

Jim Tauber, one of the guys on our floor nearest the hall phone, yelled down the hall to me. "Carson! Carson! Phone call, it's some girl—sounds upset."

"Yeah, coming!" I hollered back.

It was about 11 o'clock, and I was trying to memorize a set of geologic time tables when Jim yelled at me. As I walked down the hall his words, "Some girl, upset," worried me. I was sure it was Vi. Mr. Football, the sorry asshole had probably mistreated her again.

"Vi, what's wrong?"

"No, Sandy, it's not Vi. It's Lacy."

"What? Uh, well, are you okay?"

"No, I'm not." I heard a muffled sob.

"Lacy, what's wrong? Are you hurt?"

"Yes, I'm hurt. I need you to come and get me—please hurry," she sobbed as she broke into uncontrollable crying.

"Okay, okay, I'm coming. Hey, wait a minute. Where are you?"

Lacy took a few moments to compose herself and said, "I'll be standing outside Hinson's Truck Stop on Highway 71 North. Do you know the place?"

"Yeah, I'll be right there."

I hung up, dashed down the hall to Billy Rob's room, and pounded on the door.

"Billy Rob! Billy Rob! I need to borrow your car!"

In a couple of minutes, a sleepy Billy Rob opened the door and held out his hand.

"Ten bucks, Sandy, you know the rules."

"Okay, yeah, but this is an emergency."

"So what? It's ten bucks for dates and ten bucks for emergencies. Ten bucks, or I'm going back to bed."

"Here." I handed Billy Rob a ten, and he tossed me the keys.

"It's parked down the hill by Drake House. When you bring it back be sure to park in a legal parking place, or you won't ever get to borrow the car again," he hollered.

I was already sprinting down the hall. "Yeah! You bet!" I yelled back. In a few minutes I was driving north on Highway 71, heading for Hinson's Truck Stop. As I approached the truck stop, I saw someone on the right side of the road. It was Lacy.

I pulled up, and Lacy managed to open the door and slip into the front seat. She was limping, and even with a cursory glance, I knew that something was seriously wrong.

"My God, Lacy! What happened?" She looked terrible.

As soon as I said that, Lacy began to sob. Her whole body was shaking, she was crying so hard. The side of her dress was ripped, and there were a scrape and a bruise on her cheek. Her mascara had run down both sides of her face, and she had lost both shoes.

"Oh, my God!" I gasped. I scooted over beside her to comfort her. Lacy put both hands over her face and buried her head in her lap as she continued to sob.

"Lacy! Lacy! Here, let me see your face." I pulled her hands back and made her sit up.

Lacy raised her head, and when I looked at the most beautiful girl on campus, I was shocked. Her long, blonde hair was matted in blood around her left temple, and her left lip had been split. Blood was dribbling from the side of her mouth.

"Oh, my God! Oh, my God! Lacy, what happened to your face? How did you get here?"

Lacy finally composed herself, looked over at me, and, between sobs, said, "Sandy...hated to call you so late...didn't know who else to call. Thanks for coming. Just take me to the sorority house."

"What? Lacy, before I move this car you've got to tell me what happened."

"Sandy, I can't. I know it sounds stupid, but I just can't tell you." And with that statement Lacy began to cry again.

"Lacy, we're friends, and I promise not to tell a soul anything you tell me. Did someone hit you?"

There was a long minute of silence, punctuated by Lacy's sobs.

"Did they? Lacy! Did they?"

"Yes, but I can't tell you anymore."

Lacy was almost out of control with her crying, and, as I looked at her, my temper soared.

"Damn, probably one of those sorry guys you've been dating," I muttered.

"No."

"No?"

"It wasn't one of the guys."

"No, not one of the guys I've been dating. Okay, let's skip the who did it. How did you get out here on the edge of town?"

Lacy began to cry again, and I reached over to put my arm around her.

"Lacy, I'm here; you're going to be okay." I tried to comfort her, but she was so distraught that she couldn't stop crying.

"Oh, Sandy, it was horrible," she said between sobs.

"He hit me, again and again, and then he opened the door and kicked me until I fell out on the side of the road! When I hit the ground my dress ripped, and my hip was bruised! I can barely walk! My shoes fell off in the car, and it took me nearly an hour to walk on that rocky side road to the truck stop!" Lacy was so hurt and embarrassed that she dropped her head in her lap and continued to cry.

"We're going to the police station, Lacy." I pulled out on the highway and headed back toward Fayetteville.

"Sandy, no! No! I can't! I can't!" Lacy screamed. She sat up in the seat and tried to grab the steering wheel.

"What? Why on earth can't you?"

"I'll be ruined if I do."

"That doesn't make a bit of sense, Lacy. Somebody needs to be arrested for beating you up and throwing you out on the side of the road. Hell, one look at you, and a police car will be on its way to get him."

"Sandy, stop this car! If you head for the police station, I'm jumping out!"

"Lacy, you can't let someone beat you half to death and not do anything about it. You've got to tell me what happened."

Lacy took a deep breath and composed herself somewhat. With a look of resignation she said, "I can't go to the police station, Sandy. Pull over, and I'll tell you why."

I pulled into the IGA grocery store parking lot. Lacy wiped her eyes, looked over at me, and started trying to tell me what had happened.

"Sandy, you're the only person in the world who will ever know what happened to me tonight. As far as my sorority sisters are concerned, I've been in a minor car wreck."

Lacy wiped the blood off her lip, and a tear ran down the side of her face as she continued.

"I had a date with Chuck, one of the guys I've been dating, and he was supposed to pick me up at eight o'clock. But, at about a quarter to eight, he called and told me he couldn't make it. Then he said he wanted me to do him a big favor and go out with one of his friends. It sounded a little fishy, but, after he begged me, I finally agreed. He said that his friend was very shy, and he didn't want to come in the house to pick me up. I was to walk up to the corner, and at eight o'clock he'd pick me up. Sandy, I know I should have hung up the phone right then and there, but he kept talking and finally convinced me. At eight o'clock I walked to the corner and stood there, and, about five minutes later, a flashy blue Chevy pulled up, and this man called out to me. I nodded and walked over to the car.

I thought I recognized the car, but, before I could remember where I'd seen it, he reached across and pushed the door open, and I got in. I should have jumped right back out, because, when I looked across at the man driving, I knew it wasn't a student. It was Bull Jenkins. First, I told him to stop the car and let me out, and I reached for the door handle to open the door.

"'Wait a minute, Lacy,' he said to me, and he pulled away from the curb before I could get out. 'I'm Jim Jenkins, a good friend of Chuck's.'

"I don't care. Take me back to the sorority house right now!" I yelled. "Sandy, he was so drunk that I could smell alcohol on his breath, and he was slurring his words. He said he wanted to take me to the drive-in, but I kept telling him no. And then I could tell he was getting mad and I wanted out of that car so bad, but he wouldn't pull over. Finally, he said that I must think I was too good for him, and he started calling me the most horrible names. Sandy, I was scared, and I started to beg him. I'd heard some terrible things about Bull Jenkins, and the way he was looking at me was scaring me to death.

He started talking about some of the guys I've been out with and he made me feel so dirty. Sure, I've made love to some of the guys I've dated, but I knew right then and there that I wasn't going to let this drunken coach touch me. He didn't take no for an answer. I was praying that a State Trooper would stop us, because he was so drunk that he was weaving all over the road. He headed north, and, when he couldn't get me to agree to stop at the drive-in, he pulled off the highway and drove about a mile down a little rocky side road until he came to a place to park. Then it was just horrible. He moved over by me, pawed me, and tried to force me into having sex with him. After a struggle, I slapped him, and then he started getting violent, screaming the vilest things, then all of a sudden, he hit me, knocking me back against the window. When I screamed he hit me again and again, and then he opened my door and kicked me until I fell on that rocky road."

"My God, Lacy, why won't you let me turn him in to the police? They'll not only charge him with assault, but attempted rape."

"I can't do it, Sandy. It would ruin me."

"Ruin you?"

"Yes, after he kicked me out of the car he walked around to where I was laying on the ground and said that if I told anybody or went to the police he would ruin me."

"How could he ruin you? It looks like he's the one who would be in trouble."

"Sandy, he told me if I went to the police he would have all the guys I've had sex with stand up and testify to how easy I was. He told me that everybody on campus would hate me because I was accusing one of the coaches right before the big Texas game. I'm not going to the police, Sandy."

I sat there, stunned, so angry that I was gritting my teeth. Then I looked over at Lacy, who was covered with bruises, scrapes, and blood. Even as battered as she was, she wasn't going to the police. I understood.

"Okay, Lacy, I know you're not going to the police, but we've got to clean you up enough to go back to your sorority house."

Lacy smiled a faint smile and nodded. I pulled out and drove down the street to an all-night wash-a-teria. After about thirty minutes, Lacy had managed to clean the scratches, wipe off the blood, and put on a little make-up.

She sat there in silence as I drove her back to the sorority house. I walked her to the door, and she stopped on the front steps for a moment, looked back at me, and softly said, "Sandy, you're a wonderful friend. I don't know what I'd have done without you. Thanks." She leaned down and kissed me very lightly on the cheek, but then, before she walked into the house, she drew herself up and said, "Sandy, that's it. I'm never going out on another date as long as I'm in school here."

"Lacy, you're a wonderful girl. Don't let something like this foul up your life."

"No, Sandy, maybe this was what I needed to make me stop the stupid stuff I've been doing! Never again, and I mean it! Something like this will never happen again!"

She looked as determined as anyone I've ever seen. Then she smiled and said, "Goodnight, Sandy, and thanks again."

"Goodnight, Lacy." I turned around and started back to the car; still thinking about how bad Lacy had looked when I picked her up. I'd walked around to the driver's side of the car when I heard someone call out, "Hey, you, come here."

The man's voice sounded slurred, and I thought it was some drunk asking for directions.

I turned around and saw a man in a blue '57 Chevy motioning me to come over. I thought I recognized the car, but it didn't occur to me that it could be Bull Jenkins. When I walked back to where he was parked, he stuck his head out the window and asked, "Hey, did you just drop off Lacy Darnell?"

"Huh?"

"Lacy Darnell, was that Lacy Darnell?"

"Yeah, why?"

"Oh, I was just checking up on her. We had a date tonight, and she was a little upset. I wanted to be sure that she got back okay."

I was beside the car now, and, when I looked at the driver, who was obviously drunk, I recognized him. He cocked his flushed red face out the car window, waiting for me to answer.

"You were out with Lacy tonight?" I started to see red.

"Yeah, you know, she puts out, and I thought I'd get a little, but she turned out to be a real bitch. I had to make her get out of the car." He gave me a drunken smirk, and I exploded.

"You worthless drunk!" I yelled. "You beat her up!"

"Hey, hold your mouth down, boy. She's just a whore. What if I did rough her up a little bit? Damn her anyway, putting out like Santa Claus and too good to screw me." He laughed a stupid, drunk laugh as if he thought his "Santa Claus" line was funny. Then he continued.

"Hell, she deserved a kick in the ass. You think she's gonna keep her mouth shut?" He was still grinning as if he had just had a little argument with someone, and, from the way he talked about Lacy, I knew that he wasn't worried about beating her up. I was in a blind rage. If I'd had a gun I would have blown his brains out right then and there, but all I had were my fists. As I looked at the fat, red-faced, drunken coach sitting there, I decided I had to do something, even if it got me kicked out of school. I leaned against the car door with my knee so that he couldn't open it, reached in, grabbed his full head of hair with one hand, jerked his head into the open window, and began to punch him in the face with my left hand. After two summers of throwing bales of hay on a flatbed truck, my shoulders and arms were strong and well developed. The first couple of punches shocked him, and he tried to jerk away and push the car door open, but I kept a death grip on his hair, and my whole body was pressed against the car door to keep him from opening it. He was so drunk that he could hardly resist, and the next three punches dazed him so that he was unable to defend himself.

I know I should have stopped, but the anger wouldn't let me. Finally, as his head went limp in my hand, I turned loose, shoved him down in the front seat, and walked back to my car. On the way back to the dorm I wondered if he'd call the police when he came to, but, considering what he'd done to Lacy, I figured that he wouldn't. He didn't.

26.

Mr. Football, Vi, Lacy, and...Bull

I met Vi at the Union the following Monday, and all she could talk about was Mr. Football and the upcoming game, the Texas game. My God, it was two weeks away, and everybody—but me—was already getting ready for next week, which would be Beat Texas Week. We talked for a few minutes, and then Vi leaned over the table.

"Sandy, I probably shouldn't tell you this, but Bill is going to be the star of the Texas game."

"Oh, really? How do you know that before the game's even been played?" I could barely conceal my disgust.

"Coach Jenkins has come up with several new plays and two trick plays. Bill will be the one who stars in them. You know, Bill was a quarterback in high school, and they made him a running back in college. Well, he's a good passer, but Coach has never let him throw a pass in college. The last thing Texas will expect is for Bill to throw a pass when he takes a pitchout."

"Well, maybe, but he can't just drop back and pass. They're not that stupid."

"Of course not. Some of the trick plays include one of the ends and the quarterback. Bill said everybody will expect him to run when they pitch out to him, but he'll fake a run and then pass back to the quarterback, who will pass back to him, and then—well—but it's a lot more complicated than that. Bill has been trying to memorize the plays, and he even takes the playbook with him when we go on dates."

I nodded. Yeah, I'll bet the dumb jock is about to go blind looking at all those X's and O's.

"Oh, Vi, plays like that are usually a disaster. Surely Arkansas can beat Texas without a bunch of trick plays? Hell, we've beaten 'em two years in a row."

"Sandy, so far this has been a terrible year for Arkansas, so I don't care how we beat those jerks. If Coach thinks these plays will help, then I think it's great. God, I hate those damn 'horns!"

I could see Vi's eyes flash when she talked about beating Texas. Of course, even I wanted to beat Texas. Then Vi acted as if she'd just remembered something important, and she leaned across the table to tell me.

"Oh, Sandy, something terrible happened, and Bill is all upset about it. A gang right in downtown Fayetteville attacked Coach Jenkins, the coach who coaches Bill. They beat him so badly that you couldn't recognize him. Both eyes were black, and his nose is broken."

Hell, it was hard to keep from smiling—two black eyes and a broken nose. Yes!

"Did he say who did it?" I said. I leaned back in the booth, holding back a smile, waiting to hear the details about the "gang."

"Yes, it was five big guys, and he recognized one of them."

I gave Vi a little smirk and said, "Sounds like Bull Jenkins got a dose of the same medicine he's been passing out. You know he's bisexual, and every semester he ends up fooling around with some of the new guys. Hell, he slaps those freshmen around like they're rag dolls."

"Oh, Sandy, surely you don't believe that gossip."

"Gossip my ass! It's true, Vi. Hell, you know damn well the

sororities have even warned the girls about letting him give the girls rides."

Vi knew that was true, and she nodded her head. "Well, maybe he is a little different."

"A little different? If he wasn't a good coach, his ass would be in jail right now."

Then I thought of a little zinger. "I've heard that he and Mr. Football are fooling around." Well, that was a lie, but I couldn't resist the opportunity to trash Bill Tucker, even if he was an Assistant Scoutmaster and blood donor.

"Sandy, it's terrible to say that about Bill and Coach Jenkins! Bill sure isn't a homosexual, and I believe Coach Jenkins, if he says that a gang beat him up."

"Well, just tell me, Vi. Have you ever heard of a Fayetteville gang or a university gang?"

"No, but it must be a gang we don't know about, and I'd hate to be that gang member he recognized. Coach Jenkins has gotten several guys together to teach him a lesson."

Well, that little statement worried me, but I'd decided I wanted Vi to know I was the gang.

"It wasn't a gang, Vi."

"Just how do you know?"

"Vi, I'm going to tell you something, but you've got to promise never to tell a soul, especially Bill Tucker."

"What?"

"I'm serious, Vi. I'm not going to tell you anything if you don't promise to keep it a secret."

"Sandy, we're friends. I won't breathe a thing you tell me."

"Okay, Vi, here goes. Last Saturday night I was sitting around studying when Lacy Darnell called me." I continued with the story, and when I got to the part about Bull beating Lacy up, Vi was irate. I finished with the beating I'd given Bull.

"I'm the five man gang, Vi."

"Sandy, I can't believe he'd beat up Lacy! Is she all right?"

"Yes, she still has some bad bruises and several cuts. But she's going to be okay."

"God, I can't believe that low-life, Bull Jenkins." She gritted her teeth and said, "I'm glad you worked him over, Sandy. Men like that need to be put in jail."

Well, women stick together, and even though Vi was ticked off when she saw me having a Coke with Lacy, the very idea of someone like Bull beating up a woman was more important.

"Remember, Vi, you can't tell a soul."

"I won't Sandy, but I think, from what Bill said, he knows you beat him up. You'd better watch out. Bull's got several guys who will do just about anything he wants them to, and, according to Bill, they're going after whoever beat up Bull."

"They must be the guys he's fooling around with. God, he is one lowlife. I'll watch out for them, Vi. Thanks for telling me. Now remember, don't mention this to anyone."

Vi got up and left after another few minutes, and I sat there, thinking about Bull getting several guys to beat me up. I didn't think they'd jump me during the day, on campus, and risk getting caught, but I would probably run into them down at the bowling alley or at George's. I'd make it a point not to be by myself when I left campus.

After a couple of days, I'd pretty much forgotten about anybody being out to get me, and the next night I walked down the street to George's and spent a couple of hours drinking beer and flirting with Millie. It was almost 12 o'clock when I walked around to the back door of the dorm, and, as I approached the door, I noticed three guys walk out from behind a parked car and start toward me. I was almost to the steps of the dorm when I heard one of them call my name.

"Hey, you! Sandy?"

"Yeah. Why?" I turned around and stopped, puzzled as to why someone would be looking for me so late.

The three guys hurried up to where I was standing, and the

one in front said, "Well, you asshole, we're here to give you something, compliments of Coach Jenkins."

Oh, my God! It's Billy Ray Schmidt. He was the guy I'd embarrassed at George's when he made Millie drop a tray of dishes. As he approached me, I saw him clench his fists and draw back to swing. The other two were right behind him, and, as they approached, they blocked any possible way I could run. My mind was racing. There was no way I could get in the dorm, and a scream for help was useless. Billy Ray was already drawing back to throw the first punch when I kicked him as hard as I could—right in the groin.

"Aaaaaa! I'm gonna kill you for that!"

He bent over, grabbed his groin, and lowered his head down in front of me. I swung with all my might and hit his bent-over face, knocking him back, but now the two other guys were all over me, pounding me from both sides. I ducked most of the punches initially, but then I felt a fist hit the side of my head, and I banged back against the dorm door and fell onto the sidewalk, both of them still kicking me. I backed up against the door, trying to get up, but two good blows smacked me right in the face and knocked me back down, and a vicious kick in the ribs nearly killed me. I rolled over, trying to dodge the kicks and blows as I pulled my pocketknife out. Finally, I got the knife open, gripped it in my fist, and stabbed straight down into the top of the foot of the fellow who had just kicked me.

"Ahaaaaa! He stabbed me!"

I pulled the knife out of the top of his foot and began to slash and stab at anything in sight. The first swipe cut the pants and leg of another one of the jerks, and blood streamed down his leg as he cursed and yelled. I was up on my knees now, and another sweep caught an outstretched fist, sending blood all over the steps. They were backing away now, and I was screaming, slashing, and yelling as I went after them.

"You tell Bull that he's going to regret the hell out of this!" I yelled at them, cursing and waving the knife. Well, a little pocketknife with the three inch blade turned the tide, but they had done some damage—serious damage.

"Damn," I muttered, as every breath sent excruciating pain through my rib cage, "That worthless bastard broke some ribs when he kicked me!" I went into the dorm and tried to lie down, but my aching ribs were killing me, and I couldn't rest. Every time I took a deep breath, pain shot through my chest. I was having trouble even breathing.

After trying to get some relief for a couple of hours, I got up and stood there in the room, still muttering about what to do about Bull Jenkins. The pain had me wild, and I was crazy to get back at him. As I looked over at my coffeepot and sugar bowl, an idea popped into my mind.

"Sugar! Yeah, sugar. I need a pound of sugar for that worthless coach, and hey, this golf ball will work just fine." I picked up a golf ball that was sitting on my dresser, a can of sugar that I used to sweeten my coffee, and, in a few minutes, I'd poured the sugar into a sack and was out the door.

"This'll teach the worthless so-in-so a lesson," I muttered in a fit of rage. In my entire life I'd never been so mad—or hurt so badly. I headed down the hill to Carlson Terrace, the new university housing complex near the stadium. Hell, with Bull's reputation, everybody on campus knew where he lived. As I walked down the hill from Williams House, the ache in my chest was so bad that every step I took sent a shooting pain through my rib cage, and, by the time I reached the apartment complex, I was wild with pain. I was looking for Bull's '57 Chevy with the special deep-blue paint job. Finally, on the north parking lot, I found Bull's pride and joy. The special paint job literally sparkled as the car sat under a streetlight.

"Okay, Mr. Big Shot Football Coach, here's something from Lacy and me. This'll make your fancy car freeze up like its got lockjaw," I mumbled. I looked to see if anybody was around, and then I took the gasoline cap off, poured the sack of sugar into the gas tank, and dropped the golf ball in. When I finished with the sugar and golf ball, I stood back and looked at Bull's freshly waxed car.

"Well, I wonder if that's some of that new wax that won't scratch," I muttered. I reached into my pocket and pulled out a set of keys, stuck the biggest key between my index finger and thumb, and walked beside the car, digging the key into the custom paint job. I circled the car twice, and then made a big S on the top of the hood.

"I'll be; that's just ordinary wax." I stepped back to admire the two deep gouges that cut into the metallic blue paint and the S on the hood. "I'll bet you'll regret having me beat up when you see an S for Sandy—big-deal football coach!"

Then, before I left, I pulled out my pocketknife and slit all four tires.

"Have your goons beat me up, will ya," I mumbled. I walked away, and, with every step I took, pain shot through my side. As I left the parking lot, I could still hear the air hissing from the slit tires.

Thinking back on what I did, I realize I was totally out of control, but my cracked ribs were hurting so badly I'd lost all sense of reason. Hell, I'd gone overboard, and, before I got back up the hill, I was regretting what I'd done. I knew my ribs needed medical attention, so I walked across campus to the Washington County Hospital Emergency Room, and, in a few minutes, I was meeting with the doctor on duty. An x-ray showed two cracked ribs. My God, when he wrapped my chest and tightened that bandage I nearly blacked out from the pain.

After a couple of days, the pain subsidized enough for me to work at the bookstore and return to class. I phoned Vi and told her what happened in the dorm parking lot, but I didn't tell her anything about Bull's car. Vi rushed into the bookstore that afternoon and motioned for me to come outside.

"Sandy, I know those guys shouldn't have beat you up, but what you did to Bull's car has him absolutely wild. You must have been totally out of control."

"Heck, Vi, how do you know it was me? Shoot, a lot of people hate Bull's guts."

"Oh, come on, Sandy, you're talking to me. Don't you think a big S on the hood was a little obvious?"

"Vi, I was hurting so badly I could barely walk. I wanted him to know I was paying him back for what he did to Lacy and for those goons breaking my ribs."

"Well, Sandy, Bill told me what happened when Bull found his car. Evidently, he made such a racket screaming out in the parking lot that you could hear him from all over Carson Terrace. But what was strange was that he didn't call the police. He managed to change his tires and get the car started, but halfway to town it quit on him. The motor froze up, and later that day a mechanic drilled out the cylinders, which he said were full of sugar. Bull got his car back only to have it run for a few minutes and then stall. The mechanic told him that something was blocking the gas fuel line intake."

"A golf ball."

"What?"

"Yeah, I dropped a golf ball in his fuel tank after I poured in the sugar."

"Sandy, don't you think you went a little overboard? You've stirred up more trouble than you can imagine."

"Well, hell, Vi. What am I supposed to do after that goon beats up Lacy and has his thugs break my ribs? I was in so much pain that I couldn't think clearly. Maybe I did get carried away."

"You sure did, Sandy. Bull has been crazy ever since you vandalized his car. He's got a terrible temper, and I'm afraid he may do something irrational. Bill said he swears that he'll get the guy who vandalized his car."

"Well, let him come after me. I'm sure not afraid of a fat, fifty year old coach. I hope that car drives him crazy."

"Don't say that, Sandy. Just before I came over here I talked to Bill, and he told me that Bull is so distraught that he's threatened to kill the person who did it."

"Huh, well, do you think he knows who did it?"

"Yes, he mentioned to Bill that he knew."

"Did he give Bill a name?"

"No, he didn't Sandy, but he knows it's you."

I took a deep breath and didn't say a word. Oh my God, an out-of-his-mind nut of a coach out to kill me.

She shook her head, moved closer to me, and whispered in my ear, "Sandy, he's got a gun, and Bill is afraid that he's going to shoot the person who vandalized his car. That's why I'm here. After those thugs beat you up, I don't blame you for what you did. But you were right about him; he's crazy. Be careful. I don't want anything to happen to you."

Vi rushed off to class, and I went back to the bookstore, so worried that I could hardly breathe. That sorry coach obviously knew where I lived, since he'd sent his thugs to beat me up, and he probably knew that I worked in the bookstore. If he was going to shoot me, I didn't think it would be in the bookstore or the Student Union, in front of everybody. He'd probably try something around the dorm or on campus after dark. Honestly, I hadn't been concerned about Bull coming after me until Vi told me that he had a gun. Now all I could think about was him slinking around campus, looking for me. Hell, from what Vi had told me, I figured he was about one step from going totally crazy.

Tuesday night I was coming back from a movie with Benny, and we'd just separated, heading for different dorms. As I walked under the streetlight in front of my dorm, I saw a shadowy figure move out from the edge of the building and walk hurriedly to the front door of the dorm, where he would arrive before I could get there. Normally, I'd just have kept walking to the front door, but I was so jumpy after what Vi had told me that I broke, ran back toward the parking lot across the street, and ducked behind a car. God, my heart was thumping so loud that I could hear it. I held my breath and looked out from around the back of a car. Oh, my God, the man was running toward the parking lot. I dropped down, slipped under a car, and waited. In a few seconds, I heard the crunching of gravel as someone moved through the lot. Those next couple of minutes were the longest in my life as I lay under that car, trying not to make a sound. He began to walk around the lot, looking behind and under cars, and then, just before he came to where I was hiding, a car full of guys pulled in to park and began to scramble out. He left. I pulled myself out from under the car and ran across the street to my dorm.

Oh, my God! Oh, my God! I was terrified.

Well, looking back on it, I guess I didn't know for sure that it was Bull, but hell, in my state of mind I was jumping every time someone walked out from behind a car or building.

I slept very little that night. There was not a doubt in my mind he was crazy, and I was sure he was determined to kill me. The next day I was so jumpy and nervous that I couldn't concentrate on anything but Bull. I helped Bob close up the bookstore for the night, and I started back across campus, thinking about what I could do about that sorry nut of a coach. It was dark. All of a sudden, I realized that someone was following me, and, as I passed the library, I caught a glimpse of him when he stepped out from behind a tree.

I tried to act as if I hadn't seen him, and, when I turned the corner at the west end of the Chemistry building, I sprinted toward the Greek Theatre. I wasn't quick enough, and he saw me. There was the sound of running on the sidewalk behind me, and I jumped behind some evergreens on the upper west end of the Theatre, hoping to hide behind one. But suddenly the person burst out of the shadows. He wasn't twenty yards behind me, and I could see the gun in his outstretched hand.

Oh, my God! It's Bull, and he's going to kill me, flashed across my mind. I jumped, ducked, and sprinted toward the street as I heard a loud pop, almost like a firecracker, then another and another. A bullet ripped through some leaves right beside my head as I cleared the bushes near the street. I ran as fast as I could up the street, and then it was quiet, deathly quiet. There wasn't a sound or any trace of Bull. He'd vanished. I knew the guys in the dorms across the street would just ignore the shots, thinking that they were firecrackers. I was trembling by the time I reached my room, and, as I sat on the edge of my bed with my ribs throbbing, I tried to come up with some way to stop the crazy idiot. Going to the police was useless. Bull was a popular coach, and they sure would believe him over me. And anyway, I'd have to tell them about vandalizing his car. With my luck, they'd arrest me and forget about Bull. I knew right then that I'd have to come up with some kind of a plan, or sooner or later he'd kill me. I really thought he'd lost his mind and was determined to do something totally irrational.

The next day my ribs were starting to feel a little better. Vi came by the bookstore and we walked into the Union to get a Coke. We talked about Bull, and Vi told me how he had continued to rave on and on about how he was going to get whoever had vandalized his car. When it was time for us to leave for class, Vi and I got out of the booth at about the same time that several football players walked into the Union. One of them was Mr. Football. Vi didn't see him, but I saw him stop, stand there, and watch us leave. I gave Vi a squeeze around the shoulders and kissed her on the cheek, just for his benefit. She looked a little surprised, but smiled and walked on out of the Union without ever seeing her boyfriend.

That afternoon I was finishing my shift at the bookstore, and I was about to leave when Mr. Football strutted in. He walked straight over to the counter where I was standing. Bob and I were the only ones left in the store, and he was back in the storeroom, stacking up used books.

"You Sandy Carson?"

"Uh, yeah."

"You the guy I saw with Vi Botner this morning?"

"Uh huh, why?"

"Leave my girl alone, or I'm gonna beat the crap outta you." He leaned over the counter and got right up in my face.

"What are you talking about?"

"Don't give me that bull. I saw you in the Union with her this morning."

"Hell, we were just having a Coke and talking. And if we want to have a Coke and talk, it's none of your damn business."

"Huh? Listen, you worthless lowlife, I'm not gonna stand here and argue with you. Stay away from her! Do you know who I am?"

Well, Mr. Big Shot puffed up and stood on his toes so that he could look me in the eye and tried to act like some tough guy who was going to knock the crap out of me. I was standing behind the counter, and I sure didn't think that I had anything to be concerned about, at least not right that minute. Then, instead of trying to calm him down, my in-your-face streak took over.

"Yeah, I know who you are! You muscle-headed moron! Get lost!" I leaned over the counter until our faces were inches apart. I was just about to smirk when his fist hit my jaw, sending me staggering back against the rack of books behind me.

"You worthless bastard!" I yelled as he turned and left the bookstore. "Damn! Damn!" I muttered, rubbing my jaw. His fist had busted the side of my lip and cut the inside of my jaw. Blood was filling my mouth. I ran to the restroom, not really believing what had happened: slugged in the mouth for having a Coke with Vi. God, what a gorilla. Well, I guessed my mouthing off had something to do with it, but hell, hitting someone working in a bookstore just for mouthing off is just about the most redneck, stupid, goon-like thing I can think of—at least that's what I thought right after it happened. The next day I was waiting on Vi when she finished Civics class.

"Vi, over here," I called out from the bottom of the stairs. She saw me, hurried over close, and whispered, "Sandy, I can't have a Coke with you. Bill saw us yesterday, and he got upset about it." She walked over to me, and I turned my face up to her.

"Yeah, I know. Look at my lip."

"He hit you?"

"Uh huh, while I was standing behind the counter in the bookstore."

"I can't believe he'd do such a thing."

"Well, he did, and he's lucky that I didn't call the police and have him arrested."

"Oh, Sandy, don't do anything like that. He's too important to the football team. You want us to beat Texas, don't you? Daddy would just have a heart attack if Bill didn't play."

"Beat Texas? Oh, for God's sake, Vi! Surely there's more to life than football! Damn, I can't believe you'd take up for him! We didn't do anything!"

"I know it, Sandy, but he's uptight about the big game, and he's real irritable. He's still trying to memorize all those new plays. You know, those trick plays that I told you about."

"Really?"

"Yes, we're going out tonight, and he told me that he'd have to spend some time studying them while we were out."

Something clicked, and I asked Vi, "Uh, where are y'all going on your date?"

"Just to the movies at the UARK. Bill wants to see that new French star, Bridget Bardot. I've gotta go, Sandy. Maybe we can meet and talk while Bill is at football practice."

"Yeah, okay, I'll see you later."

I was already thinking about Bill, the new plays, and the big game. I guess my broken ribs, a battered Lacy, and a punch in the mouth had poisoned my mind as far as Arkansas football was concerned, because what I was thinking would have infuriated any Razorback fan. Over the years, that compulsive, obsessive attitude has caused me a lot of trouble, and now, against my better judgment, I was considering a betrayal of my school. I'd blanked everything from my mind except the overriding desire to get even with that sorry Bill Tucker and his worthless coach. I had a plan.

Late that afternoon I stopped by John Dorman's room. John was in one of my classes, and he mouthed off constantly about his stupid brother, who was attending the University of Texas. It seems he was a rabid Longhorn fan who was always calling John and telling him how Texas was going to kick Arkansas's ass.

John was sitting in his room studying when I walked in.

"Hey, John, heard from that tea-sipping brother of yours lately?"

"Yeah, the dumb clown called a few minutes ago, bragging about how they were gonna whip our butts."

"Is he a fraternity man?"

"Yeah, an Alpha Chi."

I'd heard all that I wanted to hear.

"Well, I'll let you get back to studying. He'll really have to eat crow when we kick the crap out of 'em."

"Yeah, see you, Sandy."

I walked back to the dorm, checked to be sure the hall was empty, and dialed information for Austin, Texas, on the hall phone. Soon I had the Alpha Chi fraternity on the line.

"Let me speak to Buddy Dorman."

In a few minutes Buddy picked up the phone.

"Yeah, this is Buddy."

"Buddy, do you want some insurance to be sure that Texas wins next week's game against Arkansas?"

"What?"

"Yeah, some insurance. I've got something that would give Texas an edge in the game. Hell, after getting your ass kicked for the last two years, it looks like you guys need something extra."

"Who is this, and what in the hell are you talking about?"

"You can call me Randy, and I'm talking about providing you with a copy of some new trick plays that Arkansas will use against Texas."

"Is this some stupid joke?"

"It might be, but what if it were the truth? Do you have any interest?"

"Uh, well, yeah, maybe."

"Maybe isn't good enough. If I provide you with the trick plays, are you interested enough to pay 500 bucks for them?"

"Are you serious?"

"Yeah, I sure am. Now, can we do business?"

"Well, yeah, I think so, but I don't have 500 bucks right now."

"Shit, Buddy, there's a 1000 Texas alumni who will step up with the money if you tell them what you can get." I didn't care about the money, but I thought if I offered to sell the trick plays, he might believe they were real.

"Uh huh, that's probably right, but how am I going to know that the plays are legit?"

"Bring along someone who understands football and how coaches' diagram plays. They can check the plays before any money changes hands."

"Okay, that sounds fair. But how are we going to get together?"

"I've thought it out, and this is what I've come up with. Sunday afternoon at one o'clock I'll be sitting in my car on the side of the road on State Line Avenue in Texarkana, just on the Arkansas side of the line. My car is a green 1950 Ford, and there'll be a white handkerchief tied to the radio antenna."

"Well, I'm not sure I can raise the money by then. Can I call you back and tell you if I have it?"

"Nope, this is the only time we'll talk. I'll be sitting in that 1950 Ford at one o'clock. If you want Texas to beat Arkansas, you'll be there to meet me. Goodbye." Damn, when I said that, I had a queasy, sick feeling come over me. I couldn't believe what I had just agreed to.

That night I waited until after the Bridget Bardot movie had started and walked down to the UARK Theater on Dixon Street to look for Mr. Football's car. He'd have to park back behind the theater on a side street, because Dixon Street on Friday night was always packed with cars. It didn't take 15 minutes to find his car.

I had a clothes hanger bent in the shape of a hook to unlock his car door with. However, Mr. Football hadn't locked his car. In the backseat there was a folder with the trick plays. I put the folder under my arm, walked across the street to the bowling alley, found an empty table, and proceed to copy and trace the plays. I was finished and had the folder back in his car long before the movie was over. I folded up the paper with the plays on it and walked up the street to the Delta House. It had only taken 30 minutes to get the trick plays, and I was early for the Saturday poker game.

The next morning I rented Billy Rob's car for the day, left Fayetteville, and headed for Texarkana. As I drove south from Fayetteville on Highway 71 I started thinking about what I was doing. I'd been born and raised in Arkansas, and ever since I could remember, the Razorbacks had been idolized by everyone, including me. Of course, there were several important games on Arkansas's schedule, but the hated Texas Longhorns topped everybody's list of teams you wanted to beat. A win over Texas insured a successful season, even if Arkansas lost every other game, which, so far that season, they had. However, the Razorbacks had been improving in each game, and had only lost by a few points to several ranked teams. Everyone was expecting them to start winning.

I thought of all the glum faces in Arkansas if Texas clobbered the Hogs, and I began to have some doubts. Hell, they were more than doubts. I was almost ready to back out. However, as I rubbed my busted lip, felt the pain from my cracked ribs, and thought about Lacy and her blood-matted hair, I started seeing red, and it wasn't Razorback red. Yes, I'd made up my mind. I was going to betray my school and state by selling the plays to Buddy Dorman, knowing they'd be heading straight to Texas's defensive line coach. I've always looked back on that moment, which I considered the low point in my college life.

By noon I was in Texarkana. I stopped by Bryces's Cafeteria for lunch, and at one o'clock I drove to State Line Avenue, pulled over onto the shoulder of the road, and tied a white handkerchief on my radio antenna. At 15 minutes, past one I noticed a car driving very slowly. As it approached where I was parked, it pulled in behind me and two guys got out and walked up to my car.

"You Randy?"

"Yeah, get in the back seat and let's talk."

"I'm Buddy, and I brought Delbert Williamson. He knows football."

One glance at Delbert, a beefy, no-neck lineman, and I was sure that those plays would go straight to his defensive line coach. I had that queasy feeling again, but I was committed.

"Sure, get in, and I'll let y'all take a look at the plays."

Delbert poured over the plays, and ten minutes later, he nodded.

"Yeah, these came from an Arkansas coach all right. There're good."

"Okay, have you got the cash, Buddy?"

"Yeah, right here." Buddy handed me a fat envelope containing $500.00, and I stuck it in my pocket.

Delbert looked a little uncomfortable, still gripping the plays in his meaty hand as he leaned forward in the seat to speak to me.

"Uh, one thing before we go. I thought all y'all Arkansas guys were rabid Razorback fans. Why in the hell would you betray Arkansas? Hell, when we spot 'em trying to run these plays, we're gonna put nails in Arkansas's coffin."

Damn, I nearly choked when he said that, but I took a deep breath and said, "It's a long story that includes a woman, cracked ribs, a sorry coach, and a busted face."

"Huh, well, it sounds like somebody is tryin' to get even," Buddy said.

"I'd hate to be Bill Tucker when he tries to fool our defensive line with some of this crap," said Delbert. He grinned at me, shaking the paper with the plays on it.

I put on a little fake macho for Delbert's benefit, "Nail him! He damn sure deserves it!"

"I sure as hell will. You know, when a trick play is spotted, it's usually one hell of a loss for the team that tries to run it," said Delbert. He chuckled in anticipation.

I was beginning to feel more and more uncomfortable talking about how my betrayal of the Razorbacks was going to result in disaster next Saturday. I needed to get away from those guys.

"Listen, I gotta go. It's a long drive back to Fayetteville."

"Yeah, us too."

Buddy and Delbert got out and started walking back to their car. Delbert waved the plays at me and yelled, "Thank youuu-uuuu!" They were grinning and joking back and forth as they pulled around me and headed back to Austin. I had a sick feeling as I turned the car around and headed north.

The six hour drive back to Fayetteville gave me plenty of time to think about what I'd just done, and my thoughts drifted from regret to satisfaction. When I was almost to Mountainburg, I reached in my jacket pocket and took out the envelope with the $500.00 in it. As I opened it, the sight of those five one hundred dollar bills nearly sent me over the edge. I couldn't stand it any longer, and as I crossed the White River, I threw the envelope with the $500.00 in it out the window, hopping that would ease my mind. For the rest of the trip, just to keep from feeling like such a lowlife, I'd think of Lacy's battered face and my cracked ribs, and I'd rub my tongue over my busted lip. By the time I pulled into the dorm parking lot, I felt a little better. Just a little payback for Mr. Football and his worthless coach.

The Beat Texas Pep Rally was on Thursday night, and I went by the Greek Theatre with Benny and some of our friends from the dorm, and, after about 20 minutes of constant yelling and listening to several thousand Razorback fans who were all screaming "Beat Texas" I began to have second thoughts again. I started wondering if I should alert the Arkansas coaches that the trick plays were out, but I changed my mind when Mr. Football walked on stage to say a few words.

"Hey! Y'all! We're gonna whip their sorry ass!" he screamed, and then he yelled, "Go Hogs!"

He was strutting around on the stage, acting as if he were God's gift to co-eds. I wanted to throw up when he got right out in front of the crowd and started pumping his fists like a locomotive as he screamed, "Beat Texas! Beat Texas! Whoooooo! Pig! Sooie!" Hell, after about five minutes of that, everybody was so worked up yelling that one cheerleader fainted and the Razorback band went into a crazy rendition of the fight song while Mr. Football strutted across the stage, pumping his fist and continuing to scream, "Beat Texas!" The pep rally seemed to go on forever.

For the rest of the week the hype about the game continued until even I was interested in it. The game was to be played at Memorial Stadium in Austin, and, that Saturday afternoon at about 1:30, I walked over to the Union just in time to hear the Arkansas announcer say that the Razorbacks were so pumped up that he was almost certain they were going to slaughter Texas. Of course, nobody ever believed those homer announcers, but I could feel the excitement in the air.

I joined about 200 students in the Student Union Grill, where a radio was blaring into loudspeakers, which were so loud that you could hardly hear yourself think. The Razorback Band played our alma mater, which a few girls tried to sing, and then the band broke into "Arkansas Fight," and everybody jumped up and yelled for about three minutes.

We were just settling down to listen to the game when, booming out of the speakers, we heard "The Eyes of Texas." I had a sick feeling as about 80,000 Texas fans roared out their alma mater. The Arkansas group in the Union tried to boo loudly enough that you couldn't hear, but, even with all the booing, that damn song almost blew us away. It ended with, "Till Gabriel blows his horn." I can tell you that the Razorback team that was standing on the sidelines waiting to play might not have been intimidated, but the 200 fans sitting in the Union who had listened to "The Eyes of Texas" played at ear-splitting levels sure were.

The game started, and it looked as if it was going to be a real cliffhanger. Then, right after the half, with Texas leading 7 to 3, The Razorbacks held Texas at midfield on the fourth down. Everybody in the Union went crazy, and the Arkansas offensive team ran onto the field, jumping around as if they were wired. I can still hear the Arkansas announcer.

"Folks, we have a fired-up Arkansas offensive team on the

241

field, and the small contingent of Arkansas fans in the end zone are screaming their heads off! Man, oh man, this is the break the Razorbacks have been looking for all day! If Arkansas can move down the field and score, the momentum will definitely be in the Hogs' favor! They're calling the Hogs down in the end zone, and everybody in the stadium is standing.

"First play from the Texas 49—Hogs at the line of scrimmage—Simmons takes the handoff—moves down the line—pitches back to Tucker. Tucker cuts back against the grain—breaks a tackle at the line of scrimmage, sidesteps the linebacker! He may go all the way! No, he's hit by the safety and is finally dropped on the Texas 42, for a big, big seven-yard gain! The Arkansas fans are going wild, and the Arkansas team is jumping around on the sidelines, so fired up that we can feel it up here in the booth! Second down and three from the Texas 42: Simmons takes the handoff again and immediately pitches back to Tucker—Tucker heads for the sidelines, trying to cut the corner, but is knocked out of bounds for no gain. The Texas band is playing "The Eyes of Texas," and the Texas fans are screaming for the 'horns to hold 'em! This could be the play of the game, folks! Wait a minute! The Hogs call time-out! The whole Arkansas team comes to the sidelines, and the Razorback coaches are talking with Simmons and Tucker. Folks, Bill Tucker can't stand still, he's so fired up! The Arkansas team runs back out on the field and lines up at the line of scrimmage. Oh, look at that!! There's only a single running back behind the quarterback! Bill Tucker is lined up three yards deeper than usual, and Davis and Blevins are split wide right. We haven't seen a formation like this today, folks. The Texas defensive captain is changing signals, and everybody in the stadium is standing. Hogs are ready: Simmons takes the handoff from center—drops back to pass! No, he laterals to Tucker, who is running right toward the Texas sidelines!—Tucker stops and is dropping back!—Bill Tucker is going to pass!—He passes back to Simmons, who hands off to the left end coming around!—My

God, he's dropping back to pass!—He passes to Tucker in the right flat!—oh, my God!"

And then there was a pause, and everybody in the Union held their breath. I knew something very good for Texas was happening, because 80,000 Texas fans in Memorial Stadium were screaming their lungs out. Then the Arkansas announcer finally got his tongue back and said, "Tucker was hit while trying to pass, and Texas picked off his wobbly pass. The Texas defensive back is at the 20, 10, 5, Texas touchdown—Tucker is still down, folks, and he's clutching his shoulder. He was hit just as he released the ball by Delbert Williamson, the 260 pound Texas All-American tackle. He really smelled out that play."

Well, after that it was all downhill for Arkansas, and Texas won 24 to 6. A thoroughly whipped bunch of Razorbacks crawled back to Fayetteville with their star, Bill Tucker, wrapped in an elastic bandage. Yeah, I felt sick about what happened.

Next Wednesday I saw Vi and asked how the game went.

"Sandy, it was terrible, and Bill got hurt when he tried that trick play. He told me the whole Texas team acted as if they were watching for that play. Some big old tackle hit him so hard that he got a terrible bruised shoulder and had to leave the game."

I nodded my head as I thought about old Delbert, the big tackle, waiting on that play. I smiled and said, "Maybe they did know about those trick plays."

"Oh, they couldn't have. What?" Vi looked at me questioningly. "Sandy, do you know something?"

"Naw, it's just possible that they did know," I teased Vi.

Well, I might occasionally do or say some stupid things, but telling a rabid Arkansas fan, who just happened to be the girl of my dreams, I'd given the Razorback's trick plays to the hated Texas Longhorns was beyond even considering.

"Umm, oh, well, Coach Jenkins said Bill will be able to play next week, and, if he finishes out the season like he started, he'll make All Southwest Conference and maybe All-American."

"Oh, come on, Vi. All-American? He's not that good."

"Sandy, you're just jealous."

Jealous? Me, jealous of a football machine? Hell, I'm not that stupid. But let me tell you something about that coach of his. Vi, that sorry coach is bad news, and I'm not kidding."

"Well, you may be right about that. Even Bill is nervous around him, but he said that Coach Jenkins has stopped talking about his car, so maybe things will blow over, and you won't have anything to worry about."

I'd decided to not tell Vi about Bull trying to shoot me. She couldn't do anything about it, and it would just worry her.

"Oh, shoot, Vi, let's don't keep talking about that stuff. How about meeting me on the front steps of Old Main tonight so that we can really talk? Meeting here in the bookstore isn't very private. I want to ask your advice about something."

Vi looked at me and smiled.

"Sandy, you asking me for advice has gotten both of us in trouble. Are you sure you want my advice?"

"No."

"No?"

"Vi, I can't help it. I want to see you, and I'd tell you anything to get you to be with me."

Vi looked shocked for a moment, and then she smiled. "I'll be there at seven." She squeezed my hand and walked away.

I was elated. It seemed that Vi did care about me, and maybe tonight would be special.

Bob came over and told me that he'd close up, so I could clock out. It was a dead time of day, and I thought about walking across the hall to the Student Union Grill for a Coke before I went back to the dorm. Then I saw someone walk through the door. Oh, my God! No! That crazy coach had walked into the bookstore.

27.

Bull, Vi, and Dickie

I was so shocked I just stood there as he walked over to the literature section and started thumbing through textbooks while he looked around. Oh, my God! Oh, my God! Sure enough, he saw me standing there, about to go out the door. I hurried out, considering that, if I went into the Union where there were 50 or 60 students, I'd be safer than if I let him follow me outside, where it was almost dark. I didn't see a soul I knew when I walked into the Union, so I took an empty booth, picked up a Coke, and pretended as if I were reading *The Traveler*, the university newspaper. I glanced over the top of the newspaper to see Bull walk through the door and head straight for me. Surely to God he's not going to do something right here in front of all these people. I stopped breathing for a moment. He walked over and got right in front of my booth, acting as if he hadn't seen me until he suddenly smiled at me.

"Hi, Sandy, it's good to see you again." He stood there and glared at me.

I could hardly open my mouth I was so scared, but I managed to say, "Hello, Coach."

He gave me a little smirk and then started to walk away. When he was about halfway across the room he looked back, patted a bulge under his shirt, and smiled at me again. He sat across the room, watching me like a hawk. When I got up to leave as a group of about ten guys started for the door, I looked over my shoulder, and, sure enough, he was following me. As soon as I walked up the basement steps and made it outside, I started running. I knew one thing for damn sure: with any head start, I could outrun that fat coach. I was gasping for breath when I made it back to my dorm room. Do something! Do something! Was all I could think. Now he'd started coming into the Union, and I was sure that he was following me around the campus like some wild man. I wondered if losing to Texas had sent him over the edge.

At around 5:30 I walked over to the dining hall and ate supper, and, although I hated to go outside and risk running into Bull, at 6:30, I slipped out a side door of the dorm, dashed down the hill through some bushes, and circled the west side of the campus. After I finished the circle, I headed for Old Main to meet Vi. That afternoon the wind had picked up, blowing right out of the north, and by seven o'clock it was gusting at about 25 miles-per-hour. My God, the wind chill was terrible, and I'd wondered all afternoon if Vi would show up for our meeting. At ten minutes till seven I was huddled in the front doorway of Old Main. Hell, I was so cold that there was no way I could sit on those icy steps. Vi was late, as usual, and it was 15 after 7 before I heard her call my name.

"Sandy?"

"Yes, Vi, over here, I'm in the doorway at the top of the stairs."

Vi hurried over and climbed the steps. She looked at me shivering and shook her head.

"Sandy, this is the stupidest thing either of us has ever done. Let's have our talk some other time, when we're not freezing to death."

I reached out and pulled her close to me. "Vi, thanks for coming. But before we go, I want to tell you something." We were so close; she turned her head up to me, and we kissed long and passionately.

"Oh, Vi, I love you. I can't help it, I always have. Please drop that sorry Bill Tucker."

"Sandy, you're sweet, and you're so special, but I can't break up with Bill. Daddy would; well, uh, Daddy would be real upset," she managed to say. "Maybe I will sometime, but not right now."

I was dejected, but I muttered, "Okay, I understand."

"Sandy, don't be that way. Didn't I come here to meet you in this horrible weather? I have some feelings for you, or I wouldn't be here."

"Yeah, I guess so," I mumbled.

"I've got to go before I freeze to death. Come here." Vi pulled me close and turned her head up for a goodbye kiss.

"Oh, Vi, you're wonderful. I love you so much." I kissed her and held her close until she pulled away.

"Bye, Sandy. See you next week at the bookstore."

"Vi, just a minute. I'm worried about something." I decided that I had to tell someone, in case Bull did kill me.

"What?"

"That crazy Bull Jenkins has been following me, and I think he's totally lost it."

"Oh, Sandy, are you sure?"

"Yeah, Vi, I am." Then, as quickly as I could, I told her some of the things that Bull had done.

"My gosh, Sandy! You've got to go to the police!"

"I can't, Vi. Who would they believe? And heck, if I told them it was because I vandalized his car, they'd probably arrest me."

"You're right, but be careful. I couldn't stand it if something happened to you."

Vi reached out and hugged me for a long minute.

"I've got to go. Please take care."

"Don't worry, I'm watching for him, and I've got a plan. See ya, Vi."

***

Saturday was a home football game for the Razorbacks. Bull would have his hands full all weekend, and that would give me

Saturday and Sunday to get ready for him. I didn't have much of a plan, but it was all I could come up with.

Saturday morning I got up early, rented Billy Rob's car, and headed for Pine Valley, telling my mother that I was homesick and wanted to see her and my friends. Actually, I'd come for one thing: The rattlesnake shooter; my .22 caliber pistol I carried when I went squirrel hunting. Living on a farm all my life and hunting since I was eight years old had made me a crack shot. The only plan I could come up with was to defend myself, and I figured that if that crazy coach tried to shoot me, at least I could shoot back. Of course, as I look back on things, I realize that was a crazy idea.

Saturday afternoon I drove back to school with a gun tucked under my shirt. It was loaded with long-rifle, hollow-point cartridges. A regular .22 short wouldn't have enough impact to stop someone as big as Bull. The long-rifle hollow-point slug would expand when it hit him and deliver a potent punch. My God, I was shaking just loading the gun.

I pulled into the dorm parking lot at 7:30, gave Billy Rob his keys back, and headed for the Delta house and the Saturday night poker game. As I walked down Dixon Street and the wind bit into me, I smiled as I thought about Vi braving the weather to come talk with me. I was convinced that I had a chance with her. I was determined more than ever to win her over.

As I walked up to the door of the Delta house, I began to think about the poker game and whether or not I should lose a couple of big hands, just to keep from discouraging some of those sorry players. Not tonight, boys went through my mind. I need the money.

I'd started a savings account at a local bank, where I was trying to put aside enough money to rent an apartment and buy a car. That was the goal for my senior year, but the damn ticket the crooked Monticello cop had given me had put a dent in it.

I was hoping to recover some of that ticket money by playing porker. Dickie, who had become more of a heavy, beer drinker during our poker games, came in for the game almost drunk, and I could hardly wipe the smile off my face. Hell, he was a lousy poker player sober, and I figured he'd be easy pickings when drunk. We started playing, and Dickie, who could hardly shuffle the cards, looked like an easy mark. But he was unbelievable lucky that night, winning hand after hand by drawing to stuff no serious poker player would ever do. My God, sitting there being cleaned out by a lucky drunk was hard to do, and naturally, he hooted and yelled, "I'm cleaning Farm Boy's plow," every time he won a pot I was in. I'd had a few good hands toward the end of the evening, and there was a good stack of chips in front of me when another one of those situations came up where only Dickie and I were left in the game.

We were playing seven-card stud, one-eyed jacks wild. I had a pair of kings in the hole, and, on the fourth card, which was an up card, I got another king. I was already eying the pot, thinking of how I could suck Dickie in to build it up when the totally unexpected happened: We were both dealt one-eyed jacks, wild cards that could be used for anything. That gave me four kings, and, the way it looked, Dickie would also have four of something, though probably less than kings. Dickie lit up like a Christmas tree and started shoving money toward the middle of the table. We each bet and raised the limit, and then the last card was dealt, another hole card. I peeked: a king. I couldn't believe my eyes, and I looked again, holding my composure and trying to indicate that it didn't help me. Now, with the one-eyed jack's wild, I had five kings and, looking at Dickie's hand, I knew that it was impossible for him to have a better hand than mine. He probably had four of a kind or maybe, if the last card helped him, he could have five of a kind, but not five of a kind that would beat five kings. When Dickie looked at his last hole card, he could hardly contain himself. My God, talk about giving away your hand. Hell, it was a cinch that Dickie had five of a kind. With the two tens on the table and his one-eyed jack, I was certain that he had a pair of tens in the hole, which would give him five tens to my five kings. The only thing on my mind was how much money I could milk out of that knee-walking drunk. I had a lock to win the pot, and Dickie was so smashed it hadn't occurred to him he could lose the hand.

It was Dickie's turn to bet, and, sure enough, out came the ten dollar bill and a sick, drunken smile. Hey, Farm Boy, wanna play this one for some decent money?"

"Make it light on yourself," I spit back.

"Okay, I'm raising you ten bucks, you worthless hick."

I'd been thinking of what to do when Dickie pulled out the ten dollar bill, and, when he threw it in the pot, I pulled out two tens and raised him. Knowing Dickie, he wasn't going to let me out-raise him, and, sure enough, he didn't.

Dickie was leaning back, chewing on his cigarette and digging in his billfold. He smiled, pulled out a handful of bills, and slurred, "I'll call Mr. Farm Boy's ten and raise him fifty-bucks." He tossed two-twenties and two-tens into the pot.

My God, that was the biggest pot we had ever played, and now everyone was leaning over the table, expecting me to fold, since it took $50.00 to call, but I surprised them. I reached into my billfold and pulled out a blank check, which I kept for emergencies, wrote "cash" and "$150.00," and then tossed it in the pot. Hell, this hand was turning out to be a spigot of money from that sorry drunk.

"Call your 50 and raise you a 100."

Dickie looked stunned for a minute and shook his head, trying to sober up and make the right decision. After a gasp from the other players, there was a deathly silence in the room. Dickie was clicking a couple of chips while he stared at my hand. I knew him well enough to know that he was going to call. Just the possibility of being bluffed out of the biggest pot anyone had ever seen was enough for him to pull out his checkbook and write the check. However, what he did surprised even me.

The check hit the pot and Dickie announced, "I call and raise you a 100."

"Oh, my God," somebody murmured as a buzz went around the table.

I sat there a minute, stunned that Dickie would make such a

bet when he didn't have a lock on the pot. His cards told the story: He was certain that I was playing four kings, and he had five tens. The possibility that I could have a better hand had never crossed his drunken brain. I looked at my hole card again to make sure that I hadn't misread it. Only five aces could beat my hand, and Dickie didn't have an ace showing.

"Come on, Farm Boy, put up or shut up," Dickie mouthed. He sucked on his cigarette and blew smoke in my direction.

"Don't blow smoke on me, you asshole!" I yelled. Dickie leaned back, looking smug.

I was trying to figure out how much Dickie would call. He was drunk, but even a drunken Dickie wouldn't call an over-the-top bet. Finally, I had my number.

"I only have one check. Can I change it?" I said, looking at Peter, who ruled on everything.

"Sure, go ahead."

I pulled my check out of the pot and made a couple of changes in the numbers.

"Call your 100 and raise you 500," I said, to Dickie's amazement. No mercy is the only way to win at poker.

"What? You raised me $500.00?" said a shocked Dickie.

"That's right, Mr. Big Shot, now it's your turn to put up or shut up."

Dickie was sobering up now, and the realization that I thought I had the winning hand flooded over him. He was as nervous as a psychotic cat, not knowing what to do. Minutes passed, and finally he jerked out his checkbook and wrote the check.

"Call."

"Five kings." I turned over my three hole cards, which were all kings, and then put them with the wild card jack and the other king. Dickie went ballistic.

"Damn it to hell! You lucky hick! You probably cheated!" Dickie screamed and knocked chips and cards everywhere.

"Okay, hold it down. Dickie, you're out of the game. Jeff, pick up the chips and cards. Sandy, take the pot," said Peter.

That ended the game, and, for the rest of the year, Dickie was a humbled player. As Dickie would say, I'd cleaned his plow. I stuffed my winnings into my pocket and headed back to the dorm, thinking about what I'd do with all the fresh cash I had.

28.

Bull!

The next day, before I left the room, I tucked the gun into my belt and wore a blousy shirt, which I didn't tuck in. God, I hated the thought of carrying a loaded gun under my shirt all the time, but I didn't walk out of my room without it. Working in the bookstore or sitting in class with a loaded gun stuck in my belt made me nervous at first, but, after a few days, I got used to feeling the gun, and I stopped running around campus like a scared rabbit. The bastard was still coming in the bookstore and glaring at me, and he frequently strolled through the Union while I was in there, but, gradually, I began to see less and less of him. I wondered if he'd cooled off and was going to quit stalking me, but every time I started to relax he'd show up and, from the looks he gave me, I knew that he hadn't given up. I was okay on campus, but the dark parking lot and the area around the dorm still gave me shivers when I came back in late at night. Several times, I thought that I saw him in the shadows, but I hurried in before he could come my way.

I hadn't seen Lacy since her disastrous so-called date with Bull, and, that Friday, when I saw her standing on the steps of the library waving at me, I hurried across the street to meet her.

I almost didn't recognize Lacy. She was dressed conservatively, and was wearing only a slight amount of makeup: a total change from the flashy, sexy woman who was every guy's dream date. Well, I was shocked at the way she looked, but pleasantly shocked. Hell, she looked a lot better than she did wearing those tight clothes and too much makeup. She was also one big smile.

"Sandy, let's go sit on the bench. I can't wait to hear about Bull's car," she whispered, grinning from ear to ear.

"Lacy, what are you talking about?" We walked over to the bench and sat down.

"Oh, Sandy, come on. I know it had to be you. You're so wonderful to do that for me. I heard all about Bull getting beat up, and then, when his car was vandalized, I knew there was only one person on campus who could have done it."

Lacy and I had shared almost everything, so it sure didn't seem like much to admit that I was the one who had beat up Bull and vandalized his car.

"Well, yeah, I did it, but I'm not sure that it was such a good idea. That sorry coach has gone nuts over his car, and I'm afraid he might do something crazy." I didn't tell Lacy about Bull stalking me. There was no use in worrying her, since I'd already told Vi, and, if anything happened, Vi would go to the police.

"Sandy, he's an evil man, and after what he did to me, I wouldn't care what happened to him. But that kind is all mouth, or he wouldn't beat up a woman. I wouldn't worry about him."

"I hope you're right, Lacy," I said, but I knew better.

"I am, Sandy, and guess what?"

"What?"

"I haven't had a date since that night, and you know what? I've never been happier. I just hang up the phone when those sorry guys call."

"Well, Lacy, after that night it wasn't but a few days until I heard that you had quit dating. Someone said you were thinking about becoming a nun." I gave her a little nudge on the shoulder and grinned.

Lacy laughed out loud and moved over closer to me. "Do you

really think I could become a nun?" She grabbed my stomach, and I almost jumped off the bench.

"Damn, Lacy!—No, you'd never make it as a nun." Then I took another long look at Lacy. She smiled as she saw me look her over.

"Sandy, after that date with Bull, I realized that the cheap way I dressed wasn't me. Something deep within me was making me dress like that, and God, I get sick at my stomach when I think about the way I've acted, but that's all behind me now."

Well, Lacy didn't look like the sexiest woman on campus any more, but she was still one gorgeous woman. I smiled, put my arm around her, and gave her a hug. "Heck, Lacy, you don't need to dress like that to be the foxiest chick on campus."

"Sandy, I believe you'd tell a girl anything."

We kidded and talked for another 45 minutes, until Lacy had to leave for class.

***

After the big win playing poker, I felt rich, and I decided to find an apartment so that I could get away from the dorm and that dark parking lot. I thought maybe I could shake Bull if I moved off campus, so, for the next several days, I scoured the area north of the main campus behind Sorority Row until I found a small, one-bedroom unit tucked away on a side street. I moved in the following weekend, and, for the first time in a while, I relaxed as I walked back from class or the bookstore to my new apartment.

Another week passed. I didn't see Bull, and I was thinking that this whole mess was about to blow over. I'd been down at George's drinking beer with Benny and Bob while I flirted with Millie. It was about 11 o'clock when I got back to my apartment complex and started for my front door, and, as I pulled out my keys, I heard footsteps behind me in the parking lot. I turned around and saw a shadow between two cars. Someone was starting to come my way. Then, suddenly, he started to run straight at me. There was a loud noise, a blinding flash, and then another. Two bullets hit the front of my apartment, not a foot from me. My God, at first I was so shocked I couldn't move, and I didn't know what was happening. Then he yelled, "I'm going to kill you for what you did to my car!" He slurred more words as he staggered toward me. Oh, my God, it's Bull! Damn, he's drunk and crazy!

It was one of those moments I'll never forget. Shock turned to panic and I glanced around to see if I could run, but there was nowhere to go. I guess it was desperation combined with the terror of the situation that took over as I ducked down behind the rail of the entryway to my apartment. Hell, I nearly ripped my shirt off trying to get my gun out. I can remember expecting to feel a slug tearing through me as I crouched, half exposed behind the rail, trying to pull out the gun and cock the hammer back. It only took seconds, but everything seemed to be in slow motion, and I was sure he was going to kill me before I could do anything. He was no more than ten yards away when I jumped up with my gun. I never had a thought about not shooting. It was shoot or be shot. He was raising his pistol to shoot again when I fired my first shot.

I know the old-time sheriffs in the movies would have calmly shot the gun out of his hand, but hell, when you're just trying to keep from being killed, it's just point and pull the trigger. I think I fired several times. After the second shot, I heard Bull scream. My God, my hair stood on end as it flashed across my mind that I had shot him and maybe killed him. The panic of thinking I was about to be killed was then replaced with absolute terror that I had ruined my life by killing someone. I ran down the steps, expecting to see him lying on the ground, but evidently, one of my .22 hollow-point slugs had just hit his outstretched arm. He had dropped his pistol, and he was bending over, holding his arm.

For a few seconds I didn't know what to do. I could have put a slug in his head and finished him off, but I couldn't make myself. There was no way I could kill him, but I had to stop him from stalking me. The bullet had just creased his fat arm, and I breathed a sigh of relief. He obviously wasn't seriously wounded.

Then something came to mind, and I rushed over to where he was standing, grabbed him by his hair, and stuck my pistol in his face.

"Bull, I'm going to kill you! Do you understand?"

Suddenly Bull seemed to sober up and began to beg.

"No! No! Please don't! Please!"

I pressed the pistol against his temple and pretended that I was about to shoot him.

"I don't have any choice! You're trying to kill me, and if I let you go you'll come back after me in a few days!" I was yelling as loudly as I could, and I acted out of control. The hammer clicked back on my pistol, and Bull looked terrified.

"No, Sandy! Don't! No, don't shoot me! I promise! I'll never try anything again! You have my word! Nothing! I'll never bother you again! Please don't shoot me!"

A light came on in an upstairs apartment, and I knew I had to finish and get out of the parking lot before the police came.

"Okay, Bull, but let me tell you something!" I was still screaming. Then I tapped his temple with the cocked pistol to get his attention. He was trembling, and I got right up in his face and said, "If I so much as see you following me or coming in the Union to glare at me, and God forbid, if I ever see you in a dark parking lot stalking me, I'll come after you and kill your sorry ass! Do you understand?"

"Yeah—I won't ever come around you again. Now please, lower that pistol. What if it went off?"

"You'd be dead," I said in a matter-of-fact tone.

"Okay, Bull, get your sorry ass out of here, and I better not ever see you again." I slapped the barrel of the .22 pistol against the side of his head and gave him a shove toward the street. Bull stumbled across the parking lot, still clutching his arm, and ran down the street as fast as he could, leaving his gun on the ground. I picked up Bull's gun and ran in the other direction. I wasn't worried about Bull, but I knew that the neighbors had called the police when they heard shots. Bull turned off down a side street, and I jumped into a drainage ditch just as I heard police sirens heading down the street.

I ran down the drainage ditch until I came to a side street that connects with Maple Street, crossed it, and, in a few minutes, I was at the front of Old Main. It took me awhile to regain my composure, but eventually I sorted everything out. The best I could tell, no one had seen the actual shooting, and I was the only one besides Vi who knew that Bull was trying to kill me. He had ended up wounded, but not seriously, and since he was the one who had attempted to kill me, he probably wouldn't go to the police. Of course, if the police came around checking on the reported gunfire I'd tell them that I hadn't been home. It would be hard to tie me to anything.

I guess my adrenalin had been pumping to get me through that situation, because in a few minutes it left me, and I could hardly sit up, I was so drained. Depression swept over me, and I worried about the police coming to arrest me on some trumped-up charge. It took me several hours to get back to normal, but finally, after walking around campus to calm down, I started back to my apartment. On my way back, I walked by a trash dumpster, wiped my fingerprints off both guns, and tossed them in. My hands were shaking so badly I could hardly throw the guns. When the garbage men dumped the dumpster in the city dump the next day, the guns would disappear forever.

I stayed away from the apartment for several hours, and, when I returned, everything was quiet. There were no police or anything out of the ordinary. I went to bed expecting a knock on the door any minute from the police, who I assumed would be questioning everybody in the complex about the sound of gunfire, but nobody showed up. Of course, for the rest of the night, I worried non-stop, but by the time I headed for my first class I had convinced myself that if they were coming they would have already been there.

Vi walked into the bookstore the next day, and I motioned for her to come outside. I couldn't wait to tell her what had happened.

"Vi, I'm going to tell you something because you know that Bull has been threatening to kill me, but please don't breathe a word of what I'm about to tell you to anyone. Promise?"

"I won't, Sandy."

"Vi, Bull was waiting for me last night." Then I told Vi every detail of the confrontation. She put her hand over her mouth.

"Oh, Sandy! You didn't really shoot him, did you?"

"Vi, I'd be dead right now if I hadn't. What would you do if a drunken madman was coming at you, firing a pistol?"

"It's just such a shock. I just can't see you shooting someone."

"Vi, it's bothered me ever since I did it, but there was no other way. Maybe I scared him enough when I put that pistol against his head that he won't bother me again."

"I hope you're right. Let's don't ever talk about this again. I promise you that I'll never tell a soul what you just told me."

"Thanks, Vi."

For the next few days, I worried constantly about the police digging up something on the shooting, or Bull going to the emergency room with a gunshot wound and implicating me, but evidently Bull bandaged his arm himself and didn't go to the hospital. That was the last time I had a run-in with Bull. The university didn't renew his contract after the disastrous Texas game, and, when he left Fayetteville at semester break, I felt relieved.

The problems with Bull had been so intense that I forgot about stealing tests for the Deltas, but, after I got that sorry coach out of my mind and Ten Weeks Tests approached, I started getting call after call from them. The Saturday night before Test Week, I was besieged by several guys begging me to provide them with tests. I refused. It was a good feeling to know that I finally had enough will power to say no, even though every time someone asked me to get a test, I had the strongest urge to say yes. However, that week, after the Saturday night poker game was over and everyone had left, I was finishing up a beer when Jeff, who had become a good friend, came up to me and asked me to come back to his room to talk. Jeff seemed very hesitant to bring up the topic he had asked me to come back to his room to talk about. Finally, he managed to start the conversation.

"Sandy, I hate to ask you this, but I don't have a choice. We're friends, and if you say no, I'll understand." Jeff hesitated as if he was embarrassed to go on. Then he said, "I'm about to flunk out of school."

"What?"

"Yeah, I'm on probation, and if I don't make a two point this semester, I'm out of here."

"Hell, Jeff, change majors. Electrical Engineering is a tough cookie."

"It's too late, Sandy. I'll still get booted out if I don't make my grades this semester."

I could see where Jeff was going, but I let him finish.

"Sandy, on Four Weeks Tests I made a flat F in Quantum Physics, and if I don't make a B on Ten Weeks Tests I don't have a prayer of making a two point this semester. Hell, I know the stuff now, but I can't possibly pull up an F without some help. If I had the Quantum Physics test and made a B, I could make that two point this semester. Could you get me that test?"

I was about to say no, but Jeff continued.

"Oh, another thing—I can't pay you. My dad lost his job, and I barely have enough money to stay in school. Sandy, you're my only hope. If you don't help me, I'm finished with college."

I looked at Jeff, who was embarrassed for having to ask me to get a test. His lips were trembling, and I was afraid he was going to start crying. I didn't have the heart to say no.

Finally, I said, "Okay, give me the course and room number of your professor."

Jeff never said a word as he handed me the slip of paper. There was an awkward silence and then Jeff muttered, "Thanks, Sandy." And then, much to my surprise, he gave me a big hug.

A desperate friend and four beers had knocked me off the wagon again. The next night at one o'clock, I picked the lock, slipped in the side door of the physics building, and got the test.

29.

Mother

After Ten Weeks Tests finished, it was only a few days until school let out for a short Thanksgiving vacation. I was anxious to get home and see my mother. Before I left for school at the end of the summer, I'd noticed a marked decline in her strength. She was tired all the time and had continued to lose weight. I knew something was wrong, but I didn't know what.

On the Wednesday afternoon before Thanksgiving, I caught a ride with a friend from Magnolia, and by six o'clock, I was in Pine Valley. I walked into the house. Mother was sitting in her recliner. She was so tired that she could hardly get up, and I was shocked at the way she looked. Her face was gaunt, she had a terrible cough, and she'd lost weight. However, she had two days off for Thanksgiving, and, after a couple of days of rest, she seemed better, but I knew that something was wrong. I made her promise that she'd see a doctor on Monday.

After I got back to school, I kept waiting on Mother to call to tell me what the doctor had said, but days passed and I didn't hear a thing. Finally, I called her, and, after that conversation, I knew that something was terribly wrong. Mother wouldn't tell me what the doctor had said. She kept evading the question, but when she told me that she was quitting her job, I knew it was serious.

Between Thanksgiving and Christmas things were hectic

around the campus. There was a lot going on, and I barely had time to meet Lacy to take our long afternoon walks. Vi kept coming by the bookstore to talk, but I couldn't get her to meet me on the front steps of Old Main again. Finally, on December 23rd, I finished with my last class and headed for south Arkansas, riding with Billy Caruthers from Magnolia.

It was almost seven o'clock when Billy let me out in front of my house. When I didn't see Mother's car out front, I thought she might be in Pine Valley, buying groceries. The house was dark. I opened the door, walked into the living room, and heard a sound from Mother's bedroom. I called out, "Mother? Are you here?"

I heard a faint, "Stuart?" from the bedroom.

"Yes, Mother." I walked into the bedroom, but I wasn't prepared for what I saw, and I gasped as I looked at my mother's drawn, withered face.

"Stuart, help me up, and I'll fix you some supper."

I tried to compose myself as I stared at my mother, who was struggling to get up. She was so frail that she could barely raise her head.

"Mother, don't try to get up, lie back down, and I'll fix myself something in a few minutes."

"Okay, Stuart. Today has been such a bad day for me. I'm so weak. My Sunday School class brought supper by earlier, and I haven't felt like getting up to eat anything."

"Mother, I didn't see the car out front. I thought you might be in town. Where's your car?"

"Oh, Stuart, I couldn't keep up on the payments, and the bank came by a few days ago and repossessed it."

"Mother! Why didn't you let me know? I could have helped you with the payments."

"Stuart, it won't make any difference if I have a car. I'm not able to drive."

"What's wrong, Mother? You never did say what the doctor told you."

"I didn't want you to worry about me. After I met with the

doctor, I realized that it wouldn't do a bit of good to tell you. You would have just worried for nothing."

"Mother, what did the doctor tell you?"

"Stuart, I've been having terrible pains in my chest, and, right before I went to the doctor, I started coughing up some terrible looking stuff. I thought it was bronchitis, and that I just had an infection."

Mother was having a difficult time breathing, and she paused to catch her breath as a cold sweat popped out on her forehead.

"Stuart, I'm so tired, and I can't see you very well. Please come over a little closer." She took my hand, and I sat on the edge of the bed as we continued to talk.

"What did the doctor find when he examined you?"

"He took chest x-rays and did some other tests." Mother's eyes filled with tears as she squeezed my hand. It was several minutes before she said anything.

"I have advanced lung cancer in both lungs, and I only have a few weeks to live." Mother closed her eyes and tried to catch her breath, but she couldn't. I began to shake my head no, no, as she tried to breathe. There was a lump in my throat as big as my fist as I sat there and tried not to lose my composure.

"Oh, my God, no, Mother, surely not." I managed to say. "Maybe you need to see a doctor in Little Rock. I just know there's something they can do." My breath was coming in little short gasps now as I looked at Mother and tried desperately to think of anything I could do for her. God, don't let me break down and cry, I prayed. Then a peace came over me, and I reached over and kissed her on the cheek. I knew there was nothing I could do except be with her.

"No, Stuart," she said when she was able to speak again. "I know by the way I feel that life is slipping away, and it won't be long until I'm gone." Mother stopped again to catch her breath, and then, with great effort, she said, "I've been praying all day that I would get to see you one more time. I'm so glad you're here.

Just sit down on the bed and hold my hand for a few minutes." Mother's voice trailed off, and she closed her eyes.

Those were the last words I heard my mother speak. She shook slightly and made a small cough, and her head dropped back on the pillow. I felt her hand give my hand a final squeeze, and then in a few seconds it went limp. I stood up, numb, and walked into the kitchen to call an ambulance, but I knew even before they arrived that Mother was gone.

I spent Christmas Eve picking out my mother's casket and greeting friends who dropped by to pay their respects. We had the funeral the day after Christmas, and Uncle Hosie, accompanied by a guard, came down from Tucker Penitentiary to attend. Finally, late that afternoon, when the last of Mother's friends had left the house, I sat down in her recliner, exhausted. Everything had happened so fast that the impact of Mother's death hadn't hit me, and, even during the long funeral and graveside service, I hadn't shed a tear. I thought that maybe, sitting there in Mother's recliner, her death would sink in, and I'd cry and relieve the pent-up grief that I was holding in. But no, an hour passed, and I was still sitting there stone-faced. I'd just started to get up when the phone rang. No doubt it was another one of Mother's friends calling to offer their condolences.

"Hello."

"Hello, Sandy?"

"Yes, Vi? Oh, Vi! Oh, Vi!" I couldn't make myself say another word as I broke down and cried for the first time since Mother had died.

It took me a few minutes to regain my composure, but finally, Vi and I started talking again.

"Sandy, I read your mother's obituary in the Gazette today. I'm so sorry that I couldn't come to the funeral. I think you understand."

"Yes, Vi, I do."

We talked on for another 20 minutes, and finally, as we hung up, I said to her, "Vi, you'll never know how much your phone call meant to me."

The phone call from Vi was the catalyst I needed to put Mother's death behind me and begin work on the dozens of items that had to be taken care of before I went back to school. For the next several days, I worked from daylight to dark, doing everything from buying a small monument for Mother's grave to closing out her checking account. The checking account had $21.00 in it.

With only a couple of days before I would return to school, I was stunned by an unexpected visit. Doctor Carl Davidson, the man who owned the house where Mother and I had lived for the past five years, stopped by late that afternoon. After a few pleasantries about Mother and a few other comments, he said, "Sandy, as you know, I'm an old friend of your folks, and I was glad to help your mother out after your dad died."

"Oh, Doctor Davidson, we couldn't have made it without you. Thank you so much."

"Well, Sandy, I expect you'll be spending most of your time up in Fayetteville, since you don't have any family left down here in Pine Valley."

"Yes, sir, I probably will."

"I know I should have stopped by earlier in the week to tell you this, but I've been busy."

I was puzzled, but from the way Doctor Davidson was looking at me, I knew that what he was going to tell me wasn't going to be good.

"Sandy, I've rented this house to the Stover family, and, I hate to tell you this, but I need you and all your things out of the house before you go back to school."

"But Doctor Davidson, that only leaves me two days. I thought I'd come back here after school was out this summer, have a sale, and empty the house."

"Sorry, Sandy, but I can't wait around that long. Why don't

you go see Ned Kelley? He buys used furniture, and he'll probably work something out with you."

I was stunned. Settling up Mother's estate had been coming along, but now I was faced with a total liquidation of everything, and it had to be done by tomorrow afternoon.

"I'm sure you'll work it out, Sandy," said Doctor Davidson as he turned and walked back to his truck. "Your mom's death was a terrible shock to everyone in town."

My mind was spinning as I thought of all that I had to do with only a day left before I went back to the university. I ran into the house, found a paper and pencil, and started to list and evaluate everything in the house, giving each item a greatly discounted value. At eleven o'clock, I finished and totaled it up. It came to almost $3000. The next morning I walked into Pine Valley, looking for Ned, and found him making a purchase down at the feed store.

"Ned, if you've got a minute, I need to talk to you."

"Sure, Sandy. It was just terrible to watch your mother go down like she did."

"I know it, Ned, and I want to thank you for all you did for her while she was sick and for being one of the pallbearers."

"I was happy to do it, Sandy. Now, what do you need to talk about?"

"Well, Ned, I thought it might be better if I sold all Mother's household goods before I went back to school."

Ned nodded, and I continued. "I know you're always buying lots of furniture, and I thought you might be interested in buying Mother's goods, everything in the house."

"I don't know, Sandy. I'm pretty stocked up, but let me think about it for a day or two."

"Uh, Ned, I need to get this done today. I have to leave for school tomorrow. Here's a list of furnishings, and I've noted a price by everything. Look, it comes up to nearly $3000," I said as I pointed to the total. "I've been thinking about it, and, if you could pay me 2000 for the whole lot, I believe it would be a fair trade."

Well, 2000 was a lot more than a fair trade, but I was desperate. I started to hand Ned the inventory, but he waved it back.

"Sandy, I don't need to see that to know what I can pay, and I sure can't get to no 2000."

I wasn't surprised that Ned had started to bargain, and, although 2000 was almost giving my mother's stuff away, I decided to drop the price.

"Uh, well, Ned, what can you do? How about 1500?" He was shaking his head before the words left my mouth. I knew that he was about to low-ball me, but I never expected the figure that he threw out.

"I'll take everything off your hands for 200."

"What? Ned, Mother's mahogany dining room table is worth at least $500. You're not being fair with me." My God, I was so shocked that I could hardly speak, but in a few seconds, I understood everything.

"Sandy, you ain't in much position to bargain. This here's a little town, and I knowed about Doc Davidson renting your place to the Stovers 'fore you did. Now, I'm trying to do you a favor by taking all that stuff off your hands. I can do 225, but that's it, take it or leave it."

I'd been surprised several times during the last week, but now, having an old family friend trying to steal Mother's estate was crushing. I stood there and stared at Ned while he pulled a plug of tobacco out of his pocket and cut himself off a chew.

"Whata you say, Sandy?" he said as he stuck the tobacco in his jaw.

My mind had been racing ever since Ned made his final offer. I didn't have a choice, and he knew it: so much for old family friends. Damn, I couldn't believe it.

"I'll take it," I managed to say.

"Good, just leave the key to the house under the front door mat when you leave, and I'll take care of the rest."

I nodded. Ned pulled out his billfold and counted out the $225.00, then turned and walked toward his truck. "Shor was terrible 'bout yor mom," he said as he spit a stream of tobacco juice on the sidewalk.

I wanted to yell, "Go to hell!" as loudly as I could, but I just dropped my head and started walking back to the farm.

The next day Billy pulled up in front of my house, and I walked out for the last time. I stopped beside the car and looked back at the little white frame house, and, for just a moment, I could see Mother standing at the door and Uncle Hosie sitting in the porch swing while I sat on the steps. There had been some fun times living there, and I already missed my mother so much. I got in the car and, for the last time, I glanced back at the house. The last two weeks had been the most painful of my life, and I was anxious to put Pine Valley behind me and move on.

After I got back on campus and started back to work in the bookstore, Vi stopped in and talked and talked. She was wonderful.

I was so depressed about Mother's death that I almost didn't go to the Deltas' poker game that Saturday night. When we finished, the subject of providing final tests came up, but I wasn't in the mood to talk about anything, much less the sordid part of my college life. However, as I started to leave, Peter handed me a list of five tests that they wanted me to provide. I told him I didn't know, but I'd consider it. Maybe my resistance was down from the ordeal of Mother's death, but, for whatever reason, I called Peter the next day and told him that I'd get the tests. Finals were a week away.

The next day, I met Lacy on the bench beside the library. Since it was early January, the temperature was hovering just above freezing, but the wind wasn't blowing, so we sat down. I put my heavy trench coat around both of us, and we began to talk. After I told Lacy about Mother's death, and having to sell all of her belongings for almost nothing, Lacy began to cry, and soon both of us were huddled under the trench coat, crying our eyes out.

The next week I started going after the Final Tests. The first two were easy, and I decided to stop by the Chemistry building that same night to get an Organic Chemistry test before I called it a night. I was anxious to finish, and I was like a zombie as I hurried along the dark hallway after picking the side door lock. The office door had one of those push button locks, and I opened it easily. I was sitting on the floor, copying the test, when I saw a flashlight beam sweep the side of the building. I crouched down, turned off my flashlight, and waited for the campus cop to pass. The front door rattled as he checked it, and then, in a couple of minutes, I heard him pull the side door where I'd come in. Suddenly there were footsteps in the hall clicking down the tile floor. I jumped to my feet and peered around the door facing, and, sure enough, a campus cop was coming down the hall, checking each office door. I must have left the side door open when I came in, and he would be caught up to where I was standing in seconds. I turned around, put the test back in the drawer, dashed out into the hall, and pulled the office door shut behind me. There wasn't any doubt he'd hear me as I ran down the dark hall on the tile floor.

"Hey! You! Stop!"

I headed for the stairs at the end of the hall and sprinted up to the second floor, trying to think of how I could get out of the building. I knew that if I turned down the long end of the hall it was a dead end, and I'd be caught for sure. When I came to the top of the stairs, I turned in the opposite direction from the long hallway and stepped into the nearest doorway. If he turned his light in my direction, I was done for. I could hear him puffing as he started up the last flight of stairs to the second floor. Before he reached the top of the stairs, I reached into my pocket and pulled out a coin. Just before he got to where I was standing, I threw the coin as far as I could down the long, dark hallway, where it rattled and hit the wall at the end of the hall. Without even glancing my way, he turned and ran down the hall. As soon as he got halfway down the hall, I slipped out of the doorway and silently went down the stairs to the first floor. I was out of the building in seconds. I dashed to the Greek Theatre to pick up my clothes, and only one thing was going through my mind: Never again!

I dropped the two tests that I had gotten earlier by the Delta house the next day, and told them that was it. After nearly being caught, I wasn't about to break into another building. Finished, no more of that sleazy mess; it was all behind me. Thank God I didn't get caught. I'd come close to ending my college career, my future professional life, and any romantic hopes I had for Vi.

30.

Millie!

My last final was on Wednesday, and, since I couldn't go back to Pine Valley, I stayed in Fayetteville between semesters. Most of my friends were gone, and, after working at the bookstore, stocking for the coming semester, I usually went back to my apartment and settled in to read a good novel. After a few days of that, I was bored and horny, and I began to get itchy to see Millie. Friday night rolled around, and I couldn't get Millie off my mind. After a movie, I stopped by George's, slipped into my regular booth, and waited for Millie to come by. A few minutes passed, and then I saw Millie pick up a pitcher of beer and head toward my booth.

"Hi, Sandy, all alone tonight?"

"Yeah, you know how it is between semesters. Everybody heads out of town. I stayed here to rest up. Last semester nearly worked me to death."

I kidded back and forth with Millie, and, after about ten minutes of shooting the bull, she was leaning against my shoulder and rubbing her hand on the back of my neck. Soon the conversation drifted around to when she would get off work and, with a smile and a wink, Millie nodded. I'd be standing at the side door when Millie got off at 12.

It was a little before 12 when I walked around to the side door and waited for Millie. A cold front had roared in a couple of days earlier, and it was clear and cold. I pulled my jacket up around my neck and thought about cuddling with Millie in a warm bed. The door opened. Millie stepped out and grabbed my hand.

"Let's go, Sandy, 'fore we freeze to death." Millie started pulling me along, heading for her apartment.

I stopped and said, "Hey, Millie, why don't we go to my apartment? You haven't seen it yet, and I'd like to show it to you. I need some help decorating." I knew that most girls couldn't resist the urge to decorate, and Millie was no exception, but I had other reasons for Millie to come to my place. When we finished making love it would be well after midnight, and Millie wouldn't want to walk back across a dark, cold campus by herself. Spending the night at my place was the obvious choice.

Millie hesitated, and I said, "I decorated it myself, and I thought you might give me some pointers." Of course, outside of putting a few mineral specimens from a field trip on a windowsill, I hadn't done anything. It was about as bare as an apartment could be; bed, desk, table, two chairs, and a lamp. Millie's curiosity got the best of her.

"Well, okay, Sandy, but I can't stay long."

We started across campus to my apartment, walking into a cold, north wind, and, by the time we got there, we were frozen.

The "I need help decorating" statement got Millie to my apartment, but, before I could get her to bed, she wanted to go over every detail and made me make notes of what to put where. Finally, she finished, and, after we courted and kissed for a few minutes, she nodded toward the bed.

"Am I the first one you've taken to bed here?" she giggled.

"Yep, you should do this one free, since you're breaking in a new bed."

"Sandy, you know I don't like to talk 'bout money. Now, come on, let's get in bed," she said as she started to undress.

Millie watched me as I pulled out my billfold and put a ten dollar bill on the table. I hadn't been with Millie for weeks, and I was determined to take my time and enjoy this sexy woman. However, I was horny, and, as soon as Millie and I were tangled up in a passionate sexual embrace, my plans to take my time went out the window, and the lovemaking turned out to be a lot shorter than I'd planned.

After we finished, I opened a couple of beers, and we leaned back on the pillows and talked for 30 or 40 minutes as we sipped our beers. Millie mentioned that she needed to get back to her apartment, but, as she looked out the door at the dark street and thought about walking across campus after midnight, my suggestion that she spend the night was accepted. Millie and I made love again a few minutes later. The next morning we had a cup of coffee in bed, and, before we got out of bed, we had sex. That had been my plan when I insisted Millie come to my apartment. But thinking back on that time with Millie, I can tell you it was more than that. The more I was with her the more I wanted to be around her, and it wasn't just for the sex. She was a neat gal and fun to be with.

Millie was about dressed when she looked at me and said, "Sandy, don't you think that I was worth more than a measly $10.00? After all, we did it three times."

How do you answer a question like that? Of course "yes" is the only answer, and when you answer "yes" you'd better be pulling out your billfold.

"Millie, you were wonderful, absolutely out of this world." I pulled out a five and stuck it in her hand.

Millie hung her head and slipped the money in her purse.

"Sandy, it just kills me to charge you. You're the best lover any girl could want, and taking your money makes me feel so cheap."

I walked over and hugged Millie as she stood there with a tear in her eye.

"Millie, I understand. I know how hard it is to get by, and working for that stingy Mary won't do it."

"Thanks, Sandy, you're wonderful. Well, I'd better go—see you soon."

I opened the door for Millie, but, just before she stepped out, I pulled her around and we kissed. Not a passionate "let's have sex" kiss, but one that expressed our affection for each other. Ever since the incident with Billy Ray Schmidt, we had a special bond. Millie smiled and whispered in my ear, "Sandy, you're so wonderful." Then she goosed me in the ribs and snickered, "Can't wait till next time."

"Yeah, me too—bye, Millie."

Millie pulled her jacket up around her ears and started walking down the side street toward campus. I stood in the doorway, watching her until she reached the corner and was out of sight. I was still smiling and thinking about Millie as I closed the door and walked back into my apartment. There was something between us, and I knew it was a lot more than sexual attraction. Over the next few weeks, I began to have more and more thoughts about Millie, and I knew that I'd developed a genuine affection for her. My trips to George's became daily, and, as soon as I opened the door, Millie would rush over and grab me. Millie was becoming a lot more than a sexual partner. I had fallen in love with her.

However, after being with Millie I always felt guilty the next time I met Vi. And, sure enough, the Monday afternoon after classes started back up, I was leaning against the bookstore counter, thinking about Millie, when I felt someone squeeze the back of my neck. I jumped straight up and turned around to see Vi standing there, laughing.

"My gosh, Sandy, you were out of it. What on earth were you thinking about?" Vi laughed at my shocked look.

I know I must have had a stunned look on my face as I desperately tried to think of something to say, but I knew that even mentioning Millie would send Vi into fits.

"Uh, uh, oh, just stuff. I guess I was in another world, and I sure didn't hear you walk up."

"Sandy, you sure were in another world. Are you sure it wasn't some girl's world?"

"Oh, Vi, you know me. I never date."

"What about Millie, you know, the girl down at George's?"

I know my mouth must have dropped open as I looked at Vi, wondering how she could possibly have known about Millie.

"Uh, what do you mean?"

"Oh, Sandy, I've been in George's when you and Benny were having a beer, and Millie flirted with you like crazy. Sure you're not fooling around with Millie?"

I could tell by the tone of Vi's voice that she was just kidding, and she didn't really know anything. It was just one of those girl's intuition things. Damn! How does she do that?

"Gosh, Vi, who doesn't Millie flirt with? I heard she gets more tips than any of the other waitresses at George's." Vi didn't completely buy that line, but, since it was obvious that Millie was a big flirt, she couldn't just dismiss it.

"Just flirting, huh?" She poked me in the ribs and leaned closer to me. "Bull!"

"Oh, Vi, come on, Millie's nearly 40," I exaggerated. "You must think I'm hard up. Heck, you know I'm saving myself for you."

Well, that turned the tide of the conversation, and Vi stammered and blushed.

"Well, uh, how are your classes shaping up?" she said, trying to change the subject.

I grinned and said, "Good, couldn't be better." We talked for a few more minutes, and Vi left for class. Damn! Women, I'll never understand 'em.

***

After the close call with the campus cops, my test procurement service, as I was calling it, was unavailable at Four Weeks

Tests. It was a relief to turn down the few who asked. My God, I was glad to have that sordid episode behind me.

I kept seeing Vi at the bookstore, and Lacy and I met at least once a week on the library bench to talk. It was a quiet semester.

Millie was still around and available, and every Friday and Saturday night I stopped by George's and flirted with her. We'd become good friends since the incident with the big tackle, and, of course, after Millie spent the night at my apartment and we had sex all night, there was a special bond between us. As the weeks passed, I found myself looking forward to talking with Millie, and I was writing more and more about her in The Journal. I was starting to think about her more than Vi. I tried to tell myself that it was the sex, but I knew that it was more than that. I was in love with Millie.

It had been six weeks since I'd been with Millie away from George's, and I was getting a strong urge to take her to my apartment. That Friday night I was by myself when I slipped into my usual booth. I sat there and waited for Millie, and, as soon as she walked over, I knew that something was wrong. No smiles, flirts, or small talk. Millie looked at me and said through tight lips, "Sandy, I'm pregnant."

31.

The Wedding

I couldn't believe it, but I knew from the way Millie was acting that she wasn't kidding.

"But...but...I thought you said you'd taken care of everything."

"I thought so, too, but evidently something happened, and the doctor told me that I'm six weeks pregnant."

"Whose—?"

"You."

"Me? But it's been weeks since we were together."

"Yeah, Sandy, about six weeks, and I'm six weeks pregnant. If you'll remember, we did it so many times I was sore the next day. I've checked my calendar, and I'm certain it's you. And Sandy, if it had to happen, I'm glad it was you. You're the most wonderful guy I know. I'll be right back with your beer."

Oh, my God! I sat there for a few minutes, stunned, as Millie went to get me a beer. She seemed so certain that I was the father. Was I? Maybe. It seemed so unreal, but a pregnant Millie was sure real. The first thing that came to my mind was to marry her, but then I realized that a marriage with Millie, if I didn't love her, would be bad for both of us. But maybe I did love her. Oh, my God! Oh, my God!

In a few minutes, Millie returned with my beer, and we continued our conversation.

"Sandy, if you don't love me and don't want the baby to have a father, I'll probably go live with my Aunt Claudia down in Clarksville, and, after the baby is born, I'll give it up for adoption. Think it over for a few days. I know you want to do what's right for the baby. Sandy, I love you, and you're such a fine person. You'll do the right thing. I'm sure of it."

When Millie said that she loved me I felt weak all over, and the strangest feeling came over me. "Millie, I...uh, well, I love you, too." I did love her, but I couldn't get the idea that she was pregnant out of my mind. "It's just such a shock. I can't believe it."

"Sandy, it just happened. It wasn't anybody's fault, and maybe I shouldn't have told you, but, since you're the father, I thought you had a right to know. Let me know what you want to do."

The father! My God, a shock ran through me as if I'd stuck my finger in a light socket. I sat there, trying to start breathing again, as Millie started going on about naming the baby Stuart Carson, Jr. I could hardly form my words. About that time, Mary yelled for Millie to pick up a tray of food from the kitchen. I didn't talk with Millie for the rest of the night, and, at about 11 o'clock, I went back to my apartment, where I spent a sleepless night. For days all I could think about was Millie being pregnant with my baby. Finally, just the thought of Millie giving up a baby that I had fathered had me so upset I couldn't sleep or study. Vi, Lacy, Bull, and even the Saturday night poker games all seemed so distant. Millie was on my mind every hour of the day. Did I love her? Yes, I did, she was such a great girl. Should I do the right thing and marry her? What about Vi? How in the world am I going to tell her? I was a nervous wreck. And Lacy, oh my God.

The next Saturday morning, after a fitful night's sleep, I woke up determined to marry Millie. It had been a week since Millie had told me that she was pregnant and that I was the father. It wasn't fair for Millie to have my baby down in Clarksville, and then send a baby I had fathered off for adoption. No, she can't send our baby off for adoption. After making that decision, I felt a little better, and I'd even rehearsed what I'd say to Vi and Lacy when I had to tell them that I was marrying Millie. I was planning to go to George's that night before the poker game and tell Millie we'd get married, and then we could plan when and where. Since I had an apartment, Millie could move in with me, and I could continue in school. My poker winnings and test procurement service had fattened my bank account enough that I thought we could make it. By noon I was actually looking forward to marrying Millie and being a father. Maybe the baby will look like me. And then, after a few hours, I was sure about it. Yeah, I do love Millie; I really do, and we're going to get married.

That Saturday afternoon I was propped up on my bed, leaning back on a pillow and trying to read a magazine, when Benny, my ex-roommate, barged through the door.

Sandy, get your ass outta bed! We're going to a wedding."

"What?"

"Yeah, you won't believe this. Millie and my brother, Bob, are getting married down at George's, and the wedding starts in 45 minutes."

"Millie and Bob are getting married? You're kidding. Millie can't be getting married to Bob, she's marrying—" And then I caught myself. "Are you sure?"

"You're damn right, I'm sure. Bob and Millie are out rounding up all their friends. Bob's got a marriage license, and even a ring. Come on, we're going to be late. Hell, Mary is gonna serve free beer."

I still didn't believe Benny, but I dressed, and, in a few minutes, Benny and I were heading down Dixon Street to George's, where we found a crowd of guys and a few girls milling around, looking a little puzzled at what was about to happen. Most of us thought this was a joke, and we'd all have a beer and leave. But no, Bob walked in wearing a rented tux. In a few minutes, a Justice of the Peace was standing by the bar, ready to conduct the ceremony.

One of the girls had brought a portable record player, and soon wedding music was playing. Then, out of the kitchen came the bridesmaids, George's waitresses, each holding a white rose.

They walked slowly up to the bar and positioned themselves beside the Justice of the Peace. There was a little scratchy sound as the girl handling the record player moved the needle over to the wedding march, and then, as the music started, Millie came out of the kitchen on Mary's arm. She looked absolutely drop-dead gorgeous in a beautiful, long white wedding gown, carrying white roses.

I know my mouth must have been hanging open because, an hour ago, I had been excited about marrying Millie, and now, as she walked toward me, I had to pinch myself to be sure this wasn't a dream. Millie walked by me, and her deep blue eyes cut over and caught my eyes. She smiled and gave me one of her winks. I guess that, deep down inside, I didn't really want to marry Millie and give up on Vi, but the thought of abandoning a baby I'd possibly fathered had me ready to do the right thing. But it was more than that—I really did love Millie.

A surge of relief and, believe it or not, regret swept over me as Millie and Mary continued on to the bar, where the Justice of the Peace was waiting. I started to come out of shock, and as the ceremony continued, I thought back on Millie's rather active sex life. It seemed pretty obvious that Bob could easily be the father of Millie's baby. Of course, there were at least 15 other guys in the room, including me, who might have been the one. Benny mentioned to me later that Millie had told Bob she was absolutely certain he was the father, and Bob, who was crazy about Millie anyway and had been with her a lot longer and more frequently than any of the other guys, wanted to marry her.

I guess, thinking back on it, Millie didn't have any intentions of going to Clarksville to live with her aunt. She was going to find her baby a father, and that father was going to be one of the guys who could be made to believe he was the father and couldn't stand for his baby to go up for adoption.

I stood there, listening to the wedding march, wishing I were standing there beside Millie. It was one of the most painful moments of my life, watching someone I loved marrying another person. Then I thought back on Doris and my love for her. Millie...Doris—I'd wanted to marry both of them, but it was not to be. I was puzzled by the way I felt.

I was depressed for a few weeks after the wedding, but, as spring finally made it to northwest Arkansas and the weather warmed up, I got into better spirits. Ten Weeks Tests would be starting the following week, but I had no intentions of breaking into any buildings. One close call was enough. Of course, the Deltas wouldn't take no for an answer. After the next Saturday night poker game broke up, Peter handed me a list of tests they wanted, but I shook my head and told him there was no way I was going back into a university building in the middle of the night. Hell, coming within an inch of ruining my life was enough to put any test-stealing thoughts I had on the back burner. Well, Peter stuffed the list in my front pocket and told me to keep it in case I changed my mind. No way–I was through with that slimy part of college.

It was a warm, sunny day that next Monday morning, and Lacy and I met at the library bench and talked for at almost an hour. She was still the talk of the campus, but not because of her sexual reputation. Since her disastrous date with Bull, she'd kept her word; Lacy had not had a date, and, not only that, she'd changed the way she dressed until she didn't even resemble the old Lacy. Well, let me just say this. She didn't look like a walking sexpot anymore, but she was still a damned foxy woman.

32.

Lacy

The semester was slowly winding down. Millie had quit George's when she was five months pregnant, and Vi was still going steady with Mr. Football, but she was also still coming by to see me at the bookstore, usually telling me about the ring she'd picked out and even describing it to me. I did see Lacy almost every week, and we'd invariably go sit on the bench beside the library to talk. I wasn't dating and neither was Lacy.

I was getting irritated with Vi because she wouldn't meet me on the front steps of Old Main anymore, and, heck, who wouldn't have been discouraged, because it seemed as if her domineering, crazy father was looming over us every time we talked. Not a conversation passed in which Vi didn't mention his name, and not once did I see her smile when she talked about him. I was convinced Vi was only dating Mr. Football because of the grip her father had on her.

It was the first weekend in May, and that clear, warm Saturday morning I left my apartment behind the Delta Chi House and started walking across campus.

"Sandy! Sandy! Come here!"

I looked around and saw Lacy lying on a chaise, surrounded by a bunch of her sorority sisters. They were all lying out, sunbathing, and, from what I could see, they were trying to tan as much of their bodies as possible without getting completely nude.

"Sandy, come on over and talk to me while I'm sunbathing," yelled Lacy.

Well, I'd intended to walk down to the Palace Drug Store and buy some toothpaste, but one look at a backyard full of half-naked, sorority girls changed my mind.

I walked over and sat down on the ground beside Lacy's chaise, and we started to talk about the upcoming finals and what we were going to do during the summer. Of course, I was heading back to work on an offshore drilling rig. The money was too good not to, and the idea of playing poker during every waking hour I wasn't on shift appealed to me. Lacy had a job in a Tulsa department store, selling makeup.

When I took a good look at Lacy, I just shook my head. She was hard to believe. Her long, blonde hair was draped over her shoulders, and my God, what a figure. She had rolled her swimsuit back until it was barely covering her breasts, and she was lying on her back when I walked up. The other girls who were sunbathing all had two- piece swimsuits on, but when you looked at the group, there was Lacy, and then there were the other girls. I was doing okay until Lacy turned over on her stomach, unsnapped her swimsuit top, and looked over at me.

"Sandy, would you do me a big favor?" She handed me the suntan lotion and smiled.

I'd been around Lacy since I was a freshman, and this last school year we'd spent at least a couple of hours every week talking on the bench by the library, but this was different. I was already breathing heavily when I squirted the suntan lotion on my hand and started rubbing Lacy's shoulders.

"That's good, Sandy, but a little lower, and don't miss a spot."

"Okay," I mumbled. I sat there and rubbed Lacy's back, and then my hands drifted down to her waist and, finally, down until my fingers were under her swimsuit bottom. I was glad I was sitting down because, by the time my fingers were under her swimsuit bottom, I was panting like some old bull in heat. I finally had to quit, or I was going to do something stupid.

Lacy looked up at me and smiled as she purred, "Oh, Sandy, that felt so good."

"Damn, Lacy," I whispered, "I can't stand this."

"Sandy, we're just friends. Remember?" Then Lacy gave me a wink that I still remember.

I grinned and poked her in the ribs, and she jerked and deliberately exposed one of her breasts.

"Oh, pardon me," she said as she gave me a big smile.

Damn, I had to sit there another 20 minutes so I could stand up without embarrassing myself. I walked away from the Delta Chi's backyard that morning with only Lacy on my mind. It took days for me to quit thinking about her. Friends? Are we just friends? Do I want to be just a friend? I couldn't answer that question.

***

Finals were coming up, and the Deltas were all over me to provide them with tests. It took a lot of will power, but I said no. I'd decided that if I could turn the Deltas down, maybe I could put the test-stealing behind me. Finals arrived, and I refused to get any tests for the Deltas. I was proud of myself for resisting the temptation.

Only a few days were left in the semester, and I could hardly wait for them to be over. God, that semester had been tough. I walked down to the Delta House that last Saturday night of the semester to play the last game of poker before the school year was over. I settled into my regular chair after that worthless Dickie and I glared at each other and spit out a couple of our usual slurs. The game got under way. As the night progressed, I built up a fair stack of chips. It was about time to call it a night when someone called a weird game that made all deuces wild, with both jokers still in the deck. The betting got out of hand after the sixth card was dealt. Since it was nearly the end of the game, almost everybody stayed in, and there was quite a pot on the table. Finally, it was just Peter, Dickie, and me. Dickie pulled out that ten dollar bill again, and challenged Peter and me to call it. I figured that Peter, who was in graduate school now, but still ran the poker game, would remind that asshole the limit was 25 cents, but he didn't. Well, when Peter was ready to take a ten dollar bet, I started taking a serious look at everyone's up cards, especially Peter's. Hell, I had a damn good hand, and I was anticipating winning the pot. It took me a minute to see it, but, putting the wild cards into the blanks, I had a straight flush, king high. Since Dickie had taken off the limit, Peter and I had agreed that there was no limit now. I raised another ten dollars, and Dickie called. Peter looked at his cards, studied them for a minute, and then wrote out a check for a $120.00. He had raised Dickie and me a $100.00.

I knew in an instant that Peter thought he had a lock on the hand, and I folded. Hell, with all those wild cards, he could easily have five of a kind. Dickie hesitated for a long time, and then he called. Peter had been bluffing. He had nothing, and the hand that I'd folded would have won the pot.

"Damn," I said, "look at this." I turned my hand over so that Dickie would know I'd been bluffed out of a winning hand. You could have heard Dickie holler from across the street.

"Plow cleaning time again, you hick Farm Boy. Whooo! Whooo! Whooo!" he yelled.

I'd been stung, and I came out a loser that night, but getting bluffed out of a winning hand would stick in Dickie's stupid little mind. Some night, folding that winning hand would pay for itself, and Dickie would find himself in deep poker water.

***

The next Monday I stopped by the bookstore to work for a few hours before I went back to the apartment and packed for the summer. I still had one final to take on Monday afternoon, and then, on Tuesday, I'd store everything in my apartment except a suitcase full of work clothes, hitchhike down to Morgan City, Louisiana, and spend the night in a cheap motel. On Wednesday I'd catch a crew boat to the offshore drilling rig, the Mr. Charlie, where I'd spend my summer working twelve-hour days. I had about 15 minutes left to work when Vi came in and walked over to the counter where I was standing. Honestly, I was disgusted with her for keeping me at arm's length all semester. Hell, just another flirty conversation, and she'd be gone out of my life for three months.

"Sandy, I just stopped in to say goodbye. We probably won't see each other till fall. I don't think you're coming to Monticello this summer."

I smiled. "Not unless I get the urge to have a sorry cop beat me up again," I smirked. We talked for a few more minutes, and Vi was about to leave when I had an idea.

"Vi, let's don't say goodbye now. Meet me on the front steps of Old Main tonight, and let's say goodbye then."

Vi was shaking her head before I got the words out of my mouth.

"I just can't, Sandy. I'll be in more trouble than you can imagine, and you know what I promised Daddy."

"Oh, come on Vi, we're not going to see each other for months. Let's meet late, at 11. No one can possibly see you then, and you can be back in the house before they lock the doors at 12."

I could see Vi wavering, and I pressed the point. "Please, Vi, we won't see each other for three months." Well, most women have soft hearts, and, when you beg them, they'll usually give in. Vi nodded her head and, without saying a word, she walked out.

It was a warm, late spring night, and I got to the steps early. I sat there and listened to the tree frogs croak. As I thought about how I'd pursued Vi for the past three years, I started to get depressed. I wondered if I should give up. This last semester she hadn't given me much encouragement at all. Maybe I should start dating that sorority sister of Lacy's, Glenda. Yeah, she sure looks like a hot date, and I'll bet she'd go out with me.

"Sandy?" Vi called from the shadows on the edge of the building.

"Vi, here." I stood up as the thoughts of Glenda quickly passed out of my mind.

"Well, it's been a long time since we've met here," Vi said.

"Yeah, way too long." We talked for a few minutes, and I was enjoying myself, but the thoughts about wasting my time pursuing her kept going through my mind. Finally, I just blurted it out. "Vi, are you here just because you feel sorry for me?"

"Sandy, what do you mean?"

"Oh, you know, Vi. I've made a fool out of myself chasing after you ever since I was a freshman. And now, here we sit, almost seniors, and it seems hopeless."

God, I couldn't believe I'd said that. I was embarrassed now, and I turned away from Vi as she hesitated. Well, I'm right. She just feels sorry for me, and she's trying to come up with a way to let me down easy.

"Sandy, I, well—" There was a long pause as Vi looked away from me and tried to come up with the right words.

Here it comes.

"Oh, Sandy, no, I don't feel sorry for you. I...I...care about you."

Did Vi almost say she loved me?

"Thanks, Vi." I put my arms around her shoulders and felt Vi's arms circle my waist. Then she reached up and kissed me with such intensity that it shocked me.

For the next thirty minutes, we courted and petted like two crazy lovers, rubbing and touching until Vi pulled back, smiling. "Sandy, we can't go any farther than this sitting on these cold steps."

"Why don't you come to my apartment? It's just right behind your sorority house."

Before Vi could answer, I kissed her again, rubbing her back and pressing against her, whispering in her ear how much I loved her.

Then, very quietly, she whispered, "Okay, let's go."

We walked across Maple Street, up the alley to my apartment, and, in minutes, we were rolling on my bed making love. After we had finished and Vi had touched up her makeup, I walked her back to her sorority house. We stood on the doorsteps, kissed, and said goodbye.

Sex with Vi was totally different than sex with any girl I'd ever been with. When we walked into the apartment we were both so worked up it didn't take ten minutes until we were in bed. We started to make love, and, as we did, Vi clasped me close and kissed me passionately with her eyes closed. She continued to kiss and caress me in the most affectionate way during all the time that we made love. When we finished, Vi hurried off to the bathroom, and when she came back into the bedroom she gave me a shy smile, a kiss, and a hug.

Suddenly life seemed worth living again. Vi would be mine next fall. I was certain of it.

33.

Temptation

My God, working on that roustabout crew 12 hours a day for 14 days in a row nearly killed me. When I wasn't sleeping, I played in the nonstop poker game to pass the time, and, by the end of the summer, I was so tired I'd pushed the guilt of stealing and selling tests to the back of my mind. However, as the end of the summer approached, I began to think about school, and stealing tests always crossed my mind. I resolved there'd be no test-stealing my senior year. I was certain of it. With my roustabout's salary and my poker winnings, I wouldn't have any money problems to tempt me. I remembered my junior year, when the addiction to test stealing overcame all my resistance, and I felt like an alcoholic at a bar, unable to turn down a drink. I called it the Uncle Hosie Disease.

During the summer, there wasn't a day that passed when I didn't think about Vi and the end-of-school love-making at my apartment. I was anxious to see her when I arrived back on campus, confident that I could convince her to break up with that sorry, Mr. Football. There wasn't a doubt in my mind that Vi and I were meant to be together.

I hitchhiked from Morgan City, Louisiana, to Magnolia and then caught a ride back to school with one of my friends. We pulled into Fayetteville around three o'clock, and, after tossing my bags in my apartment, I took a leisurely stroll across campus. During the summer, the 12 hour roustabout shifts had almost worn me out, and I was sure glad to be away from that noisy drilling rig. As I passed the Chemistry building, I looked at the side door and felt a little tingle go up my spine. Then I noticed a girl ahead of me.

"Lacy, wait up!"

Lacy turned, saw me, and ran to meet me, throwing her arms around me.

"Sandy, oh, it's great to see you! I've missed our long walks. How was your summer?"

"Well, it was mostly hard work. I didn't leave the drilling rig for weeks on end."

"Didn't find a girlfriend?"

"Ha, I didn't even see a girl. Come on, Lacy, our bench is just waiting for us."

Lacy and I walked over to the bench beside the library and sat there for at least an hour, catching up on the latest campus gossip and talking about what we had done during the summer. Lacy had worked in a department store in Tulsa, selling make-up. I told her about working on the offshore drilling rig, and how I nearly lost my ring finger when my senior ring got jammed between two joints of drill pipe. My finger healed, but my senior ring didn't. Lacy took my hand and rubbed the finger, which was still red and a little sore.

"Sandy, that's terrible! You could have been scarred for life! Thank goodness you didn't lose the finger."

She kept holding and rubbing my hand as we talked.

I didn't realize how much I had missed Lacy until we sat down to talk. When Lacy told me that she still wasn't dating, I couldn't believe it. If anything, she looked even more beautiful than last year.

***

The next day I ran into Vi and, as we talked about our summer, I proposed that we meet on the front steps of Old Main that night to talk, or better yet, go to my apartment. Picking up where we had left off at the end of the spring semester was what I had in mind.

"No, Sandy, I've had the summer to think about everything, and what we did at the end of school last year was a one-time fling. Daddy talked to me all summer about how I shouldn't do anything to affect my relationship with Bill. Daddy even called Bill and got him to come down for a few days. Daddy is right, Sandy; we can't be more than friends. It just has to be that way. I can't say anymore about it."

That last statement felt as if someone had hit me, it went so deep. I shook my head as I thought about her domineering father. I was stunned, but honestly not that surprised. After thinking about it, I knew that Vi's sorry father would've worked on her all summer, and she seemed to have an unnatural fear of crossing him.

"Oh, Vi, surely not. You have so much more in common with me than Mr. Football. Let's just take some time together this semester and get to know each other better. There's nothing wrong with that."

"I don't know, Sandy, maybe. But I can't meet you on the steps of Old Main any more, at least not for a while."

Vi had an almost frightened look in her eyes and immediately changed the subject. I knew better than to press it. My God, I couldn't believe how he controlled her. The way Vi was acting I knew there was something more, but I couldn't figure it out. We talked for a few minutes more, and then she had to go. I was depressed. It seemed as if I would take a step forward with Vi, and then her father or that sorry Mr. Football would intervene, and I would be pushed back two steps. I thought about it for several days and almost decided to give up on her. For once, it really did seem like a lost cause.

During the summer I'd saved almost $2000.00 from my

roustabout's salary and poker winnings, enough to pay for my final year of college.

One of my goals as a senior was to buy a car, and I started the semester hoping that a few good nights playing poker with the Deltas would put enough money in my pocket to make a down payment. Saturday rolled around, and I walked down to the Delta house for the poker game. When I entered the room, I noticed there were all new players, except for Dickie, who was at the head of the table. My seat was taken.

"Hey, guys, I need a seat," I said to the group in general.

"No seats available, Farm Boy. You're outta the game," said Dickie.

"What?"

"Yep, I'm the Delta president this year, and I suggested that you not be invited back. You know all those winning hands? Well, we think your playing was a little fishy." He leaned back, sucked on his cigarette, and blew smoke across the table. I could feel the blood flushing my face, and I spit out, "Well, I'll be damned. If you can't beat 'em, kick 'em out of the game."

I was disgusted and ready to quit everything that had to do with the Deltas. Of course, I'd already decided that I wasn't going to get any tests for them, but I was sure disappointed at not being able to clean them out playing poker. Hell, that bunch of coon-asses in south Louisiana had taught me every trick in the book over the summer.

"Hey, you hick Farm Boy, take a hike," spit Dickie. He gave me the finger and leaned back in his chair, sucking on that damned cigarette.

"You bet I will, you creep, and I'll still be hiking when Four Week, Ten Week, and Final Tests come up." Of course, I didn't have any intentions of getting those tests for them. Even though I was ticked off about being kicked out of the poker game, I felt a weight lifted off my shoulders. Maybe, without the Deltas begging me to steal tests, I could kick the habit. It was such a relief to walk back to my apartment, knowing that sordid episode of my life was behind me. Hell, I wasn't surprised about being kicked out of the poker game. After two summers working on an offshore drilling rig and playing poker night and day with some real poker whizzes, I'd honed my skills until a college boy's poker game was a piece of cake. Of course, with that worthless Dickie running the show, I wanted to clean him out again like I did last year.

***

Three weeks passed, and I thought the Deltas, their poker game, and the test stealing were behind me. However, after several frantic phone calls from Billy Faison, a good friend, and several other guys from the Delta House, I agreed to at least come talk to them about providing tests. The next night I took in a movie and stopped back by the Delta house for the meeting. We went to the basement where we usually played poker, and five of the Deltas and I sat down around the table. Dickie was sitting in his usual seat, and he started the conversation.

"Uh, Sandy,"

I looked up, startled. It was the first time Dickie had called me anything but Farm Boy. "The arrangement we had with you last year was good for everybody. Let's let bygones be bygones and do business again."

I knew one thing for sure, they hadn't been keeping their end of the deal, and I was going to use that to drop the whole thing.

"Humm, I don't know, you guys haven't been keeping our deal. One of you buys the test and passes it around to everybody in the house."

It was deathly quiet for at least a minute.

"Uh, no, Sandy."

"Don't lie about it," I interrupted. "Or I won't ever get another test."

"Okay, Sandy, maybe we did pass some of the tests around, but we can work something out," said Billy.

"We had better, or you're not going to see a thing from me."

I didn't intend to get tests for them again, but I figured that I could at least pull Dickie's chain. Hell, just jerking him around was what I had in mind.

"Whata you think's fair?" said Dickie.

Then I hit them. "Oh, I don't know, maybe something like $500.00 a test for everyone who gets to use it, and everyone in the house who takes the course has to pay up." I knew that astronomical figure would send them into orbit, and, after a little more arguing with Dickie, I could stalk out, and forget about the Deltas.

"Are you crazy?" yelled Dickie. "We'll never pay that!" Then the little weasel leaned forward, almost whispering as he bit down on his cigarette between his front teeth, "I'd worry about some of these guys ratting on you to the school administration about last year's test-stealing if you don't come through this year." Dickie leaned back, blew a smoke ring, and acted as if he'd just nailed me.

I couldn't believe that he was trying to blackmail me. He'll regret the hell out of that. "Meeting's over! I hope every one of you flunks out!"

"Wait, Sandy!—Dickie, quit screwing everything up, damn it! Now, Sandy, let's everybody calm down and talk this thing out," said Billy.

I'd started to walk out, but, when Billy said that, I stopped for a moment and looked back at the table of guys. Suddenly I had the urge to rejoin their poker game, and even the possibility of providing tests was creeping into my mind. After a few more minutes of conversation I said, "I'll tell you what. Since we're all hacked off tonight, I'll come back tomorrow night with a proposal, and we can discuss it."

Everybody nodded, and I left the meeting. Walking back to my apartment, I had the nagging feeling that I was being sucked in to something that I knew was terrible for me, but I couldn't shake the desire. However, there was one part of that conversation I wanted to counter; the blackmail threat from Dickie. I couldn't wait to get back to the apartment. I rushed in, pulled out The Journal, and started copying some of the details about last year's sales. It took me the better part of an hour, but, when I finished, I knew Dickie would find it fascinating reading.

I was early for the meeting the next night, and, after everybody had taken their seats, I pulled out my copies of The Journal.

"Here, guys, I want you to read something before we get started." I passed out the copies. I'm sure that the group expected to read my proposal to furnish the tests, including the costs per test and other stuff.

"What the hell?" said Billy. "Damn, have you been writing down every time we bought a test?"

"Yep."

"Why are you showing this stuff to us?" said Dickie.

"Okay, hand me the copies back, and I'll tell you," I said as I took them up. "I've kept a journal of everything I've done since I sold you the first test. Yesterday, Dickie threatened to turn me in if I didn't produce this semester's tests, and I just wanted to show you my ammunition, in case he does. If the administration gets its hands on my journal, they'll go back and change your grades, expel you from school, and kick this fraternity off campus. Now, Mr. Big Shot," I said to Dickie. "Still planning to turn me in?"

It was so quiet that you could have heard a pin drop. Now it was time to make my proposal. I'd wrestled with my conscience for the past 24 hours, and I'd finally come up with something that I was sure they'd turn down. Then I could forget about test stealing. But I knew that if they accepted my proposal, it would be difficult for me to walk away. I couldn't believe I was even making a pitch to them.

"Okay, I think we understand each other. Here's my proposal. Number one: $200.00 for each person who uses any test I procure, and every member of the fraternity who is in the class must buy the test, even if he doesn't use it. Number two: I will only provide five tests. Number three: any selling to other fraternities or independents is prohibited. I want a registration card from everybody in the house. And one last condition: I'm back in the game. Take it or leave it. Y'all talk it over and call me tomorrow. Four Weeks

Tests start next Monday, so you better decide pretty quick, or it'll be too late for those tests."

I left the room as they started discussing the proposal. As I walked back to my apartment, I felt relieved. Surely $200.00 per test per person would be too much for them, and making Dickie eat crow and let me back into the poker game should be the final blow. I was through with test stealing, thank God.

The next morning Billy called me and tried to trade me down. It took a lot of will power, but I finally said, "No, there's no trading, take it or leave it." I hung up the phone, relieved again.

However, I had underestimated their desire to have the tests. Billy called again that night to ask for more tests and for me to stay out of the poker game. I told him to forget it and hung up the phone. He was back on the phone in less than an hour.

"Sandy, we've agreed to the deal. You can stop by the house tomorrow, pick up the registration cards, list of tests and faculty offices, and, yeah, you're back in the poker game. Oh, one more thing. We're going to pass on the Four Weeks Tests. That's too much money, and we can catch up on the Ten Weeks Tests and the final."

I stood there holding the phone for almost a minute, too stunned to speak. Would I go back on my word? Finally, I mumbled an "Okay" to Billy and sat down on the bed. At least I wouldn't have to go after the Four Weeks Tests, and, since they had changed the deal, I could refuse to get the Ten Weeks Tests, but I knew I was committed to get at least five finals for them. I had tears in my eyes as I considered what to do, but, as I sat there and thought about playing poker and picking those locks, I could feel my breath quicken, my hands sweat, and a rush of adrenalin surge through my body. I couldn't resist. I was hooked again. The Uncle Hosie Disease had returned.

34.

The Sting

The next day, between classes, I stopped to sit on the library bench where Lacy and I usually met. I was still trying to sort out the deal I had made with the Deltas, and I was trying to shake the guilt I felt as I contemplated another series of break-ins and test stealing. It was an early autumn day, and the first cold front of the season had ushered some real fall weather into Arkansas. I was bundled up in a big trench coat, bent over and deep in thought, when someone sat down beside me.

"Thought I might find you here."

"Lacy!"

"Well, Sandy, aren't you going to keep me warm?"

I smiled and put the trench coat around both of us, and we huddled together, talking. Lacy, who looked prettier than ever, was in a great mood. She still hadn't had a single date since the experience with Bull, and she seemed to relish not dating.

"Sandy, I feel like a free woman. I don't feel a bit pressure on me to do anything. My grades are good, and I can sit here and talk to you, knowing we're best friends, and you respect me. My God, when I think back on what I did with some of those guys, it makes me never want to date again."

Well, I winced when Lacy said that, because I was one of those guys who had taken her out strictly for sex.

I took a good look at Lacy as she sat on the bench beside me. The Lacy with the tight fitting, sexy clothes had been replaced by a demure, conservatively dressed woman who actually exuded a sensuality stronger than the flashy, on-the-make Lacy of last year. As I sat there, thoughts about asking her out crept into my mind. Damn, it was about the most difficult thing I have ever done to be close friends with someone as beautiful as Lacy and not lay a hand on her. However, as I thought about it, and about how Lacy had responded when she quit dating, I decided not to ask her out. Honestly, I felt so guilty about taking advantage of her that I couldn't bring myself to ask her out. She'd think I was after more sex, and we were such good friends that I didn't want her to get that idea.

"Lacy, you'll meet the right guy someday, and you'll put this no-dating behind you."

"Maybe, Sandy, but he'll sure have to be special. No more of those grab, grab guys who only have one thing in mind."

When Lacy said that our eyes met, and our faces weren't eight inches apart. There was an instant where I wanted to kiss Lacy so bad I could taste it, but I didn't. After a few more minutes, we started shivering from the north wind that was almost blowing the trench coat off our backs. After making plans to meet at least a couple of times a week on the bench to talk, we left for class.

***

Saturday night I walked down to the Delta house, and, sure enough, my regular chair was empty. Dickie seemed in a better mood, and the game started with some good-natured kidding. Soon we were in the throes of another poker game. However, as the game progressed, Dickie seemed to have a seventh sense about when to raise and when to fold. Every time I came up with a good hand he dropped out, and, when he had the winning hand, he'd back me into a corner and raise me until I called or dropped out. He won every one of those hands, and I couldn't figure it out.

Dickie, who was one of the worst poker players I've ever been around, was playing like a pro. As the night wore on, I started watching Dickie intently. Was he doing anything differently? He was winning whether he dealt or not, hollering about cleaning someone's plow, usually mine. Then I noticed something different. Dickie seemed to stare intently at everybody's cards for just a minute, and then he'd bet, raise, or fold his hand. Could he be cheating? How?

I thought back to last summer, when I had played poker every day with the coon-ass roughnecks on the offshore rig, and then I realized how Dickie was cheating. One of the roughnecks brought a deck of marked cards out to the rig as a joke and started cutting cards for ten dollars a pop, betting on the cut before he turned the cards over. He won every time, and I couldn't believe it until he laughed and showed us how the deck was marked. I looked at the cards we were playing with: Bicycle Playing Cards, the same as the roughneck had brought out to the rig. I wanted to stop the game and accuse Dickie of cheating, but I held my peace. The game would break for a beer at about midnight, and I'd have a chance to check the cards.

"Well, I believe this two pair is gonna win the pot," hooted Dickie. He scooped up the chips and leaned back in his chair, posturing like a winner. "Say, let's take a break and get a beer."

Everyone nodded; we got up, stretched, and went upstairs for a beer. I walked back downstairs, pretending I was going to the bathroom, and headed straight for the card table. The cards were neatly stacked, and I picked them up and flipped them, looking at their backs. On Bicycle playing cards, there is a scene in the background of a flock of individual birds. I thumbed the cards. They rattled in my hand, and the flock of birds changed on almost every card: They were marked. Dickie had marked the cards about as simply as possible. He had blotted out the birds from the upper left-hand side of the card, leaving a single bird if it was an ace, two birds if it was a king, and so forth.

I sat there for a few minutes, wondering what to do. If I

accused Dickie of marking the cards, he'd deny it and try to blame someone else. Next week would be the same—or would it? I had a plan. In a few minutes everyone was back at the table, and Dickie picked up where he left off, winning every hand. I stayed around for another hour, feigned a sore throat, and got up to leave.

"Hey, Farm Boy, tired of getting your plow cleaned?"

"Naaaah, you're just lucky tonight, Dickie. Next week you'll be right back where you were, losing you ass off."

"Ha, we'll see," hooted Dickie. He was really relishing his big winning night.

The next morning I stopped by the Palace Drug Store, bought a deck of Bicycle playing cards and some matching fingernail polish, and spent the rest of the day marking my deck of cards. I was ready for Saturday night, and Dickie was going to be in deep poker water when we played again. I was going to sting him so bad that he'd never forget it.

***

Saturday night rolled around, and I walked in, carrying a half empty can of beer, which I made a show of finishing before we started. Then I yelled for a pledge to bring me another. We started playing promptly at eight o'clock. Each time I went to the restroom, I carried my beer, poured it out, and got another one when I sat back down at the table.

"Damn, Sandy, you're drinking like a fish. What's the deal?" said one of the guys.

"Ah, some girl dropped me like a hot potato."

"Ha, no wonder, Farm Boy. You can't get any decent women if they can smell the horse manure on your shoes. Hooo! Hooo! Ha, ha," Dickie hooted. I could hardly wait to nail that loudmouth.

When it was my turn to shuffle, I thumbed the cards to see if they were marked. They were. I played fairly conservatively, loosing steadily to Dickie as the night wore on. By break time, I was slurring my words and spilling beer on the table as I lost hand after hand. Dickie was beside himself, hollering, "Plowing clean-ing! Plow cleaning!" every time he won a pot.

"Hey, I need to pee again. Let's take a break," I mumbled.

Everyone nodded, and the room empted. I slipped out, stepped into the bathroom, and then stepped right back out. I got back to the room before anybody else did, and switched decks from Dickie's marked deck to mine. I'd marked my deck exactly opposite from Dickie's. If this sting was going to work, I needed to get a good hand, just a little better than Dickie's, pretty quick, or Dickie would recognize that the markings on the cards were dif-ferent.

I held my breath as we sat down and began to play.

Dickie leaned across the table, smirked, and said, "Well, Farm Boy, before this night's over I'm gonna have cleaned your ass out."

On the next hand, Lady Luck smiled on me. It was the hand I'd been waiting for. After all seven cards had been dealt, my three down cards indicated to Dickie, who thought he could tell from the marked cards, that I had two pair, sevens and deuces. Dickie, on the other hand, also had two pair, but since they were my marked deck of cards, I knew that they were kings and tens. My cards, which Dickie thought were deuces, were actually aces. Dickie was grinning ear to ear, as I seemed to just push chips across the table to him. God, I'm going to enjoy this. I'd been wait-ing for the sting hand and this was it.

"Better make it light on yourself, Farm Boy. I'm on a run," groused Dickie.

"You've just been lucky. Now, it's just me and you. Let's take the lid off the bets. Got the balls to do it?" I deliberately slurred my words, and knocked my can of beer over on the floor.

"Damn, I hate to take all of Farm Boy's money, but maybe he needs a lesson in poker playing," Dickie said to the rest of the table. "Come on, Farm Boy, pull out that moth-eaten billfold, and take out that one lousy check you keep in there."

I fumbled around, dropping my billfold on the floor as the players watched my antics. They were sure that the beer had completely obliterated my judgment and Dickie was going to clean me out.

"Gimme a pen," I mumbled to Jeff.

"Sandy, are you sure you wanna do this?" Jeff was my best friend at the fraternity, and he was worried that I was so drunk that I was about to lose every cent I had.

"Yeah, I'm gonna teach that blowhard a lesson he won't forget," I slurred.

"Come on, Farm Boy, make it light on yourself. I'll call anything you put on the table."

That was music to my ears as I wrote the check and dropped it in the pot.

"I raise you a $1000.00."

"What?"

"Yeah, I said a $1000.00." When you have a winning hand, never show mercy.

There was a collective gasp around the table as Dickie leaned over to stare at my cards. I could almost see his little pea brain count the birds on the back of my cards. He nodded.

"I call," he said. He scribbled out a check and dropped it in the pot.

"Two pair," I said and hesitated.

Dickie grinned, thinking his kings and tens would beat my two pair.

I turned my cards over slowly.

"A pair of sevens and a pair of aces," I said, flipping the hole cards over.

Dickie's smile left him as his face turned white.

"No, uh, no, you can't have a pair of aces! The cards, uh, oh, it can't be! You cheated me, you lousy, hick!"

"Really? How? Just tell me, Dickie. How did I cheat you?"

Dickie fumed as he sat there, not knowing what to say. Jeff grinned at me and said, "Come on Dickie, you lost the hand. Get over it."

The sting had worked perfectly, and now I knew it was time to leave.

"Listen, fellows, I hate to leave a winner, but I've gotta go." I was suddenly as sober as a judge, and, as a bunch of startled guys watched, I scooped up the pot and Dickie's check and left the Deltas' poker game forever. After what I'd done to Dickie, I knew playing poker with the Deltas was history.

***

Lacy was waiting for me at the bench when I walked up that next Monday. She looked absolutely radiant.

"Hey, Lacy, guess what?"

"Tell me, Sandy. I don't have a clue."

"Look at this." I showed Lacy the check from Dickie.

"My gosh, Sandy, where did you get a $1000.00 check?"

"Well, it was courtesy of Dickie Barnett's trust fund. He tried to cheat playing poker, and I turned the tables on him. I'm going to go buy a car. How about going with me to help pick it out?"

"Sure, let's go."

"Uh, well, we'll have to walk to the car lots on Highway 71. But it's a nice day, and it won't take us very long."

Lacy and I walked the half mile down Dixon Street and started car shopping at the various used car lots that were along Highway 71. We'd gone through three lots without finding the right car, and Lacy and I had split up to cover an unusually large lot when I heard her calling me.

"Sandy, come here," Lacy yelled from the back of the lot. "I've found your car."

I walked back to where Lacy was standing, and there was a 1952 Ford, which had been repainted bright red.

"I know red's your favorite color, Sandy. This is the car you should buy."

It was that simple. One look and I knew she was right. An hour later we were driving back to the university. I dropped Lacy off at her sorority house and headed back to my apartment, where I waxed and polished the car most of the afternoon.

***

The semester seemed to fly by. Vi and I saw each other at the Union, and, if she was sure that Mr. Football, was in class or practicing football, we'd have one of our Coke dates. After a while, I stopped asking Vi to meet me on the front steps of Old Main. Her crazy, domineering daddy had put the fear of something in her. What, I could never figure out. Maybe I should have given up, but there was that something deep within me, something that I'm sure both of us felt, which kept me coming back to her. I was certain, even when things looked bleak, that someday we'd be together. If the best I could do was a Coke date, then I'd have to settle for that. Not much romance, but it did keep Vi on my mind.

That semester I provided the Deltas with Final Tests only. Hell, nobody wanted to pay that kind of money for a Four Weeks Test, and, when they turned me down and wouldn't pay for the Four Weeks Tests, I refused to get any of the Ten Weeks Tests. I hadn't broken the addiction, but at least I'd tapered off.

***

That fall, between Four and Ten Weeks Tests, North Arkansas had some great autumn days. When we had an especially gorgeous day, Lacy and I would walk over to the old Fayetteville cemetery and sit on the bench where she had told me about being abused as a teenager. There was something about that setting, or maybe it was the bench itself, which made us talk as if it were confession time. Lacy told me in detail about her first two years at the university, shaking her head in disbelief as if she couldn't believe she had done all those things. Of course, her active dating life was no secret, but the details were. I was fascinated.

Over the weeks, I told her almost everything about my life.

The only thing I left out was the arrangement with the Deltas. I just couldn't make myself tell her that I was a common thief.

The only thing that brought a rise out of Lacy was when I told her I had had a crush on Vi. She frowned. Lacy quickly changed the subject, and I knew better than to bring it up again. I'd thought I completely understood Lacy, but, after that fall afternoon, I wasn't sure I knew everything.

***

The Deltas finally agreed to come up with the money for Final Tests. The week before finals, I made my rounds, going from building to building, picking the locks, and rummaging through desk after desk until I came up with the tests. Occasionally, I'd find a professor who hadn't left his Final Test in his desk, and I'd mark that one off my list. I sure wasn't going to attempt a home burglary for a stinking test. I began to feel like a real low life as I went from office to office pilfering tests, and at times I actually hated myself because of the person I'd become. Even with a semester to go, I was already counting the days until I could drive away from Fayetteville and put that episode of my life behind me. It had begun to bother me so much that I was having nightmares and getting very little sleep. I managed to get three of the five tests the Deltas wanted, and, the Saturday morning before Finals started, we met in the upstairs reading room and I presented them with my bill.

"Okay, first off, I couldn't get Advanced Calculus or Quantum Physics."

"Oh, you've got to be kidding! What do you mean you couldn't get them? You agreed to give us those tests! Hell, I've got one of those classes, and I was depending on you!" yelled Billy.

"Listen, remember this, before anybody gets all upset. I promised to do my best to get them, and that didn't include going to some professor's house and breaking in. Hell, I think three out of five is pretty good." Well, Billy calmed down, and I pulled out a folded-up piece of paper.

"According to your registration cards, there are seven Deltas in these classes. Our agreed price is $200 per person. That comes to $1400. I have the tests in this folder. Do you have the money?"

"Well, Sandy, that's a lot more than we'd figured. Dickie, how much did you collect?" said Jeff, who was acting as the spokesman.

"Well, Jeff, I've got less than a 1000. Say, uh, Farm, uh, Sandy, let me give you this and pay you the rest next week."

"Dickie, you must think I'm stupid to even suggest that. I want all the money, and I mean every nickel, or I keep the tests." There was some general whining around the table until Jeff yelled for everybody to shut up.

"Come back tomorrow, Sandy. We'll have the full amount then."

Sunday morning at ten o'clock I was back at the table, and Billy passed the sack of money over to me. I sat there and counted it while they waited for me to pass them the tests.

"Yeah, it's all here. Here are the tests." I handed them the tests, picked up my sack of money, and left the Deltas sorting out the tests, yelling for guys to come get their copies.

As I walked out of the Delta House, I checked my watch. "Humm, 10:45," I mumbled, "too early for lunch." I was about to cross the street when six guys, two of whom I knew, passed me on the sidewalk.

"Hey, Sandy, how's it going?" one of them yelled.

"Fine. Say, where are y'all going?"

"We're going to University Baptist, to church. Come go with us."

"Naw, I can't make it. I need to study for finals."

"Okay, see you."

My God, I didn't need that.

Boy, did I feel guilty, standing there, holding a sack of money I had received for stealing and selling tests while talking to friends who were going to church. It stuck in my mind for days.

35.

Plans

The fall semester and the break between semesters were over before I knew it, and, as the weeks passed, the trees began to bud. I was by myself, having a Coke at the Union one afternoon when it hit me: I'd be graduating in less than eight weeks. Of course, I'd thought about what I was going to do after graduation, but, outside of being interviewed by several oil companies that were hiring geologists, I hadn't done anything.

My overall grade point was only a high two point, but my geology grades were all A's. The job interviews I had went very well, especially the one with Texaco, and I'd already daydreamed about working my way up in Texaco and one day being president of one of the largest oil companies in the world. I guess I was depending on getting a job offer from one of the companies, because I hadn't made any plans at all for after graduation.

It had been two weeks since the interviews when I began to receive letters from the companies I'd interviewed. When the letter from Texaco came, my hands were shaking so badly that I could hardly open the letter. I finally opened it and, after a line or two that said how impressed they were with me, there was a paragraph that said, "We wish you well, but we are unable to offer you a job at this time." I slumped back on the bed, disappointed but still hopeful about the other interviews. Several days later, after I had received letters from all but one of the companies I'd interviewed and read the short rejection notes, I gave up hope of finding a job before I left school.

***

Of course, the Deltas were all over me to get both Four Weeks Tests and Ten Weeks Tests, naturally at a greatly reduced price. I managed to turn them down, but it wasn't easy. I knew that when they came after me with a sack of money to get the Final Tests, it would be nearly impossible to turn them down. I knew I sure wasn't cured of Uncle Hosie's Disease.

***

With only six weeks left in school, I received a reply from the last of the interviews I'd been on earlier in the semester. It was a letter from Humble Oil and Refining Company of Houston, Texas. I opened the letter and stared in amazement at a job offer. Starting pay, $550 per month, assigned to south Texas, etc., and at the end, "Please give us a call and let us know if you accept our offer."

I grabbed the phone, and, in a few minutes, I was talking with the head of personnel at Humble Oil and Refining Co.

"Yes, sir, I accept your offer."

It took a day for it to sink in. I couldn't wait to tell Vi, and, when her anthropology class in Old Main ended that morning, I was waiting for her at the foot of the stairs.

"Vi, I need to talk with you. I've got some exciting news."

"Oh, Sandy, I can't right now. I'm meeting Bill at the Union."

Damn, Mr. Football again.

"Uh, okay, how about in front of Old Main tonight?"

"Well, I don't know, Sandy."

"Oh, come on Vi. At least you can let a friend share some exciting news with you."

Vi stood there a minute, but finally she nodded. Finally. It had taken an entire school year to break the fear that her domineering daddy had put into her about seeing me.

"Okay, Sandy, but I can't be gone from the house long. Bill is picking me up at eight o'clock."

"Fine, we'll meet at seven. I'm not kidding, Vi, this is exciting news."

"Gotta go, see you tonight."

I was standing at the door of the Union, looking for a table, when Lacy walked up behind me and squeezed one of my buttocks. I almost jumped through the door.

"Damn, Lacy!" I said as I turned around. "You almost gave me a heart attack."

Lacy tossed her blonde hair back and giggled.

"You must have a sensitive ass," she whispered.

"Come on, it's such a nice day. Let's go outside and sit on the bench. I've missed seeing you the last few days."

"Yeah, me too." We walked out of the Union and past the library to the bench.

I know we could have walked into the Union and had a Coke, but I was still nervous about being seen with Lacy. Vi was in a better mood now, and I didn't want to do anything to upset her. Lacy and I were just friends, but of course, Vi wouldn't believe that.

Then it hit me; I could tell Lacy about my new job. Hell, I was having a fit to tell somebody. Before Lacy could say anything, I told her about my job offer, and where I'd be living.

"Sandy, that's wonderful news! Congratulations! I knew you'd get a good job." And with that comment Lacy turned to me and planted a big kiss right on my lips.

I was surprised, actually shocked, but I smiled, stuttered, and said, "Well, I'll miss Arkansas, but if I want to work as a geologist in the oil industry, I've got to go where they send me."

"Yeah, Sandy. In a few weeks we'll both be gone from campus, and we may never see each other again."

Lacy turned her head and her shoulders slumped.

"Oh, don't say that, Lacy. We can keep in touch. Say, what are your plans?"

"I don't have any," she said in a dejected tone of voice. "Maybe I can get a teaching certificate and teach English in some dinky, little school, or go back to Tulsa and get a job as a salesperson. But you know what, Sandy? I don't care. I'm disgusted and ready to leave school. This last year has been a rotten one for me. After that horrible experience last year with Bull Jenkins, I haven't gone out with anyone, and there have been some horrible rumors about me floating around campus."

I knew what Lacy was talking about, and there wasn't a shred of truth in any of them. The sorry guys who she had stopped dating were spreading that crap all over campus. Lacy, a lesbian? Ha, that was the biggest lie of them all.

"Lacy, I can't believe you're still not dating. There's not a guy on campus who wouldn't want to date you." Well, I was trying to cheer her up, but then she shot back with a line I couldn't counter.

"Sure, Sandy, and why? Why would the guys want to date me?"

"Uh, uh." I could feel the blood rushing to my face as I looked at Lacy.

"Oh, we both know—don't we?" She dropped her head and, for a few seconds, didn't say anything.

I mumbled, "Yeah."

"Let me ask you something, Sandy."

"What?"

"Why can't I find someone besides you who'll at least carry on an intelligent conversation with me and not just grab, grab, grab?"

"Lacy, I don't know, but I think you're a neat girl. Don't worry about finding somebody. You'll be able to start over after you graduate and go to a different town."

Lacy wiped her eyes and gave me the strangest look. Then she muttered, "No, I won't."

"What?" Lacy didn't answer. She stood up, shook her head, and said, "Oh, look at the time, I've gotta go—Great news about your new job. Keep me posted, and let's say goodbye before we leave school."

"Sure, I'll see you before I leave."

"I hope so."

I sat there for a few more minutes, thinking about Lacy and the strange conversation we'd had. She was right, every guy who asked her out was after one thing, and, before the Bull Jenkins date, they usually got what they were after. When I first met Lacy it had been hard for me to figure out why Lacy was so promiscuous. Hell, actually I didn't care, because I was after her just like all the other guys were. But after I got to know her and she told me about the abuse she'd received from her stepfather, I understood.

Well, after the horrible date with Bull, she'd had become bitter and cynical about all men. I didn't blame her, because all the guys who dated Lacy were going after sex; after all, I sure was when I traded her the History test. When I really got to know Lacy, I felt terrible about taking advantage of her. I was no better than those other sorry guys. But I could see why Lacy was having trouble finding someone. No one was about to get into a serious relationship with the girl who had been the tramp of the university. The reputation she had made as a freshman and sophomore had stayed with her, and she couldn't shake it.

36.

Vi

I sat around for most of the afternoon, trying to come up with some way to get Vi to drop that sorry Mr. Football. She and that worthless guy had been engaged since last fall, and they'd planned a June wedding. Vi had resisted meeting me on the steps of Old Main for almost a whole school year. Would she even show up? If she did it would be a step in the right direction, but was I kidding myself? Did I have any hope of ever being with Vi? Hell, a wedding in June was planned, and I was still chasing after her. If I'd been playing poker with those odds, I'd have folded the hand. It sure seemed like a lost cause.

At seven o'clock I was pacing back and forth in front of the steps of Old Main, waiting on Vi. She was only ten minutes late, and she looked radiant as she walked around the corner and up to where I was standing.

"Hi, Sandy. What's the exciting news?" She took the nine steps up to the front door of Old Main two steps at a time, sat down on the top step, and leaned back against the door.

I followed her up the steps and sat down beside her. "Vi, you wouldn't believe how gorgeous you look tonight. Maybe it's the moonlight, but I've never seen you look prettier."

"You're sweet, Sandy."

"Okay, Vi, let me tell you the news."

I proceeded to tell Vi every detail, and I even pulled out the letter from Humble Oil Company and read it to her.

"Sandy, I'm so happy for you. It sounds like a great job, and wow, 550 a month!"

Vi leaned over to hug me, and I turned my head down and kissed her on the mouth. We kissed deeply, and she pulled me to her. We never said a word, but continued to kiss and embrace. I couldn't believe that Vi and I were passionately courting. After nothing for the past two semesters except dozens of conversations, I'd about given up. Now, the girl I thought of constantly was in my arms. We continued to kiss, touch, and fondle non-stop for another 20 minutes. Vi pulled away after an extremely passionate embrace.

"Sandy, I've got to go. Bill will be at the house to pick me up in a few minutes."

"Don't go, Vi. Stand him up like he's stood you up so many times."

"Oh, I can't, Sandy. He wouldn't understand, and I just couldn't tell Daddy I'd stood up Bill."

"Listen, Vi, we were meant to be together. I've known it from the first day we met, when I helped you with your books. Break up with that sorry jock and come to Texas with me. I want to marry you."

My God, I couldn't believe I'd blurted that out. Vi looked shocked, but hesitated for a moment. I held my breath for a few seconds as she paused. Maybe I have a chance.

"Sandy, that's so sweet. You're a special friend, but you know I'm engaged to Bill."

"But what about now? What we just did?"

"Oh, Sandy, just because we courted a little bit doesn't mean I'm ready to throw Bill aside and go off with you. It's so romantic here, on these steps, in the moonlight, that I couldn't help myself."

"Okay, but think about it. I think you'd be happier with me."

She started shaking her head.

"No, Sandy, I can't. What would Daddy think? You can't even imagine how upset he would be."

I started to get desperate. "Please, Vi, don't say no right now. Give it till the end of school, okay?"

Vi, took a deep breath, smiled, and squeezed my hand. "Well, I don't think I'll change my mind, but just for you, Sandy, I will. Now, I've got to go. I'm running late, and Bill will be waiting for me."

After Vi left, I sat on the steps for nearly an hour. I thought I had a chance; she was actually considering going off to Texas with me. Now I had six weeks to convince her to drop Mr. Football and go with me, and my mind was clicking, thinking of how I could sway her. By God, I was going to convince her to go to Texas with me, or I was going to die trying.

The next morning I checked my bank account. The test selling and poker games had fattened it up to $4500. I sent Vi flowers that day, and told the florist to keep them coming every three days. The cards all said, "We were meant for each other."

Vi called a week later. I thought she was calling to thank me for the flowers, but she sounded funny and didn't even mention them. She said that she wanted to meet me on the front steps of Old Main that night. I didn't have any doubt that she was ready to say yes, and, of course, I was excited just thinking about the meeting. This was the first time she'd suggested a meeting, and I was sure that she was going to tell me she'd broken up with that sorry Mr. Football.

37.

Vi!

That night I rounded the corner of Old Main about 15 minutes early, and, to my surprise, Vi was already there, pacing back and forth on the sidewalk in front of the building. She was always late. I couldn't believe she was early.

"Oh, Sandy, I'm so glad to see you. I have to talk to somebody."

One look at Vi and I knew that she hadn't set up a meeting to tell me she'd broken up with Mr. Football. She was distraught and had been crying. Her lips were trembling.

"Vi, what in the world is wrong?"

"Come on, let's go sit down, and I'll tell you." She climbed the steps and sat down, and I sat down beside her and held her hand.

Before she could say anything, she started sobbing uncontrollably, holding her handkerchief up to her eyes.

"Oh, Sandy, I can't make myself say the words."

"Vi, what? Tell me!" I grabbed her by her shoulder and turned her around to face me.

"What's wrong?"

"Sandy, I'm pregnant...but it's worst than just that..." and her voice trailed off.

Vi dropped her head in her lap, and I sat there in shock, listening to the muffled sobbing on that quiet, spring night. It was hard to believe that Vi was pregnant. Not that I didn't think that she and that worthless jock were having sex, but being pregnant? It had never crossed my mind. I was speechless for a few moments.

"My God, Vi, are you sure?"

"Yes, I'm positive. I've gone to a doctor."

"What are you going to do, move up your wedding date?" When I said that, I felt a wave of depression sweep over me. Vi was upset, but she'd surely move up the wedding date and marry that worthless jock. I'd lost. We'd never be together. But there was more, and, when she finished, I could see why she was so upset.

"Oh, Sandy, that's why I'm crying. We're supposed to get married in Monticello this June, and my family would just die if we got married before then. Well, they'd get over it, but that's not the problem."

Vi hesitated and then, in a soft voice, she said, "Bill doesn't want to marry me right now. He said a wife and baby would drag him down just as he's talking to some pro scouts and trying to get a career started."

God, Vi was so embarrassed she could hardly get those words out. I couldn't believe he wouldn't marry her.

"What?"

"Yes, that's what he said."

"What are you going to do?"

"Oh God, Sandy, I hate to say this. Bill wants me to have an abortion."

Vi shuddered and turned her head away from me. She continued, "He's found a doctor in Springfield who will do the job for $1500, and he wants me to go by myself and get it done. That's why I'm crying. I don't know what to do."

"Oh, my God, an abortion! By yourself? No, Vi, no! Don't have an abortion! It's too dangerous. For God's sake, I can't believe he won't go ahead and marry you!"

Vi broke down and cried again as she shook her head. "He's not going to marry me, Sandy. At least not until I have an abortion. He made it very clear last night when we talked. I've got to go get the abortion. Bill said he's in heavy training for some meetings with pro scouts, and, if he misses them, he's afraid he won't get a contract."

"What? You've got to be kidding, Vi."

"I'm not, Sandy."

"Listen, Vi, you don't have to get an abortion."

"Sandy, I couldn't have a baby out of wedlock. It would kill my folks, and I'd never live it down."

"I don't mean out of wedlock." I paused, and Vi looked at me.

"Marry me, go to Texas, and have the baby."

"What? You'd marry me, pregnant with Bill's baby?"

"I sure would."

"No, Sandy, even though I care for you, it's not fair. I can't let you do it."

The thought of the girl I was desperately in love with having an abortion was almost more than I could take. I pleaded with her not to consider it, and I did everything I could to convince her to marry me.

Finally, she said in a determined, matter-of-fact voice, "Sandy, I do care for you, but I'm not going to marry you." And then Vi hesitated, and she softly said, "If I did marry you, Sandy, I wouldn't want to be pregnant with someone else's baby."

"Well, Vi, what are you going to do?"

"I don't know, that's why I'm here talking with you. There's not another soul on earth I can talk to about this. I've about decided to go to Springfield by myself and get the abortion, but I don't have the money."

"What? You don't have the money? Isn't Mr. Football going to pay for it?"

"No."

"No?"

"He said he didn't have it. He told me to ask my folks for the money, but I can't do that. I just can't."

I sat there in stunned silence for a few minutes as Vi began to cry again. Then I put my arm around her.

"Vi, I'll help you. I'll take you to Springfield, and I'll pay for the abortion." It was the only thing to say. I couldn't have walked away and left the woman I loved sitting there, still crying.

"Oh, Sandy, you're wonderful. You're the best friend a person could ever have."

"When is your appointment?"

"This Friday at three o'clock. I have the address on this slip of paper."

"Wait a minute, Vi. Abortions are against the law. Is this a legitimate doctor?"

"I'm sure he is, Sandy. Bill wouldn't let me go to someone who wasn't any good."

"Oh, God, Vi, that muscle-head doesn't have a clue if this guy is even a doctor."

"Sandy, it's settled. I'm not going to change my mind. Here's the address." Vi handed me the slip of paper, which I put in my pocket. Then I pulled Vi close and held her for several minutes. Finally, I said, "I'll pick you up right before lunch on Friday. It's about a three hour drive to Springfield. How long did the doctor say he would need to keep you?"

"He said the procedure was simple, and I would be back in school Monday morning."

"Okay, but I think it's more complicated than that. Remember, you don't have to do this. You can go to Texas with me."

"I know, Sandy, and you're so sweet to offer, but I'm going to have the abortion."

We talked a few minutes more, and, after Vi left, I sat on the steps for another 20 minutes, trying to make sense out of what had just happened. I was so mad about her being pregnant with that sorry Mr. Football's baby that I could hardly think. However, I knew that even that didn't diminish my love for Vi. Maybe the trip to have the abortion, which I was paying for, and driving her up there would let her see that I was the best man, and she'd drop that louse once and for all. I couldn't sleep that night for worrying about some sorry, criminal doctor performing an abortion on Vi.

Friday morning I drove by the bank, withdrew $1500, and picked up Vi at the Delta Chi House. She had resigned herself to the abortion, and talked most of the way to Springfield about how it was definitely the right thing for her, and for Bill. I began to wonder why I was involved.

We got to Springfield at about two o'clock, and I stopped at a gas station to fill up and get some directions. The attendant looked at the address, acted a little hesitant, and then finally gave me some general directions with the final comment, "You know, that ain't the best section of town."

That concerned me. We drove along, following his directions, and, when we turned down the last street to connect with the street on the address, I knew what he meant; we were in a slum.

"Oh, my God," I mumbled. I looked over at Vi, who also seemed concerned. "I don't know, Vi, surely a legitimate doctor doesn't have an office here. Maybe we have the wrong address."

"No, the address is correct. I copied it down myself. Look, there's 321, on the door across the street."

It was the correct address all right, but the 321 building number was over a dirty wooden door leading to an upstairs room. I parked, but, before I got out, I said to Vi, "This isn't right. The only doctor who would have an office in a building like this is probably some low-rent medical criminal. Let's call the whole thing off."

Vi hesitated for a moment and then opened the door.

"Come on, Sandy, this is the address. We might as well get this thing over with."

Vi walked to the door and pressed the doorbell.

In a couple of minutes a man's voice answered.

"Yeah, whata ya want?"

"Uh, are you Doctor Adams?" stammered Vi.

"Who wants to know?"

"I'm Virginia Botner, and I have an appointment with Doctor Adams."

"Oh, ya, just a minute, and I'll let you in."

Finally, we heard the lock click, the door opened, and there stood a man dressed in blue jeans and a dirty t-shirt, puffing on a cigarette.

"Are you a doctor?" I said in disbelief. Damn, in my wildest dreams I'd have never believed that slob was a doctor.

"Yeah, come on up to my office," he replied as he turned and started up the stairs.

After we had climbed three flights of stairs, we turned down a dimly lit hallway and followed the man until he opened an office door and started inside. I grabbed Vi's arm and pulled her back out in the hall.

"Vi, this is horrible! That man's no doctor! Let's leave!" I whispered in her ear.

Vi hesitated for a minute.

"Come on in, lady, this won't take but a few minutes." He dropped his cigarette and ground it out on the floor, and stood with his hands on his hips, waiting for us to come inside.

Vi looked up at me and said, "I don't want to do this, Sandy, but I've got to."

I had a sinking feeling when I walked into the waiting room, which was furnished with a couple of folding chairs, a beat-up old coffee table, and a file cabinet. The faded wallpaper was a sickly green, and the edges were peeling up from around the baseboards. The whole room reeked of a horrible, vaguely hospital smell, which seemed to permeate everything. I stood there with my mouth open. It looked worse than anything I could have ever imagined, and, as I looked at Vi, I knew she felt the same way. Her eyes filled with tears, and her lips were trembling as she looked over the decrepit office.

The so-called doctor opened the door to an adjoining room, and there, pushed against the back wall, was a raised hospital bed covered with a dirty sheet. In your worst nightmare, you couldn't have imagined undergoing an operation in such conditions.

I pulled Vi aside. "Don't do this, Vi! He's not a doctor and this office is filthy! You could die in this hole!"

Vi bit her lip and shook her head. "Sandy, I don't have a choice. I have to get this abortion. How could I possibly face Daddy if I didn't?"

"Damn it, Vi, for once in your life forget about your crazy daddy! It's your life that's on the line here, not his! Please don't do it, Vi!" I was begging now.

Vi looked at me, took a deep breath, and said in resignation, "I don't have a choice, Sandy. I have to get this abortion." When Vi said that she turned away from me, walked into the next room, and sat down on the hospital bed.

As Vi walked away from me I had such a sinking feeling that I could hardly stand up. I was speechless, almost in shock that Vi was actually going through with the abortion under those conditions. I was brought back to reality when the man said, "My nurse ain't in today, but I can handle everything. Son, you stay out here in the waiting room, and lady, pull off your skirt and panties and lie back on that table. I'll be with you in a minute. But first," he said, looking at me, "let me have the money, 1500 in cash. Have you got it?"

"Yeah." I pulled the wad of hundred dollar bills out of my pocket and handed them to him.

Oh, my God! Oh, my God! I kept thinking. What have we gotten into?

He stuffed the money into his pocket and left the room for a few minutes. He returned carrying a black bag, but, before he could go into the room with Vi, I stopped him.

"Uh, sir, are you a doctor?"

"Of course! Do you think I'd do an operation like this if I wasn't?"

"Well, no, but can I see your license?"

"Listen, son, I don't have time to run around looking for stuff like that. Now, does this girl want an abortion or not?"

"You're supposed to be a doctor; anyway, that's what you're telling people who call. Where's your license to practice medicine?"

"Lady," he called out to Vi. "Your boyfriend is holding this operation up. Do you want an abortion or not?"

"Yes, I do. Sandy, I'm going through with this. I've come too far to back out now."

"Sit down, son. I'll be through in a few minutes." He turned and left me standing there, feeling helpless; unable to do anything to stop what I was sure would be a horrible incident.

The door closed behind him, and I could hear him talking with Vi until she went under. In a few minutes, I heard him mumbling to himself, and then he let out a string of curse words. I jumped up out of my chair and ran to the door. Should I go in? Then it was quiet again, but I couldn't make myself go sit back down, so I stood there for the longest hour of my life as I waited on him to finish with Vi. Finally, he opened the door and walked out into the waiting room. He pulled off some bloody gloves, stuck a cigarette in his mouth, lit it, and looked at me.

"She's still a little woozy, but I think she's okay. Let her wake up and take her to some place where she can lie down for a few hours."

He turned and walked out of the room and down the hall.

I ran out in the hall, calling out to him, "Hey, where are you going? Aren't you going to check on her anymore?"

"Naw, I got other things to do. She'll be okay." And with that comment he went down the stairs, and I heard the door slam behind him.

I went in to see Vi, who was barely able to sit up. Blood was on the table and floor, and Vi was as white as a sheet.

"Oh, my God, we've got to get you out of here and take you somewhere where you can lie down and rest. Can you walk?"

Vi looked at me. Her eyes were almost glazed over, but she nodded and said, "Yes, just help me. I'm still dizzy, but I think I can make it."

Vi managed to pull on her panties and dress, but I could tell that she was hurting with every movement she made. With Vi clutching my shoulders with one hand and steadying herself on the wall with the other, we left the office and started down the hall.

"Stop, Sandy! I'm about to faint!" Vi clutched her stomach and bent over.

"Ahaaaa! Oh, please, help me, Sandy!" Vi moaned in anguish and began to throw up. I could barely hold her up, and, after a few seconds, I let her slide down and lie on the dirty hall floor while I tried to comfort her. I wiped her face with a handkerchief as I propped her up against the wall and tried to make her comfortable.

"Vi, we've got to get out of this filthy hole and get you to a bed. Can you stand up now?"

"I think so, Sandy. Maybe I was just nauseated from the operation." Vi got up with my help and took a couple of steps. "Oh! Wait! Wait! My stomach is cramping! Oh, God! It's killing me!" Vi slumped back against the wall and slid down on the floor. She sat there motionless for a couple of minutes.

Then she took a couple of deep breaths and nodded her head.

"I'm better now." She reached out to me, and I helped her to her feet. We slowly started walking down the hall, but we had taken fewer than ten steps before she collapsed again.

"Oh, God, my stomach!" she screamed, bending over again.

"Easy, Vi. When you get up, just take a step at a time."

I can't, Sandy, it hurts too badly."

I looked at Vi, and I knew that she couldn't walk, and that she certainly couldn't get down three flights of stairs. There was only one thing to do.

"Put your arm around my neck and hold on." I reached under her legs and picked her up. Damn, she's heavy, I thought. Vi, who is 5' 11" and weighed at least 140 pounds, was quiet a load.

"Sandy, no! You can't possibly carry me all the way to the car."

"Yes, I can, Vi. That's the only way to get you out of here." I began to slowly walk down the dark hall as Vi began to cry. After we got down the first flight of stairs I was exhausted, and I had to set her down and rest before I could go any farther. A bare light bulb hung over each landing on the stairs. After catching my breath, I picked Vi up and headed for the next landing. Halfway down the third flight of stairs I had to sit down again and rest. I pulled Vi back on top of me so that she could lie on me and not on those dirty stairs. How we made it down three flights of stairs, I'll never know, but finally I reached the front door. It had taken almost 20 minutes to get that far.

In another five minutes, we made it out the door and across the street to my car, where I eased Vi into the back seat, where she could lie down. I thought she looked worse, and, as I drove to a motel, I kept wondering what I'd do if she needed to see a doctor. After registering, I helped her into the room, and she collapsed on the bed.

Thank God, we're here. I plopped down on the bed beside her, exhausted. Maybe the worst is over, and tomorrow she'll be better.

A few minutes later, I heard Vi moaning again, and she called out to me, "Sandy, something's wrong. I think I'm bleeding."

I jumped up and ran around to her side of the bed. Before I even got there, I saw a pool of blood on the sheet.

"Oh, my God, Vi, you're hemorrhaging! We've got to take you to the emergency room!" I was in such a panic that I was afraid to wait for an ambulance, so I picked her up and ran to the car, placing her in the back seat.

"Sandy, hurry, I'm about to faint."

"Lie down, Vi, and don't move. I'll have you to the hospital in a few minutes."

I pulled the car up to the motel office to get directions to the hospital.

"Ma'am, I've got a girl in my car that needs to go to the emergency room! Where's a hospital?"

"It's straight down Lincoln Avenue about a mile, big building, you can't miss it."

In a few seconds, I was roaring down Lincoln Avenue, speeding and running red lights. I heard a low moan from Vi, and I looked back just as she slumped over.

"Oh, God, no, no!" I muttered. I looked at her limp body, and I honestly thought she'd died from loss of blood.

In another few minutes, I saw the big sign for Memorial Hospital directly ahead. I pulled up to the emergency room door, scooped up Vi in my arms, and ran into the hospital.

"I've got a girl who's bleeding to death!" I yelled at the nurse on duty.

Oh, God! Please don't let her die! I silently prayed.

"Follow me," said the nurse as she opened a hospital room door and motioned for me to come in.

"Put her on this table. How was she injured?"

"Uh—" I stammered.

"Tell me quickly! It could be a matter of life and death!" she shouted.

"She, she..."

"Tell me now!" she said, shaking me by the arm.

"A man who said he was a doctor gave her an abortion."

"Oh, my God, she's hemorrhaging! Go to the waiting room. I'll let you know how everything is going as soon as the doctor gets here."

The nurse was already testing her blood and preparing to give her a transfusion when I left the room. I saw the doctor enter the room about five minutes later, and I sat and waited and waited. An hour later, the doctor walked out.

"Son, are you her boyfriend—husband?"

"Uh, well, no, but I'm with her."

"What?"

"Yes, her boyfriend got her the appointment, and he wouldn't take her, so I did."

"Well, I guess it doesn't make any difference."

"How is Vi?"

"She's going to be okay, but if you had been 30 minutes later she'd have died. I've stopped the hemorrhaging, and we've given her two pints of blood. We'll give her another one in a few minutes. The nurse will put her in a room after the last transfusion is finished, and, if she doesn't start hemorrhaging again, she can leave the hospital in a couple of days."

Thank God.

"Can I go in and see her?"

"Yes, but hurry, we'll be moving her to a room in a few minutes."

I walked into the room where Vi, who was conscious now, was receiving her third transfusion.

"Sandy, the doctor said you saved my life. The bleeding has stopped, and I'm going to be all right."

"Yeah, Vi, but you've got to stay in the hospital for a couple of days. You need to call your sorority house in the morning and come up with some excuse."

"Okay, Sandy."

Vi's eyes filled with tears, and she reached out her hand for mine.

"Sandy," and then she hesitated for a few seconds. As she squeezed my hand she said, "I love you, and I always have, almost from the first time we met. There could never be anyone for me but you, especially after tonight."

I couldn't believe that she had actually said those magic words, "I love you."

"Vi, I've always known we were meant to be together. You know I've always loved you."

Vi pulled me toward her, and I leaned over and kissed her on the cheek.

I stood there and held her hand until the nurse came in and took her to a room. As I drove back to the motel I repeated, "I love you, I love you," over and over again.

The next morning Vi called the housemother and made up some excuse about her sick aunt, and we stayed the weekend in Springfield. On Monday morning, she was feeling much better, and I went by to check her out of the hospital.

"Let's see, yes, here's a printout of your bill, sir," the man behind the desk said.

"$1850?" I gasped in disbelief.

"No sir, that's just the hospital services. The doctor's bill is another $850. You owe $2700. Make the check out to Memorial Hospital."

I was in total shock. Maybe I was naive, but it had never occurred to me that Vi was running up a big hospital bill.

"Do you have a check with you, sir?"

"Uh, yes, just a minute." I took out my billfold and pulled out my one emergency check.

In a few minutes, I'd written the check and virtually depleted the last of my savings.

As Vi and I drove home we talked about the frightening experience, vowing never to let anything like that happen again. I didn't bring up her "I love you" statement, but I thought about it every minute of the way. We pulled up to the Delta Chi house before lunch. Vi got out, thanked me, and went into the house. She seemed different from when she was lying on the bed in the emergency room, telling me that she loved me. I was puzzled.

38.

The Ring

When I got back to my apartment I balanced my check book and almost choked as I looked at the lowest balance I'd had in years; $450. I had spent all the test money and the poker winnings to pay for the abortion and hospital bills. Well, I wasn't depressed because, after four years of pursuing Vi, she was finally mine, and I knew we'd get married as soon as we finished college.

Two weeks passed, and there wasn't a day when Vi didn't meet me at the Union or sit on the front steps of Old Main with me. She still wouldn't go out on a date or come to my apartment, but I didn't care. I was certain that she was getting ready to drop that sorry Mr. Football. Vi kept telling me that she needed more time to break off her engagement. Of course, I kept pressing her, and one Sunday night, after a passionate session of petting and courting on the steps of Old Main, I asked her to drop him once and for all.

"Oh, Sandy, I do love you, and I want to break-up with him, but I can't do it right now. Give me a little more time. It's going to be so hard for me to get up enough courage to tell Daddy and cancel the wedding."

"Vi, we don't have much time. In less than two weeks, I'll be leaving the university to work in south Texas. When I drive out of here, we may never see each other again. I love you more than anything in the world, and I want you to be with me when I drive away. You've got to go ahead and break the engagement."

"I know you love me, Sandy, and I love you, but I just don't know how to tell Daddy."

"Start by breaking off the engagement, Vi. You know you don't love Mr. Football. Damn, Vi, he let you go off and have that abortion, and you almost died. He's the most self-centered and certainly the most stupid person I know. Drop him, and then worry about telling your crazy daddy."

"I can't, I just can't right now. Daddy would just go off-the-wall, and he'd never forgive me. I've got to break it off with Bill slowly, and then tell Daddy that we're going to put off the wedding. It may take a couple of weeks, but I'm going to do it. I promise you."

I thought about the unnatural hold that her father obviously had over her and shook my head. Mr. Football was hard enough to push out of the way, but now her damn father was the big stumbling block.

We kissed and petted a little more, and finally Vi had to leave. I sat on the steps for another 15 minutes, trying to come up with something that would make her go ahead and drop Mr. Football. Then, just as I was about to leave, I thought of something. The next morning I called the florist and had him send Vi a dozen red roses with a card saying, "Meet me tonight at 11 o'clock on the front steps of Old Main. It's important."

Right after lunch, I stopped by Underwood's Jewelry store on Dixon Street and looked at engagement rings. Even though Vi was engaged to Mr. Football, the cheap bastard hadn't bought her an engagement ring. He kept telling her that he was waiting until he got his pro signing bonus so that he could buy her a big diamond.

Vi had always said that she wanted a solitary diamond set in white gold. I found the perfect ring, and, even though it took almost every cent I had left in my bank account, I bought it.

I was 30 minutes early that night, and I'd rehearsed over and over again what I would say when I gave her the ring.

"Sandy?"

"Yes."

Vi walked over, climbed the steps, and we embraced, kissed, and held each other for several minutes. I couldn't wait any longer.

"Vi, sit down, I've got something for you."

She looked a little puzzled, but sat there on the top step expectantly as I reached in my pocket and pulled out the ring box.

"Vi, this is for you. Will you marry me?"

"Sandy! What have you done?" she gasped as she opened the ring box.

"Oh, it's beautiful, just gorgeous. I don't know what to say."

"Just say yes."

"Oh, yes! Yes! Yes! But...well, it's such a surprise, and I want to wear the ring but, well, you know what I said about taking some time to break up with Bill? Can I have a few days?"

"Sure, Vi, but you know I'm leaving town two weeks from tomorrow. Why don't you take these last two weeks of school to drop that sorry guy. Two weeks from tonight we'll meet back here, and we can plan our wedding."

"Sandy, you're so wonderful, and there's not a girl in the world that wouldn't be happy with you. Thanks for giving me that much time. I'm under a lot of pressure from my daddy. The June wedding will have to be canceled, the invitations retracted, and a whole room full of wedding gifts will have to be returned. It's going to be hard to do, and it will sure be hard to tell Daddy. You'll never know how hard."

"If you're in love, it'll be easy."

"Sandy, I do love you, and I want to wear that ring so badly, but I'm going to wait."

We sat, talked, and courted for another hour.

As the days passed, my mind was on Vi almost every moment. For a while, I continued my meetings with Lacy, but when I was sitting there talking with her, I kept having thoughts that I was betraying Vi, so I began to make excuses to Lacy and started skipping the meetings.

39.

Tests

Finals were less than a week away, and my relationship with the Deltas was at a new low. Dickie had convinced them that I'd brought a deck of marked cards to the game and had set him up to lose the $1000 on that one hand of poker. He was so convincing that Billy Faison, my good friend and contact with the Deltas, called on Monday, a week before finals started, and told me that after the sting I put on Dickie, they didn't trust me to come up with the Finals. You'll never know how relieved I was. It was exhilarating to know that part of my college life was behind me. However, a few days later I got a surprising phone call.

"Sandy?"

"Yeah. Who is this?"

"Dickie."

Well, I know my mouth must have dropped open. I couldn't say a word for a few seconds, but then I managed to say, "What do you want."

Dickie went into a long spiel about, how as fraternity president, he couldn't admit he had used marked cards, but—to make a very long story short—Dickie desperately wanted the finals. Not only that, but he had a lowball, sleazy scheme to get the money back he had lost in the poker game by selling the tests. Hell, it sounded very as if Dickie was going to be out peddling the tests to students that were in the five classes. Of course, that was just about the lowest thing I could imagine, and I was ready to hang up the phone, when he started telling me how we would really jack up the price for his own fraternity.

"Yeah, Sandy, hell, I know some guys that will pay me just about anything to get their hands on a couple of those finals."

Ripping off his own fraternity really confirmed my opinion of Dickie. I was just about to hang up the phone when he said something that grabbed my attention.

"Yeah, Sandy, I've even got a way to guarantee the tests are real. I'll have Peter hold the money, until after the test to prove they are buying the real thing."

Well, I wasn't about to get Dickie any tests, but when he said that I started thinking. If it was just Dickie who got ripped off it might be worth it.

"Whata you say, Sandy? Hell, you owe me a favor and listen, Buster, if you don't work with me, I'll turn you in to the administration. That Journal of yours with all our names in it won't hold water and you know it."

He was probably right about the The Journal. The guys that used the tests would just say I had made it up. Of course, I would say the same, if Dickie turned me in to the administration. However, I don't like to be threatened, especially by some lowlife like Dickie. I decided to teach him another lesson.

"If I do it Dickie, it's going to cost you."

"How much?"

"I want $5000 in cash, payable when I deliver the tests."

Dickie yelled about the price, but finally he gave in and we made plans to meet after I had the tests.

So the deal was made. Of course, I didn't have any intentions of getting the tests. Hell, there were old last year's tests floating around, and, in some of the classes, I could just make something up. One thing for sure, Dickie, didn't know anything about those courses, and he wouldn't have a clue that the tests I gave him weren't originals. All those bogus tests would create an uproar like nothing you've ever heard, but my plan was to be heading out of town the day finals started. My God, I was more than ready to leave the campus and get on with the rest of my life. If Vi managed to rid herself of that sorry jock and accepted my marriage proposal, we could drive out of Fayetteville on Sunday morning with $5000 from Dickie and start a new life together. It was a perfect way to end four years of college.

I'd already made arrangements to take my finals early and leave town on the Sunday before the start of finals on Monday. When I accepted the job with Humble Oil and Refining Company, I'd written the personnel manager, requesting to start my job on the Monday that Finals started. Much to my delight, he replied in a letter stating that I was to begin employment on that Monday, and the next day I made the rounds of my professors, showing them the letter and requesting to take the Final Exam early. They all agreed, and my finals were scheduled for Wednesday, Thursday, and Friday of the week before finals started.

I finished my last final at noon on Friday, and that night I worked to make up the bogus tests. At three in the morning, I got the last test finished, and at nine o'clock that morning, I met Dickie at a downtown café. I was holding a folder with ten Final Tests, and Dickie had a paper sack stuffed with the money.

"Let's don't waste each other's time." I pushed the folder across to Dickie.

Dickie opened it and thumbed through the tests. He nodded. They were all there.

"Okay, Farm Boy, here's your money. And I hope I never see your sorry ass again."

"You won't, you worthless piece of crap."

I smiled and tucked the sack under my arm.

"Tell me, what are you going to do with these tests?" I said.

"Well, Farm Boy, after our guys pay up, I'm going to go around and sell to anybody I can find who are taking those classes. After I did a little math, it seemed to me that I might as well make a little out of it. My daddy will be shocked when I add to my trust fund instead of withdrawing from it."

Dickie was leaning back, laughing as he anticipated cleaning up by selling the tests.

"Yeah, Farm Boy, you could've gotten a hell of a lot more money for these tests, a whole lot more," chuckled Dickie. "Hell, this is a perfect way to get back all that money you cheated me out of."

"Well, a deal's a deal. You do whatever you want with them." I got up and started for the door as Dickie mouthed off again.

"Hey, Farm Boy, don't you know I'm not gonna let some south Arkansas hick get the best of me?" hooted Dickie.

I didn't reply to Dickie's comment, but, as soon as I was out of earshot, I nearly laughed my head off.

40.

Choices

Vi had met me on the front steps of Old Main every night for the last two weeks of the semester, and sometimes our kissing, touching, and rubbing became so passionate I thought we might make love right there on the steps. I was certain that Vi was going to accept my marriage proposal, and she confirmed that when we met on the last Friday night before I was to leave on Sunday. She promised to break up with Mr. Football and tell her daddy before our Saturday night meeting.

That Saturday was my last day in Fayetteville, and it seemed to slip by before I knew it. I spent the morning packing everything I owned, stuffing my clothes and other items into the trunk and back seat of my car. Late that afternoon I walked out in front of Old Main and sat on the steps where I would meet Vi that night. I was absolutely certain that by the time we met, she'd have broken up with Mr. Football, and she would tell me that she was ready to marry me. Then we could spend the rest of the time discussing where and when we would get married, and on Sunday morning, we'd drive out of Fayetteville together.

I was so excited I couldn't eat supper, and at 6:30 I was already there for our 7:00 o'clock meeting. Time seemed to drag, and at 7:15 I got up and walked around the corner of Old Main to see if I could see Vi. She was always late, but then time continued to pass; 7:30, 8:00 o'clock. Every minute I waited, I became more depressed, and, after 8:00 o'clock, I started to get mad. After four years of pursuing Vi, paying for her abortion, and giving her an engagement ring, she was standing me up. I wavered between anger and depression, and finally I stood up to leave. Then I saw somebody coming down the walk, heading my way.

"Vi?" I called.

"Sandy?"

"Yes?" I didn't recognize the voice.

"It's Beth Ann, you remember me? I'm one of Vi's sorority sisters."

"Yeah, Beth Ann, what are you doing here?"

"Sandy, Vi sent me to tell you that she's not coming to meet you."

"Is she sick?"

"No, Sandy, I saw her leave with Bill Tucker."

I can still remember those words as clearly as if they had been spoken yesterday. They penetrated my soul.

Finally, I acknowledged Beth Ann.

"Yeah, it's her damn daddy again, he's ruining her life," I mumbled.

It was a blow I hadn't foreseen. Why didn't she drop that louse and stand up to her daddy? I held my head in my hands while Beth Ann stood there in silence. I felt as if I'd been kicked in the stomach. In a couple of minutes, I looked up and nodded. "I understand. Thanks for coming over to tell me."

Beth Ann left, and I sat there for what seemed like several hours, but it was only a few minutes. I hadn't cried in sorrow since my mother died, but, as I sat there on the front steps of Old Main, thinking about losing the girl I'd dreamed about for the last four years, I couldn't hold back the tears. I broke down, and, for about five minutes, I cried my heart out. As I looked down at the steps where Vi and I had sat and talked so many nights, I decided to leave something. There were too many memories to just walk away. I took out my pocketknife, and, with the knife point, I ground "Vi" into the top concrete step. Then the realization that I'd lost her for good slowly sank in.

Damn her, anyway, at least she could have told me herself. Just when I was sure Vi would be mine, she'd walked out of my life. I stood up, wiped my eyes, and started trying to forget about her.

It was early, and, with nothing else to do, I decided to walk down to George's and have one last beer before I left Fayetteville. I had started to stroll down the sidewalk, across the big lawn area in front of Old Main, heading for Dixon Street and George's, when I noticed a girl walking toward me. At first, I didn't recognize her, but, as she got closer, I smiled.

"Lacy, what are you doing out here in the middle of the night?'
"Sandy?"
"Yes." I walked up to her, and we stopped there on the sidewalk, about halfway between Old Main and Dixon Street.

For the first time since I'd met her, Lacy seemed a little nervous.

"Uh, well, I know you're leaving tomorrow, and I called your apartment to say goodbye, but you weren't there. Since you make George's your home away from home, I thought I'd walk down and say goodbye in person. You know, Sandy, you've been so busy the last couple of weeks we haven't had time to meet on our bench and talk. I've really missed talking with you."

When Lacy said that I felt terrible, since I had canceled our regular meetings because I didn't want to upset Vi.

That night, standing there on the walk a few hundred feet from Old Main, just jilted by the woman I loved, I sure needed a friend, and I wanted to be with Lacy.

"Gosh, Lacy, I was heading to George's for one last beer before I leave this place. Why don't you join me?"

"I'd love to, Sandy."

We walked down the sidewalk, across the lawn to Dixon Street, talking and laughing about some of the times we had had together. Soon we were sitting side by side in one of George's red booths, having a last beer. Sitting there talking with a good friend sure helped take my mind off of Vi. I couldn't tell Lacy about what had just happened, because the last time I had mentioned Vi to her, I'd gotten an icy stare. We probably talked for a couple of hours before we got up to leave.

"Well, it's almost midnight, and George's will be closing in a few minutes," I said. "Come on, I'll walk you back to your sorority house." We scooted out of the booth, and I stood in the doorway for a few extra seconds, thinking about Millie, and then I thought about seeing Lacy in George's for the first time when I was a freshman. George's held a lot of memories, all of them good.

In a few minutes we'd crossed the lawn in front of Old Main and were between Old Main and the library when I stopped. There was something that I had to tell Lacy before we parted. I stopped, reached out, and took her hands.

"Lacy, I know you better than your friends, and certainly better than those guys you used to date. This is probably the last time we'll be together. South Texas and Tulsa are miles apart, but, before we part, I want to say this; you're a wonderful girl and you'll make some guy a great wife."

"Sandy, that was so sweet. I hope you're right, but you know, I haven't dated since that terrible night with Bull Jenkins."

"Oh, Lacy, you need to get over that. Don't let some worthless guy ruin your life."

"Well, there are other reasons."

"Huh? What reasons?"

"Maybe there're personal, Sandy. You don't know everything about me."

Lacy dropped my hands and tuned around when she said that. I could tell that her voice was breaking.

"Lacy?" I put my hands on her shoulders and turned her back around so that she was facing me. Her lips were trembling as if she were about to cry.

"Lacy, what's wrong?"

"Oh, Sandy, I don't know. Maybe I'm just upset about not ever seeing my best friend again."

I stood there, looking at Lacy, who was about to cry, and I couldn't resist leaning over and gently kissing her on the cheek.

"Sandy, oh, Sandy, it's so hard to say anything."

"Yes, I know, Lacy, but go ahead."

"Uh, oh, it's killing me to stand here and talk to you, knowing I may never see you again. I've never had a man treat me so kindly. You're my best friend and always will be. I'm going to miss you so much, Sandy."

"Lacy."

"Yes."

I stood there staring at Lacy as if I'd never seen her this way before, and all the conversations and good times we had had seemed to flood through my mind. Why haven't I ever looked at Lacy like this?

"Sandy? Are you all right?"

For a minute, I'd turned into a mute again, but then the strangest feeling came over me, and I smiled at her. I was struggling to keep from crying as I cleared my throat.

"Yes, Lacy, I'm fine now. You know, maybe we will see each other again."

"Oh, I doubt it, Sandy. I'll be working in Tulsa, and you'll be tramping around somewhere down in south Texas. Heck, we'll be six or seven hundred miles apart."

"Maybe not."

"Maybe not? What?"

"Lacy, this is going to sound stupid, and I won't blame you if you laugh and walk away, but when I leave tomorrow morning for south Texas..." for a moment I stopped, afraid Lacy would reject me like Vi had done. Then I regained my composure, reached out and took both of her hands, and said, "I want you to be with me."

"Sandy, are you kidding me?"

"I've never been more serious in my life." I couldn't hold it back any longer, and tears streamed down my face.

Lacy stood there with her mouth open for the longest time,

and then she shook her head and began to cry as she grabbed me around the waist.

"Sandy, you're wonderful. I can't believe it. Over the last two years I've fallen in love with you, and that's the reason I haven't been dating. I'm the happiest person alive right now, and I'd love to go to south Texas with you. What time do we leave?"

We embraced, kissed, and held each other for a few minutes. I looked down at Lacy, who was smiling with tears streaming down her cheeks.

"Sandy..."

And then she cried again. It was the happiest moment of my life.

We were standing there in the back of Old Main, facing the library, trying to get our composure back, when I noticed someone walking toward us. I gasped. It was Vi.

41.

More Choices

"Sandy? Is that you, Sandy?" Vi called out as she approached.

"Uh, yes."

"Oh, I'm so glad I found you. I tried to call you at your apartment, but there was no answer. I was on my way down to George's to see if you were there."

Vi was so excited that she could hardly get those words out, and she was smiling as she reached out to grab my hands.

About that time, she noticed Lacy standing beside me.

"Lacy, what are you doing here?"

There was an awkward silence, and then Vi couldn't contain herself. "Well, who cares, the important thing is this: I just broke up with Bill!"

God, she shouted, she was so excited, and then she said, "Sandy, I couldn't be happier. You were right, he's a louse."

I'd been shocked to see Vi walk up, but now I was in total disbelief. She was looking for me, and she had just broken up with Bill. It was unbelievable; I couldn't get words to come out of my mouth. Never in my life have I been so shocked.

Lacy, who hadn't said a word, looked up at me as she nudged my arm.

"Sandy, say something," she whispered. "Please." There was a haunting look in Lacy's eyes.

Vi ignored Lacy and took a step forward, smiling as she said, "Sandy, we need to have a long talk about your proposal, but, before you say anything, just know that I accept. I've known for a long time that I loved you, but it was hard to break up with Bill because of Daddy. I think I fell in love with you that first day we met, when you helped me with my books."

Vi reached out, took both of my hands, and looked at me.

"Sandy, I love you with all my heart."

I felt Lacy turn loose of my arm and step back.

"Uh...Vi...Lacy...I...oh," I stammered in confusion. I couldn't believe the unreal situation. The girl of my dreams, the one girl I'd pursued for four years, was ready to marry me, and all I had to do was reach out and embrace her. It had seemed so right, so perfect. I'd never had any question that Vi was the girl I was meant to be with for the rest of my life. And then there was Lacy, standing on the other side of me but beginning to back away. A couple of hours ago I'd been so mad at Vi for standing me up that I never wanted to see her again, but now, as she smiled at me, holding my hands, I knew I could never be mad at Vi for very long.

"Come on, Sandy, let's go to the front of Old Main and sit on the steps where you proposed to me." She took my hand and stepped in that direction.

When I looked into her eyes and she smiled at me, it was like the first time we met, and I squeezed her hand and started for the front steps of Old Main. Then, as we walked toward Old Main, something inside of me seemed to pull me back. I moved a few feet with Vi and glanced back over my shoulder. Lacy was now almost into the shadows, and I could barely make out her shape as she turned toward the library and started down the sidewalk beside it. Vi and I walked on toward Old Main, and I glanced over my shoulder one last time. Lacy was gone. I've never felt anything like the emotions that surged through me as I stumbled along toward the front of Old Main.

It was less than 30 yards from where we were to the front of Old Main, but, as I walked along with Vi, my feet seemed to drag.

My mind was seared with the vision of Lacy walking away, and I slowed down as we approached the front steps. As we walked up those nine steps, I could hardly pull my legs up. I could feel a weight pressing down, pulling me back, and, by the time I had reached the top step, my mind was shouting, No! No! Go back! Vi sat down, but I kept standing, and I'd just turned my shoulders to walk back down those steps when Vi realized that I was going to walk away.

"Sandy! Oh, Sandy! Please don't! I don't think I can stand it if one more person rejects me tonight."

"Vi, I..."

"Sandy, I know you'll never understand what I went through tonight." Vi stood up and held my hand. Her voice was breaking.

"I had it all planned, Sandy—call Daddy and tell him. And then, when Bill came by to pick me up, break up with him and go meet you, but the phone call—oh, it took forever. Daddy wouldn't let me hang up when I told him that I was breaking up with Bill and I was going to marry you. He kept on threatening. Finally, after an hour, my nerves were so shattered I could hardly speak, but I said, '"Daddy, I'm breaking up with Bill tonight, and I'm marrying Sandy, and that's final.'" I slammed the phone down, and I was so upset that I went to my room and told Beth Ann to tell you that I'd be late coming to meet you, but evidently she saw me leave with Bill and assumed I was going to stand you up."

"Vi, I'm sorry your father was so hard on you, but it was something you had to do. He had such a hold on you that your life would never be your own if you hadn't done that. But, Vi..." I said as I turned loose of her hand, "I can't...uh, I know it's hard..." Vi knew I was trying to tell her that I was going to Lacy, and tears began to stream down her cheeks. Then she took a deep breath, threw her shoulders back, and said, "Sandy, I'll always remember you, and I'll always remember tonight."

Vi paused, and I could tell she that wanted to tell me something else, so I hesitated.

Vi regained her composure and said, "I'll sure remember that horrible break up with Bill. Oh, Sandy, he was half-drunk when he picked me up, and I tried to get him to stop at the stadium parking lot so I could tell him that I was through with him, but he kept on driving out of town until he came to a place where we usually park. It's about two miles from campus. I tried to tell him very calmly that we weren't right for each other, and maybe we could remain friends, but then he started questioning me, and when he found out that I was leaving him for you, he went absolutely nuts. For the next 20 minutes, he raved about everything you can imagine, and I kept trying to get him to take me back to campus, but he refused. He kept saying that it would look bad for him if we broke up. Finally, after the worst cursing you can imagine, I opened the door and got out. I've walked two miles to get here, Sandy...I guess I shouldn't have come."

Vi had held it in as long as she could, and she broke down and sobbed uncontrollably. I stood there, looking at the girl I had pursued for the last four years, and I knew that she was begging me not to walk away. My heart was literally aching as I visualized Lacy walking into the darkness and Vi sobbing. I took a deep breath and tried to regain my composure, but, just as I was about to say something, Vi took my hand and looked up. He blue eyes sparkled through the tears, and her lips trembled as she tried to regain her composure. She never said a word. Everything she would ever need to say was very apparent to me. I couldn't stand it.

"Vi...I'll never walk away from you." I couldn't have said anything else.

I took Vi in my arms and held her for a long time. Then, after we had both calmed down, we sat on the top step, talking about our future. However, even while I talked with Vi about where we'd get married and what our future held, I could still see Lacy walking into the darkness. It was hard to sit there, but Vi looked so gorgeous, and she was so affectionate, that soon I'd pushed Lacy to the back recesses of my mind.

From that moment on, however, I was never sure that choosing Vi was the right choice. It bothered me then, and it has stayed on my mind for the last 45 years. Did I make the right choice? After a few minutes, we started talking about leaving Fayetteville. Of course, I had it all planned.

"Vi, I'll be by your sorority house about nine in the morning, and we can leave for south Texas." Just the idea of leaving Fayetteville and some of the sordid things I'd done took a weight off my mind. It was the perfect ending to my college life: to drive off with the woman I loved. We'd have a nest egg, thanks to Dickie, and he'd have a batch of bogus tests that would do nothing but cause him grief.

Vi nodded and said, "It won't matter if I miss a couple of finals, Sandy, but I do need to take one that starts at 8:30. Could we leave at 10?"

"Sure, Vi."

"Good, I wouldn't put off leaving with you for anything. I'm exempt on three of them anyway, and even with a F on the final in the other one, I'll still have a C."

After we made plans to leave, and even where we were going to get married, I left Vi and headed back to my apartment. After throwing the few items I hadn't packed in the backseat of my car, and dialed the Delta house.

The phone rang for at least 20 times before someone picked up.

"Let me speak to Jeff Hunsinger." I said. "Yeah, I know it's late, but it's an emergency."

They had to get Jeff out of bed to answer the call. Finally, I heard a familiar voice, "Yeah, who is this?"

"It's Sandy, Jeff."

"For Christ's sake, Sandy, why are you calling me at one o'clock in the morning?"

"Listen to me for just a minute, Jeff." Then I told Jeff about Dickie marking the cards and how I had set him up for the sting, and then I told him that Dickie had made a behind their backs deal to get tests from me, and then sell them to the guys at a greatly marked up price.

"Why that sorry, worthless creep! He would stick it to his fraternity brothers just to make a few dollars. Wait till I tell the guys what that bum is up to."

"Don't tell him, Jeff. Keep it quiet and let that sorry Dickie hang himself. He's going to let Peter hold the money so everybody will get their money back and leave Dickie holding the bag and out $5000."

"Okay, Sandy. I won't say a thing, but I'll pass the word around to not buy any of the tests from him. I can't wait until he realizes you've nailed him again. He sure deserves it."

I knew Jeff would get the word around, so most of the guys wouldn't touch those tests.

I went to bed about two, but I was so excited about Vi going off with me to Texas, I couldn't fall asleep. Finally, about seven that morning I sat straight up in bed. I knew why I couldn't go to sleep. It wasn't that I was excited about Vi. It was Lacy. My mind flashed with the memory of Lacy walking away into the darkness until I couldn't stand it any longer, and at around 8:30, I decided to call her. Maybe I'd made the wrong choice. I dialed her sorority house and asked for her. The housemother came to the phone.

"I'm sorry, but Lacy left this morning. Didn't say where she was going."

I was stunned and I hung up the phone and just sat there for a few minutes. Lacy had walked out of my life and nothing I could do could change things. I brooded about Lacy until almost ten and then I resigned myself that Lacy was gone. At five minutes till ten I pulled in behind Vi's sorority house. She was standing there with her bags packed waiting for me.

As we drove out of Fayetteville, I felt a load lift from my shoulders. Stealing tests and selling them to the Deltas had made me feel like the lowest person on earth, and this was the start of a new life for me, as I drove south toward Texas with the woman I loved sitting next to me. As we drove out of town I forced myself to quit thinking about Lacy. Vi and I were beginning a new life together, and Lacy was now just a memory.

Vi and I were married by a Justice of the Peace in Blessing, Texas, the next day, and on Monday morning I started work for Humble Oil and Refining Company in Corpus Christi, Texas.

***

I've thought back on that time when my addiction to the thrill of test-stealing caused me to commit so many break-ins, and I regret it. However, something changed when I drove off from the University of Arkansas with Vi. As I drove across the Boston Mountains leaving Fayetteville and crossed the White River, I tossed my sack of lock picking tools out the car window, and when that sack hit the water it was such a relief. Vi looked at me when I slowed down to throw out the sack.

"What are you doing, Sandy?

"Oh, Vi, I'm just getting rid of some cards and other stuff- just old poker playing crap," I lied. She just nodded her head and smiled. Of course, she knew about my poker playing at the Delta house and didn't approve.

When I drove off, it was like a bad chapter in my life was over, and I could have a fresh start with a wonderful woman and a new job, far, far away from Fayetteville, the Deltas, and the university...and Lacy.

***

Vi and I have returned to the university many times, always during the spring, around graduation. We make sure it's the Saturday a week before graduation, and at midnight we walk over to the front of Old Main and sit on the top step again. I've never told Vi, but, when we cross the area between Old Main and the library where Lacy walked away, it brings back such memories that I can hardly bear it. By the time we reach the back steps of Old Main I'm so upset thinking about that night that I can hardly speak. Did I make the right choice? I wish I knew, but it's too late now.

***

The divorce will be final in a few days, so I guess there won't ever be another walk with Vi to the front of Old Main. We've done it for the last time.

42.

BIOGRAPHY

Millie and Bob Blevins:

Bob married Millie and graduated from the university in 1959 with a degree in Animal Husbandry. He went to work for a large dairy co-op right out of college, and is currently General Manager for Animal Resources. Bob and Millie have three children and six grandchildren. Their oldest child is tall, thin, and has sandy hair.

Doris Colton:

Doris received tenure in 1963 and was made a full professor in 1969. Between semesters in 1970 she abruptly left the university with one of her students, moved to Malibu, California, and began to write romance novels under the pen name of D.C. Norris. During her 30 year writing career, Doris authored 21 books. She retired in 1996 and is currently a resident of The Oaks, a retirement home in Santa Barbara, California.

Coach Jim "Bull" Jenkins:

Bull Jenkins left the university in 1960 at midterm and became an assistant coach at Northeastern for two years. However, in 1962, he was arrested for assault and battery, found guilty, lost his coaching job, and was put on probation. A year later, Bull violated probation and was sentenced to five years in the Illinois State Penitentiary. After his release he disappeared from sight until, on March 8, 1982, he was found dead on the corner of Stanton and Glover Street on the lower South Side of Chicago. His death remains a mystery.

R. Richard "Dickie" Barnett IV:

Dickie left Fayetteville in 1962, after attending the university for five years. His grade point was below a 2.0, and he never graduated. In 1962 Dickie started working for his father's oil company and, after his father died in 1978, Dickie became President and CEO of Northwest Texas Resources, an oil and gas exploration company. During the oil and gas exploration boom in the mid-80s, Dickie expanded the company by purchasing seven immediate depth-drilling rigs. In 1987, when oil prices crashed, Northwest Texas Resources was forced into bankruptcy. Dickie managed to salvage some small royalty interests from the company, and, in 1995, he attempted to restart his bankrupt company. He was unsuccessful, and in 1997 he retired. Dickie currently lives in Dallas at Silver Threads Center, an assisted living hospice. He is suffering from lung cancer.

William "Bill" Tucker (Mr. Football):

Bill was named All-Southwest Conference and All-American, honorable mention, his senior year, and shortly afterward he signed as a free agent with the New York Giants. However, before the 1962 season started, he suffered a career-ending knee injury. He returned to the University of Arkansas and worked as an assistant coach for two years. In 1964 his contract was not renewed, and, for the next ten years, Bill worked as assistant coach at several Arkansas high schools. In 1973, he was named head coach of Eufaula High School, a small town in the Arkansas delta.

He will retire in 2006 after a mediocre career as a high school football coach.

Lacy Darnell:

Lacy never married. She moved from Tulsa to Little Rock in 1985 and opened a dress shop called Lacy's.

Virginia "Vi" and Stuart "Sandy" Carson:

Vi and I were married in the spring of 1960 in Blessing, Texas. After working for Humble Oil and Refining Company for six years, I quit and started my own company, Empire Resources. I have had an oil and gas exploration company for more than 45 years, and I have had a rewarding career. In 1975, Vi and I moved from Corpus Christi, Texas to Magnolia, Arkansas and built our dream house. We have two children and four grandchildren. I am still active in oil and gas exploration.

43.

EPILOGUE

When I finished the manuscript for this book, I dropped it off at the office of my attorney, John Dickerson. John called me a week later, and we reviewed it.

"Sandy, you better be damn sure that worthless Bull Jenkins is dead. Hell, you'd be sued before this book gets off the press, and what about Doris Colton?"

"Bull's dead, John. I heard about it several years ago. Doris is still alive, but I don't think she'd ever object to what I put in the book about her. She got even wilder in Southern California, after she left the university. Anyway, I've got the name of one of her special students who'll back up my story."

John nodded his head in satisfaction as we continued to go over each of the characters in the book.

After another hour John said, "Well, let me sum it up, Sandy. This stuff ain't gonna get you sued, but you're going to have to have a hide like an alligator to take some of the crap that's gonna be thrown at you. You can deny it forever, but there are some redneck Razorback fans who are going give you hell for that Texas football story. On the other hand, the statute of limitations has long since run out on your breaking and entering."

"Okay, John, is there anything else in there that could cost me any big money?"

"No, but I'll reserve final judgment until your publisher's attorney reads it."

John leaned back in his chair and stared at the ceiling for a few seconds. He let out a low chuckle and said, "My God, that hit you put on Dickie still has me laughing."

Jeff had told me about how Dickie just went off the wall, when he found out those tests were fakes and had to give everyone their money back.

John shuffled some papers, cocked his head, and offered one more bit of advice.

"Sandy, I know you're not gonna listen to me, but as your friend, I'm urging you to stick this thing in a back desk drawer and let your kids publish it after you're dead and gone."

"Hell, John, I worked for months writing this damn thing. It's going in the mail tomorrow."

"Okay, Sandy, but when you start catching hell, don't blame me."

"I won't, John. Hell, I may be living in Europe when this comes out. When my divorce is final, I think I'll leave Arkansas."

"Don't leave your friends, Sandy. Retirement away from friends is always a bad deal."

I reached over and picked up the manuscript from John's desk, nodded to him, and headed for Pack and Mail.

***

After I bundled up the manuscript and sent it to the publisher, it should have been a load off my shoulders, because this book had been a painful one to write. However, it was just the opposite. For days I brooded around, my appetite was almost non-existent, and I was so irritable that my friends didn't want to be around me. Maybe it was all the memories that I'd recounted and relived as I wrote the manuscript. I was sure one miserable human being.

Then I began to wonder about Lacy. After Vi and I went to Texas, I'd heard that Lacy went back to Tulsa and was working in a downtown department store. Later an old friend told me that Lacy was in Little Rock and had opened a dress shop. I never told Vi, but even after all those years I still had fond memories of Lacy. Well, to be honest, it was a hell of a lot more than fond memories, and I couldn't forget looking back over my shoulder that last night in Fayetteville and seeing Lacy walk into the darkness. Did I make the right choice when I walked away with Vi? I could never answer that question.

A few years ago, an old friend from school who kept up with everybody talked with me about Lacy.

"Sandy, she's still as gorgeous as she was back in college. And would you believe, she's never married."

Thoughts about Lacy kept running through my mind in the days after I finished this manuscript. What was she doing? Would she even speak to me after I had walked off and left her that last night in Fayetteville? Of course, during my 45 years of married life with Vi, Lacy's name had come up frequently, especially after a couple of martinis. Vi would tell me that I regretted not leaving with Lacy that night behind Old Main, and we'd yell at each other until I said, "Yeah, you're right, I should have left you and gone off with Lacy."

Vi would break into tears and leave the room. After a few hours I'd go and apologize, and we'd make up, but just the mention of Lacy's name was enough to have us screaming at each other again. There were times when I really wondered if I'd made the right choice. Maybe my feelings for Lacy were a big part of why we were getting a divorce. Hell, I'll admit it. It was more than a feeling. Over the years it had been all I could do not to call Lacy. I'd lie awake at night and think about her for hours on end. But it was different now. My divorce was almost final.

It took me days to get up the courage to call Lacy. Finally, one night, after a couple of martinis, I dialed information, got the number, and made the call. I know that holding on to my love for Lacy had been the problem in my marriage. What would my life have been if I'd walked away with her that night instead of

Vi? Maybe it was meant to be that someday Lacy and I would be together. I could remember that last night in Fayetteville, standing there between Old Main and the library, when I was absolutely certain about that.

Still as pretty as she was in college, I thought as I dialed.

"Hello."

It was Lacy, and even after not hearing her voice for 45 years, I recognized it. My mouth was open to speak, but the words wouldn't come out. I guess Lacy must have looked at her caller I. D., because she said, "Sandy? Sandy?"

Then another feeling swept over me, one I haven't felt in years, and the only words that flashed through my mind were, No! No! I hung up the phone without ever saying a word. Then I sat on the couch and just looked at the phone for over an hour. I couldn't figure out why I'd hung up on Lacy. Every time I reached for the phone, something stopped me. Finally, I gave up and went to bed.

The next day was a beautiful spring day, and all I wanted to do was walk in the woods. After about an hour of enjoying a casual stroll through the big oak and pine trees at Pigeon Hill on the Ouachita River, I started thinking about the divorce. The attorneys were preparing the final settlement papers, and everything would be final in a few days. Thinking about the divorce becoming final put me in a terrible mood, and I drove back to my apartment, where I spent the rest of the day sitting out on my deck, drinking martinis. I was pretty drunk when I first started to cry.

Crying was something I never did. The last time I'd shed a tear was over Vi not coming to meet me that night 45 years ago, and then with Lacy later the same night. Over the years, even after the death of dear friends, my eyes had never moistened. But now I was so depressed, moody, and maybe even a little suicidal, that I couldn't hold them back. I threw the martini glass and pitcher as far as I could, and then I cried some more. It got dark, and I stayed on the deck, thinking and weeping as I sobered up. Then something flashed through my mind. Is tomorrow Saturday, the front of Old Main meeting time? I ran into the apartment and grabbed the calendar.

"Yes! Yes!" I yelled. I ran around the kitchen, holding the calendar over my head like it was some trophy. Now it was clear, and I knew without a shadow of a doubt why I had been so miserable for the last few days. It was Vi. I missed her and wanted to be with her. Yeah, Sandy, you're still in love with Vi, ran through my mind.

Our meetings during the last few weeks with the divorce lawyers had been reserved and a little frosty, but last week, when the lawyers said that the divorce would be final in a matter of days, I thought I detected a bit of emotion from Vi. Should I call her? Did she feel like me, or was she ready to dump me? Finally, I came up with a plan to see if there was any hope for us. This is the letter I wrote to Vi.

Dear Vi,

You know I have trouble calling people on the phone, so I am doing just what you have told me not to do a thousand times, I' m writing another letter instead of calling.

I've thought about our life together, and I am not ready to call it quits. That morning at the university when you dropped that stack of books has never left my mind. I love you, Vi, and I'm sorry for all the grief I've caused you over the last 45 years because I couldn't forget some things in my past. Please forgive me.

Vi, I shouldn't have walked out on you after that fight when my Pre-Columbian art pieces were broken. It was my fault, and I want you to know that our marriage is a lot more important than a few pieces of old pottery.

Because of the lawyers who have kept us from talking and friends who have taken sides, I don't know whether you feel the same way. Maybe you've had it with me, and you're ready for this divorce. I honestly couldn't blame you, but if there is anything left, please take me back.

A week from this Saturday is graduation at the university. At midnight tomorrow night I'll be sitting on the top step in front of Old Main. Since we walked away together that night, you've given me everything a man could want in a woman, and you've been the best mother in the world. God, Vi, I'm hurting so badly just writing this letter. I don't think I can live without you. But you may not feel the same way, so, if you want this divorce to go through, just toss this letter in the trash.

If you don't—
Love, Sandy"

I drove to our house, where Vi was still living, and I stuck the letter in the frame of the back door, where she'd see it when she came out to pick up her morning paper.

I couldn't sleep that night, and by 4:30 I was packed and driving north toward Fayetteville. I spent the afternoon walking around, looking at all the changes that had taken place since I last was on campus. Late in the afternoon, I walked to the front of Old Main and climbed the steps. Sure enough, there was Vi's name, which I had cut in the concrete that night 45 years ago.

Some of the old buildings were just as I remembered them, almost frozen in time. The former girls' dorm, Carnell Hall, had been converted into a restaurant, and I stopped by around 7:30 and had an excellent martini and a good meal. It was 9:30 when I walked out, much too early to go to Old Main. A long walk down to the new football stadium and back took up almost an hour, and then I couldn't wait any longer.

I was in a good mood as I walked toward Old Main because I'd convinced myself that I still loved Vi and that she'd show up. Then she'd cry and we'd hug, kiss, and make up as we always had in the past, and the next day we'd drop the divorce. However, as I passed the library I started to feel uneasy, and, when I was almost to the back of Old Main, I stopped. I was standing exactly where I'd asked Lacy to marry me. My breath started coming in short little gasps, and sweat popped out on my forehead, and then I turned and looked at the walk where I had last seen Lacy as she walked away that night. All the questions I've had over all the years came flooding over me, and I was shaken to the very depths of my soul. I was upset, brooding, and unsure of myself as I walked around to the front of Old Main and climbed those nine steps. It was 11:00 o'clock, and, as I sat there and thought about my life, I didn't know whether I wanted Vi to show up or not.

I must have looked at my watch a hundred times between 11:00 and 12:00 o'clock. Finally, I watched the final minutes tick off and I looked up the walk—nothing. Then a few more minutes passed—still nothing. Well, She's not coming. Maybe it's for the best. Then, faintly, I heard footsteps on the concrete walk. I looked up, only to see a couple of girls walking down the sidewalk. But when they got closer, one of them said, "Sandy?"

What on earth?

I finally said, "Yes?" They walked into the light of a street lamp, and I almost fell off the step.

"Oh my God! Vi and...Lacy," I managed to say. "What are the two of you doing here?"

I was standing there, shifting from one foot to the next, nervous as hell, as they walked up the nine steps of Old Main until they were only an arm's length away. Everything in the world went through my mind, but I couldn't imagine in my wildest dreams why both of them were standing there in front of me. Vi stood there with her hands on her hips, seemingly enjoying my discomfort. Lacy looked a little nervous and unsure of what was going on.

God, she's still gorgeous, I thought.

Vi broke the tension as she started to talk.

"Sandy, I'm going do most of the talking—for now—so just listen for once, and try not to interrupt. Okay?"

I nodded my head.

"First off, Sandy, I got your letter this morning, and I started packing my bags to come to Fayetteville. But, as I got closer and closer to leaving, I started having doubts about whether or not that was the right thing to do. I couldn't decide, and I'd sat down to have a cup of coffee when the phone rang. It was Lacy. She saw your phone number on her caller I.D. and was calling to see if something was wrong—you know we're sorority sisters.

We started talking, and I told her about our problems—hell, Sandy, how her presence had been with us for 45 years—which finally led to us filing for divorce. Then I read her the wonderful letter you wrote me. One thing led to another, and soon I was driving to Little Rock to meet with Lacy. We had lunch, talked, and then went to her house and talked some more. Then we started driving up here, and we talked nonstop for another four hours. I told Lacy about all the fights we'd had and how many times her name had come up, and then I went over all the stuff from your journal."

"What? What are you talking about? You don't know about my journal. No one has ever seen it."

"Oh, come on, Sandy. Do you think I could live with you for as long as I have and not know about everything that's in the house? There are no secrets there. Anyway, I went over all the stuff you wrote about Lacy and me, and then I told her about Millie—"

"Oh, for God's sake, Vi! That was none of your business!"

"And Doris—"

"Vi, you didn't tell about the...the..."

"Yeah, Sandy, I did tell Lacy about the tests, and she told me about you getting her that history test."

I began to have trouble breathing, and I thought that maybe I was having a heart attack. It seemed like my worst nightmare was coming true. I sat down. I couldn't stand another minute, but Vi wasn't through. "Sandy, after Lacy and I went through all the stuff that happened at the university, and even my abortion..."

"Vi! Vi! That was so private!"

Vi took a step forward, smiled, and reached out her hand to me. "Sandy, when I had that horrible abortion, you saved my life. You're the most wonderful man I've ever known."

I was really confused now, and I looked at Lacy, who had moved over to put her arm around Vi to comfort her. Tears filled

Vi's eyes, and she took a minute to compose herself. Then she said, "One other thing, Sandy. I've spent almost every waking moment since you left gluing your Mayan Pre-Columbian art collection back together. There's a new display case in our living room, and they're all back right where they were before I threw that fossil at them. They look just like they did. Breaking your collection was the worst moment of my life. Please forgive me."

Vi broke down and cried again, sobbing on Lacy's shoulder as I sat there, frozen in place. I couldn't believe everything that was happening.

"Vi, it was my fault! My fault!" Oh, God, I was hurting now.

Where is this conversation going? What's going on? kept flashing through my mind.

Vi looked at me and continued, "Sandy, after Lacy and I talked for what seemed like forever, we have some answers, but we couldn't decide what to do. That's why we're here. First, before you jump to any conclusions, let me tell you what we've come up with. I believe that, without a shadow of a doubt, that for some reason, you haven't been able to shake that last night in Fayetteville from your mind. However, I know, from our relationship over the years, that you love me and our kids very deeply. But, Sandy, we're mature adults now, and this is not going to be a replay of 45 years ago, when you had to pick one of us. Do you understand that?"

Picking one of them was exactly what I'd thought Vi was up to, and I thought that, if I had to do that again, I was really going to have a heart attack. I was sure that Vi was going to put me through that horrible process again. I was puzzled.

What now? Why are these two women here—nothing makes sense, I thought.

"Sandy, we're here to talk, and maybe, when we're through, we'll have settled some things."

"What?" Now things seemed even more unreal, and I envisioned my life being torn to shreds as they dissected it.

"Both of you want to talk? To talk? That's it?"

"No, Sandy, not both of us, just Lacy."

"Just Lacy?"

"Yes, we've been talking about our life and her life, and she has a few things she wants to tell you."

I looked at Lacy. My God, she was still one gorgeous woman. It was all I could do not reach out and hold her hand, but it knew, with Vi standing there, it would cause a real scene. At that moment, I was thinking how Lacy and I would talk, and then Vi would say she was going to leave us together, and it would be just like that last night in Fayetteville. It was anticipation like I've never felt before. I wanted to pull the words out of her, and then we could kiss, embrace and move on with our life. As I waited for Lacy to start speaking, I felt sorry for Vi.

She's a wonderful woman and I couldn't have wanted a better wife and mother. It's too bad our marriage has to end like this.

Lacy cleared her throat, and I thought about how difficult it was going to be to tell me how much she still loved me with Vi standing there.

"Lacy go ahead, take your time and tell me everything." I smiled and took a deep breath.

"Well, Sandy, after talking with Vi, I knew I needed to come here with her and talk to you." I nodded my head, as if I understood.

"But Sandy, because of some of the things we experienced when we were here at the university, it's probably the most difficult thing I've ever done." Lacy stopped and Vi put her arm around her shoulder.

Gosh, I can't believe how understanding Vi is, I thought.

Lacy, wiped a tear from her eye, and continued. "Oh, Sandy, I don't want to cry, but when I remember how you came for me, when I'd been beaten up by Bull, I can't help it, and I'll never forget those long talks we had sitting on the bench in the old Confederate Cemetery."

Well, Lacy was getting to me, and I started to feel choked up.

Damn, I can't start crying with Vi standing there!

I got my composure back and Lacy continued, "Well, here's the hard part, Sandy. When you left with Vi that night, I thought my world had ended, and for a few weeks I couldn't even think about it without crying."

A few weeks?

"Then I pulled myself together and started to think about the life I had ahead of me. Soon, I was out looking for a job, and in a few weeks I had the most exciting job I could imagine. I was hired as an assistant buyer for Dillard's."

The conversation wasn't going exactly like I thought it would, but I leaned forward, anticipating what I was sure would be her thoughts about me.

"After working for Dillard's ten years, I quit and my good friend—actually he was more than a friend—set me up in my own dress shop."

More than a friend, I thought.

"I named the dress shop Lacy's. It was great success, and later, after I broke up with my friend, I moved it to Little Rock."

Good—broke up with her friend, I thought.

"I just love Little Rock! I have some wonderful friends and I'm dating a great guy. We've been on so many wonderful trips. My life is absolutely the best I could imagine."

What, I thought.

I couldn't believe the direction this conversation was going. Maybe it had been my imagination, but I was convinced that Lacy felt exactly as I did. Was I wrong? Well, she settled that once and for all in the next few minutes.

"Sandy, after talking with Vi, I realized you've let a little college romance keep you two from living the life you should have lived. I decided, for your sake and Vi's, that I needed to have this talk with you. I don't doubt that for a couple of years I had an infatuation with you."

Just an infatuation, I thought.

"But, Sandy, it was just that—an infatuation. I haven't thought much about you in years."

Oh, my God, I thought.

It was if someone had hit me in the chest. Lacy stood there as the words sank in.

"Sandy, I'm sorry. Vi told me how you couldn't forget that last night in Fayetteville, and how you've worried all these years if you made the right choice. I'm here to tell you once and for all" (and then Lacy almost shouted), "You did make the right choice! Now Sandy, you've got to put that old relationship of ours out of your mind and give a wonderful woman your complete love. Sandy, even when I loved you all those years ago, when we were here at the university, I knew you and Vi were destined to be together. I've never seen two people who were more suited for each other—and were more in love."

It was such a shock I couldn't speak for a few minutes. It seemed like the weight of the world was on my shoulders. I couldn't believe it. All the dreams about Lacy had just exploded in my face.

Lacy, broke the silence, "Sandy, I made this trip back to Fayetteville, because, as I thought back over my memories, I thought I owed it to you. I want you and Vi to have the happiest marriage possible, and I'm sorry your memories of me has tainted it."

Vi moved over beside Lacy and whispered, "Lacy, thanks for coming with me. I know that was hard."

Lacy and Vi hugged, as I stood there, still too shocked to speak.

Then Lacy smiled and said, "Well, I'd better be going. I think you two have a few things to talk about, and you sure don't need me in the conversation."

I still hadn't spoken. All I could do was nod as Lacy walked away. Vi and I stood there for a couple of minutes not saying a word, but my mind was racing. Hell, I went from being devastated to just plain old mad.

Damn it, I can't believe I carried a torch for that woman all these years! What an idiot! crossed my mind.

Vi broke the silence, "Sandy, can't you say anything?"

I shook my head, still not believing the turn of events. Then I remembered why I'd come back to the university. It was for Vi, I thought.

Yes, I'm here because I still love Vi!

I smiled, walked over to where she was standing, gave her a long kiss, and said, "Vi, I love you, and I always will."

THE END